OF LOFTY OUTCASTS

MELISSA GOLDSMITH

Happy

Reading

Copyright © 2025 by Melissa Goldsmith

All rights reserved.

No part of this publication may be reproduced, distributed, or transmitted in any form or by any means, including photocopying, recording, or other electronic or mechanical methods, without the prior written permission of the publisher, except as permitted by U.S. copyright law. For permission requests, contact Melissagoldsmith.com

The story, all names, characters, and incidents portrayed in this production are fictitious. No identification with actual persons (living or deceased), places, buildings, and products is intended or should be inferred.

To my mum
For the past seven years, you've listened to my lore ramblings, and for all my life before that, you fought for me. None of this would have been possible without you.

Contents

Map	IX
Raylor Family Tree	XI
1. Belladonna	1
2. Kitty	9
3. Belladonna	15
4. Kitty	25
5. Belladonna	31
6. Wyvern	39
7. Belladonna	43
8. Kitty	51
9. Belladonna	55
10. Kitty	63
11. Belladonna	73
12. Wyvern	77
13. Belladonna	81

14. Belladonna	87
15. Robin	95
16. An'neira	99
17. Belladonna	103
18. Kitty	109
19. Belladonna	117
20. Belladonna	125
21. Kitty	131
22. Belladonna	137
23. Belladonna	145
24. Lane	151
25. Kitty	153
26. Belladonna	159
27. Belladonna	167
28. Robin	171
29. Belladonna	175
30. Belladonna	181
31. Robin	191
32. Belladonna	195
33. Belladonna	201

34.	Kitty	207
35.	Kitty	213
36.	Belladonna	217
37.	Wyvern	223
38.	Wyvern	227
39.	Belladonna	229
40.	Belladonna	235
41.	Kitty	239
42.	Wyvern	247
43.	Elysa	251
44.	Belladonna	257
45.	Kitty	261
46.	Kitty	267
47.	Elysa	273
48.	Elysa	281
49.	Belladonna	285
50.	Elysa	289
51.	Wyvern	295
52.	Kitty	301
53.	Belladonna	305

54. Wyvern — 309
55. Kitty — 313
56. Elysa — 315
57. Belladonna — 319
58. Elysa — 325
59. Belladonna — 327
60. Kitty — 331
61. Belladonna — 333
62. Elysa — 335
63. Robin — 337
64. Elysa — 339
65. Belladonna — 341
66. Elysa — 343

1

Belladonna

4th of Helenai, 447, Third Age

Two moons stood proof against the endless sky. Just as all things in the world below, those moons, too, had centuries of names, but on that summer night, only those set by humans were known. That of Helena, first of a set, their Maker's Chosen, always a beacon in the dark. And that of her sister, small and dim, she with no light of her own, she who could be seen only where she blocked the stars. But her name was not one to be spoken, no, not even one to be known—lest its call turn her eye on its speaker's soul.

The city of tiled roofs that sat between sea-facing cliffs had once a proper name, too. A city of torch flame and starlight on the waves, it stood as a bastion against Helena's Dark Sister, but like that monster in the shadows of a Human faith, the city's name lay likewise unspoken. To those who knew it, High Crest was a castle, and the city down its rocky hill was called nothing more than the northwestern province's capital. Names, grand or plain, were never so simple as to stay the same for long. They tended to be tricky that way.

The host of elven runaways, all chestnut hair and honey skin, who crept through shadowed streets knew this better than most. With them, they carried a silence like glass, a crystal ring, a porcelain thing, and all to ready to be shattered on cobblestone streets.

The roaming guards took no notice of the heaviness, for why should they bother to look down at things beneath their sight?

Humans, who had long ago deemed their minds and courage superior, hadn't given themselves leave to question the tales of their excellence. Supremacy named itself a lie as the little procession slipped around the edges of their vision. Those same guards never needed to hesitate as sheathed swords tapped against their raven-crested plate mail, nor did their hearts stop as their own clattering footsteps rang through the night air.

The silence, that damnable tension, they weren't for those guards that trod through familiar routes; they only mattered to those fifteen lean shadows that snuck past them.

At the procession's head, as always, was their leader. Younger than that night's charges by decades and made distinct from them only by the fine cream dress her dark cloak hid. But even that years-worn cloak, that meagre nod to disguise, lived on by years-old habit and naivety alone. For a badge of identity far greater than her face, or even the gown, was that ancient staff she didn't dare forsake. With that staff, and by the ancestry it implied, Belladonna led the people of her mother's blood through that unseen path.

Like the moons above and the city of her birth, Belladonna, too, had many names. Those she had found, those she had lost, that one she had carried long before she ever bore a Human's. But Belladonna was the name her Human father had gifted her, and only by his name could she free her people.

With the caution of understanding, the confidence of practice, and with such silence, she cut a path through the familiar city, as a spade through damp spring earth. The first run those five years ago had freed only three; how it had grown that on that summer night, fourteen more of Belladonna's people would no longer, nor ever again, toil under a Human master.

Her's was near the final role on a ring of converging paths through the night. It had been a long route on that night, a winding snake's path as she gathered her people in groups of twos and threes from safe houses scattered around the city. But that final street she led them down signalled her journey's end. Just one more corner before the agreed upon alley and alcove, the rendezvous point chosen by Belladonna's dear friend Vixensha, the true final step that would bring the runaways to her captain's ship then on to the Obsidian Iles far away from the land humans had renamed Lyria.

When the meeting point held nothing but dark, chipped stone, her stomach dropped as if stepping off a missed stair.

Vixensha wasn't there.

"You see it?" A voice came from below, blue eyes bright in that dark – the newcomer who'd arrived at the safehouse last. Not a full-blooded Elf, her skin was too pale and her stature far too short to even pretend. Her elven blood showed in her ears but not her eyes. She claimed that heritage yet no elven name. "You see it?" the strange girl repeated into the cracked silence.

Belladonna's gaze fell to where the strange girl pointed – an alcove past the alley's coveted sanctuary. So shadowed it was that Helena's pale light scarcely touched it. There, within the darkness, the black form of a raven perched. Its golden eyes, familiar and so familiarly mismatched to the animal it mimicked, settled on Belladonna's own. Caught in those golden eyes, Belladonna scarcely noticed its short flight until it had landed at her feet.

Then it shifted.

Only its eyes stayed constant as feathers contorted to skin and leather, both with an illusion of the sun's touch, as a bird's shape twisted to that of a man. After the transformation ended, all that remained of the raven were those night-black horns that crowned his head and those gold eyes that marked Xaxirion truer than any name.

Belladonna allowed her white knuckles to relax for but a moment as her staff lowered. This man was no enemy. Ally, he was, but not the one she'd expected.

"Where's your sister?" Belladonna whispered as if the empty street could call the guards.

"Mutiny." So many questions grew in Belladonna's mind, but she hadn't a moment to ask even one, as Xaxirion's voice, cold as Northguard steel, came again. "Were you followed?"

Had the guards followed them, Belladonna surely would have heard; even only a half-blooded Elf, she should have heard that ring of plate mail through a silent city if it had been there to hear. Could she have missed them? Nay, certainly not. "We couldn't have been."

"The guards know; they're waiting."

Too loud.

Xaxirion had spoken just too loud. The fugitives knew it as another crack cut through the silence. They knew it as one of the troupe gasped. When a careless step back sent a pot of herbs clattering from its sill.

The cracking silence shattered.

The next sound that dared mock the once silent street was that which Belladonna knew she hadn't heard earlier that night: those, Fin'neshi-damned armoured footsteps as they rang in the dozens from all around. The time for blame had passed, or mayhap had not yet arrived. Regardless, there was no time for such trifles, not when there wasn't even the time to plan. "Take the lead. Wait for my signal," Belladonna said to Xax.

The questions Xaxirion didn't ask danced like embers in the eyes of Belladonna's people. Those same questions Belladonna had faced so many times that she'd stopped asking them of herself. What was she to do against so many?

Xaxirion's were the only footsteps heard as he retreated with fourteen in his wake. Their feet made no sound, and neither did Belladonna's as she stepped to the centre of the street.

Belladonna allowed her people's worries to fill her mind for only a moment before she stood firm and waited. The echoes of metal as armoured boots struck cobblestone rang from all sides; it should have been impossible to know from whence they came but not for the dim promise of torchlight from the east. So they carried torches? Perfect.

Steel was not all that echoed that night. Had the guards been wise, they would have recoiled at the crack that sounded as a staff of Ashtana, spirit wood to the Human tongue, slammed against the cobble. Belladonna could no longer be concerned with the familiar task of persevering the quiet; the guards needed to see her. They needed to focus on the hooded mage rather than the elves that vanished behind her.

What a mage they faced; hers was the old magic, birthed from the Fae and passed for thousands of years, her staff, a Hetta, so much like her magic itself, a relic of days long past, the dying echo of a fallen empire.

The guards did not slow, but neither did Belladonna falter; they didn't yet know what she did, that for once in their history, their paranoia was correct. They carried their own demise.

Belladonna sent her focus inward, past her breath, under her heartbeat, to the mana that ran through her very blood. She let it flow, pushed it through her staff and away from her body, forward to the torches that so easily could have spelled her undoing. Fire, so distinct from the air around it, heat and passion. It called to her – impossible to miss. Belladonna willed her magic forward and took hold of it. She sent a command, juvenile almost, not even a full spell. Just a command, just one, and it was simple.

Grow.

So fast it consumed them, the guards hadn't the time to slow or presence to panic, and certainly not enough of either to realize their mistake. Their charge didn't stop until their armour melted into the cobblestone street. Perhaps the front few were consumed too fast to even realize the pain before the fire carried them to Vix'xhella. Belladonna had no time to hesitate, no time to mourn the men she recognized, no time to watch as the raven crests of her own house, emblazoned on their armour, melted away. Not even that silence of all aftermath dared settle as the streets shook with a dragon's roar.

Belladonna ran to find it.

The dragon was small, not Xaxirion's true form, not nearly, all too likely, even the size of one of his brightly coloured kindred. He'd made himself small enough to fit in the market square the guards must have cornered him in. But for all the shapeshifter's form lacked in size, he had the guards' attention; not an eye turned as Belladonna dashed just a hair too fast to stop herself before the shadows ended.

Her gaze raked over the blue-lit square, past the chaos, and found her people huddled under what remained of market stalls; they cowered away from the dragon as much as they hid from the guards.

They couldn't hide anymore; the time for hiding had passed long ago, the time for cowering long before even that. Belladonna ran to them, only slowed as cobblestones, frozen from Xaxirion's breath, stuck to her overly ostentatious boots.

"The docks aren't much further. We'll have to run for it."

None of the runaways moved in response to her breathless words; they must have known as well as Belladonna did that simply getting to the ship could not guarantee freedom if the guards had made it there first. But realities were unimportant. One did not pursue a dream for any great love of reality.

She would not give up – not on her people, not that night, and she swore by her mother's namesake, not ever. "I promised you I'd get you out, I'm not a liar, and I won't be made a liar tonight. Trust me and I swear by all the gods, you'll be free."

Never would Belladonna have considered herself an orator, nor did she find her speech that night, made as she crouched under a shattered market stall, a great work. But poetry was never written in a moment, and even with words being nothing, a chance at freedom would always be better than the certainty of the contrary.

The sprint to the docks was mad.

It was nothing like the quiet, orderly, practised lurking that the other escapes had entailed. They were so close. At last, it came into sight, the stone-blue sail of *The Mariner's Bounty*, almost black in the moonlight but nonetheless a beacon, a sanctuary from the storm. The call of freedom from those who invaded the elven homeland.

The sharp clang of armour from the blackness brought the sprint to the steepest of stops. Belladonna didn't need to look for what lurked on the docks; she knew they were waiting. There would be no way past them. If Belladonna was truthful, there was no way through them either, not for her, not without a flame. What remained of those torches she could see were not but fine trails of smoke; Helena's silver light traced them into the sky, a Human hero's mockery.

"You can'ne fight them?" Blue eyes blinked up at Belladonna. "You need a distraction?" Belladonna's eyes had never quite caught the crossbow until the strange girl hefted it from her back.

Belladonna shook her head. "I'm getting all of you out, no sacrifices."

Blue eyes blinked. "I wo'ne run. Lyria's my 'ome." The strange girl left no room for argument by running onto the docks. A bolt flew from her crossbow, but it didn't hit a guard; the girl hadn't even aimed at a guard. There wasn't a small thump of a bolt hitting a barrel. No, the bolt made no sound over the girl's strange call, a sound like no language meant to be known.

Something moved, but Belladonna's eyes couldn't move from where the bolt had drawn them fast enough to catch anything but a flash of red.

The way the shadowed guard shook before his sword found a new sheath in his fellow's back was too familiar for Belladonna not to recognize.

It wasn't magecraft, but what girl of elven blood would choose to become a Blood Mage? Would choose the deep art of Daemons? An academic question Belladonna hadn't the time for, even if it were one she asked far too often. Blood magic or no, the glow from inside the dock master's cabin, visible for but a moment as the bound guard opened the door, was unmistakably fire.

As so often was her way, Belladonna didn't think; she didn't remember moving, hardly felt her mana focus as she dragged the dregs of the light, the smallest bead of flame, down the docks as the door swung shut. Was it meant to be the promised distraction? It was, wasn't it? No matter. Whatever that strange girl had planned, it was too late by far to salvage, and a better opportunity had arisen.

What Belladonna did next was no mere command; she couldn't waste such precious little fire with such a basic expression. Through her magic, through her very connection to the Fae before her, Belladonna forced her will upon the flame. She pushed mana forward recklessly; she hadn't the time to measure. No time to preserve for later. Her people needed her.

The tiny flame grew and split and grew again until the docks were splattered with floating beads of fire weaving and spinning, seeking out anyone Belladonna wished. It was by no measure quick; it took far too long. By the time Belladonna was satisfied, her mana stores were dangerously low; if she could have managed even a single spell, it would have been only by Maj'jri's grace.

As thirteen elves, no longer relegated to the shadows of their homeland, vanished upon a ship of pirates, the silence had returned, but its aspect was changed. No longer did it carry the same dread; it knew, as those it carried did, that it was no longer needed as a shroud. It faded rather than shattered as the watchtowers rang their alarms to the night. Belladonna waited in shadows until that boundless dark consumed her friend's ship. Those ships that might have hoped to catch pirates in the open sea sat far to the east, a kingdom away.

Only the cold dawn and those first hints of light over grey-tiled roofs spurred her into movement. Her walk back to the castle was long, and she had much to consider. The guards had known too much of when they would move, what route they would take, and which ship they were making for. She could have considered one a coincidence, but all the points piled together? No, there were too many to ignore. In the cold light of dawn, she knew it was no such thing. Lady Belladonna of the House Raylor had been betrayed.

2

KITTY

27TH OF HELENAI, 447, THIRD AGE

Nobody was ever happy to see a Castilla with their cat's ears and beast's blood—Breaker Spawn all of them. Impossible abominations, never fellow children of The Maker. How could they be when their own maker was but a mortal man? When he gave no denial to the blasphemy he'd created? While he still walked among the living and time hadn't the chance to ease the growing pains of five new peoples? Five new others when the people of Lyria had already chosen a favourite: Breaker Spawn indeed. Then there were the worse rumours, shadowed hands and deals with Daemons, those little truths that could turn displeasure into a rallying cry. Even unproven as they were, those words would always find her ears in a crowd's hum. Kitty had known that long before she gave up her given name.

The wind whipped Kitty's face as she ducked into another alley. Her pace slowed for but a moment as her hinged hair ring came unclasped and black curls fell over her eyes. She fumbled blindly to catch the precious trinket before it loosed itself completely.

A sharp pang shot through her arm as skin grazed against a corner she hadn't seen. The jolt of her hand tore the memento free, and for a breathless moment, Kitty dove to keep hold of it.

Were those footsteps behind her? She couldn't tell for the heartbeat in her ears. Still clutching the gold ring in one hand, Kitty tried to clear the sweat-matted hair from her eyes.

Another turn, another side street of sandy hues. A glint of light caught her eye; it could have been a guard's armour. They could catch her any moment. The air left her burning lungs as Kitty missed a step and slammed chest first into the ground. As she scrambled to her feet, she vaguely recognized that the ground beneath her was no longer cobblestone. The dirt, hard-packed as it was, provided a welcome change for her abused feet, which surely should have bled if not for years of calluses.

In the quietness of that alley, with smooth dirt beneath her feet, Kitty forced her breathing to slow. Rapidly cooling sweat down her arms raised goosebumps in the shadow of sandstone houses; if not for the summer sky, she should have expected to see breath for how she shook.

A scrape sounded from around the corner. Her cat ears turned faster than her head, all muscles tightened, primed to run again. But no guards came around the corner, and Kitty collapsed against a wall at the sight of Robin's raven-like visage. A Nestia, another of Lord Mirri's five created peoples. That didn't matter; Robin was the best of them, and he was still with her; she hadn't lost him again.

It was but a brief relief, drowned by the shame of leaving him behind; she should have escaped last. Always the leader comes last – Pa's lessons forgotten again. What an excuse for a leader she was.

Robin crouched at her side, his three-taloned feet, which no shoes could hope to accommodate, dug pits into the packed earth. "Did we lose them?"

Kitty shook her head. "I don't know." She swivelled her ears but heard none of the telltale sounds of armoured pursuit, easy to hear coming, especially with a Castilla's hearing. Had it been skill or luck? Could she claim their freedom a gift of her own ability when she'd run blind? A poor thing to be so beholden to chance even in the middle of that fourth and luckiest month. "I think so."

Robin nodded – such misplaced trust. "Do you think they got a good look at us?"

Once more, Kitty shook her head. "I don't know." She should have had a better answer. Robin trusted her enough to lead; what good was she if she couldn't even answer simple questions?

She had failed him twice already.

"I don't know if they saw us at all. I didn't want to risk it." For the first time that day, she knew she was right; a few more snatched coins wouldn't have been worth the City Guards' ire. Even being in Lyria's most populous city as they were, a pair of Mirri's creations couldn't risk the second glance.

And again, Robin didn't scoff, didn't berate her for her failure as a leader; he just nodded as if what she said had been competent, had been reasonable. "Where are we anyway?"

At a glance, she hadn't that knowledge either, but what right did she have to say it a third time? If she succeeded in only one thing that day, she had very much done so in getting them lost in the walled city's labyrinth.

Kitty couldn't name the side street they found themselves on, but then not a soul could have; if ever a map had been drawn of the Northeast Capital, it was made wrong by design, by whose design between the thieves, spymasters or the Spy Lord Tenor himself, only the Maker would know.

Nay, she knew not exactly where their flight had brought them, but that wasn't to say she couldn't guess. It was quiet, too quiet to be anywhere near the gates or docks, and dirt streets were anathema to those districts of merchant lords. But it was those sandstone-hewn houses that gave the greatest of hints; only one district still stood of those pale stones, so many of their brethren were years ago reclaimed for the wall.

For all her breath had returned, Kitty held it for Robin's scorn. "I think we're in South End."

"It's a big district." Robin's eyes fixed on the sky. "We can stay clear of the temple."

Kitty flinched before she could worry who saw; a naive fool, she had almost convinced herself that place never existed.

And that another indictment of her character, those white marble spires were the four gods' home, The Maker's gift and Mother's sanctuary, the livelihood of Speakers robed in gold, blue, and black. And from its very mention, she'd recoiled; a worse charge that it wasn't even her highest heresy.

"Come on." Kitty pushed all the confidence Robin should have rightly expected into her voice. "Let us see if South End taverns started caring where our copper comes from in the past three days."

In a city of countless districts, South End was odd even by its own measure. From the antiquated name, eternally unchanged, even as the true southern border stretched far away, to the sandstone itself, those oldest buildings of Lyria's youngest capital. A wretched place, yet one that sat within eyesight of Embercove Castle's great bridge. Both too far from the docks for sailors and too far from the gates for traders.

A massive place that could host no strangers.

Still, Kitty shouldn't have startled so when they entered the Boar's Head Tavern, a place of patchwork tables and torn-up floorboards, to find it hosted an unfamiliar face. Perhaps if Robin asked, she could have pretended her shock was for lord Tenor's Bounty Minder who sat next to the ivory-pale Fensmirri. But not for the hitched breath her ears turned to capture, Kitty may have thought the towering stranger an illusion. Another of Lord Mirri's creations, one of alligator aspect no less, so far from the Fens they called home, priests and witches alike might disbelieve it.

To say the stranger sat at the bar would be to misspeak; she wasn't inside the tavern, not fully, at least. She leaned through an open window. Only her face, not quite man or woman in appearance and dotted down the sides with ivory scales, could be considered fully within the tavern walls.

For all their entrance was unnoticed by the stranger who towered over the bounty officer; the same indifference was not granted by their fellow patrons. Glares and whispers Kitty cared not to hear followed the two as they sat. Even so, Kitty couldn't bring herself to begrudge them; having two of Lord Mirri's experiments in one place should have been enough ill omen; three may as well have been a curse.

But she couldn't begrudge those thoughts either, for she could walk the streets or pray in the temples when there was another people who couldn't. The Beast Bloods' fortune was only in part that King Elric had feared the Fensmirri would choose to fight for freedom; truthfully, their fortune was that they could never be so hated as elves.

Kitty leaned close to Robin. "Is that one of your father's?"

Robin's beak clicked a chime of struck nerves. "No, the Bastards' Fensmirri is... different."

Kitty didn't argue. She knew not of the people who stayed in the Fens, but still, she knew they weren't meant to be so pale. The stranger's hair, only a shade lighter than the muscled arms its tangles fell across, captured Kitty's attention as to driven snow. Robin's tales told of a different shade, not so dark as her own, but the tones found in those centre kingdoms of Old Nareth.

As copper coins called Gin, not earned but stolen, were traded for bowls of a broth both she and Robin knew not to ask the make of, Kitty's eyes stayed on that stranger. Even beyond the small worlds of her childhood, Kitty couldn't help but turn her ears to someone so new. Flairs of a mind's familiar war forgotten for but a moment. The whispers behind her faded to a hum as she sought the stranger's words.

"I don't doubt your integrity," said the guard.

"You think I'm lying about what I can do!" The woman's fist slammed into the windowsill.

The Minder flinched back, and perhaps rightly so for how the wood groaned at the impact. "I wouldn't say you're lying... Simply overestimating, perhaps."

"You don't know what I can do."

"I don't doubt that you think so, but I can't give this contract to a lone agent. There are plenty of bounties–"

"I'm not here for the other bounties!"

A fool, Kitty let herself drown in the conversation. She should have known better. Soft feathers against her arm tore her focus, her thoughts shunted into memories, a mind's illusion; their touch transformed into cruel hands in a bruising grip. The phantom faded between breaths. Robin's eyes showed not but guilt and worry as Kitty reconciled the touch of his feathers and forced back the memories.

It had become quiet, but that time not as a trick of her focus; nay, the din had vanished along with the Human patrons. Truly, they were never happy to see her type dining near Mirri's Creations, not but a reminder of the Purges' failure.

That telltale echo of armoured boots on hard-packed dirt echoed from outside – the worst portent for a pair of thieves. Uneaten broth mocked her as those steps grew closer, and her stomach growled its protest. For just a bare selfish moment Kitty considered delaying, rushing through a meal, stealing some small satisfaction. No, it wasn't her right to risk Robin a second time.

"Come, Robin." Kitty stood from that untouched temptation, and her friend followed before she needed to explain the thought. "We should find another district for tonight."

Kitty spared a glance at the Fensmirri woman as they left. A war of thoughts raced through her head. Pa would have called the woman kin; it would only be right to warn her and then help her from that place. But she pushed those thoughts away for all the what-ifs. What if she couldn't convince the stranger? What if her attempts drew the bounty officer's attention? What if those few seconds of delay let the guards find Robin? She promised herself, in lies she didn't believe, that it was the right choice.

3

Belladonna

25th of Helenai, 447, Third Age

The first beams of midsummer sunlight warmed Belladonna's face as they broke through the dusted glass of her windows. As if any other day, green eyes opened to the same dark wood panelling and rich green velvets that had always furnished her chambers.

Small, by the standards of the Northwest, the rooms atop High Crest's shortest tower had perhaps been gifted to her as an insult, a spurn against Lord Raylor's unwanted heir. Almost certainly, the near abandonment of the tower's lower rooms was a less subtle one.

Belladonna's chambers could not truly claim to be plural. Merely a single round room cut in twain by bookcases and a curtain that stood in for a door. Still, the modesty of size was granted no consideration when some fool chose the adornments an heir, even a bastard one, was expected to possess.

She might have been happier for her rooms to have gone without, to have been another victim of Lord Raylor's most vital quest upon receiving the appointment. How unfortunate, the wire-thin budget, her grandfather's god above the Maker, couldn't stop the court from simply moving furniture from larger rooms. The effects of the bed chamber, dressing room, sitting room and study, each of them in uniform mahogany, were crammed into two rooms that were truly one. Only those eight windows that framed the tower kept the crowding from Belladonna's mind.

In that moment of waking, as was her habit, Belladonna clung tight to that fleeting comfort of dreams; it could have stretched for a lifetime if not for the shattering racket of temple bells.

Belladonna wrapped blankets around herself and walked to the sole window fully free from obstruction. Those cursed ivory spires atop the temple, the eyesore, identical in every city, sat just within the window's view. Belladonna couldn't help the scowl that twisted across her lips. Had she half the powers those Fin'neshi-touched nobles ascribed in their rumours, she should have levelled it.

All that racket they made, and for what? Four gods paired off as good and evil? What nonsense, all the stories Belladonna took pains to ignore, naught but imaginary tales, excuses to burn those the humans feared. No, she had no need for her father's scripts, not when she learned the truth *all* elves knew through her mother's songs. What need had Belladonna for a mere four that claimed all dominion when the dozens she could name were but a breath in the gale of all that wove the world?

She should have known more of them; their names should have been her right, but all that had been lost with the invasion, like so much of her birthright. Only the Seers could recall all of them.

Even so, she should have sung for those she knew. For Arh'nen and Arh'henni, Weavers of Land and Life. For Maj'jri, new carrier of gifts passed from the Fae. She knew their songs far better than those countless melodies of war.

Belladonna knew even then that she invoked the name of Fin'neshi more than she should have, but for that, she blamed only the Human nobles; who else could hold them but the Great Fool?

Should Belladonna have given her gods every tribute they deserved, still a song would have remained that she'd never sung, one silent for centuries. Lost were the words of worship for Vix'xhella, but who would have needed them? Who would sing for She Who Waits Behind All Doors? Who would sing for Death? Perhaps the first forgot her song by design; perhaps they, too, intended to know it by only a handful of words.

And so she left and traded one strange world for another. Thei'nas annan mott'tir se't re'nnan

As the bells ceased their clamour, Belladonna's ears found a new sound under the quiet – a near-silent shuffling from the sitting room that raised the hairs on her neck. Certainly, it was no Human maid. High Crest employed but four, and none that would dare approach Belladonna's chambers. Certainly no stationed guard, Lord Raylor hadn't the gold to waste on watching bed-chamber doors. No elven slave either; what need would Belladonna's true family have to sneak about her in such a way?

Of the vanishingly few possibilities that remained, fewer still were pleasant.

Warm sun and cool air duelled across Belladonna's night dress as blankets were dropped, their place in her hands taken as she pulled her staff close. As her fingers touched the smooth wood, Belladonna could feel the mana inside reach for it in tandem, not so hot as usual and far too much in the blood, but she spared not a thought for that as the empty place in her soul filled one more.

Her footsteps echoed, and heavy velvet slammed aside as Belladonna pushed through the curtain.

Had she seen who sat in that room, his hands a blur as they worked over a book of drawings, a moment later, it would have been too late to pull back the spell as it reached for the hearth. But she saw him – recognised her tailor in time to claw back the killing intent. Belladonna allowed her grip to relax and her staff to lower, and for just a moment, she laughed at herself. "Edmund?" Elven green eyes met those of an all too Human blue. "What are you doing here?"

The aborted spell faded to a whisper, its failure taking precious drops of mana in its flight, just a hair from her reserves, but not a thing to be taken for granted. The old magic of an unbroken line was a gift, not ever to be wasted carelessly.

Of all who could have been found in her chambers, Belladonna would have named Edmund her choice. A welcome surprise truly, but a surprise, nonetheless. "You're early."

"Aren't you happy to see me?" Edmund asked as he stood. His hands left charcoal spots as he wiped them against the dull red of his second-hand shirt.

She should have been. She was. She'd awaited his return every night, but her wait should not have been over. "You know well what I mean. You weren't supposed to be back for weeks." The thought stuck as thunder in a summer storm. "Did something happen to Jacob?"

That was where Edmund should have been, somewhere far off in the Southeast, pretending to be nothing but her tailor while Belladonna's idiot cousin partook in some pantomime of manhood. That Fin'neshi-held boy with the good fortune to be the only remaining heir to the throne. Had his fortunes changed?

"Now you want to talk about him?" It wasn't an answer, yet somehow, it broke through the dread.

Belladonna's eyebrow raised just slightly as she let her free hand lace into Edmund's. "Don't be jealous," she said as she pressed into his lips. "It's unbecoming."

"I'm not jealous." Edmund's eyes danced over Belladonna's staff until she let it fall against an overstuffed chair. The loss of contact stung only just less than letting go of Edmund's hand would have.

"I'm sure you're not," Belladonna said. "The way you glare at Vix could certainly never be that."

How pleased he had been those years Vixensha had been absent from their smuggling ring, how disappointed he had been just that past spring when she returned. He had, perchance, thought that the only living Half-Dragon had been gone forever. Belladonna certainly had.

"It's not jealously." Edmund's hand left a cold spot, a frost in summer, as he pulled it away, "She's not good for you to be around. Every time she's here, she makes you think you can do whatever you want."

"Should I stop doing what I want, love?" Belladonna's voice strained as she crouched to pull a discarded slip from beneath her desk. "I don't know that chastity would suit either of us."

Edmund's words came out muffled as he busied himself digging through the wardrobe. "You know we need to be more careful. Vixensha may be able to get away with whoring up and down the coast—"

"Edmund!" Belladonna let the warning hang until her lover turned. Cold air played along her skin as she let the night dress drop. Those moments she waited before stepping into the slip were of a pure kind. What idiot gods would claim pureness as chastity? "When has it ever been anyone but you?"

The silence hung as Belladonna kicked the crumped night dress aside, and still, it lingered until she pulled a corset off the ground. "Do you tidy at all when I'm away?" Edmund's teasing came as the sweetest of sounds.

"No." Belladonna cast a look over her shoulder. "Lace me up, will you?"

Edmund's breath ticked Belladonna's neck as he stepped close; even after so many years, his touch called goosebumps in its wake. "I just don't want to lose you."

Belladonna leaned against her love for just a moment. "You won't."

"Please, promise me we'll be more careful."

"Alright," Belladonna said, "just for you, love, I won't use my sinister magic tricks to destroy Lyria today."

Edmund's warmth faded as he leaned away. "Donna, please. You know making jokes like that only makes them more nervous."

Belladonna allowed only a sigh for that part of her heart which mourned the lost moment. "What would you have me do?" she asked. "I can't make those idiots less afraid of everything."

"They're afraid of magic."

"I am magic," Belladonna snapped, "and so is everything else in Lyria, come to that."

Edmund shook his head, his back again turned. "You don't have to carry a staff. They'd be happy enough to forget you're a mage if you'd let them." He shouldn't have kept talking. No, he shouldn't have started. "Whatever lies you told your grandfather to get it, just say you've grown out of it."

Seven years it had taken; Belladonna had passed her twelfth birthday before the lie had stuck properly. Uncontrolled magic, she'd said; all mages had it, she'd said. A sloppy, juvenile lie, that entangled Alyria in it's fiction and played on fear in such a way Belladonna knew her sister hated. What other choice was she given?

Emotions were no different than the four base elements, malleable to one who knew control, but a mage could only bend what already surrounded her and when it came to magic, humans gave only fear. Perhaps she could almost call herself grateful for the fear of those Speakers, all too eager to call mundane fire magical. What her maternal grandmother had said for Lord Raylor to send for a true staff of the old times, Belladonna would never know.

And he wished for her to give it up. "Edmund, love, why would I ever do that?"

Edmund turned back, his arms filled with fine clothes made by his own hands. The grey overdress, of course, his favourite, not hers, the sole beneficiary of his skill with an embroidery needle. His scowl lasted only a second too long to pretend it was anything else. "You know why."

"Strange that they don't have the same concerns about Alyria." Belladonna shrugged. She swore, for her own mind, that the dark feelings in her chest weren't jealousy for her sister named in honour of the kingdom and her first queen. "It doesn't matter anyway. It's still illegal for me to use it."

"And yet you still use it," Edmund said as he wrapped a skirt of green brocade around Belladonna's waist.

"Not that anyone sees."

"But they could. What if someone saw?"

"I'd make up a lie," Belladonna snapped. "Grandfather made such a fuss to say I'm part of the Mage Guard. I'd come up with something."

"It's a ceremonial position; they'll burn you or Blood Bind you; your position won't matter. The deal your father made, the Speakers and the king, they… nobody could help you." Edmund's breaths came as gasps.

Belladonna pulled her love into an embrace. "I know," she whispered, "And you're right, and I won't let that happen."

"I need you to be safe until your Calling. Lady Raylor will be safe."

Her Calling, her coming of age, her twentieth birthday just five months away. In that embrace, neither of their naivety needed refuting.

"I know," Belladonna said again as she pulled away.

Her mind burned with the question she was never given an answer to. For a moment, she couldn't help the worry that the return had been caused by the same incident that plagued her mind for weeks – the all too perfect trap on the docks. But nay, it couldn't have been, if but for the size of the party perhaps, but for such a grand parade of nobility to return from the Southeast. No, whatever it was, it must have been weeks before the escape. What could warrant pulling the heir to the throne away from his Seeking? "Now, tell me what happened to my idiot cousin."

There were no words in the common tongue for how the air changed at that question. Perhaps lightened would be the nearest. "There was some kind of trouble at a brothel–"

Belladonna couldn't help the smile that grew. "What was this you said about Vix spending her life whoring?"

Edmund froze for a moment before he moved as if underwater to thread the robe-like overdress of grey summer wool over Belladonna's arms. "Donna, I-I didn't–"

"Edmund." Belladonna caught her lover's eyes; what fear she saw broke her heart. "I know you wouldn't."

Still, Edmund's hands shook as he fastened the glass buttons down the front – a hint of scorn aimed where the top of her corset peaked just above her overdress dress, the style of the season rather than the fashion season that had persisted, all but unaltered, for the past eleven years, that glacial pace so often lamented as the first victim of Lord Raylor's budget. The greater tragedy in the hours Edmund and his like wasted keeping frilly corsets spotless for the sake of that fashion. "I didn't see what happened; all I know is that Lord Tenor got spooked and called off the whole trip."

"Tenor's here?" Belladonna spun at the name of the king's former spymaster. So soon after the trap and such a man, he would surely have heard what happened. His presence could only mean his involvement. A thought darker than poison. Already, Belladonna had too few allies to move without Edmund. If Lord Tenor—

"He's not here." Edmund's voice cut through her thoughts. "He left for his city before we arrived. What happened? What's wrong?"

Belladonna shook her head as she reclaimed her staff, its weight a comfort even then. Betrayal, such a simple word, yet so impossible to say; why was that? There was no failure in being betrayed, but perhaps that was wrong; it was a failure – one of trust. She had trusted the wrong person, and so many of her people could have been ruined for it. "I need you to check in on Nadia."

Refocus, the mantra of her mind as she forced it towards a problem she could manage. The Human in charge of her safe houses and hideaways in the city had been silent since that night, but that was a problem, so simply rectified now, she could send Edmund to speak with her.

An exercise in grounding shattered when Edmund failed to know Belladonna's thoughts.

"I told you we can't sell any more of your jewels until the autumn markets," Edmund said. "The favours she wants are gold, not promises."

Her knuckles turned white around the staff; mana pushed desperately at Belladonna's hand while words failed. "It's not to pay her; I just need to know if she's alright. I haven't heard from her since...."

"Since what? You know how she is when I show up without the gold."

"Since somebody told the guards about our friends!" Belladonna snapped. "We've been betrayed, and I can't figure this out alone, so I need your help!"

Edmund took a step back. "They can't have. But... How can you be sure?"

She dug her nails into her palm at the memory of how close they had come to failure. "They were waiting for us; somebody has to have told them something."

"You could ask your grandmother. I'm sure she knows."

Belladonna scoffed. Her mother's mother would have known, would have know before it happened, before Belladonna had ever started the ring, before she'd ever been born come to that, but still not a word of warning. "It would be easier for me to go see Nadia myself than get clear answers from a Seer. Please? Just make sure Nadia is alright."

"Okay, I'll go," he said.

Some of the weight Belladonna had become so accustomed to lifted from her chest as she once more kissed her lover. As always, there was more to say, but none of those sweet words were spoken as a shiver ran down her back. Her mana's flame grew hotter but less constant in her blood, more her own. A piece of physicality none but her own could have named returned. Belladonna opened the door before Alyria ever needed to knock.

There stood her sister, far more their father than mother and perfect in every way, punctual, tidy, ears hidden away beneath her hair, as always the model of a perfect mongrel. She wore the same robe-like dress, but the softest of pink and with sleeves that only brushed Alyria's fingertips, the mode of childhood, likely her last of the style since her first aging had ended. That amulet she'd never used tucked away under layers of that pink wool present but always so easy to forget. Still, Alyira already looked tired and so very small. Belladonna knew both that it was her fault and that she had wasted her sister's gift.

Edmund looked at the ground, his eyes wide, "I'll be going then."

Alyria giggled as he slipped past her.

"Oh, quiet!" Belladonna scolded. "How did you know he was here?"

"I saw the carriages last night," Alyria said, her voice dropping low. "Did you have fun?"

Belladonna's head shook before the question had time to finish. "When you're twenty, Lyri, we can talk about it." If not for how Alyria giggled, Belladonna might have thought her sister's question a misstep. "Now, where shall we go? The fountain garden should still be tended."

Tended as a generous term for the long dry fountains and unswept stone paths, but it wouldn't be overgrown. Nor would it be overrun.

"Grandfather is expecting you. He sent me to get you." Alyria's hands shifted under her shawl.

"Brilliant, Lyri, absolutely brilliant." Belladonna tugged her fingers through knotted hair.

"What was I supposed to do?" Alyria put her hands on her hips. "I already lied about where you are whenever you sneak out and how much time you spend with that tailor."

"Don't act so innocent. I lie for you, too," Belladonna hissed. Alyria's face fell, and so quickly, Belladonna regretted saying anything at all. "Don't worry about that. No doubt this is my fault somehow. We'll have to see what Grandfather has to say."

Alyria's smile, as their arms linked together, may almost have been bright enough to weather whatever Lord Raylor planned. Even after so many years, Belladonna couldn't help but glance at the contrast where her sister's aura met her own.

4
Kitty
27th of Helenai, 447, Third Age

*S*moke; it always started with smoke. That acrid smell – just a whisper against the spring morning, but that smell was only ever the beginning. Then came the flames, all around all at once, too hot and more real than the memories reduced to cinders in their wake, more solid than those wagons they drove into the earth.

Those who survived the flames jostled the little girl in their flight to the river; they would find no sanctuary there. But the little girl pushed against the tide of survivors; she never saw the massacre that awaited those who ran, but the screams echoed as every step towards her wagon drove shattered pots into soft feet. She didn't run; she never ran.

Her wagon, her home, its painted canvas already burned away, memories of a child's paintings gone with it. The healing herbs and blood-soaked wood burned into a bitter smoke, sharp and foul; nothing of that savoury scent of home remained. The girl's steps never stopped, but with each one, the wagon only drifted further from her reach; she never ran, no matter how she wished it. She fought with all her meagre strength against the force that pulled her from her home; how she fought, but she knew what she would see.

Rough hands seized her arms and yanked her from the path; Hanson's grin burned just the same as the flames she fell into.

"Kitty!" Robin's voice tore her from the nightmare. As wakefulness crashed over her, Kitty's hand found her wand before her mind could stop it. A white streak of pure cold shot from it and cast a layer of frost over the hay loft's far wall.

Neither Kitty nor Robin dared move in the moments that followed. Nights in such a city could never boast true silence, but they were quiet, a subtle distinction that made quite some difference to those with no right to the refuge they took.

The shuffling of the stable's horses carried gently into the loft that a pair of thieves dared spend only one night in. Frost, already melting in the late summer air, dripped a silent symphony onto the straw. As moments stretched, the two let themselves relax again; nobody had heard, or at least not anybody who cared to find them. They hadn't been caught yet.

The witch's craft – more like a dragon's breath than a mage's control. She'd been fortunate, a blessing of the fourth month, her addled mind reached for the cold grip of ice. In fire and lightning she may have found weapons, but never subtlety.

Only as the forced quiet of the aftermath lifted, did Kitty allow herself to thank Maker and Mother for their kindness in discretion. They had come to the edge of another true disaster, and just like Robin's missing fingers, it would have been her fault. Already, she had him marked a thief, punished twice to account for the leader the guards didn't catch. Had she gotten him caught sharing a witch's company… No, she couldn't live with that, not even for the brief days before she wouldn't have to.

Robin's voice carried softly through the night, his black-feathered visage nearly invisible in the darkness. "They're getting worse."

"Not worse." Kitty sighed. "Just more frequent. I'll find some Willow Tail next time a caravan comes through."

If Robin saw through the lie – that promise of an herb that was years past having any effect – he didn't question her on it, only silently lay down next to her. He was so close that if either of them dared stretch an arm out, they would be touching. But Robin wouldn't; he knew better. Kitty couldn't.

Kitty broke the silence. "You aren't sleeping?"

"Neither are you."

Kitty stared deep into the wooden roof. There had been another in that loft once, a Half-Elf born free, or so she said. They hadn't known her, hadn't even known her name. Kitty hoped she had simply moved on, tired of sharing a space with unnatural beasts. She so hoped it wasn't because her claim to the so-called Half-Elf exception that allowed those born into freedom to as such had been proven a lie.

Another would come along, true privacy was for those who lived by the law. To have a place within the law, even a place as damp and drafty as that latest hiding spot lay far beyond her means. The price of rooms, even the least of rooms was measured in Silver Kell; she measured her means in Copper Gin and she hadn't a prayer of lifting the three hundred copper needed to make a single silver. "I'll stay up for a while in case."

Her head turned to the stable's high window. The sky was still dark– still grey-toned to Kitty's eyes. Those white spires, lit by ever-burning braziers below, glowed against the dark. The Maker's gold-robed speakers would be in bed, their preaching the work of daylight, but those of The Mother and her darker counterpart would ply their trades by candlelight. The dying and dead took no rest. Wounds would be mended, and graves dug before and after the sun rose again. By the look of the sky, that shift change didn't yet draw near. Still, without seeing precious Helena's position, there was no way of knowing just how little sleep Kitty's risk had earned her. "It can't be too long until dawn."

The quiet bustle of the city floated through the sea air; somewhere not such a long way off, a ship's bell rang into the night. It was a long time before the hayloft's personal silence was broken again. "I wonder what happened to that woman," Robin said.

"What woman?" Kitty let herself be pulled away from the welcome darkness of the window.

"The Fensmirri. From earlier, I wonder what happened to her."

For all The Mother's love, Kitty had tried not to think of the Fensmirri woman. They should have warned her. No, that was wrong. Robin had left the tavern only by Kitty's word. She should have warned that strange woman. New to the city and without Kitty's hearing, how could Kitty have left her? What if she didn't see the guards until it was too late?

She tried not to imagine the enchanting white hair stained red, that scale-dotted flesh torn asunder. That Fensmirri woman's blood was as much on her own hands as any guard's. But these were not thoughts she could impose on Robin, not least that he might claim blame for himself where he could rightly take none. "I don't think the guards want to fight a Fensmirri anymore than we would."

"Of course," Robin said. His eyes widened by just a hair, "What can you bury if someone's been eaten?"

In but a moment, Kitty was sat up, her eyes turned to Robin. "What?"

"Sir Emmet said—" Kitty didn't let him finish.

"What would Sir Emmet know about anything?"

Robin's beak clicked. "He fought in the Seventh. He would know if anyone does."

"He thinks I'm your wife."

The next click of Robin's beak carried nothing but silence for a long moment before he shrugged. "He taught me everything I know."

Kitty lay back. If she knew nothing else, she was certain the woman hadn't eaten any of the guards, the thoughts of an old knight couldn't say whisper against that fact. Still, seeing the Fensmirri had been odd; Kitty couldn't banish the pale woman from her mind.

"Do you think..." Kitty started before she shook her head. "Did Sir Emmet say anything else about the Fensmirri?"

"Not much," Robin said, "you wouldn't believe most of it, probably. Why?"

"They don't usually leave the Fens. Why would she be so far north?"

"You said she was looking for work; maybe she's with a company."

Kitty shook her head. "If she had people, she would have mentioned them. The Bounty Minder seemed to think she was alone."

"Oh." Robin's words hung like a miscast spell in the night air.

"Oh?" Kitty asked, more awake than the moment she had been pulled from the nightmare.

Robin shook his head. "It's just... Nothing. You don't need to worry about it."

"No, what were you going to say? I want to know." Reassurances were useless; however unsure she was of Robin's first words, she knew his latest were lies.

The eyes of a raven met those of a cat, and finally, Robin spoke true. "You've never really been on your own in this city. There are a lot of people who would want a Fensmirri on her own."

Kitty pushed herself to her feet. "We're going."

Robin tipped his head but followed. "Where?"

Kitty dropped down from the loft. The horses shifted but raised no alarm at the familiar trespassers. "You're right; nobody should be alone in this city."

5

Belladonna

25th of Helenai, 447, Third Age

On stockinged feet, for her boots lay precisely where she had kicked them aside, and Edmund had no more patience for finding the handcraft of another than Belladonna did for the ridiculous frilled things her grandfather had intended as a pacifying gift, Belladonna allowed herself to be led through the stone halls.

It came to Belladonna as both surprise and disappointment when her sister's path led not to the family dining room in the east wing but rather to the shadow of those great dark doors that stood guard at the dining hall proper. The guards, their plate armour no more than glamorous decoration, stood as they were behind so many walls of stone, made no true acknowledgement but to pull those great doors open.

With the doors' opening came the rich smell that could only come with such vast quantities of food, promises of meats and sweet pastries danced into the corridor. Summer fruits from the south added their light tones to the mix, and behind it all, the slight haze of wood smoke. Just under those familiar scents came another, that sharp tang of winter strong drink; still but mid-summer, and as ever, not a day too early for Southerners to remember how cold and miserable they found the northern provinces when viewed through sober eyes.

Gray stone and dark mahogany near glowed with the light of four fireplaces. Knights of old Narreth, the Human homeland of conquest and civil war, chased their quarry across interconnected tapestries like the pages of a storybook. A new scene compared to the age of the castle, the room showed no hint of remembering those last tapestries torn from its walls, dragons of thread cast to flame, replaced on the king's own orders. A grand spectacle when set against the family's private dining room, yet, the size did nothing in the face of such a hoard. Crowded as they were, it was easy to tell the strangers; brightly coloured silks and jewels clashed harshly against the earthier palettes imposed upon the Northwestern court. The guests must have arrived with her idiot cousin, Jacob, in the night. For people so obsessed with their etiquette and rules, the nobility never seemed to care enough about manners to leave before they became a nuisance.

Some may have called Lord Hamish Raylor a great man. King Elric's first brother born and grown under the Sixth Mage Rebellion. The stoic brother, the practical brother. The middle child given a job in the Northwest, while the youngest was given the Southeast's luxury.

All Belladonna saw at that table was a Human well past the centre of his life, with that great misfortune to have naught but bastard granddaughters for heirs. Great or otherwise, he sat soberly at the head of the table, a rock against the chaos of strangers. His plate was tall with piled food but pushed to the side in favour of a greater stack of letters. A sash of red satin with embroidered ravens perched atop thread branches hung from his chair.

Despite all of Belladonna's efforts to ignore his lessons, she couldn't help but notice the play – to display a sash of office, even at an event that would be inappropriate to *wear* one. His eyes locked on the sisters as those doors squealed open, but his gaze lingered for a mere moment before it returned to his work.

All the careful steadiness Alyria had brought crumbled as the younger sister pulled her arm away and strode, as if watched by only friends, to their grandfather's side. Had Belladonna walked by her sister's side, perhaps the eyes would have lessened, but linger as she did by those great dark doors, only more eyes turned on her. It took every one of her fifteen years of experience to stand tall against the scrutiny.

Still, there was something strange about the eyes – an unfamiliar weight to it. Had it been only her family in the hall, or perhaps even those Northerners she knew to be worth nothing, she could have left, sought sanctuary in the gardens. But under the scrutiny of strangers, of those who took shelter in her home – as near to uninvited as the distinction would allow – no, she would not have them know her as a coward, lest only they think she cared for them.

Those first steps into the dining hall were the worst of them, for it was those that brought into view the Bound Mages, those poor souls who hadn't kept their secret as well as Belladonna's mother. They waited at the walls like ghosts, their cheeks branded with ravens. To see their eyes was to pretend they were empty, for the alternative, if life lived on in their minds as their bodies moved to another's whims – a fate far worse than being rendered mindless puppets.

She wouldn't see the others, the first faces of her childhood; those with their own minds couldn't be trusted with the lord's food. They would be tucked out of sight; their lye scarred hands too unseemly for the people who made them that way. But strange, the Bound Mages were not all that served on that day. Human servants, none dressed in Raylor reds, flitted about the table as if houseflies. The arrogance of Southerners to think a northern house couldn't serve them without assistance.

Belladonna took the vacated seat beside Alyria and allowed her staff to rest against the table. Unlike those nobles who tried to play at subtlety as they shuffled away, Belladonna made no attempt to hide her smirk as she noticed their retreat.

"Good morning, my dear," Lord Raylor said.

Belladonna nearly blanched. Why would he break so early? But no, he wouldn't be playing that game in front of strangers, too much respect for their opinions.

"I'm sure," Belladonna said as she pulled a tray of sweet pastries away from Alyria before she could empty it completely.

Belladonna hadn't the time to place even one pastry on her plate before her grandfather set upon it a stack of letters. "These came for you," he said.

Belladonna took in the stack of broken seals. They reeked of perfume and desperation. Without reading a single one, she would have wagered her grandfather's yearly budget that she knew their contents. "How thoughtful of you – reading them first. I need not bother with them now."

"A lady makes the receipt of a letter known with a response."

"A lord wouldn't waste my time." Even as she spoke, Belladonna gathered the letters in hand and stood, such unsubtle gaps sounded as her staff, tucked under her arm, swung just too close to those strangers who dared encroach.

Again, she felt their eyes as she strode to the fireplace. Shameless– the lot of them. If only they had the same subtlety as Vix. Belladonna could have placed herself above it, ignored the petty idiots, but no, she couldn't care to hold back the glare she sent across the table.

Only her eyes couldn't sweep its entirety, caught as they were by those of a servant girl, her ears and flame-red hair covered with a cloth. Anyone else's focus might have locked on the scarred over burns that covered near half the girl's face. There was something about those amber eyes. Belladonna shook her head as she forced her attention back to the letters.

Perhaps she was wrong about the letters' contents; perhaps what she held were more than the desperate calls of suitors, pathetic, as if the humans didn't know their own rules. They could have had the courtesy to wait until she was Called before their imaginary gods as they were supposed to. Still, of course, those who would write to an underage girl were sons so far down the line of succession they could scarcely afford the ink, sixteen year old boys freshly back from their Seekings, newly declared to be men and still revelling in supposed maturity, as well as all the rest of those without far to fall if they were revealed.

It gave Belladonna pause when the nine-branched tree of House Mirri rose to the top of her pile. It certainly couldn't be called a boring house. Until not so long ago, their current patriarch had ensured it had been the most troublesome of the southern houses. Intriguing, certainly, but not so much to be worth reading. Not with the nature of the Mirri boys, an heir who stood to gain nothing from her, a younger brother betrothed to his grandfather's creation.

Perhaps the letters contained more than Belladonna thought, but she would never find out as she cast the lot into the flames.

A glare from her grandfather. "I think I can do better," Belladonna called across the room.

"If I were in your position, I should count myself lucky," Lord Raylor said as he picked up his goblet and inspected the contents. Belladonna may have missed it under the racket if not for her elven ears.

"My position as the uncontested heir to the Northwest?" Belladonna leaned against warm stones around the hearth. What a sorry state of succession, the king's son dead, the Northwest's heir a fool to invoke his privilege and step out of line – none left but a bastard for the province and a traitor's son for the throne.

"Your father could have another child yet."

She had to suppress a laugh at the decade-old threat. "He can have as many bastards as he wants; I'll still be the eldest."

More than a few indignant looks flickered across the swarm as if they never said such things themselves, as if they knew at all how well elves could hear.

"My son could easily find a wife," Lord Raylor hissed with more venom than Belladonna could have expected. It was strange though, he turned away with those words. Not even the decency to look in her direction when spitting another over-said threat.

But it was that turn that drove her past reason's frayed edge. "Then why was he bedding an Elf for so long?" she snapped.

Belladonna promised herself it hadn't been intentional, that it had been a mistake. The instant silence that fell over the room almost brought a smile to her face. If not for Alyria's stricken expression and the fork she pushed into her thumb, Belladonna may have even laughed.

Belladonna shook her head, strode back to the table, and placed a hand on Alyria's back while she leaned in close to her grandfather. "Let's not forget that my father stepped out of line for me. I doubt he would intentionally displace me."

A defence built from truth, but only just. It wasn't a great love that had her father exercise the heir's right to give their place to any blood relative. He hadn't any other option if he wished to keep his daughters together. None would have looked twice if Alyria had been called free under the so called "Half-Elf exception", but not even her father, King Elric's beloved nephew, could have claimed a slave of five years had been born free. Not without a claim added to her name.

Perhaps Lord Raylor meant to say more. Certainly, his open mouth would suggest he did. But whatever words he had to repeat in the decade-old argument went unspoken as those great doors squealed open once more, and into the room stepped their newly crowned prince.

Half-drunk nobles staggered to their feet as Jacob, just sixteen and by any Human laws, a man ready to inherit his uncle's throne, lingered in the doorway. By his birth, his right should have been a chance at the Southeast. If not for the idiocy of King Elric's only son, the late Prince Michael, it may still have been.

What shapes would have landed if Lyan'nyea hadn't taken Fin'neshi's hand that cursed year? What would have happened if fate had chosen a lesser fool for her model?

The doors closed at Jacob's back as his lingering stretched far beyond an announcement of arrival. In those weeks of his absence, Belladonna had become complacent, forgotten those safeguards she'd long enforced; she made the mistake of meeting his gaze, of seeing that half longing, more than half pathetic, look he cast upon her. After so many years, Belladonna needn't see her sister to know Alyria wore the same towards him.

Had she not tossed the letters, Belladonna could have pretended to busy herself with them. As it was, she held no distractions as Jacob strode across the room and crouched to meet her eyes. "Beautiful morning, cousin," he said.

"Indeed," Belladonna said and hoped to the gods that her tone would be some manner of hint.

As it always had been, the gods were silent. "I was hoping to find you this morning; I wanted to tell you about my Seeking."

"That is *fascinating*," Belladonna said as she turned and walked back to her sister's side. If only her cousin had not been so dense, she would have been walking alone.

It broke Belladonna's heart to see her little sister's face light up as Jacob sat beside her, only to fall as he ignored her and turned again to face Belladonna. Once, his ignorance may have been charming, but for one who claimed to be grown...

There were few excuses for his behaviour, fewer still that he continued, "Yes, I wanted to tell you about the Southeast. You were always interested in it when we were kids."

No, not the Southeast, not the province, or the lands, or the Dwarves exiled down below. Only Torren Raylor, its leader, father to the newly crowned prince, youngest brother to the king, and the power and backing for her people's Eighth Rebellion. An interest born and died a decade past in hopes that Jacob might follow his father's footsteps.

The vain hope crushed by Human schemes, by the King's cruellest justice, that his brother should live on named blameless, his every move watched by spies of every court. That the prince, the last true born option since one died and the other stepped aside, should be raised by family far from his father and he should never know himself to be a hostage. But those facts of interests and politics long had eluded Belladonna's fool cousin, and on that day,

Belladonna held so very little faith that explanation could bring him clarity.

"I didn't see the Dwarven tunnels," he prattled on, "but we got close to the entry under Varrinae Keep."

"I don't care about Dwarves," Belladonna snapped, perhaps some long forgotten part of her, some vestige of that decade old hope for an ally, would have wished to apologise for how Jacob's face fell.

Lord Raylor saved her from that fate by standing and tapping his glass. A far less abrupt silence came over the hall. "By the will of the Maker, my dear nephew has returned to us quite early."

A chorus of murmuring rippled across the hall. Lord Raylor raised a hand, and again silence fell. "Wiser and holier men than I can debate the Maker's will. But I know a sign when I'm shown one. I've consulted with my Seer."

Belladonna raised an eyebrow at his lie. Lord Raylor caught her eye for but a moment before continuing. "The Seer has revealed that our prince will find what he seeks when we open the Dark Sky Festival. I pray he finds his bride, and we have cause for a fourth celebration." He raised his goblet, and the hall erupted into its racket once again. How they loved their fours.

A fourth celebration? What was the third? Belladonna was pulled from that thought by the feeling of those amber eyes burning into her back again. She tried to ignore it, but the room felt, all at once, far too hot. Any further argument with Lord Raylor would have to wait until Jacob wasn't present, lest he had the need to be involved again. At least the other nobles had the good courtesy to pretend they didn't hear them.

"Dear, could you do me a favour?" Belladonna asked Jacob.

"Of course!" Jacob said in the eternally eager way. It was proof enough that he had not miraculously matured into a man.

"Would you accompany Alyria through the gardens for me?" Belladonna asked. Jacob had already agreed, and he had some false notion about honour. Belladonna knew he would keep his word; still, she would not give him time to rescind it.

She stood and retrieved her staff. "Thank you, dear," she said as she stood. But before she could make for the door, a weathered hand caught her wrist.

"You will make an effort," Lord Raylor whispered.

Belladonna made no effort to hide the force with which she ripped her arm from his grasp, and as she stepped out of those great doors, her eyes caught those of the red-haired servant girl once more; those amber eyes burned into Belladonna's mind long after the doors closed behind her.

6

Wyvern

28th of Helenai, 447, Third Age

She knew the world beyond the Fens to be strange, but those comfortable cities of the South did nothing at all to prepare Wyvern for those absurd contradictions of the Northeast. In precious few days, the city people had shown themselves capable of naught but dishonour and treachery, and nevertheless, they dared question her own integrity. Those who would claim to uphold order in that awful place knew nothing of true honour. The Fensmirri elders had been correct; leaving hadn't been her right.

Next to the wrong ocean, the dawn air hadn't nearly the same biting cold it held inland; even still, the northern air raised gooseflesh between the scales that dotted her pale skin and sent aches through bruised muscles. Did the North ever grow truly warm? Surely, summers shouldn't have been so frigid. Wyvern knew that even with the respite of sea air, she had scant weeks left in that strange northern city. Wandering the streets could not be abided when the frosts came, not if she wanted to keep those few tenets she had left.

Perhaps she should have celebrated her return south as she had in other years. Perhaps the next year, she would once more celebrate a return to the cat and mouse hunt that awaited in her home province. There could be no celebration that year. A point she shoved aside; it wasn't time for her to leave the North's safety of distance, not while there was more good she could do.

Those moisture-stained window shutters had far too readily crumpled beneath her scale-dotted hand on her first visit. On that misty morning of her fourth, Wyvern scarcely dared knock at all for their poor craftsmanship. But knock she did, for she had come to the blighted city for that contract.

Children stolen from their beds. It had been a rumour in the lesser port cities, what good fortune that Wyvern had heard it; the merchants who pointed her to the Northeast capital had clearly thought the same for how readily they gave directions. They knew she would see those children safely home. If only the Bounty Minder agreed.

All Parsifal had told her of a guard's honour; they knew nothing of such things should they think she would leave without it. Should they think she would allow children to be stolen from their beds with not a word to the contrary? None born Fensmirri would dare such cowardice.

That tavern window swung open once again at Wyvern's lightest prompt. That same thrice familiar guard showed naught but surprise in his eyes and ran a hand down his face. "You again?" he growled alongside words Wyvern couldn't hear.

He made to close the shutter once more, but the frail wood snapped from its hinge as Wyvern's hand shot out to stop it. "Listen," he hissed as the broken shutter fell to the dirt, "I've told you thrice now—"

"You doubt my word!" Wyvern said.

The guard stepped back from the window. "I thought my fellows made it clear to you yesterday. This contract cannot go to a lone agent."

"Who said she's alone?" a voice called from the dawn mists. Wyvern spun around, her hand flew to her greatsword, and she couldn't help how she winced at the movement of fresh bruises. But from those corners, obscured by her poor vision, emerged not a guard, but a woman of such magnificence; Parsifal hadn't taught Wyvern the words to do her justice. "She's with us."

The words that the guard exchanged with the Castilla woman were nothing to Wyvern's mind. She became as she had never been before, a being of no ears, no voice, no mind but to know she was unworthy of what her eyes saw, yet still so desperate to memorize the newcomer's beauty forever.

Those Castilla whom Wyvern had met so long ago, them that sheltered her from summer storms under their wagons, had called her kin. Could she be kin to such a woman? Could she be so fortunate?

"Are you coming?" The new voice, though soft and songlike, was enough to startle Wyvern from her trance. She hadn't seen the raven-black Nestia that stepped from the shadows. Even as she watched him stand by the Castilla's side, his form grew shapeless with every blink in that morning shade.

All in a moment, her mind waged war; a hope the pair hadn't noticed her staring and the signs of her girlhood steward, an admonishment for the will to deceive those she had only just met.

But it was a war shorter-lived than the Seventh, for as the pair retreated into those endless streets, Wyvern found her legs moved without her biding.

"Wait! Who are you?" Wyvern's hand grasped the woman's shoulder, but a moment was the only contact Wyvern had before she ripped her hand back; a moment was all she needed to feel how the woman stopped breathing.

Even above water, even with the mist, Wyvern's eyes couldn't miss how the woman shook as she turned. That spark that cowed guards was shrouded by a veil behind her eyes. Those eyes, such a perfect green that Wyvern could meet them for but a moment. "They call me Kitty; this is Robin."

Kitty. There could be no words for her in the Talish sign language, a sign for cat, perhaps. Black Cat. Swift Cat. No signs for beautiful.

Wyvern's tongue was stone as she met those eyes once more. She had scared Kitty, but how? Nonetheless, Kitty had given her name; she still thought Wyvern a friend. Two voices echoed around her; she heard not what they said, but they would want her name. They knew not how her voice had fled to the winds; they would know not that she still thought them friends.

Only as a parchment, rolled and rumpled at the edge, entered her vision did Wyvern's sense return. "This is for you...." Kitty started.

"Wyvern." She jumped at her own voice as her hand followed in Talish signs. "My name is Wyvern."

Parsifal had a gift. He knew faces, and he always knew what Wyvern thought. Only that day, so near a half-lifetime apart, did Wyvern envy that gift. No price would have been too much if she could only have known what Kitty thought as she once again held out the contract.

"You want to do it alone?" Kitty asked.

So close, and yet Wyvern couldn't will her arm to move. "I must," she said. "I can't leave them."

"You don't have to."

"I must," Wyvern repeated as she finally grasped the parchment. She hadn't the will to rip it away, but neither did Kitty relinquish the precious document. Those green eyes turned for long moments to Robin.

"You don't have to go alone."

Wyvern had words; Parsifal had taught her all she could learn. There were so many ways to say yes in common. But a nod was all Wyvern managed as her fingers slipped from the contract. As she fell into step behind Kitty, so unlike all else in the North, it felt like home.

7

BELLADONNA

25TH OF HELENAI, 447, THIRD AGE

She hadn't thought to notice it at the time; it wasn't until hours later, when sunbeams beat through the western windows of the elevated passage between wings, that Belladonna remembered her father's absence at breakfast. She should have noticed it, the empty chair beside her grandfather, but only in that corridor overlooking the gardens and Shivering Sea did his absence strike her.

Even as her mind turned to it, she couldn't give the feeling a name. Would she have preferred his presence? Truly? Perhaps for the sake of his preferred child, but that was a thought cast aside; there was no place for resentment where Belladonna swore none existed. Distance, perhaps, was preferable; nothing could be gained from contact when, fifteen years later, there was still too much room for blame.

The movement beyond the windows, polished to a mirror sheen by her true family, called it back to the present. She hadn't realized how she wandered with her mind filled with thoughts of traitors. Her search had no place to begin; silence from Nadia should have heralded safety; she had sent no alarm. And still, Belladonna awaited the return of Vix and Xax, but not as she had once. Not as she so often had longed for her friends. Their names carried only more dread for her mind to carry.

Belladonna didn't feel herself move until her forehead pressed to the window. The largest of the gardens that still remained sprawled far below, with paths of roses all in white. Once, perhaps only the better times all nobles longed for, those flowers had bloomed in all their Maker's colours. The ambitions of the North's first lords, what a thing it must have been to be culled by frost.

If only such things could have been said of that hoard of Southerners who prattled along Belladonna's garden, shivering in borrowed shawls, so much like those who drove the province into debt ignoring its realities. She would have let Fin'neshi take them all, damned them as not more than fools, if not for that feeling in her gut. Sailors claimed it their own, an instinct to steer from storms, but any former slave remembered when to run.

Another worry. Perhaps if Belladonna had sung as she should have, the gods would have sent her problems one at a time. A vain hope when the goddess Lyan'nyea had taken Bann'ni's hand. Fate's portent for a hard year, no ease would come from change, not even from changing seasons.

Had Belladonna taken even but a moment to scowl at that crowd and spent her focus hoping the growing clouds would cast down lightning, she may well have missed the voices that carried in hushed whispers through the corridor.

Belladonna pressed herself against the corner where the voices were coming from, keenly listening to the conversation on the other side while she held her skirts and staff close. She knew the voice from memories older than her Human name, but his name was nothing to her; surely Alyria knew it. Even after fifteen years, Belladonna so nearly gave in to her urge to run, to hide behind her grandmother's skirts for fear of the bruises he left. But that desire was pushed back by a new voice, a stranger's voice.

"I saw it, didn't I?" A stranger but no highborn either, a new guard. Belladonna's skirts fell from her hands as both gripped her staff. A replacement. How many had it been that night? How many guards would she no longer recognize? How many that Nadia would not know to turn away? All the sooner, she needed to hear from what allies remained.

The old guard scoffed. "I heard you, but I know you didn't fight a dozen mages."

"I know there were at least ten. And I saw their ears; they couldn't have been human."

"So you saw *elves*, if anything."

"I said that."

"You said mages." The old guard's voice drew near Belladonna's hiding place. "Not many where you're from then? Thank the

Maker, most of that lot aren't those Breaker-touched Daemon's spawn."

They invoked the name – the old enemy, the patrons of witches, the first blood mages – as humans so loved to do. Invoke the name of an enemy they never fought to curse the descendants of those who did. So readily, they claimed the Fae's enemy, still trapped in The Other Place, as if they had ever heard them before The Landing War.

"It's just, the ladies—"

"You've not met the Seer; she would send mages to fake a lineage." There was a silence in the wake of the accusation, one of thought, of wonder. A tale long dismissed, but its hate passed to another, and for but a moment, Belladonna might have thought the guards had moved along. "Come on then, show me where you saw them. Maybe you can still avenge your predecessor."

Belladonna pressed hard into the stone as the voices retreated. She could follow, but the new guard's words had to be lies; her people knew better than to travel in such numbers; it was a risk only allowable on nights of escape.

The choice was taken from her as tiny, rough hands grasped her shoulders. Belladonna's staff, already clutched tight, hummed its potential as she spun. But for the second time that day, no enemy lay before her. Lady Anika Redsail's face held not a hint of worry as her eyes met Belladonna's.

For a moment, as the pair stood, the hall held a comfortable silence, one of familiarity, as if nothing was wrong, as if they hadn't been weeks apart. Belladonna's gaze skipped over those scars of fire that marred so much of Anika's body to find her friend's eyes, to see that kindness, those eyes that never dashed to the staff that shared their colour.

A true innocent among nobles, perhaps the last of her kind. Though sent as a tool, a child just the right age to befriend an heir wanted by none, far from the only one, but the sole to remain. Such unwanted children could be tools for the games nobles played, to be pulled away, to run home when their goal proved impossible. Yet still, Anika had stayed, two souls in an empty tower.

As it always had been, it was Anika who broke that silence; her finger twisted around the auburn strands of her wig. "Miss me, Donna?"

"Don't do it again," Belladonna breathed as Anika pulled her close.

Anika stepped back. Her embrace stopped short. "What did I do?"

Belladonna put on that teasing tone so few humans knew. "You left me here with these people."

That flash of hurt hadn't the chance to form truly on Anika's face before it vanished with a laugh. "I wasn't gone so long."

"Weeks, Ani." Belladonna let herself laugh along; it was what she had wanted, her friend's laugh if not her own. "I could have killed everyone by now."

Belladonna allowed one hand free of her staff, only for the joy of linking her arm with Anika's. As wool slipped against sea blue silk Belladonna, let her eyes leave Anika's face.

Her clothes had changed, still, in the sea blue that backed her family's sigil, but the angles were sharper the waist more defined. The front of her dress was held closed with a panel and two rows of buttons rather than the strings it had been before. Where before her sleeves had been tied on with bows, the seams had been covered with some kind of short sleeveless coat. So that was how they showed it in the Northeast, the change from girl to woman, her family would have furnished her with a new wardrobe during her Calling. Once the Northwest would have had a similar tradition, perhaps there she could have found common ground in her grandfather's decisions to do away with such a thing. Perhaps if she cared to.

"I've not noticed anyone missing," Anika said as the pair passed that view of white roses. "Seems you've rather picked up a few."

"Jacob's homecoming. It would seem you've missed it."

"Lord Raylor told me the ball isn't until the Opening. Will you miss it this year?"

A smile crossed Belladonna's face as summer air rushed through the opening doors. "I might; since you're back now, you can cover for me."

"I didn't mean to be so late." the ghost of a frown pulled against stiff scars. "Some fool claimed he saw a dragon rider near Northguard. The soldiers closed the pass."

A fool notion. The dragon riders were gone from Lyria; they'd fled back north or made new allies in the ever waring nations of old Narreth. Their images had been torn from the walls; their statutes reduced to dust. Not one sighting had proved true since the young yellow had been felled over the capital, and even she hadn't been a true dragon. Nit had been her name.

And still, border towns claimed sightings, stories of the dragon riders returning for vengeance grew up with all those younger than the banishment. But Belladonna knew, from those stories only dragons told, from all Xaxirion had shared, no dragon rider longed for Lyria; nothing awaited them, not after Rider Valisteir killed that fool prince.

But history was not all that Anika's words implied. "You went through the Wildlands?" Belladonna asked.

"No, the messenger came before we left."

"But you were going to?"

"Lord Aroch was kind to offer his routes and Holceina's still little more than ashes; I wanted to be home." Anika halted so suddenly that Belladonna very nearly tripped. But her friend's eyes were not for the near accident; Belladonna's own followed their gaze across the rows of roses. A single bound-mage stood alone amongst set tables. "Everyone was different."

Belladonna pulled just slightly on her friend's arm; the roses were no place to talk unheard, and Anika always cared so very much about what the Fin'neshi-touched thought. Roses turned to wild hedges as the pair strode through gardens abandoned after the Eighth, then to those left to rot after Lord Raylor was gifted the castle. No racket of the crowd reached the two nestled between branches in the Queen's Maze.

"Talk to me, Ani," Belladonna said.

"He purged them." Anika's voice came as a whisper. "One of the elves, she was a mage; he had the Speakers burn them all."

Belladonna had no words for her friend, none she would know, but for the dead. "Thei'nas annan mott'tir se't re'nnan." One strange world for another.

"And here I am crying about it to you. I'm so stupid."

"You're not stupid, Anika."

Tears left black streaks along Anika's sleeves. "I had plans. After I got married, I'd have my own castle, and I'd free them."

What irony, the friend she had left from her scheme had dreamt her own. The only friend who couldn't have betrayed her ring for her ignorance of it. What a strange irony that it was only then that Belladonna discovered her as the one who never would have. What they could have done had she confided all those years ago, but it was then too late.

Belladonna shook her head; somewhere deep in her mind screamed she had dropped her staff. "My people can't be free here; I wish I could free them too."

"I could have called them all half-elves or petitioned the King Elric. Jacob's always liked me. I could have waited until he took the throne. I'm just so useless now."

"You could still try." But Belladonna's voice broke at her friend's renewed tears. "Your Calling. What happened?"

"They were right, all of them," Anika started. "Nobody wants to be stuck with me as their wife."

"That's not true."

"You weren't there. The ball was for me, and still, they wouldn't even look at me."

There was a piece of Belladonna's mind, one that burned guards so her people might live that yearned for names, to know who would dare hurt her friend. But there would be time for that in later days. No, she asked for no names but laid a hand on Anika's shoulder. "We will find you someone. There are plenty of eligible men around these days."

"There were plenty of young men at my Calling Ball, but none of them wanted me."

"Then your father didn't invite the right ones. I refuse to believe that there's nobody for you."

Anika pulled away with a shake of her head. "Forget it. My father invited every man in Lyria."

"Then we'll find someone in Narreth." Belladonna grabbed her staff from the earth, but careless anger set slip a spell she had never learned. Wind, as if from a summer storm, raced through the maze, its screams like the old foe.

That wasted mana should have been her only regret, could have been, too, if not for those soft footsteps that sounded over the soft ground. Belladonna spun to face a stranger, but a familiar one at that; the amber eyes and flame-scarred cheek marked that serving girl even without a name. She had found them, but how? How long had she been followed?

The servant girl tipped her head to the side just slightly. "Sorry, m'lady, I didn't realize you had company." Her voice had the sharp tinge of a low-born but that edge of an actress.

"Wait—" Belladonna called, but the servant girl had retreated into the maze.

Ankia stepped to Belladonna's side and grabbed a hand Belladonna hadn't realized was shaking. "Who was that?" she asked.

Belladonna shook her head and kept staring at the corner as if the girl would reappear. "I don't – I don't know."

It was only the soft breeze, pulling storm clouds ever closer, that saved the pair from silence until Anika spoke. "Everyone was surprised I came back here."

"They were?" Belladonna asked, the laughter from just moments ago gone from her voice.

Anika nodded. "They thought I was going to live with James and Elisabeth."

"Why? Did they think something's changed now that you're of age?"

"They must have. James said that I'm welcome to move into his estate now that Father won't want me around."

It wasn't so much the words but the ease with which Anika said them that gave the feel of a stone in Belladonna's chest. "Your father said that?"

"Not the words, no... but—" The face of calm Anika had pulled from tears teetered for but a moment, "but I'm glad of it, really. If he wanted me, he would have taken me back before I got you to like me."

"Anika," Belladonna said, "it's just me; you don't need to—"

"I'm alright. I told James that I couldn't live with him because the future Queen needs me." Without their years together, her tone may well have sounded earnest.

Belladonna sighed. "Why? Why must you lot pretend I'll marry Jacob?"

"He certainly wants to marry you. You couldn't ask for a better match."

"Without a doubt. There is, however, a part of the arrangement that you, and it seems Jacob, have missed."

"What's that?"

"My uncle would never approve of that match."

"Which one?" Anika asked with a grin.

Belladonna sent a sharp look. "Neither?"

"Don't be a fool, Donna; Lord Raylor, the younger, loves you more than his son."

"Of course he does; he's never had to meet me," Belladonna said.

"He committed treason for your people."

"Not for any great love of me; I was seven."

Ankia hummed, "Perhaps I should convince our peers that at a mere seven years of age, you were the true power behind the Eighth."

Belladonna shook her head. "They'd believe you. I'm an Elf."

"You're a Half-Elf."

Belladonna's eyes narrowed at the Human concept. "There isn't such a thing, as I'm no human; I must be an Elf."

Anika sighed. Belladonna had said nothing new to the debate repeated many times before. "But you do have Human blood, just the same as Alyria, and you champion her match."

"People tend to like Alyria a fair bit more than me."

"Only because she cares to make people like her. If you wished it, you could be just the same. Besides, she's five years your junior. I've never known Jacob to wait."

"He'll have to learn then. He won't have me," Belladonna said, and as the first raindrops fell, any rebuttal was silenced.

Even as that was, Belladonna felt Anika's eyes on her as they ran. It could have been the end of it, if not the debate, then the day, but a guard, decorative at the doors, signalled the pair to a stop.

"My Ladies." His bow stilted, from rain or from armour, marked him as another newcomer, "Your presence is required in the Great Hall by Lord Raylor."

Another argument not yet come to an end. If not for the memory of a governess's switch, Belladonna may well have rolled her eyes; so soon after the last fight and her grandfather wanted another. "I wonder what it is I've done," Belladonna said to Anika. "I'll find you at dinner."

But the girls hadn't the time to step apart before the novice guard interrupted. "Apologies, my Lady, Lord Raylor requires both of you."

Curiosity, that dammed thing, it wound through her mind and twisted until it warped to worry. No, he wouldn't want an argument then, not before an audience. Plans, all that lot and their plans, such pains Belladonna took to be excluded, but her grandfather's would not be avoided, not when he had called her already. Belladonna found her arm hooked through Anika's, her dear friend's steadiness a blessing as they journeyed to whatever awaited in the Great Hall.

8
KITTY

28TH OF HELENAI, 447, THIRD AGE

"Never see the wall." Pa's words, a distraction he had so often called it. *"See the wall, and you'll forget the eyes. Paint the wagons, and they miss our wands."*

Eyes, walls, the Great Bridge to Tenor's castle – Kitty saw them all – but the city was brick and sand. To beggars, it gave only brick and sand.

"We aren't going to the wall?" Wyvern asked as dirt streets turned to sun-baked cobble. Perhaps Wyvern could have said more; surely she would have, but for how she faltered under Kitty's gaze.

Not a day passed, and few words had been spoken, so soon to have done wrong by her new companion. Had her eyes truly been so cruel? Kitty dared not meet Wyvern's gaze again, not for the risk that those red eyes would lose their light once more. "Supplies," Kitty said. "We don't have enough saved."

Had Maker or Mother any mercy, Kitty's companions couldn't hear the slight lie, the small difference between not enough and none.

"We've passed shops."

Kitty could only shake her head, shops of bricks. "We don't have the coin for them." Only by her aspect's gifts could Kitty hear Robin's beak click; he knew the lie as well as she, but as it would seem, Wyvern did not.

"What will we do?" Wyvern asked.

In that city, Kitty had seen her people and kin play along with the lie, the near self-made delusion that it was their poverty and not their blood that would see them turned away. But Wyvern's words held none of those liar's tells. Didn't she know?

"There's a place," Robin said, directing his words to Wyvern but keeping his eyes on Kitty alone. "Emmit's been good to us, Kitty; he could help."

"Maker, help us," Kitty hissed. The traditional Speaker's chain pierced to her ribs and navel, and wrapped around her wand rattled a song for her mind only. When had her god's name become a curse in her mouth? What an odd plea it was when the Speakers had made it so clear the god they shared with Kitty would never smile upon her let alone help her.

But Robin's words were true; she knew this, just as her feet knew where to lead before her head had made its choice.

The forge was a smudge, a blemish trapped between wall and sea; perhaps it never had a name. Perhaps that, too, had been buried in the soot that crept over its neighbours like Wild Lands vines.

A chorus of shouts reached Kitty's ears just moments before a column of smoke drifted above the roofline. A beacon Robin would have known far better than she. But Kitty hadn't a moment to look at her friend's face; no, it wasn't until she saw the tiny shop, all black against white marble, that Kitty realise she had started running.

Had the forge not been stone beneath the soot, it surely would have been ablaze, for all the smoke that poured from that ever-missing door. Perhaps it was the Maker's blessing such places were built to stand against dragons. Kitty held her breath as she searched the smoke-heavy square until her eyes caught Sir Emmit, hunched and still wearing those flower-crested bracers of some southern house. And as the heartbeat calmed from Kitty's ears, she heard it was he who yelled, all alone, great bellowing threats to nothing, despite the smoke.

Kitty hadn't the time to catch her breath nor imagine a veneer of composure before Robin pushed past her.

"Sir?" Robin called. "Sir, can you hear me?"

All in a moment, Sir Emmit spun; his hammer raised just as suddenly as Kitty's hand found her wand. But Emmit's arm lowered, and his eyes softened as they fixed on Robin. "Robin!" he called. "You're late; you know that you start at dawn."

On the edge of Kitty's sight, Wyvern reached for her sword as Emmit strode towards Robin, but Kitty raised a hand, and her new companion stilled.

"Let Robin talk to him," she said. Robin's ally, Robin's contact, had Kitty not been so focused on her friend, she might have thought it a failure that she brought none of her own.

Robin sighed – that whistling hum of Nestias alone – as he stepped to the soot-covered knight. "I don't work here anymore, Sir. I lost my apprenticeship ten years ago, do you remember?"

For all a Castilla's hearing, Kitty understood nothing of what Emmit grumbled as he pulled Robin to the smoking shop. She very nearly followed them, just until her eyes caught how Wyvern didn't, how those eyes, more like Kitty's own than any Human's, lingered on the door and how her hand again twitched towards that sword.

"It's not his fault," Kitty said as, finally, smoke ceased to flow.

"He was a knight?" Wyvern asked. "Why—"

"He *is* a knight." A paradoxical urge to defend the man she so often derided rose in Kitty's chest. "You must have heard stories about the Seventh."

White hair danced in the summer sun as Wyvern nodded. "My steward took us to the Brackish; I saw the castle burning."

"Aye, it burned." Emmit's voice startled Kitty as he strode from his shop with Robin on his heels. "In all the ways, no fires burn, and all came black as Lyria tore east from west."

Wyvern took just a step closer. "You were at the siege break?"

Emmit gave Wyvern no answer as he pointed just above Kitty's head. "See! Still fixed!" he cried.

Just slightly, and for just a moment, Robin's feathers ruffled. "I know you fixed her hair-ring; that doesn't mean she's my wife."

Had Sir Emmit heard him at all, he gave no sign as he once more retreated to the forge. And again, Robin followed, but for just a moment, he hesitated in the doorway. "He doesn't mean anything by it; we aren't like that, Kitty and I."

"I've never met a Human from the siege break." Wyvern's eyes still watched the forge but with a reverence Kitty had never caught before.

"He wasn't," Kitty corrected.

"You said he fought in the Seventh."

"He did, but he followed a mage into the Deep Woods. Robin said they found him months after the rebellion. He doesn't talk about it, not to me anyway."

For all the travels of Mari group, for all their routes through the provinces, never had Kitty seen those cursed trees, that place the Fae brought along, that hid the realm of Daemons, that Other Place. Those half-elves of her troop, that would take its trees for their mages' amulets would find their prize alone. It had been part of Pa's promise to protect and heal just the same as those leaders of elves and humans. No faster routes, no shortcuts.

They should have been safe.

Should have been, yet the purges lay seventeen years in the past and only Kitty remained. The only survivor and not half the leader her father had been on his worst day. How had she fooled another into following her by accident? "You don't have to follow me," Kitty said after the silence grew too much.

Wyvern's face flashed with something Kitty couldn't name. "I'd follow you any—" Wyvern cut herself off. "I can't lead... I want to follow you."

And what could Kitty say against such words?

The sun had gone as Kitty led her party from the shop, a day spent for naught but a day's food and burned maps. No, Kitty couldn't be ungrateful, not when Sir Emmit could give only what he had. A better leader would have had her own contacts; perhaps a better leader would have waited until morning to leave those walls. But she had a feeling, somewhere deeper than a thief's instinct, that cried to leave the city, as Robin's song said, from one strange world to another.

9

Belladonna

25th of Helenai, 447, Third Age

Lyrian Humans didn't raise armies against each other, at least not while the mages were a passable threat, yet of eight Mage Rebellions, only the First and Sixth ever reached so far into the Northwest. Those petty exceptions to the story of unity, the eternal wars of thieves and spies, scarcely crossed the Ridgeline that tore Lyria down the center. The only battle High Crest had truly needed to stand against was that of cold, but in the case of the Great Hall, just like those once-loved gardens, she had been built for that separate battle of ego.

The Lords that came before had no need for the realities of the cold; certainly, they had no concept of Lord Raylor's budget, his first and favourite child. They had gold to spend, then they had gold to borrow. What use had the second lords had for hearths? For tapestries and rugs? What fear had Carsari lords of cold when they brought that white marble of temple walls?

Fear there should have been, for those stones gave no god's protection, and that great white hall, that proud affront against modesty, drew gooseflesh and white breath even deep in those months of summer; a frigid effigy to the winter its master so scorned.

And such an affair for nothing, those so self-important to demand such a setting were those same so ready to scorn a mere provincial capital. Still, all the better to Belladonna's mind, let the fools be seen by the grandest fool of her blood, let them all flock to the true capital.

Where Belladonna expected a crowd behind the hall's side doors, she was met instead by a wall, a press of bodies that swayed and writhed as one, like the old enemy's beasts of blood magic. In but a step into that mass, Belladonna's hand was wrenched apart from Anika's, and no matter how Belladonna searched, she hadn't the height to see her friend beyond the crowd.

Like swimming through the tar sand beyond Elody's Point, each push gained only the pain of the hoard's retaliation; had Belladonna even a Fensmirri's strength, she couldn't have moved those that pressed from all sides. Only by the fear, those panicked steps back as humans saw her staff, did she wade through the bodies. Still, even as nobles trampled each other to escape, they jostled Belladonna. Elven strength wasn't enough to hold against a single human, and so she fluttered through the crowd, a leaf in a summer storm, until an elbow she never saw coming sent her stumbling against a stranger's back. His cape, with patterns of grey birds, all drawn as if by a child, caught around Belladonna's staff.

"Watch it, half-breed," he hissed.

What tolerance Anika's presence bought her friend's people fractured with so few words. Belladonna made no move but to allow the crowd to push her staff further against the fool's back. "I'm still the heir to this province, On'ik."

That strange insult from before their enemies were human, before they were dwarves and witches but still dragons and Onari fell past her lips; how simple the common tongue was that he failed to understand even the feeling behind the word.

And how little he could have understood, for he only scoffed, "We'll see."

Those amateurish birds tore as Belladonna yanked her staff back, their meaning still lost to her as the stranger gaped at their loss, perhaps an answer only Southerners would care for. But its place vanished from Belladonna's mind as, for only a moment, the crowd shifted, and Alyria's aura shone through, a sunset over choppy seas. As if a ship to such a beacon, Belladonna followed its light until the crowd abated and, once more, she was by her sister's side.

"What's happening, Lyri?" Belladonna's breath came as a cloud in the eternal cold outside the hoard. "Why has Grandfather gathered everyone?"

Alyria shook her head. "It won't be good news, will it? It's never good news."

What answer could she give her sister when uncertainty gave no more comfort than the promise of damnation? What, when she knew so little of such times? How many times had High Crest truly gathered? Few enough in her own lifetime, and none since the Eighth, since Jacob's first arrival. But what to tell her sister? Too clever to be fooled, Alyria, too, knew they could only hope for stagnation for some months yet.

At the periphery of that shifting mass, it became so much less one entity. Familiar faces pushed and vanished between strange ones. No, not a Daemon-cursed creature at all, but a shipwreck, all those faces fighting to the surface, the moment of triumph only to be pulled back. Still, one was missing again, and no more was his absence a twice-forgotten thought.

"Where's Father?" Belladonna whispered for elven ears alone under the pounding hum of voices. But even as Alyria turned at the words, she gave no answer but to once again shake her head.

The hoard all at once was silenced as those great pulleys and winches whined their warning of the great doors opening. A crowd with no space to breathe moved as one to form a path as Lord Raylor strode between them. Those guards that followed were not given the same courtesy, but still, not a sound was made as they added their number to the beast. Not a soul breathed a word until Lord Raylor took his place at Hall's head. His smile may well have seemed genuine to the strangers, perhaps too to the locals who'd never seen him smile at Alyria. "Thank you all for joining me in today's most joyous news."

Was that joy behind his eyes? No, but neither was it sorrow; if Belladonna had watched him show much beyond anger in all her years, perhaps she would have its name. But her grandfather's words allowed no pause for contemplation. "It is the hope of every parent that they will find a suitable match for their child. And at long last, after thirty six years, I too have found one."

A lesser warning cry came from the ill-used doors, and after so long apart, Belladonna saw her father, his hair longer and clothes looser, but those storm-grey eyes still matched Alyria's. A man unchanged and yet so different for the stranger on his arm. She was tall and thin, darker than a northerner of the usual descent, lighter than an Elf, but still, the silk of her gown and goosebumps along her bare arms spoke truer than any family name to her origin. Only as she walked past did Belladonna truly see her face, her youth. She couldn't have been more than a few years past her Calling.

Lord Raylor waited only until they reached his side to speak once more. His words were no surprise to any who recognized the strange grey birds stitched on the stranger's gown. "It is with great pride that I announce the engagement of my son and Lady Eugenia Gavire."

No force could have made Belladonna join that raucous applause that rose from the room; not even Alyria's eyes could sway her that day. She tried to meet her father's eyes, to read a man she'd never before needed to wonder about, but no power of hers could draw them as her grandfather once more raised a hand. "We will open The Dark Sky with the beginning of one man's search; it seems only right to close with the end of another's. They will be married on Helena's Triumph."

Was that what hid behind her grandfather's eyes? Was its name triumph? Was he so pleased that his threat had come true? Less than a month until that celebrated centre day of the Dark Sky Festival and only just five until her father's promise could be made true. But in that moment, she named her father a liar. He met her eyes, without guilt, without remorse, nothing but a Fin'neshi-touched kind of joy, a child's joy. No liar but worse, to be a fool.

The applause all around her faded, patterns and echoes, or perhaps it was only the storm that raged beyond the walls. Belladonna saw only a glimpse of understanding from those gray eyes as she tore her gaze away and pushed past the wall of bodies. She should have done the same all those years ago.

Her master's eyes caught Av'vella even as she hid behind her grandmother's skirts; he saw Liv'vella. No, he couldn't see her; the masters could never see her, she'd promised Mother.

Mother. Thei'nas annan mott'tir se't re'nnan.

"You'll take both, or you'll have neither." Grandmother's voice didn't waver; she was important. Why was she so important?

The master scoffed, white breath in the white room, "You forget yourself; I won't have my son's name tarnished, not by your lot."

"Ask him then, ask him what my daughter was to him," Grandmother spat, and Av'vella held her sister ever tighter. "Just look at the babe; I'm sure you'll recognize your son's eyes."

Some sign she didn't see, but Av'vella heard the guards as they moved to her, only the guards, her grandmother's voice lost to the racket. Mother's amulet – All that was left after every image of Mother had been burned with her body – she shouldn't have taken it; *grandmother said to hide it away; the carved wood fit just perfectly in her hand.*

An iron hand clamped around her arm for just a moment before torches grew into wildfires. Someone screamed; perhaps it was her own voice. White walls blackened, and mana slipped away in rivers until the precious trinket was knocked from her grip.

None moved as the amulet fell. "Don't touch her," *Av'vella sobbed.* "You can't hurt her."

"An'neira," *the master growled,* "you swore to me."

"You took my son." *Grandmother's shadow fell long over Av'vella.* "Will you do differently, Hamish? Will you give them to the Speakers now that it's your blood?"

Av'vella pressed her face to her sister's blankets as the master stood. "Take the Bastards."

"No!" *the master's son spoke at last.* "Father, please, they're my daughters; I claim them."

"You can have the younger."

Grandmother only pulled Av'vella close. "You will take both."

"I won't have a slave in the family colours, An'neira. Give it to the Speakers, and I'll call the younger free."

"Father, you can't Bind her. I'll– I cede my position. I give it to my oldest daughter. You can't send away your heir." *Av'vella looked up, past her grandmother, to the man who was her father, even if those words would take so many years to understand.* "I'm already meant to cede the throne. Torren's boy can have it. I'm going to protect my girls."

Av'vella then still knew nothing of a Human's face, but the fury in the lord's eyes was far too familiar even then. "Fine then," *the once master said,* "if you're to have a pet, you might name it."

"Belladonna!" her father's voice carried down the storm-dark corridor. The footsteps in chase echoed against her own, a melancholy duet against the pouring rain. "Donna!" his voice echoed again.

She could have run, lengthened her stride, but against a taller man, no, she willed her feet to a stop. Had her staff been of mortal wood, surely it would have snapped from her grip before her father caught up.

"Belladonna," her father's breath came in gasps as he stepped to her side, "What is the matter with you?"

Belladonna rounded on her father. "With me? I haven't seen you in weeks, and now you're to be married?"

"Why shouldn't I be married? A father doesn't need his daughter's blessing, but I'd rather like it. So, tell me why, Donna?"

"Loyalty," Belladonna spat.

"Loyalty?" The silence of his question stretched for a long moment. "Donna, it's been fifteen years. I—I, I loved your mother, but—"

"You owned her!" For the second time in a day, mana leapt from her anger and became a screaming gale down the corridor. "You owned me as well, come to that."

A lesser fool would have left. "Donna, it was never like that. The two of us, we—"

"You let Mirri use her! Was it worth it, Father? For whatever he gave you? Did you promise you would protect her, too?" Had she control, her words would have stopped along with the tears. "I believed you! You promised, and I believed you!"

His hand was cold, yet burned as if flame for that bare moment it touched her shoulder. "I never stopped trying to protect you."

"You're to be married. We'll have a Lady Raylor before the winter."

"No, I gave you my place here." His head shook as if denial mattered. "My wife will have no more claim than I do; she knows this. She agreed."

"Father," Belladonna said, "Jacob is more liked than I, but few would complain if Torren's son was displaced. If there was another option..." The two of them knew just the same, the crest on the gown so quick to become a brand on the cheek.

In a moment, her father was no longer by her side, and a crack rang through the dark as his fist found the window. A spiderweb of cracks and blood welcomed the storm in a silent symphony of hail that echoed for long moments. Only the reflection of those eyes matching the storm met Belladonna's. A waiting kind of quiet.

"I won't have any more children. Eugenia will understand." As the storm soaked his hair, he looked, perhaps, just as any father would, chasing his child through the night. His eyes were ready with promises of home.

But Belladonna turned from him, her lone footsteps, a new kind of sorrow. "And Fin'neshi claims me that I trusted you once."

If his footsteps joined the pattern, she knew not over the growing storm, or for her own heart that pounded in her ears, or tears that still fell. No, the stone hall was by all signs empty, not a soul to be found, and even to elven ears, Belladonna thought herself alone until she was yanked by the arm to a side passage.

In an instant, Belladonna's staff was levelled to her assailant, but that low light kept no secrets for the servant girl with strange amber eyes. Those eyes that caught the light when none could be seen, had Belladonna been blind, she'd have known them for that watched feeling they brought. Pressed so close in that half-light, she could count those ridged valleys of the girl's scars, but, as with those on a friend, Belladonna's eyes skipped the flame marks for those eyes. "You've been watching me," she said.

The girl nodded. "I needed you alone."

Belladonna's grip didn't waver for a moment. "Why?"

"I heard you can get people out," the girl said. "I need your help."

10

Kitty

29th of Helenai, 447, Third Age

On that day, she learned a single truth for all travellers, land and sea: The Maker's Heart had no love for those bound to their own two feet. A traveller should have known such truths, but that life from lifetimes ago drew no rhymes to a day on foot. She had thought she'd known travel by a childhood on the roads – novel towns, no two days of the same sights, so many memories of roads passing beneath, rivers to a sailing ship. She'd known nothing, for even as the dark forced their pace to a stop, those city walls loomed still on the horizon.

That stained and torn map, packed alongside the meagre food Kitty had pushed to her companions, lay just before her knees. It was a soldier's map indeed, with routes and notes all along the Southwest. To the right noble or perhaps rather the right fence, it could be a true treasure indeed. The promise of plenty was a near temptation to retreat. However, had her wand been to hand, Kitty would have surely set the parchment ablaze. Inked moors and mountains offered no more hint to the thrice-damned puzzle of that contract than Sir Emmit's smudged battle notes.

And what hints of the contract? Hardly a note itself, not more than twenty words, a call for aid, a promise of riches, a liar the same as any from the province. Truly, she should have read it before she intervened. Only such hesitance burned as Breaker's damnation. For what number could she expect? If they had promised one hundred Golden Favours, would it be less of a lie than the idea of riches? Were vague lies truly worth less than those made precise?

Could she reject the pleas of parents begging for their children's return? Surely Robin would never forgive such an act, nor would Wyvern; she'd only face it alone. White hair matted red, pleas for a rescue snuffed, no, Wyvern need not go alone ever again. Kitty had given her word. True, it was the word of a thief but those blue beads on the chain beneath her dress were meant to mark her as a healer, a protector, and they need not be liars either.

"Why this contract?" Kitty asked.

"Nobody else wanted it," Wyvern said. "I was at the bounty board for days waiting to see who would take it, but nobody did. Somebody needs to."

Not simply unwanted but left to age. Still, Kitty couldn't help how she nodded to Wyvern's words for but a moment before she caught herself. Simple agreement helped nothing; to know its necessity was for her companions; to make sense of it was Kitty's role.

Her eyes cast again to that parchment.

"Great reward to any who can find our missing children." But ten words that made up the body, a list of names followed matched with hair colours and ages, seventeen names, the lot of them under ten.

Those scant words held but one hint, beyond the promise and prayer, the name signed at the bottom, the one who listed the bounty, a Lord Greyson of Gentea. A lord's name for attention, a crossing town its source. Surely, it was as right a place as any to search for the rest.

They'd stay on the King's Road, follow it west until the burned-out ruins of New Anaire, then turn to follow a lesser road north. The Coast Road would have been faster, safer too for the patrols along its length, if only the mark of a thief in Robin's two missing fingers didn't forbid them entry. Her fault.

"We might find something in Gentea. If—"

"You're right," Wyvern's voice cut through Kitty's. Her white face flushed red, a near glow against the firelight. "I mean, I think so too."

Kitty's own cheeks grew hot in turn, so her companions had thought of such things first. Was the shame wrong? Had she thought herself so above that none could see the obvious but her? She carried on. "If Gentea is the source, someone must have seen something."

Kitty could have been as blind as any other in the half-light, but still, she would have known how Wyvern bit her lip. A quiet of tension fell over that camp; only the fire's pops dared break it.

"Wyvern"—Robin's hands moved in turn with the name—"would you move the log? It's getting too high."

Kitty held her tongue to Robin's lie; that fire of grassland twigs died no slower for the silence, but neither did Wyvern question his words. So soon to know trust, to know a benign kind of lie, to know how Robin used them. Or had she not seen it? Her face gave no sign as great muscles hefted the sword, nearly Kitty's full height, to prod the embers. Childhood memories of the world beyond failed her; were the other provinces truly places so innocent?

But those were questions for Kitty's mind alone. From Wyvern, there came another entirely. "Where did you learn Talish?"

"Oh, um..." Robin's talons curled deep into the ground. "Was that wrong? I never knew much, I just saw when you said your name, so I thought..."

"When did you learn?" Kitty's words slipped as the answer came to her. "Did Sir Emmit teach you?"

Grey tones of the night broke into gleaming amber where fire light danced across ruffled feathers. "He worried about us being overheard and said his methods were to be kept secret."

A discordant chime rang through the night as Wyvern's sword fell back to the ground. "You didn't know?" Her eyes danced between the two. "You never told her?"

Robin's hands worked over each other, a fruitless battle to smooth his feathers. "I don't know much, and we never needed another language to be discreet. Kitty can hear a whisper from across this field. And we never met many Fensmirri in the city."

Kitty felt her ears flatten unbidden. "He wasn't much interested in talking to us."

His battle lost, Robin pulled hard on rag-patched sleeves, the click of his beak like a snapped bone. "No. He wasn't."

Maker, all she had sworn to protect him, all he trusted in her. She couldn't save him from memories any better than she had from the guards; what a leader she was. What crime of Robin's deserved such penance? But still, he carried her regret, her guilt, her burden. "You could have taught me. We could tell Emmit I'm not your wife in two languages."

"There's no sign for wife." Wyvern's hand dragged over her great scaled tail. "We don't have that."

"Oh," Kitty said as her mind yearned for more. She wanted to know more, to understand all that was Wyvern's life. But no, the heat of flame was nothing to those hidden beads, nothing more private than a reason to flee; none in the city mourned those who asked too much.

"I didn't know that," Robin said. "I only know a bit; I wouldn't be such a good teacher, maybe Wyvern—"

Wyvern's tail called forth a cloud of dust as she came to her feet. "It would be my honour." Twigs and grass joined their brethren dust as Wyvern scrambled to sit once more. "I mean, if you wanted to learn, it's not such a hard language; I'm sure you could. That is not to say you couldn't if—"

The rest of Wyvern's words were drowned out by a snapped twig. That grey night, a lonely sea, the waves of grass—all that stirred in that empty world beyond their fire's light. No, not empty, all too perfectly quiet. That old friend, that thief's instinct, carried her wand from its hiding place just as the night carried that feeling of eyes.

"Just the basics then—"

"Shh," Kitty hissed. Silence filled the place Wyvern's voice had been. And by a handful of dirt, the warm circle of light vanished, and that grey-toned night overtook the party.

A silent breath, a waiting breath. A third and a fourth. Pa's watching count.

One.

Two.

Three.

From silence: a cacophony. From all sides, they sprang on the once-haven.

Too many and none at all; cloaks as to the night, holes cut in the grey. All around, nowhere to run, no escape.

White light, colder than Helana's own shine, banished night for day, and Kitty's eyes followed its blessing to Wyvern, her sword alight with black flame as attackers rushed the halo. And as if moths cleft from their wing, they fell to pieces.

Robin. She couldn't hear him, and dark as night, he vanished to the grey. Only too late, she turned; she had searched too long.

There was a hatchet in a gloved hand and a man who raised it over his head. It glinted in the strange flame. No, Kitty saw not man nor axe.

Too close, he was too close.

No thought, no call, no incantation on the wind. A movement she didn't remember, and the gout of her own flames that rent through wild grasses behind the pile of ash that used to be a man.

The world danced and wobbled around Kitty's eyes. The ground that rushed to meet her played no part in reality until she was yanked back by her hair.

"Out of mana, little witch?" A voice Kitty couldn't realize was unfamiliar hissed. "Not so clever now." The bite of steel on her neck so much less present than the hand in her hair.

She couldn't breathe for his knee on her back nor for the cold floor pressed against her face. "You're a test," he hissed.

Stolen daylight vanished, and void rushed back for its claim. A camp of slow chaos and screams in her own voice. A great sword clattered to the stone ground.

"His words," his breath ghosted over her ears, "are wasted on such a creature."

Kitty's head was yanked to the side, and that wicked blade carved a shallow line across her neck. Dark rivulets of crimson blood dripped onto the grass beneath her knees. When had she fallen?

Time and reality snapped back, and her head spun at the sound of Robin's cry. The once-blazing grass had burned down to a smoulder. In the half-light, Kitty saw a woman atop Robin's form. Black feathers and dark rag-bin clothes, usually so indistinct from the night, lost their refuge as they tangled about the woman Robin grappled with. His shaking hand clamped around the stranger's wrists, a desperate final defence against the bloody blade that shook just a hair above his eye.

Never again.

Kitty's feet moved before she could think to call a spell she had no means for. Two women rolled as one. Kitty's shoulder cried its wails of grinding bone from the hit. A tumble through the air, seconds that felt longer than her own life. All ended in a heap on the ground. Only by the Maker's blessing did Kitty end atop the prone woman. But she hadn't a moment nor the strength to resist as the bandit flipped their positions.

Kitty called for a spell, another torrent, a blaze to banish dark forever back to its master, but not half a spark came from that wand as that grinning woman plunged down with her knife. Only so few things could outdraw a cat's own hand; before that knife could taste Kitty's blood again, her wand's flame-hot crystal found its home in the bandit's eye.

The woman reared back, the scream of a stuck pig, a lurch so fast it wrenched Kitty's wand from her hand. That longing moment of theft, that empty place it left, nothing to how her mind already screamed. The wand was only half a stopper for blood that poured a torrent from the ruined eye. Another nothing as the stranger once more raised her blade.

The blade fell as one, with arms and chest, and apart entirely from the waist and legs that followed.

Kitty heard her own voice cry out against the aftermath quiet as a great calloused hand pulled her from beneath the dead woman. She struck with bare fists at the wall of iron that clutched her arms. But there was no man, no monster to haunt shadows of a lifetime long past, only Wyvern, only furrowed brows and white hair, a halo under Helena's silence.

"Don't touch me!" Kitty gasped as she pulled away. Loose hair fell across her eyes, an ebony curtain against the night's renewed grey stillness. "Just don't... Robin! Where's Robin?"

"I'm here," he called out. Kitty spun to his voice just fast enough to catch how he pulled her wand from the bandit's eye. Just too fast to catch how Wyvern's eyes hardened.

No measure of moments passed before she reached his side. Her hands hovered just moments above his arms. "Are you okay?" she asked, cat's eyes strained to see signs of that telling dark in a world without colour. "Did she hurt you?"

Robin's head tipped in no slight way. "I'm fine, but Kitty, you're bleeding."

Unbidden, her hand found the stinging spot on her own neck, darkness against darkness in a world of greys, but she knew blood for that smell, always under the herbs of Pa's wagon. Her own breath may have kept steady if not for the sound of Wyvern's catching as mundane firelight reclaimed the camp.

A catch of breath, and not even her own, but how it sent her heart to a rabbit's beat. "Robin, my pack." Her voice trembled. "There are herbs from—" How long had she truly held on to what little was left? Surely not so long to have forgotten, but no, not a memory came from her stumbled words.

In his way, Robin voiced no question but launched a scrambled search of the carrion camp's remains.

The question came from Wyvern with a twitched hand and an aborted step. "Isn't there some magic you could do?"

Disappointment came in waves. Kitty couldn't quite name the feeling, like a shame from another life, such a strange thing for it to be aimed at another.

"I'm not a Blood Mage," she spat, but her own heart recoiled. Had she not bought her magic? Spilled blood for a Daemon's deal? Was being a witch so dissimilar? Yes, instinct older than a thief's whispered in trickled mana, change without control, a senseless comfort, but one for her mind alone, and Wyvern's eyes hid nothing of her hurt nor her fear. "But my pa taught me plenty without."

Helena walked her silent quest over the three as they sat just quietly in a camp of the dead. Herbs, long bereft of scent, stung with what little potency time had spared, secured by a rag stolen from a dead man. Her wand was once again wrapped by her acolyte's chain, its warmth stolen by The Mother's blue beads. Comfort, a near answer for forgiveness, was louder to her mind than chanted sermons. She so nearly missed when Wyvern broke the silence.

"Robin needs a weapon." Wyvern's eyes strayed not from the sword across her lap but, in reflection, met Kitty's own.

"I don't," Robin said.

Matted hair cascaded over Wyvern's shoulders as her head shook. "You're no Warrior vocation. You aren't strong enough to fight with your hands."

"I don't need to be." Robin's beak clicked. "I don't... I don't need to kill anyone."

"We have to."

Kitty felt the eyes settle on her back, but she had no words for them, her own eyes cast over the broken bodies. So many years fighting hunger and winter, had they truly never killed? Surely they must have, every coin to their pocket was one taken from another; surely there had been others she never saw. A pile of ash, once a man. So simply he had gone, and how little guilt he left. The lone black bead on her chain, ever frigid, rejecting its companion's warmth. How many would she give to The Dark Mother? To the Mother's opposite and adversary?

By rights and by the Maker's doctrine, it should have been none at all until she joined those black robed Speakers to carry the executioner's burden. An early temple law, one of the very first, the bedrock under Lyrian justice, none but those who spoke for The Dark Mother could send others to her grasp. Beggars and kings alike were to be powerless over death. Perhaps in Helena's time, the scripture had spoken true.

Or perhaps it never had.

Queens waged war, and beggars fought in the street. Spies vanished, and mages rebelled. An acolyte knew death sacred, but a thief knew it cheap, so readily given in a city that gave so very little, so common in a kingdom of eight rebellions — The Dark Mother's a familiar face in a land cut with steel and sundered by mana. Even so, execution, that calmest violence, remained the sole domain of the black robed Speakers, by headsman's sword or witch's pyre, it was their responsibility and privilege alone. Likewise, all that came after.

There wouldn't be a Dark Mother's Speaker to tend the bodies in that field, to clean and dress and make them whole before burial. There wouldn't be a burial; The Dark Mother could take the twisted things they'd become or leave them to watch the sky forever. A wicked thought formed and was struck down in a moment; only the taste of it lingered. Her judgment mattered not; none present could grant peace to the dead.

"Not all fights end in death," Robin said, "there are other ways."

"You need one." Kitty didn't wait for protests that would never come as she found her prize, another once man; perhaps his body would have retained the title if not for the rent torn from shoulder to hip, cauterised it would seem by those strange black flames Wyvern had summoned. Such thoughts held no heed, and she pried a hatchet from stiff fingers.

Robin looked away as she held it out. "Kitty, I don't—"

"You do," Kitty cut him off. "I can't protect you here. I haven't – if I'm the leader, you need it."

Robin turned back to her; green eyes met black in silence for a long moment before a feathered hand took the dead man's hatchet.

A truer leader perhaps would have spoken to how talons dug through blood-spattered earth, but for Kitty's eyes, another prize showed itself and drew her back to the once man. Not eyes locked forever open, too slow to know their own pain or a glimpse of a heart torn apart behind kindling bones.

It wasn't the many-pointed-star amulet, identical on every chest, though those would stay in her mind. No, what caught her eyes was a bundle of scrolls all the wrong colour for a scavenger's parchment, clean of soil if not of blood. Be it the guide thief's instinct or Maker's Eye; those too-clean scrolls found their way to

Kitty's hand. There were six, all identical, with broken seals of a crossroads house and bearing not more than twenty words.

She knew the words they held at a glance. They were the very same she had been puzzling over on her own copy of the contract.

"They weren't bandits," Kitty's voice echoed to her own ears.

"What?" Robin asked.

Kitty held out the bundle. "They were waiting. For others. For us."

Wyvern's voice carried over the wind. "There were others? They tried to help." Bones, with no more use, cracked as her sword struck against the chest of an already still body. "How could they? Why?"

There were reasons Kitty wished not to voice, reasons none should stray alone in her home city, reasons girls never wandered the docks at night. Perhaps she had hoped children would have been safer inland, far from the ports young acolytes and urchins alike never returned from. She couldn't make her voice form those words, that the not-bandits could have been the lookouts for such monsters.

Instead she shook her head. "We have to keep moving if they were camped here—" Cat's ears turned on a shifting wind, grief for strangers forgotten if only just for a moment, just a hint on the breeze, but a kick of dirt killed the low fire as she stood. No attack and such a familiar cadence; a lifetime ago, they sounded so different in the city.

Kitty waited only for her companions to stand before she made for the sound. "Where are we going?" Robin asked.

"Shh," Kitty hushed. There was another breeze, and on it, another hint.

With each shifting wind, she became certain for those long moments she had imagined such sounds, certainty broken by a breeze.

Slow steps turned to a sprint as she saw the camp, empty in the grey-toned night and still for all but creatures of the Mother's own hand. Horses, unwary of strangers, unknowing of their masters' fate.

"Hurry," Kitty whispered, as she grabbed hold of a pale horse's reins, "there might still be more of them." For the first time in a lifetime, her smile reached her eyes.

Before Helena sunk below the western sky, the little band rode. Hooves thundered on the well-trod King's Road. As those great walls finally disappeared over the eastern horizon, Kitty could almost imagine the sound of wagon wheels and the smell of herbs alongside them.

11

Belladonna

25th of Helenai, 447, Third Age

Few knew the true nature of aptitudes. Fewer more who were born beyond Fae's empire cared to expose the lie inherent in a mage's control — the central myth that all four of water, fire, earth and air were held in equal sway by all. A fiction pushed forever by the outsiders' reverence for that number, but a people of ten thousand gods understood a deeper complexity, and any novice mage knew which truly called her.

A chance of birth, fascination, and the Eighth had laid bare the power of fire to those who survived its onslaught. For all a sword could rend, no wound held sway against those savage lines of a fire cast; no scar like those who escaped its never grasp, for all Belladonna's eyes caught those knights who found She Who Waits on smoking fields, the red-haired Human's face gave no fascination, no more reproach than a friend's.

Flickers of torchlight lingered on the servant girl's pitted cheek as if they, too, remembered where their kin had touched. In that dim storm's light, Belladonna could look nowhere but those too-canny eyes.

A test perhaps, but no, she had no help for a human, none such that a stranger should have known. Should the traitor have been so bold? No, but a spy perhaps, a trap laid, though such an odd trap, to send one without elven blood. Or perhaps not a trap at all then, but no words worth the risk in belief.

"I'm not sure what you heard..." Belladonna began.

"Please," the girl cried, her eyes growing wide, "they tell me you can help; please don't say it was a lie."

A tale grew behind the stranger's words, some subtle call that drew an instinct, some lesson not quite ignored. Belladonna found her staff gripped tighter than she recalled. "This isn't who you are. Is it?"

Hunched shoulders unfolded with a breath, such a small change in height, such a great deal to one so small. "No." Her voice remained unchanged, but that hidden edge of panic vanished behind narrowed eyes. "But I do need your help. And you'd only listen to somebody weak."

A tether severed as Belladonna dragged her eyes away. "You're mistaken; I don't know what you're talking about." A story, a word, perhaps a truth, her own if not the stranger's, and still not worth the risk of saying more; she turned her back. "I must go."

"Av'vella." It was her oldest name, the eldest's name, only her own until death. That old name, never spoken by her father, halted the step Belladonna had yet to take. "That is you, innit?"

"Who gave you that name?"

"Erh'henni."

Belladonna dared not look back even faced with the name of her ring's first member. "Who sent you to her?"

"I wasn't looking for you." The voice was all too close for lack of footsteps. "I knew nothing of this until we arrived, but this is my only chance."

"What help could you need of me? There is no Human slavery in Lyria." Belladonna risked a glance back to the eyes she could still feel.

"Isn't there?" the girl tucked a hair back into her handkerchief. "What would you call it then? When I'm sold to settle a debt? When I can't leave without being dragged back? I can't make you help me, but don't lie; don't tell me there's nothing you can do."

Those tales she had been told, those truths of her people, were they more real than that girl's? Or were they mayhap only more worth the words for them being of her own people? No dream came from any great love of reality, but no words, not even those, the last of her mother, could force it to change for a tale. "I'm truly sorry, but I can't help you."

"Are tragedies fair when they fall beyond your bloodline?"

Knuckles turned white around her staff. "I never said that."

"But you would leave me to this?" the girl asked. "If the mask had been real, if I were the little lamb afraid of the woods, you wouldn't have hesitated."

Belladonna didn't know if that was true. "I'm sorry, I—"

"I was once." The girl's right hand, just as burned as her face, traced the damaged skin. Something broke behind those eyes – something forced back down in an instant. "But I wouldn't have survived staying that way. I didn't escape quickly enough, and now I'm not worth saving?"

"I can't help you, and I can't change that either." Somewhere, the roll of thunder caught Belladonna in how loud she'd become. She stepped to the servant. Humans so often stood tall – loomed over those of Onari descent, yet even in stockinged feet, Belladonna's chin tipped down to meet those amber eyes. "It's no longer safe."

"I can't imagine it was ever very safe."

The girl's scars looked so like Anika's; they covered so much less, but for a moment, Belladonna's eyes lingered on them the way they never did on her friend's. Perhaps the new understanding that the servant's had been no accident. Excuses of safety rang hollow for even her own mind.

Of all Belladonna could have said, it should never have been the truth. "There is a traitor, someone spying for the guards. I don't know who, but I can't take risks while they're unknown."

"I'm sorry." Of the tales that girl had told that night, perhaps it was Belladonna's own hope that it was that last one which sounded most true. "I didn't know."

The tone caught Belladonna more than the words, something that had her feeling wrongfooted as if she were the interloper demanding things in a stranger's home.

"No, you had no way of knowing." A thought, perhaps another instinct, flared to life. Thoughts she had discarded connected under that feeling, the too-perfect trap, the dread she felt beside her friends' names, the ease she had with indisputably innocent Anika. How could that same ease come from a stranger? "You truly could have had no part in it. You knew nothing. Perhaps—"

Some small vicious part of her bade her not to trust any of that girl's kind. No, she couldn't listen to such things, not when she'd only just realized how little she must have known of her allies for one to have fooled her with such ease. Belladonna straightened. "Perhaps we can find a way to help each other."

"You'd have me help you?" the girl asked.

"I don't know which of my allies I can't trust. I need somebody I know isn't involved." Somebody whose heartstrings couldn't be pulled.

"It's no small thing you ask; they can't find out you've asked me to watch them." Belladonna didn't quite notice how close the girl had gotten until she was pulled away from those eyes. "And I need your word: if I help you, you'll help me. You must swear you'll not leave me to his mercy."

A vow to such, to something Belladonna need not question she would do; it was the easiest in the world. "I swear I'll get you out once we find the traitor."

"By the Dark Sky's Open."

"What?" A step back took Belladonna only a breath from the girl.

"Swear you'll get me out before the Open."

"Before? The lords won't leave until after the festival."

What small distance Belladonna had bought, the girl closed. "More will come, and there are those who prefer I don't see the festival end; I must be away before they find me. Can you swear it?"

"Yes, I give you my word. I'll have you out by the festival's open." Another instinct, perhaps some vestige of a Seer's blood, or perhaps that well-used paranoia, told a new tale, a warning, some far-off regret she couldn't know, some ignorant wish for itself, and that cold grasp behind all doors.

Echoes of chatter cascaded down the halls, and the servant girl, the new ally, ducked into the shadows before she cast one last glance back. "You never asked, but they call me Elysa."

12

Wyvern

30th of Helenai, 447, Third Age

No delicate thing had ever found refuge in the beauty of Wyvern's homeland, not even in words beyond sentiments of "small" and "weak"; those no pretty thing to be either. She wondered, as Kitty's fingers danced through the pair of signs if she wished it was the first time she had seen her language being broken by such grace.

The trespasser had returned, a stranger in the Fens without leave of the Elders, no friend. And yet he'd returned. Those blue eyes as much a beacon against the woods as her own skin in that tannic river. Why had he returned? Had he thought her a liar — believed she wouldn't tell her Steward of his trespass? Had he known she hadn't? Her first tenet broken before she had reached her first decade.

"Like this?" Kitty asked.

For a bare and weak moment, Wyvern hardly wanted to correct Kitty's mistake, if only because the lesson would add a few-second delay to the time Wyvern could see her make the signs again.

"Almost, but—" she faltered. It wasn't until the short distance reduced Kitty's form to a blur against the glaring light that Wyvern noticed how her horse had once more fallen behind. Even the beast was clever enough to know how unworthy she still was. "Y—You have to use your right hand."

"Really?" Kitty's brows furrowed. "You used your left."

"It isn't my name; I couldn't sign it as if it were. That would be a lie." Right hand for signing about oneself, left hand for everyone else. That was the way, and that was always the way.

"Even if it was a demonstration? Isn't that a bit confusing?"
The book of drawn hands made not a sound as black water ate its pages. "I don't understand." *The boy grasped for its sodden remains.* "Why can't I draw the signs? You won't have to repeat them anymore."

Wyvern couldn't help the growl. Human words—she had so few. "Don't write. Don't share."

Those blue eyes turned from the lost book, his hands red from autumn-chilled water. "That's not...I wasn't going to. Don't you trust me?"

Wyvern kicked another twig to the near-stopped river. It would not be long until frosts turned their clearing into winter pools. "Can't write," she said. "Dwarf elders didn't."

"Who? The Onari?" *He didn't cease when the only response was another growl.* "Everybody writes now, even the dwarves. Anyone can learn it."

No, he misunderstood. Such a Human condition. "No! I can't."

"Why not?"

"You don't—" *Another growl. A sapling splintered beneath her fist. She hadn't the words; he hadn't the signs.*

Mud splashed where the boy scrambled to his feet. Neither of them even nearly grown and already he was near a head shorter than she. "If you'd let me teach you more, you could say."

"No! Only Elders speak."

"If your people don't have secrets, why are only some allowed to know Common?"

Secrets were lies, secrets broke the first tenet. The elders weren't capable of breaking that rule simply by following the final tenet. She hadn't the words to explain, or perhaps she had too many already; too many foreign words confusing her mind, drawing her astray from the rightness of the rules. That boy's questions that she could no longer pretend that she didn't, in a cold moment on that colder bank, understand.

"We don't get confused." She shouldn't have snapped. Her horse stumbled, and Kitty's ears flattened. "I mean, we don't lie, so nobody has to misunderstand."

In moments that could have been Wyvern's entire life, Kitty's ears straightened, and her shoulders fell back. "Okay," she said as the reins traded hands., It was a single fluid movement; it could have been a dancer's as her hand found a rhythm with her horse's gait, a wrong kind of tranquillity across those signs for name and cat.

"Suppose it means your name is Cat," Robin said. "It's closer than Red Bird."

He had a name. Of course, he knew Talish — stolen by an outsider, but not by Robin. What could be stolen by those with all rights to know? Hadn't he the right? No secrets from kin. Weren't all Mirri's works kin? Could it matter when he had learned, perhaps? He knew, nonetheless. Springtime always brought mimicking birds to steal the winter's songs until they sounded just as their own. How appropriate then, the strange symmetry of his names. A raven named Robin. A blackbird signed Red.

"Suppose it's lucky enough we can get close then," Kitty said. "It would be difficult, wouldn't it, if we had other ones?"

"I don't know how to call you." Glass ice clung to winter furs across her back, endless flat white across the brackish sea, a windless year it had been.

Parsifal sat still as the silent night, still so afraid to fall through, so convinced by his people he wouldn't return as one of hers. "You know my name."

"I don't have a sign."

"Trespassers don't get Talish names, you said."

Always so worried. Perhaps he was right, too, but her Steward had always said how often wrong humans were. "You're a friend; friends share names."

"You have a sign for Mirri," he said with a laugh.

Wyvern only frowned at his laughter; he didn't understand. "It's not a nice one."

Another word she couldn't translate. What could be nice beyond being good or perhaps useful?

She still hadn't the signs for Parsifal.

Kitty was smiling as she turned to Wyvern's lagging horse. For a moment, Wyvern saw nothing but blue eyes, fine clothes, and fair hair matted with mud. She heard nothing of the question in Kitty's voice nor the answer Robin gave for her silence.

Mayhap it was the sun, or mayhap the journey had got to her, but, no, Wyvern couldn't lie to herself any longer. No more could she promise her heart was free from dishonour. Perhaps she could have lived with the dishonour of it all, with the lies in her own mind, if not for Kitty's smile.

They looked nothing alike, but for just a moment, in some way deeper than appearance she had looked to be such a true reflection of Parsifal. Of Wyvern's first love, first lie, first and final broken word. The warring duties that lay behind her two rings, both of which barred her any right to the joy in her heart when she watched Kitty's grace butcher her language.

"Wyvern?" Kitty's voice rang across the planes. "Do you want to keep going?"

Wyvern knew not if it was truly Kitty she was answering; she knew only that she could lie no longer. "It wouldn't be right," Wyvern heard herself say. "I'll scout ahead."

Wyvern's horse cried its protest as she urged it ahead. She couldn't bring her eyes to Kitty, not to those perfect hands, for even a moment. She hadn't been fair, not by half, not to either of them.

13

Belladonna

28th of Helenai, 447, Third Age

Morning frost tore through scant night things as Belladonna's blankets were ripped from her bed. Body moved before mind as she curled closer to Edmund's warmth. It was almost such a nice moment until her mind awoke.

"Well now, what's all this then?" Elysa's voice pierced the pre-dawn.

Belladonna gave not but a glance to the thief and her prize. Eyes strained against the sunless dark before she pressed further against her lover's side. "You're early."

"I'm only following your orders. It's before dawn, innit?"

"Helena can't be half sunk yet."

"Donna?" Edmund's chest rumbled as he cut in. "Who is this?"

That last bastion against the frigid dark fled as Belladonna pushed herself from her lover's chest. "Elysa is..." Her excuses faltered; what lie for someone so close? "She's going to be around until we can get her out."

"I didn't think we were still running this," Edmund said as his hand snaked around Belladonna's waist. "I never thought you cared about indentured servants. "Why now?"

"We don't have any in this castle. I never *knew*." Belladonna pried his hand away as she stepped from the bed. "No one ever *told* me." The true words beneath, such accusations they cried, a Human's ears could have heard them.

"What about her master, then? You don't think he'll notice the time she spends with you?"

"He won't, not during the day. Besides," Elysa said, "he's imposing on our lady's hospitality; if she wants something of his he ought to give it over."

Edmund ignored Elysa's comment. "I didn't think you would risk your people with it. Don't we risk enough for them already? We don't need another burden."

"Oi now." Elysa ripped what blankets remained from beneath Edmund. Perchance a weaker man would have faltered; Belladonna and Elysa had shared so few words since their meeting in that storm, none with such easy venom, but blue eyes set, as if iron, against amber. "I'd hate to think I was a burden."

Belladonna needn't have turned to see how both turned to her. "You aren't," she said. Her eyes caught Edmund's. "We're helping her."

What words Edmund's mouth opened to say were cut short by Elysa's. "I suppose that's settled then." So simple as it arrived, the venom in her voice lifted. "Now, I assume you have a clean slip."

It took more than mere moments to spy that fallen garment, knocked from where Edmund had laid it and buried beneath the previous day's ruined gown—such a waste of Edmund's work to be torn in haste but not a loss for the memories it harboured. Flame-bright hair held steady just within sight until that breath and heartbeat where Belladonna pulled the rumpled slip passed her eyes.

No, she heard no footsteps either, not a hint of movement in that moment of blindness until the corset was pressed to Belladonna's chest, the breath of one far too low to be her lover's raised goosebumps over Belladonna's neck. A moment of subtle eternities until Elysa leaned away, her hands danced through lacing with that deftness of ladies and maids.

"Do you—" Edmund's protest caught.

"Oi now, I should think I can lace a corset." Elysa's tone could have held a mirror to the smugness of any lord. "I've laced mine for longer than our lady has owned one."

No Elf should have welcomed the silence as Edmund vanished from Belladonna's sight. Then perhaps Belladonna was so wrong to crave its return as her love emerged from the sitting room, his arms laden with wool and silk of charcoal and night-blue. "You must have been young."

"If you must know, I was seven."

"Isn't that a bit odd?" His voice had that same green edge of envy and scorn as it did when he spoke to Vix. "Even a free common girl wouldn't start so young. How did you have the means?"

"Edmund!" For all the warning in her tone, Belladonna shouldn't have dared hope it would end the matter.

"Was I born to this? Do you know me so well to presume?" Elysa asked. "Perhaps my parents had ambitions before the Dark Mother took them. Didn't yours? Or have you seduced a noble girl without learning your letters? You seem the type."

"Elysa," Belladonna warned.

"I know my letters just fine," Edmund cut in.

"Certainly, I'm sure," Elysa hummed.

What illusion Belladonna held of control slipped as if stolen by summer storms, as laces and bundles all at once were abandoned. For a moment, she stood, only watching as a pair that called themselves servants crowded around her desk, all scattered with half-forgotten things. It seemed almost as if a truce was approaching until the quill shook in Edmund's hand.

"I'll make it easy then," Elysa said. "You should know our lady's name. You share her bed."

"That's enough," Belladonna snapped over the quill's scratch. Pages flew, knocked as the pair turned as one. She nearly missed how Elysa snatched the note from Edmund's hand. "Are you, children?"

"I'm sorry, Donna." Edmund made just half a move for her hand. "I didn't expect to take on someone ungrateful."

"Suppose that's me in my place then," Elysa said. "Is the lacing to your liking, my lady?"

Belladonna allowed those amber eyes to catch hers for but a moment. They would be having words, but not for an audience. "Edmund," she said as her eyes shifted, "you've been stalling. I need you to speak with Nadia today."

"Of course, Donna." And perhaps his words could have promised truth if he hadn't stood so still.

"Oi now!" Belladonna couldn't help but spin as Elysa's voice rang from behind her. "Better run along before somebody sees you here."

"I'll be back as soon as I can, Donna." Edmund fixed a glare at Elysa. "Don't cause trouble."

Not another word passed until that off-key, brass and wood chime echoed against the chilled stone, and footsteps sounded down that echoing tower.

"So that's one then," Elysa said.

Belladonna couldn't find the care to hide her sigh as she gathered the abandoned garments scattered across her bed. "And I suppose that was subtle."

Midnight silk, so fine to spark lightning in winter air, yet so soft in humid summer, wrapped around Belladonna's waist as Elysa settled on her knees. "You could have had a perfectly sweet girl, but you liked this better."

"Is this another mask, then? I wanted the *real* you."

Those amber eyes flicked up, then, just the hint of a smile. "Is there so much difference in our world?"

"It's not my world," Belladonna snapped.

"More yours than his."

"And Edmund?" A forced change from that debate Anika and Edmund couldn't understand after decades of trying, that truth humans never tried to see when they called elves half. "What was that about?"

"That?" Elysa came to her feet. "Oh, that's natural. North-easterners and all."

An odd chord Belladonna couldn't quite reach, so much like Alyria giving up a surprise too soon. "I never told you where he's from."

"Suppose I heard it in his voice then." The silence in that lie was heavier than the wool Elysa draped over Belladonna's arms. "What of the other two then?" Elysa asked into the tension.

Two who used to be three. Nit had been her name.

"Vixensha and Xaxirion," Belladonna corrected, though she knew the girl hadn't forgotten the names *accidentally*. "Not back yet. If it was them, I don't know if they will ever be."

"They'll have to; whoever laid the trap, they'll need to try again." There came no pause, not a moment to consider a coming trap. "Should pin your hair."

"No." It was not a thing to be debated, not a thing to share with outsiders either. None but a true enemy would see the legions of her people with hair tied back. But not on that day; none of the Seven Hundred held domain that day, no war, not beyond that which raged across her mind. A personal war wasn't nearly enough of one to dress for battle.

"Oh? And I suppose you can't tell me why?" Perhaps what Belladonna gave in silence was the only answer Elysa had needed. "Your people might have allies if they didn't hate everyone else."

"We don't."

"I'm sure, and nobody hates Mirri's lot either."

Belladonna so nearly cried out as Elysa took her staff from the wall. She felt a kind of tension she never before had the need to name grow. A mould that propagated in her chest a rot so quickly spread but so readily withered as Elysa held out the ancient weapon.

She dared not name nor truly acknowledge that feeling as she snatched the staff back. Perhaps only to be spared what amber eyes might show in their reflection, she spoke, "Come now; it's past time we spoke to my grandmother."

14

Belladonna

28th of Helenai, 447, Third Age

To a human, perhaps the castle was silent, and to those beasts of Lord Mirri's creation, perhaps a symphony of fallen dust and cat's feet, but to Belladonna's ears, only one melody echoed beneath night's silence. From that sound came calmness — no stranger hid behind those decades-known footsteps.

"I thought you swore to never have a maid." That sweet, familiar voice echoed through halls, empty but for three souls.

Belladonna stopped but didn't dare turn to her friend. Instead, perhaps of Fin'neshi's own bidding, she kept her eyes on Elysa. "Are you following me, Anika?"

"I heard talking in your room. I know where you go so early." Still wrapped in night clothes, Anika walked a wide circle to meet Belladonna's eyes. "Is this a good idea? I won't try to stop you."

What a notion. For a moment, Belladonna wanted to feel outraged. How dare anyone judge her for seeing her own true family, for wanting to lay eyes on and share songs with people she should have seen sooner. No, it was shame that flooded her mind, for she knew those weren't her reasons. Her motives hadn't been unimpeachable. She hadn't risen before dawn for any purer reason than the hope that a grandmother's love could surpass a Seer's vow. "I won't be long."

Anika's scarred fingers worked over cream silks never meant to be seen. "You always say that. You know you don't need to lie to me."

Blood charged to Belladonna's cheeks, the heat of another shame, another call to how she should have known to trust a friend. Trust, what an odd word that was, and to deny it to the one she knew deserved it most.

"You're right," Belladonna said, but honesty died in her throat before her tongue could admit uncertainty. "But I should be back before the castle wakes."

"You needn't worry, Lady Anika," Elysa cut in. "I'll keep her out of trouble."

The barest ghost of a smile crossed Anika's face. "You truly are new then," she said. "You complained of feeling ill last night — if I don't see you at breakfast."

For but a moment, Belladonna relinquished her staff to the wall. The emptiness hadn't the chance to sink its claws, as all the warmth of Anika's embrace set in as an iron-strong bulwark against the chill. "Thank you."

Her quest resumed. It should have been silent — that journey through corridors rarely trod, it so nearly was. So near that those twinges of doubt, those which kept Belladonna from sharing the passages between walls with any at all, turned to shame for casting them over her new ally. There was a kinship she should have expected but nonetheless did not; they moved the same way through those dark halls — so few had the need for footsteps devoid of sound.

But it was under that silence new footsteps heralded another, no metal echo of a guard, and graceless beyond a hint of Belladonna's kind, an intruder in that place humans rarely ventured.

Belladonna stopped as those steps drew near and, in a whirl of skirts, faced the stranger. She felt an odd kind of disappointment. He was plain and pale, with hair dark as night sea and eyes to match, a northerner, a stranger beyond the hoard. A visitor like so many thousands before him, he might have been beneath remark, but for the hour in that nearly abandoned place.

The man with no sigil on his night clothes showed every piece of his shock, perhaps for being caught, perhaps for seeing another at all. It was a question Belladonna would never know the answer to, as, after meeting her eyes, he turned on his heel and ran.

"Go on then," Elysa said as she followed the stranger's path with that stalking pace of ambush predators. "I'll not be a moment."

Belladonna caught a but glance of the girl reaching beneath her skirts before she rounded the corner out of sight.

Should the castle have been awake, should that prying hoard have wandered those ancient halls, those corridors to the undercroft with their never-warmed stones would still boast no visitors. Even those most Fin'neshi-touched nobles dared not risk being seen for accusations of making her father's same mistake. They dared not, yet still their half-breed children were born. The graceful steps of her people would not be heard either; none knew so little to be seen beyond those secret places between the walls her grandmother rediscovered.

Those torches, dark and cold for fifty years, gave no ward against the morning chill. Belladonna could expect nothing more from those empty places; so many years seeing them only long before Helena took her rest, she'd long forgotten their feel by daylight.

No dust fell from the last door before that place and prison of her people; Belladonna hoped it implied the end of Alyria's stubbornness, her ignorance of true family. It was a barren hope when she knew the door's true users. Her grandfather, after all, had the Blood Bound Mages openly stationed around the castle, a pageant for strangers.

Each step down those stairs was as much a new world as the portal her ancestors left behind. The bittersweet longing of a storm rose with smells of handmade soap and food that couldn't be touched. Desperate homesickness clawed its way from hiding as the quiet melodies of the mother tongue reached her ears.

The stairs ended in packed earth and for a time, she lingered in that last doorway as those who worked in that never-sleeping kitchen, lit only by woodburning ovens, moved beyond. It was an odd kind of feeling to watch unnoticed, so much like an intruder in the place she had been born. How many could she still recognize? How many could say the same of her? So many new in the sea of honey skin, of wild hair so like her own, to replace the few she helped, for so many she hadn't, too late, too careful, too worried for the eyes it might draw.

Of all those few left she knew, the cooks *couldn't* know her, branded cheeks told that more than their empty eyes. They were the same she had seen at the breakfast feast, the same three since her childhood, their auras still a perfect mage's green, no matter Alyria's claims.

Those auras, a mage's way to see another, so like the grace they moved with, it could have been so easy to pretend they moved by their own will. So long she thought them her greatest danger, all her sister's protests forgotten, so long they had been, moved by that great hypocrisy, to live, to work, to spy on their own people by that very same blood magic their masters called evil. It didn't matter that the Dark Mother's Speakers – undertakers turned executioners, turned something worse – refused to acknowledge the truth behind their binding power. Lyn'nearri, Aih'han, Lih'han; they couldn't be helped.

All around were children, unlike the adults, a mix of boys and girls; for the boys were not yet old enough to be taken away to the labour camps of the interior. The children were the true source of that welcome melody, a song to the goddess Kye'enai, a song for play as they wove between washing buckets full of bitter lye soaps. A Human would call them half-elves, so long it had been since the men or mage guard had last been brought, those of pure blood had grown past the time for play while parents slept. Half-elven blood perhaps, but the song, the words they spoke in a singer's language, they called the name a lie, there were no halves. So small, but already bruises that littered those skeletal frames flashed in glimpses through rags.

She should have gotten more out.

"Look! Av'vella's back!" the sound of Laih'henni's voice broke Belladonna from her thoughts.

The meaning of the child's name was a secret from outsiders but clear as daylight to those who knew the rules of Mai'iaha, The Names Keeper. The same secret hidden in the child's aura hidden away, from mages free and bound alike, by those Fae secrets only a Seer knew.

Another mage, given the first prefix of Belladonna's mother, that which she held, before she inherited the eldest's. Before firstborn Ash'herien died and Laih'heiren took his name as her own; another of Mai'iaha's rules kept just so secret. And the suffix of stones rounded by the sea, chosen for the eldest but shared by all siblings as was the way. A strong name, a lasting name. The child would endure, if only until Erh'henni would let her go alone.

The song didn't stop all at once but lost voices until its end as little soldiers followed in Laih'henni's wake. Belladonna had hardly a moment to wonder after the motives behind five sets of green eyes before the children erupted into a chorus of voices that she could make neither rhyme nor sense from. Laih'henni held her arm out to the followers, and, in their way, the rest quieted.

"Magic Av'vella, show us the magic."

Belladonna so nearly could have laughed. Such waste and risk, and for such small pleasure, a wise woman wouldn't consider such things. But she saw those faces, noses too pointed for round cheeks made hollow. What right had she to deny a request made in the kind of earnest years too old for the faces before her? A glance for the Bound, perhaps subtlety, would give them no need to take notice.

She lowered her voice to a whisper and nodded to a discarded bucket. "Bring that here then."

Laih'henni and her soldiers moved as one to their prize. A muddy slick across the packed dirt floor was left in the wake of their haste. Belladonna took her staff in both hands. She had in mind an old spell, a simple spell from that time before she knew her true aptitude. It was nothing so impressive, but a rarity to find a water spell in the repertoire of one so called to flame.

She took a breath and her mana found the water, just drops at first, rain in reverse. It rose and grew together into a ball. Just a tiny sphere, but how the children squealed as Belladonna sent it dancing around them. She hadn't half the heart to heed them keep quiet.

With another breath she called forth control of its shape – a star, a tear, a wave on the sea. No true change, absolute control, such simplicity, the pure heart of magecraft. Had her blood run cool with water, she could have shown more – to freeze it, to make ice so sharp it could shatter swords. She could have run with them, shown them freedom beyond the song's escape. To learn ice, to compromise the flame in her blood, to free five and damn thousands. It was an avenue she could scarcely bear not to take.

She was rescued by another voice of her childhood. "Go off the lot of you; stop bothering Av'vella," Erh'henni scolded.

The children didn't complain; they already knew better. As one, they followed their leader into the next game, a song to Maj'jri taken up at once.

"You shouldn't do that," Erh'henni said with a scolding tone that would have called her the eldest sibling if not for how her name proved otherwise. "It's not right to dangle false hope in front of them like that."

"It's not false hope," Belladonna said, "not when we'll get them out."

Grandmother so often said Erh'henni looked more like Belladonna's sister than Alyria, with the same brown-green eyes and the same hands. Both yet to finish their first aging. Behind the bruises, if not for fifteen years of hunger or the scars they didn't share, they might have still been a match. But that voice Belladonna knew so well turned cold. "A few at a time. How many can you get before they're all sent off somewhere?"

"We agreed we can't take many from here; it's too much risk," Belladonna said, "if they get transferred away, we can get them out sooner."

"I know you think we can, but what happened last time?"

"What happened changes nothing; we just have to be careful until I find who talked."

Erh'henni shook her head. "You've been living with the humans too long if you think that'll fix it."

Like so many wasps, those words burrowed a stinging burn through Belladonna's heart. "So you'd give up?"

Something iron formed behind Erh'henni's eyes. "No, but we won't win from escape."

"What else is there?"

"We won the surface from the dragons when the Onari couldn't; this is our homeland. I won't let the humans just have it. Sing for the Seven Hundred. We would have fought in the Eighth if we were older."

Smoke on the hills, her mother's friends vanished, that boy delivered when the ash stopped falling. Belladonna's knuckles turned white around her staff. "We lost the Eighth."

"We wouldn't have if we weren't following a human," Erh'henni said. "The Ninth could be you; you're strong."

"I can't fight a country." Guards fell like candle wax, but how could she fight those trained for her? How could she fight her own in the Mage Guard? Fifteen years from the Seventh and twelve since the Eighth, so many losses to the free mages. "How many mages are truly left?"

"Enough if we have the conduits; my sister could raze this castle with the amulet Liv'vella stole."

Those words and Alyria's elven name were a poisonous hurt she hadn't felt in so long. Beneath it, she mourned a friend she hadn't quite realized, had become someone else without her, a friendship she'd never realized was gone.

Belladonna forced herself to breathe. She hadn't the time to mourn one who still lived. "Where is my grandmother?"

"Where is she always? She doesn't bother with us since Ash'herien died."

Belladonna had no words for that as she walked to her grandmother's room. Perhaps her once close friend, too, understood how little was left to say.

15

ROBIN

32ND OF HELENAI, 447, THIRD AGE

A beast needed a name; all things deserved a name. The only lesson that elven gods had the right to speak on, that first lesson, so far from the betrayal to be uncorrupted. Robin named his horse Ria, drawing from the one his mother's parents rode out of the Southwest, a matched name to fit the matching cream hair the two shared.

How a life of the city had denied him. How Ria could run. The winds of the road swept past fast enough to tear back his scarf, to let air flow between so often covered feathers. With his eyes closed, he could imagine he was taking to the wings of his aspect, wings his people were denied in their creation. Each day, bare fields broke for farming villages that vanished just as they appeared – dots of civilization on the King's road, too small for even a mark on the map, their names for locals alone.

Those little farms they passed under that midday sun, some welcome shade against inland heat not tempered by the ocean breeze, bore orchards heavy with apples, so ready to be picked, so many to be wasted on the branch before the traditions of old Narreth deemed it right to benefit from the year's labours. Just under three weeks until the total eclipse, just twenty-nine days until Helena's Triumph.

All around, those fruits gleamed, and Robin's stomach cried its protest. What little food they found after Sir Emit's gifts were gone

Kitty had pushed away, and of that, Wyvern took the lion's share. That was not a statement of blame nor one of reproach. Wyvern had no need for guilt in that matter for that same reason Robin felt none for the coins he lifted. There was no selfishness in stark necessity.

Again his stomach growled, a matching sound to the three-day song of Kitty's. That thing she denied, she endured, but at that first sound from Robin's, her ears turned. She made no comment, but there was a rare confidence in her frame as she pulled the horse, which she'd named Shale, to a stop. Robin followed her. Ria and the horse that Wyvern had given no name slowed as one.

He couldn't quite say what Kitty looked for as her eyes danced across those verdant trees or what her ears turned to on that sweltering wind until she jumped from Shale's back and pulled an apple from the grass.

"It's not harvesting if it's fallen," she said as she held the fruit to Robin. The red fruit was framed by that amber glow within her and all witches. Her words held an argument for herself, for her own beliefs, the rules of her gods, not his. For what argument would be needed for them two known thieves to steal? For Robin to forsake the rules of a divinity he didn't believe in? His gods were elven and had they any ruling in the matter, he surely would have broken it for the small joy of spiting them.

But it was not law, mortal nor divine, that spurred a war across his mind, to take what she freely gave, to relive his own pain at the cost of hers, no, impossible selfishness when she had long given her portions. But with hesitance, he saw the surety in her eyes crack, a rift to all the usual doubt, the blame she claimed for all ills. "There's got to be more around here," he said as he took the offered fruit.

"We can't leave the horses," she said, even as her eyes searched the trees.

"Wyvern and I can watch them." Not a contradiction, so carefully not anything of that kind, and by just an inch, Kitty's shoulders relaxed, the right thing to say, a treasure greater than the fruit in his hand.

She nodded. "I won't be long," she said before dark hair and once-coloured clothes disappeared behind those trees, steps as silent on grass and earth as they ever were against cobbled streets.

Even the greatest fool could have felt how that lingering tension, a frayed ship's line between his companions, vanished at her disappearance. A blind man could have seen how Wyvern relaxed. "Why won't you talk to her anymore?" Robin asked.

Wyvern shook her head, even in the orchard's shade, she squinted against the sunlight. "I've behaved badly around her."

"Would she think so?"

There was a long pause as if Wyvern, so sure of imagined missteps, didn't know the answer. "If she understood, she would."

"She thinks it's her fault." The sweet fruit in his hand bruised beneath his fingers.

"It couldn't be."

And he knew, knew the same force that drove Kitty to find a stranger in the night drove Wyvern just as far. And how desperately he wished to speak, to show their hopes true. But for that one force, he had no right to speak on. Instead, he focused on the meagre bites of his meal. It was not his place to say a word.

"Why are we stealing?" Wyvern's voice rang from the silence; it brought his mind back to the remnants of the stolen fruit he held — a thing that should have been left to rot by all laws.

He threw the handful of seeds back into the grass. "We can't buy them."

"Because we have no coin?"

Because they had no coin. Because the farmers wouldn't risk the wrath of their god by harvesting early. Because so far from the great port cities, the creatures of Lord Mirri couldn't count on the same tiny bastions of tolerance.

"Because inland humans won't sell to us," he said. "Gentea might help after we help them."

Wyvern's horse huffed a protest as she turned, her hair a cloud as she towered over Robin. "They sold to me."

"They had to, Wyvern," he said. "You're a citizen." The arrangements of Mirri's creatures, a siege broken for citizenship, a dragon slain for fame, and perhaps a child saved would grant kindness. "And there aren't enough of us in the country anymore."

"Castilla live in the country."

A question Robin didn't want to ask, a story he was certain he didn't want to know and yet one so needed, needed to know if his new friend understood. "Were The Fens safe? In the spring of 430?" The silence gave so much more answer than he wanted to force. He nodded. "We all have Purge stories."

"Did you lose people?"

"No." And he almost wished he could have been as he was before Kitty if only to keep back the reason. "My father was a guard; they protected us."

Only the song of trees played for a long time. "Did she?" Wyvern asked.

He hadn't the time to deny an answer. The dry inland wind shifted, and on it a racket of shrill squeals, that portent of execution. Talons dug trenches as Robin hit the ground running. He didn't need Kitty's ears to know the source; he'd seen her path through the trees, so many years by her side, hiding from that sound.

What grasses were spared from his talons soon were crushed by Wyvern as she ran alongside him. The branches that missed his stature broke against hers.

It was a great boar, all grey in coat, with an eternal silver glow from within. Its shrieks filled that dry air as it paced the base of one of those fruit-heavy trees, its snout pointed to where Kitty perched within its branches, that amber glow pulled toward the silver. It made no move as Robin threw his hatchet against the tree. No, such beasts, the Ashkari Hogs, wouldn't startle, all blind and deaf; it'd have no mind for him, for any without the scent of magic.

Even as Robin stopped beyond the reach of those killing tusks, Wyvern barrelled forward, leaves and twigs caught in her hair, an effigy of a hunter's disguise. The run was graceless, but for that last move — her hand so fast Robin hadn't the chance to call out before Wyvern pulled her sword and cleft through the great hog.

He couldn't look down, couldn't see what remained, so focused to not see, he missed Kitty's silent dissent. "You shouldn't have done that," Kitty said, not fury in her voice, for anger needed injustice. No, hers had only fear.

"But it would have..." Wyvern's voice faltered as Kitty retreated down the path, footsteps almost audible in her haste. "I thought..."

Robin could only guide her from the scene. "We have to go."

Stolen apples and hunger took no space in Robin's mind as they spurred the horses away from that place that would soon know their trap had caught a witch. As midday cooled to red evening, that silent tension turned, a frayed line snapped and rebuilt with each glance. It was not a thing he had the right to interfere with; the phrase danced through his mind, not his place to speak.

16

AN'NEIRA

MOTARI, 304, THIRD AGE

The Wastes were death, scars of two invasions, a fever that failed to kill the coming sickness, those places with no built structures, yet still haunted by She Who Waits Behind All Doors. But a runaway had so little choice. How many had been found near-dead in the Sand or the Fens? How many drowned in tar, a merciful thing they never reached the Poison Fields proper. An'neira knew; she saw each, just as if they'd happened before her own eyes. Of her people dammed to those empty places, none yet lived who could brave their madness, and none ever should have.

But just as those who chose the tar and gas were never found, those who faced the oldest wasteland could have faith they'd go unfollowed. Fin'neshi himself was not such a fool to test those ageless trees. However, she was no fool to know and cherish that she had no choice but to follow Ellivar's orders, to give not a moment of hesitation when she was told in that never-spoken tongue to run north.

A Seer, one who ran but a Seer still, she would have been forgiven if only she had stopped running. That thought hunted her just the same as the Mirri soldiers. It was that thought that raged when she stepped off the future path, and the Sight failed her when she could see no future beyond the moment, no past beyond her own thirty two years of memory. Had the White Dragon truly forsaken her to such blindness, to wander dazed as any other? Such was the temptation to stop, to return to her safe island of banal luxury in that sea of her master's cruelty. To die in her time by his mad son's hand.

But no, she had no right to stop, to doubt Ellivar's plans, Not when her failure would surely bring forth the Old Gods' wrath all the sooner. So on she ran, through the muck of spring earth too poisoned by war to ever grow again.

Those soldiers of the nine-branched tree overtook her lead that same day An'neira found her sanctuary, but, as she passed those first eternal trees, the clamour of horses, the yells of guards, none passed the silence of the tree line. Before that first step, An'eira had thought herself so above the fear of that place. She knew the tales, and she knew the truth of the moment it came to be — an accident, a piece of The Other Place, dragged along by the Fae when they tore the Veil.

An'neira had thought herself too clever, too wise, to care for the Human tales of Daemons that lurked beyond, hunting eternally that they might one day find the portal left behind. However, it came to her with that first step how very little she knew – not if the first enemy had found that gateway, nor if they ever would. Their forsaken home was beyond even Ellivar's sight of all futures.

All the same, as the spring sun vanished for endless green twilight, An'neira knew how little she had understood the old stories, and how little those tales knew. No sun for that shifting velvet canopy, no night for the eternal gloom. Branches stood within reach, a near beckoning thing, but one that brought no temptation to climb, for she knew, with primal understanding, she would find no sky beyond that canopy, not even as spring rains fell silent, unfettered by the endless green expanse.

In another place, she should have grown hungry, and her legs should have ached for running; in another place, she may have hoped for relief in sleep. But the time she couldn't count brought no change. Valire hadn't brought time to her creation. An'neira knew the story but it wasn't hers to tell that oldest tale of another people's gods.

An'neira grew to know the fear of those times when the silence seemed so natural, how leaves shook with no wind, the earth trod down with not a soul to see. For what she once might have thought a long time, she didn't dare speak. She worried that the woods wouldn't allow it, that they might steal her voice too. For fear they already had.

An'neira, she knew her name, the only child, none older to inherit from; it should have been wasted before she ran, an eldest with no children, but it was hers. Even as those trees took all else, she held her name, only perhaps because she knew something of those trees, familiar as it rested in her own soul.

Not a gift from She who had forsaken rights to that place, another, one An'neira's people gave no name, who met his death before their birth, for they only saw the replacement they made in Maj'jri. But there was a spark there, a spec of divinity from the nameless one, some part of her that still claimed the Faes' realm as home. Just a whisper.

Only by a thousand voices had her ancestors travelled that place; only by those songs so loud to break the Wood's spell had they called them home. What of those who strayed? Did the woods keep them still, wandering forever between those trees unbeholden to time? What claim would she have to escape their grasp?

She found her voice, curled under the trees of Ashtana and Noria, first just those dozen words, the prayer that couldn't be answered in those woods.

Thei'nas annan mott'tir se't re'nnan.

But the rest, like a flood, her footing found to the song of fools. And she dared snap a twig to tie back mud-caked hair as her voice carried the countless marches of seven hundred war gods. One voice, but carried with the weight of ten thousand as her feet pounded across damp earth.

She knew the edge only as her song was accompanied by those silver sweet northern birds and as her heart came to understand seven years lost.

The scar of farms cut across the foothills just beyond the last tree. She knew not what to expect when she passed that last boundary of the once homeland, only that it would be the true end of her flight. The lord of the Northwest so insignificant to the world but for two points: first, that a descendant would one day, in the way of northwestern lords, sink the province deeply enough into debt to lose his title to a brother of a future king and, more immediately, that while he lived, he would never see the North's first Seer lost.

Dew soaked An'neira's back as her legs gave out in a garden just steps past her goal. She was too exhausted to feel the cold as the first snow fell. The wind turned north, and with it came an unfamiliar strange feeling. However, as she opened her eyes in that three-hundred and fifteenth year, it took on a name she always knew.

Like the falling snow, it came; slow at first, then all at once. The Sight returned, changed as fate moulded itself to the new reality so far beyond her own life. The mage guard man she would meet only once. The son torn from her arms, and the daughter to one day share her father's gift. That same girl to see only her first aging, only twenty of two hundred years owed. Her granddaughters with gifts that were, in equal parts, given and forsaken. And that boy. Her new place in the White Dragon's plans.

    And the beginnings of the war, which, on that day, and in days one hundred and forty-three years yet to come, could still have been averted.

17

Belladonna

28th of Helenai, 447, Third Age

Knowledge and understanding had proved, once more, to be separate qualities. Belladonna had heard the tale of her grandmother's escape from Castle Mirri many times. She marvelled at the weight of a single detail that had been omitted. All the implications of a name she should never have heard before. An overheard thing from a conversation not meant for her when it passed Xaxirion's lips.

"Who is she? Ellivar?" Belladonna asked as she pushed herself upright on the bed of straw.

An'neira tipped her head, such a benign gesture if not for who she was. "I would have thought Xaxirion could have told you."

A shade of the other family leaked into her mind, and Belladonna pushed it off like the parasite she knew it to be. "Grandmother, I'm not playing this game."

"My dear, I don't see what I don't look for; I thought I might learn of your friends on your own terms." Honey-toned hands, weathered by the start of her fourth aging yet preserved from labour, took Belladonna's own. "I *couldn't* tell you of the White Dragon; I never thought that he wouldn't."

He hadn't. He'd shared a glimpse of his world only after the false yellow dragon had been felled over the capitol, only after his youngest sister's tapestry of gifted secrets was left forever unfinished — a consolation coloured by warnings to keep well away.

The colour was the key, not any of the four hues dragons aligned to their breath's element, but white, one of their elders. She'd been allowed to learn that much of the four Elder Dragons: Gold, Silver, Black and White. But just as she knew transformation was the domain of the Black Dragon and magic the heretical claim of the Silver, she knew not those of the other two.

Had her staff not been left at the door of that tiny room, Belladonna might have sought its comfort. "He's warned me away from his kind enough times."

"I hadn't thought to look," An'neira said as her hands closed tight. "I hadn't thought there was any truth in it."

"What?"

"There have been whispers. I thought them to be the young Seers' gossip."

"What Seers?" she asked, for she knew there were no others with her grandmother's gift north of the True Capital. "What rumours?"

Matching eyes met as An'neira released Belladonna's hand. "They say you're giving up, my dear."

"What?" Belladonna couldn't help how she scrambled for her grandmother's hand. "I've not given up anything."

"We've all seen the great kingdoms fall; a small thing always leads. The White Dragon carries the domain of prophecy; she sees every path, just as I see the path we walk. She would have kept it from me; had I seen this, I might have strayed." No truer regret than that of her grandmother's voice.

It struck Belladonna then where her grandmother had spoken to the other Seers, how distance had meant nothing to their gossip. Had they truly been born of the White Dragon's domain, the dragons' language between minds would be their own. The mother tongue of all Dragon Kin, or so the Changeling Nit had told her. That language gifted to dragon riders. That same language Xaxirion refused to share with her.

He'd refused to share. But the Seers would call it her failing for what she didn't know.

"Because I haven't pursued Xax about dragons? That's not giving up. I—" Belladonna's words, like stones, tumbled forth. "You've spoken to her, this White Dragon?"

"I have."

"Then ask her — ask her if he would have told me if I kept asking."

"My dear..." An'neira gave Belladonna's hand a final squeeze before she pulled away entirely. Emptiness hit Belladonna — greater than if she had lost her magic. "You know I bend so many rules for you, but I can't say if he would answer every question."

Belladonna's fingers tangled in her hair. It was a pointless hesitation, a pointless grasp for warmth, an attempt to hide her motives from a Seer. "What if I asked about Seralie, then?" Another name from Xaxirion, not overhear but but freely given with such scorn. "In the Dragon Lands, to the north."

"I know the one." An'neira looked away from her granddaughter, those ancient green eyes fixed somewhere far from that place. "He would have told you of his blood sister."

"And that's why I don't ask." If only comfort came from that confirmation if only she'd wavered in the choice so that knowing its correctness could lift her mind. "You never told me The Sight came from dragons."

Her grandmother's gaze returned to the dust-filled air that hung between them. "You must know by now why I can't tell you everything."

"You're Dragonkin?"

"No more than the Ashkari."

Those frozen islands so far north, their people of silver hair and those hogs Lyrians imported to smell magic, vestiges on the Silver Dragon's border. Such distant issues, in Xaxirion's words. Had they, too, been given the dragons' language between minds? She could have known, like so much of Xaxirion's world after his youngest sister's trickle of secrets had stopped, she could have known if only she'd been willing to lose another friend.

How her mind rebelled from the word, a friend she couldn't trust, how far he'd kept her from his kin who might reveal a traitor.

"Why tell me now?" Belladonna asked.

"Things have shifted, and without Ellivar's say," An'neira said, "I've felt four in these past five years. And again, on that night, you wish to speak of."

"Grandmother, please, what's more important than our people?"

"There are things coming." An'niera's eyes never moved, but Belladonna knew her gaze once more fell beyond that room. "A blue-eyed girl you've met with no elven name; she's the key."

Nails dug hard into Belladonna's palms. How she wished for her staff, which still sat just out of reach. "That doesn't make sense."

"When you find her—"

"Find her?" Belladonna stood. It was a stumbled step as that long, tattered blanket tangled about her legs. "I can't leave now."

"Av'vella, sit," An'neira said as she pulled Belladonna back to her side. "Far greater forces than this castle are stirring, and you were born for your role in this fight."

Belladonna scoffed. "I wasn't born for anything; I was a mistake."

"Nothing in Ellivar's plan is a mistake! Ash'herien knew her part of this; our family has a responsibility to the world. We've already lost your sister."

That tone so like Erh'henni's. Anger brought the worst of Alyria's ignorance to them, but that tone forged iron in Belladonna's heart. "I can't abandon our people. If I leave now—"

"In this war, our family fights, we sacrifice what we must, and Ellivar provides. You could give so much more with two elder dragons."

"Has Ellivar told you to say nothing more?" Belladonna asked. The silence that followed was all the answer she could ever expect. "She must have seen that this wouldn't work when all Xax tells me is how little he trusts his kind."

"You'd still take his word? Even when you're not sure he can be trusted?"

"You told me Seers can't read minds."

"My dear..." Again, those hands gave Belladonna warmth, but An'neira's eyes didn't stray. "I speak as your grandmother; I wouldn't need to read thoughts; I see your conflict behind your eyes, not on your path."

"Grandmother, please. You know who the traitor is — you know that keeping it from me won't convince me to do Ellivar's task."

Finally, An'neira looked away from that far-off place. "But neither would telling you. I'm truly sorry I can't help you, my dear."

Belladonna knew herself a fool; she'd known it when she'd dared to hope some bond of family could tempt her grandmother's help. When had it ever before? An'neira had watched a century of rebellions fall to dust before they began. She hadn't given a word of warning for dear Nit's death, hadn't made a move to forestall her own daughter's. What power had love over the mandate of dragons?

Still, Belladonna held tight to her grandmother's hands, six years old all over again, begging to come home. "Anything? Just a hint?"

Her grandmother pulled her fingers across Belladonna's curls and held them for just a moment, aged fingers a near effigy of hairpins. "It won't make it any easier."

A hint, or perhaps a warning, she wouldn't find out until the season's end, for she had no dragon's power, no sight for what lay beyond the moment, no knowledge but for the sounds beyond her grandmother's door and their promises of dawn. The loss of her grandmother's hand when Belladonna stood was only soothed by the spark as her hand found her staff. "I shouldn't keep Anika waiting."

Perhaps she imagined how cold the room became at those words.

Hardly a step lay between the bed and door, but Belladonna was halted by the wrinkled hand that took hers once more. "I wish you'd come here more; I'd see you before Helena's Triumph."

"I know, and I will. Jacob's back now; I should be able to sneak away." An excuse of convenience, a lie to even her own ears. But the only words she knew to say.

Only as she stepped through the door did her grandmother speak again. "Vixensha has returned; I trust you know where."

So, they had returned after all. But for another run or another trap? Another thread to pull, and she hoped, so nearly a contradiction against her urgency, that it wouldn't be the one to ruin everything.

18

Kitty

34th of Helenai, 447, Third Age

She hadn't let them stop that night, nor the one before; only brief pauses, as clouds covered Helena, spared the horses. Two bitter nights of silence, none yet pursued, the chimes of black beaded chains only in her mind. And yet she couldn't find anger for Wyvern when panic turned stale, a feeling she had no name for, not envy that Wyvern could so easily do what so many witches wished for. Could it be she felt gratitude that Wyvern had come to her aid? Perhaps not, for how Kitty wished she hadn't. Who would kill such a guard but a witch? Another thought crept in, had her party any options beyond the slaughter?

No running from hogs faster than a horse, no way to hide from the scent of her magic. But Pa had so many times turned them from the caravan, their masters none the wiser, a pointless thought; his gifts were not hers.

There was one way, but had she wanted it? Had she been wishing her party had left her to the Speakers' mercy? Perhaps if she knew such a path would have kept the other two from harm, she might have admitted to herself that she had.

It had been by morning's first pitiful light they passed what remained of New Anaire, abandoned and never rebuilt after the Eighth.

She'd nearly missed it amongst the tall grass; the rainbow of half-remembered market stalls and banners of a house that no longer existed were gone. Even the burned shells of homes were invisible for the grasses that grew over their toppled husks. One could imagine there had never been a city at all until they came to the lone remaining signpost.

The sign had been wrong, out of date; it still named the overgrown path to what was once Holceina Crossing as a branch of the King's Road. From that place rose a certain melancholy, beyond that of silence on the open road. Like seeing a memory frozen under the flame-scarred wood, that last remnant in the center point of the plains didn't need to know that the Jewel of the Ridgeline had met its same fate in the same war.

The roads grew rougher north of the King's road and as the sun climbed from another sleepless night, with nothing but knee high grasses as far as the eye could see, something unseen lifted from her companions. Too focused on the road, Kitty hadn't seen their hands until Wyvern spoke. "You said the humans wouldn't help us."

"What?" Kitty asked at that moment before she remembered Wyvern wouldn't have spoken to her.

Perhaps she had been wrong about that. Wyvern urged her horse to Kitty's side. "Robin told me we might get help after we save the children, but before he said they wouldn't."

Kitty's tail drummed against Shale's back. "They won't help us."

"They might after—" Robin cut himself off, but those first words stuck. What had he called his father's fame? A creature's bargain? Perhaps then, or perhaps the end of the thought he never voiced, would dispute that hope, too.

"But why won't they?" Guileless pink eyes pinned Kitty.

Lessons, and those four books, forbidden to touch until she earned their beads, and beads out of reach until she knew the words. All the words so different from Pa's. A switch on her knuckles as she reached to understand.

"Because they think The Breaker made us." That notch left from a once broken bone ached a second heartbeat as her tail drummed.

"That doesn't make sense," Wyvern said. "Our kinds are higher than theirs."

Kitty turned as Wyvern's voice faltered, as she pulled her horse away, but Robin's words came first. "No, we aren't," he said, "and they aren't either; there's no such thing."

"There is," Wyvern snapped. "If you do good, you're reborn higher."

Kitty gave her eyes back to the empty road. It was a debate she had no words for. It couldn't be anything but pointless to argue the merits of a thing she knew nothing of, beyond disbelief.

"Who chose the order?" Robin asked.

"The Ancestors."

"Your ancestors?"

"Yes!" Wyvern growled. "The highest choose, and the strongest are the highest."

Robin's beak clicked. "The strongest woman I've ever known didn't get it as a reward, and she wasn't born that way either."

Those stories he hadn't told for those first years, that kindness in his mother's eyes long after sickness took them piece by piece, courage for the sake of someone else. "I wish I'd known Opal," Kitty said as she turned to meet his eyes, taking a moment to share grief's burden.

But his eyes returned nothing but confusion. "I—it, it wasn't her. It was"—he shook his head—"someone else."

Kitty had to turn from the sadness in those black eyes. She had thought she knew every tragedy of a short life; what right could she have to ask of a woman he had never once before spoken to her of? One who could cause such pain at a mention. No, she had no rights at all to that.

But the debate that should surely die if Kitty added her voice no longer reached her ears, for all her mind turned to what lay across the road. She first thought it a snake, a long blackness that ran the width of the road. From how Shale spooked, he must have thought the same. But a second glance told a far different story. No living thing could lie so still. No once-living could be so empty. No, the burned branches portended an entirely darker tale indeed.

Her last hope the blemish had been an error, carried by the wind, rubbish from a burn pile, was dashed as she dismounted. As she stood, her feet so near to the line, she saw how it burrowed deep into tall grasses on either side of the road. She needn't have seen the curved trail it followed to know the ring it formed. Had there always been a town? She couldn't remember; the map held no marking, such a young town for such a fate.

"Is something wrong?" Robin called from behind.

Kitty nodded, for her own mind more than either of the others. "Eisalie's Crest."

"What's that?" Wyvern asked. Only her second words for Kitty in near on two days, and they were for such a thing.

Kitty scarcely dared answer, for all the strife her last words had caused, for fear of the distance she had caused returning. The Maker's own blessing in Robin saved her from such a choice. "Do you really not have it in the South?" he asked. "Rings of boils? Coughing blood. It's terrible; they say Elves spread it."

"Oh. We have that; they call it—"

"Never mind that," Kitty cut in. She had no need the hear those words ever again. "It isn't true — what they say about Elves; they don't get sick, but they don't spread it either. Pa always said Dwarves wouldn't get it either."

"I never meant—" Wyvern started, but like Robin so often did, she cut herself off.

Kitty's ears flattened as silence reigned. She had known the matter of Wyvern delicate, and yet so easily snapped, such the fool she was, when her tone did war with her words, to cause pain when she spoke true. Apologies that would discredit her words hung in Kitty's throat, her eyes too heavy to meet Wyvern's lingered on those hands. Still carved of temple marble and decorated by a ring of pewter and a ring of nine ruby stones. Still, an illusion of blood haunted her dreams as if she had already failed. Would Wyvern still wish to have her company when they reached Gentea? It was a question she had none of the courage to ask.

"Nothing to be done for it then," Kitty said. "We'll have to go around."

Ebony hair burned her scalp under that sun. Wyvern had dismounted to break a trail through the long grass. Even with that great tail of hers, it wasn't enough to keep stray stalks from brushing Kitty's bare feet. The blazing heat drove sweat to soak Kitty's back. But even as Wyvern cut through the long grass on foot, she showed no sign of tiring from the summer heat and didn't so much as a glance back during those long midday hours.

The distance hadn't been born from her debate with Robin, nor even the hog. The origin that Kitty searched for was some point before then. It was some mistake she had made, something she couldn't reach. A question she had asked, perhaps? What awful thing for Wyvern, who gave so freely, to balk. Kitty the fool to forget what words made Wyvern hate her so.

"Careful," Robin's voice snapped through her thoughts. She halted a moment before Shale's hoof would have crossed the hateful burned line.

"How many times will it come back?" The Maker's Speakers thought she couldn't hear, or perhaps they knew she could.
"Three towns burned black; it's the Breaker's work; he wouldn't lose his spy."
Her eyes fell to Wyvern's back as she steered Shale from the quarantine line. A line that couldn't be uncrossed. Could her newest friend have been spared the hurt if Kitty had been called to the Dark Mother in all those doomed towns she tended to?

"Do you think?" Kitty said before she could think. "Never mind." It wouldn't have been right to worry Robin about it; he needn't know how she worried and unsure she truly was.

"Give her time, I'm sure—" Robin faltered, as the tall grass ended and his eyes fixed somewhere far ahead. Kitty hadn't the time to turn before he had long since spurred Ria on. She didn't see those dark shapes in those temple-fine, white and blue robes before he was long out of her reach.

But his eyes didn't fall on the Speakers. No, Kitty saw too late in her pursuit how his eyes were locked to those figures that cowered at the feet of robes that should have meant mercy.

Rain ran tracks through the soot where tears had not. "I expect you to be grateful for this," the white-robed man with the gold-beaded chain said. *"The Maker has mercy for even a creature such as yourself."*

"Wyvern!" Kitty called. The Maker above couldn't have detected even a moment's hesitation in Wyvern. No one of such size should have had the right to jump so far, but in a heartbeat, black feathers were enveloped by white scales as Wyvern pulled him from Ria's back.

Such a commotion drew far too much attention, and before Kitty could remember her fear, the Speakers turned to the little group.

"You three," their leader, marked by four bands of blue, called, muffled through her plague veil stained by too much red for any hope of homecoming. "Back to town with the rest of them."

No place to hide; the tall grass was far behind them, and nothing but empty prairie lay ahead.

"No!" one of the sick cried. "It's death; you drag us to the Dark Mother."

Kitty couldn't hear what the Speakers said as they raised clubs to the protester, so transfixed she was by those beaded chains that hung through slits in their robes, all blue beads, such violence from those sworn to heal. Had she been so different when she called the black-robed Speakers on those who ran? Was an executioner's sword better than a healer's club?

Her trance was banished like the night when Robin slipped Wyvern's grasp and, without a glance, returned in his flight to the sick.

When Robin's foot crossed that cursed threshold, the acolytes turned on him. A hand, stained with blood not its own, reached for him. Pa's first lesson for plague towns returned like thunder's crack — don't touch the sick, don't touch the cloth, it lives in the blood. Kitty hadn't the thought to move until after her heels dug into Shale's sides, until after she steered him between Wyvern and her unnamed horse to cut between Robin and the Speaker.

"Don't touch him," Kitty hissed, her ears pinned back.

"You will not interfere in the Mother's work," the Speaker hissed.

The Mother's work, once Kitty's own. To bring life. To heal the hopeless, to stand – to fail – against the Dark Mother until her call becomes their own. To forsake all the methods Pa had to save those a Speaker would fail; all those Kitty failed in the years she heard his gifts called wicked.

Kitty hadn't noticed Wyvern until Robin let out a squawk at being lifted onto the horse.

The lead Speaker pulled down her veil. "You've crossed the line; you can't leave."

Kitty tried not to see the Speaker's face, not to think about how she knew it was a stranger only because of the youth hidden behind the rings of boils. What had that little girl done? To deserve a plague town, to hold the sick, to carry the cloth, to invite sickness into her blood?

A question Kitty hadn't the time to ask, for the chance the Speaker would force her, too, to break the rules the temples never taught. So, she tried not to think of anything at all as she urged Shale around.

"Heretics!" the Speaker screamed to their backs.

Lightning scars burned against temple stones, smoking bodies that still moved, but the Nestia dropped from Hanson's grasp. "You'll burn for this."

For a bare moment, Kitty imagined pulling her wand as she had before. It could have been a good death; to die for Robin. But she didn't, too afraid to fight still; what a coward she was.

As she crossed the line to that place the Speakers couldn't follow, accusation sang from the weight of her own chain, so hidden, so heavy, three beads of blue, one bead of black. Already, she'd strayed farther from The Mother than those children ever would have a chance to.

Both the black circle and the daylight had long passed before they once again found Ria. It was long after that before Robin spoke. "We could have helped them."

Kitty shook her head. "We couldn't have. Pa had a way, but without him," she said, and the night pressed in with its silence. "It's in the Mother's hands."

"Didn't your father teach you?" Wyvern asked.

"I told you already; I'm no Blood Mage."

19

Belladonna

28th of Helenai, 447, Third Age

An orchard had been built for the first lord's daughter, a lace of dancing paths and trees from her homeland, fruits of a different coast and blossoming things that should have never known the cold. Just as the roses turned white and the Queen's maze formed a labyrinth, those trees did, too, turn wild.

There was a place in Lady Cassia's abandoned orchard, beyond the wasps and under the wall, where the earth never settled anymore. Once, it had been as rock-filled as its kin, but after so many times being dug and replaced, only a shallow dip told of the space stones used to take. It was that spot, under the odd crochet of neglected trees, that Belladonna claimed as her escape.

"Did she give you anything?" Belladonna spun at the voice; she needn't have searched; Elysa's hair stood as an ember against the green as the girl slunk through the pathless wild.

"I don't know yet," Belladonna said as she turned from those eyes. "I didn't think I'd see you until I got back."

Amber eyes found Belladonna's gaze in spite of her efforts. As Elysa came to her side, a hand with the same scars as her face tugged the handkerchief that still covered her ears. "I hope you hadn't planned on it." Elysa tossed the boots Belladonna had neglected to remember across the short distance. "Were you planning to leave these behind as well?"

"Its a bit hard to move silently in heels," Belladonna said as she crouched to slip them on, the relief from the undergrowth thorns almost worth the hassle of the laces. Almost.

"Harder to sneak off without a word, more like."

"I didn't know how long you planned to take with…" Belladonna faltered in both voice and pace. How little she had cared for the man that she'd never thought after his name. Chestnut curls shook as she stepped through brambles. "Have you finished with him?"

"Oh, I do think I've made him understand the merits of silence."

"What did you do?" She recalled her glimpse of a knife's edge.

"I asked him nicely."

Belladonna stopped at the piece of the wall that was never patrolled for fear of wasps and their nest in the towers. "I'm sure I believe that," she said. "Who was he?"

"Oi now, at least give me the benefit of the present tense. His name is Aroch."

"I've not heard of it."

"No?" Elysa asked. "They hold the Wildlands. You have heard of that?"

Ko'e'a Kai't, that last place her ancestors could never hold, both equal and opposite to their first home. Dark wood matched by white, eternal summer by early autumn. An equal in damnation for the wanderer without jealously guarded routes. So quickly, invaders named the two forests cousins. Foolishly called the Deep Woods the greater for its stories and conquered the mortal wood, which stood older and in an entirely different manner of strange.

Strands of untamed hair broke as Belladonna worked her fingers through the knots brought on by straying twigs. "And you convinced *him*? By *asking*?"

"Oi now," came that familiar protest. "I'm not without my uses. You wouldn't have heard the sorry tale of the Hunters?"

"Who?"

Elysa hummed. "Hasn't your lover told you? We all grew up on it out east."

"Edmund knows I don't care about that kind of thing."

A wrong turn of the head and Belladonna was caught in those depthless eyes as they narrowed. "You should."

Belladonna yanked back from that pull and jerked her head to the side, as her curls snagged a branch. But anger rose before either action and only grew in their wakes. "Some Human took something from some other human; why would I?" she hissed.

The burn-scarred hand rose again, in an almost absent movement, to tug the handkerchief tied over her ears. "Bold, for mixed company," Elysa said.

"Tell me the story or don't," Belladonna snapped. "I don't have time for games."

"Very well, I'll leave out the bits you won't care about. The Hunters were the house that Aroch stole the Wilds from. And Arochs are fools to have accepted Tenor's offer when he let the Hunters live," Elysa said, "and since I've answered yours, what did the Seer say to have you sneak out?"

"The other members, the pirates are back," Belladonna said. "I might catch Vix alone if it's her first day on shore."

"Do you think it's her, then?" Elysa asked.

"She never met us that night. The reason Xax gave..." She shook her head. "Mutiny can mean a lot of things."

"You'd go alone?"

"It will be better this way."

But Elysa carried on, relentless. "You're sure?"

"Yes!" How little Belladonna had grown if needling words could still irk her so. Earth-scented air filled her chest as she took a breath, grounding, rebuilding the core that words had so readily eroded. "That is. I need you here for when Edmund returns."

Elysa tipped her head just slightly as a smile crept over her lips. "If you didn't disdain The Game, so," she said, "you might be a better liar."

Belladonna gave no heed to whatever riddle those words hid as her newest ally turned from her and vanished to those wild trees.

Had Belladonna been true to her aptitude as the ancients were, her chosen escape would have been locked to her, but with their castles and gardens, the humans brought nothing so much as the compromise they all so adored.

An inch of her true potential was lost forever for the need of tools, and the crush of earth was a tool in her reach. She had cleared that tunnel many times, and yet so many times a perfect path eluded her, a turn the wrong way, a stone she hadn't felt to dig around, failed gambles that cost precious mana. And she dared not waste the gift in her blood for all those echoes in her grandmother's voice, that she who spent with none left to replenish could never again feel mana through her veins.

But a tunnel dug and a tunnel filled, and she was not so much nearer to that final betrayal of the Fae's gift. Belladonna pulled her hood forward as she stepped again into the Northwest Capitol. In the tones of sky and ocean, their market was a grey place in summer; in those weeks before the turn to autumn, the picked things left from spring, too, were grey. Amongst the clay-tiled roofs on lumber framed houses and between those beiges and browns of the people that lived in them, there was no way to mistake Vixensha.

Uniform only in how brightly she stood apart. A horned woman who stood a head above the crowds she walked through could scarcely pray for anonymity even if she'd not chosen to string charms through her hair, to glitter with belts and beads hung across the colours of southern nobility, to stride so far north in cuts that should have raised goosebumps on any but the only living half dragon.

She was alone that day, her adopted brother staying away, her adopted sister gone. Had they been together, none would have questioned they were sibling by blood. None would have known they were only family by choice. But that appearance of shared blood was as much a lie as their claim to be Draknai, those elusive northern neighbours. Had Vix's horns not been dull and Xax's not black, the disguise might have fooled more than those who had never seen the northern dragonkin in person.

A cloak could only hope to hide a staff so well, and wilful ignorance reached only to that which stayed out of sight. With every bump of the crowd, Belladonna's grip grew tighter on staff and wool as she followed the beacon of her ally past stalls of guard recruiters and fish sellers.

Belladonna might have guessed where Vix's journey would take her, the kind of people she chose to spend her money on. As it was, Belladonna felt an odd cold in the brothel's shadow. It was a place that was neither grand nor subtle in what it was, an undeniable kind of thing beyond the temple's sight. But strange as she felt there, her hair itching beneath her hood, Belladonna truly hadn't any intention to follow Vix beyond the threshold. That was, until a pair of guards, still adorned in raven-crested plate, entered. The voices that warned of a second trap won over those that scoffed at dereliction.

Any thought of those guards – their motives and traps – fled as Belladonna crossed the threshold. There was a smell to that place, beneath the silk-covered windows and carpets dragged to cover stained wood, one Belladonna knew well only for its threat to her own affairs should it have been discovered in her chambers. She pulled her hood low, her eyes to the floor if only to keep them from the patrons.

Belladonna had been bold to enter, but she hadn't thought herself unsubtle, a thought that hadn't mattered, as she stumbled blind through a door that held Vix's voice. Her ally's back had been turned; tattooed dragons and nine-branched trees adorned her arms, tributes to families past and present, and those sun-bright flowers across her shoulders, such stunning memorial.

A sun against the night sky, the gold-eyed canary perched in Belladonna's window, a sight impossible for the winter beyond, a sight made all the stranger as the bird shifted, and left in its place that yellow-horned girl with dark braids and golden eyes. A child, even through the eyes of one just two years older. "They'll come around."

"They said no."

Rags of clothing made fine and whole by illusion fluttered as Nit came to Belladonna's side. "They don't mean it. Xax forgot how to stop being mad, and Vix forgot to disagree with him. Find us tomorrow; I'll make them say yes."

With that promise, so simply made by a child too wise for her years and kindness, the young girl stood, and a yellow bird flew from the lonely tower, once more brighter than any sun and vanished too soon.

"Morning, Vella."

Shaken from memories and against all reason, Belladonna was drawn to that voice, a Vale fly to flame.

"You can go, love," Vix said as she pulled a robe of red brocade from its peg. Her command hadn't been for Belladonna. Honeyed words for the women Belladonna hadn't noticed until they brushed past her. "I never thought I'd find you here."

All at once, she felt Fin'neshi's touch wash over her, and Belladonna's eyes caught on the retreating forms. No guards, no secret trap, not but Vix's preferred company.

"What's the matter, Vella?" Vix's voice drew her back. "Didn't you like them?"

Belladonna tore off the cloak, suddenly hot as she met eyes brown and white. "They're human," she said.

"Of course, they are, love, that is what I paid for." Vix smiled. "I'm not like you; I can't hate all of them."

Belladonna's brow furrowed. "I don't—"

"Oh, of course, you do," Vix cut in. "You've stopped hating a few after a while, but not enough to make a difference."

Heat pooled in Belladonna's cheeks, her hair itched with sweat, and she turned from her ally. "I should go," she said with a step to the door.

"Vella, wait," Vix said as she lay an ember-warm hand on Belladonna's arm. "I didn't say I blame you for it. I don't even know if you're wrong, but I don't have that luxury."

The hand slipped as Belladonna spun. Had she any less presence of mind, she may have reached for it. "What luxury?"

Vix shrugged. There was a thoughtful silence as she sat on the bed. "You could wage war on every human, and your people would stand behind you. Not all of them, maybe, but you wouldn't be alone, would you?"

"No." Belladonna shook her head as she sat next to Vix. "Erh'henni wants me to do just that."

There came a pause as Vix nodded. That claw scar through her brow stretched as her eyes closed. "Vella, I don't have that. I don't have a people. I had two, and now I only have Xax. So, I'm friends with everyone."

"My people would stand with you. I..." Belladonna's voice faltered before a personal oath as doubt caught her voice. "After all you've done for us."

"Vella," Vix sighed as her hand brushed Belladonna's arm. "I've never learned much elvish, but I know more than nothing. I know As are for the eldest and Ls are your mages and I certainly know what it means to put Vix in a name. Forgive me if I don't trust the unconditional support of people who named me as if I were already dead."

Belladonna stood at that. Her free hand ran through sweat-matted hair as her knuckles turned white around her staff. A mistake in Vix's words, perhaps only a mistake, but how clever she would be to hide a lie between truths. "No support is unconditional."

Not fully, never entirely without, and thought the support of Elves had but one condition: the act of being one wasn't so simple as shared blood.

"Isn't it? Why are you here?" Vix asked. "What's happened?"

For a weak moment, Belladonna let herself float on that voice, any goals she had in coming to that place forgotten. If she'd intended a conversation, she'd come unprepared. "Xax said there was a mutiny."

As Vix turned her head, the growing sunlight danced as if fireflies off those charms in her hair, and they sang a song of silver bells so gentle next to how her eyes hardened. "The late captain, some of the crew, they thought the guards had caught on; they wanted to abandon the runs."

Belladonna felt her heart stop just as it pounded in her ears. "How did they know?"

"Never mind that, love, we took care of it, and besides, Xax decides who lives on the Obsidian Isles." Vix's mouth curved a wicked grin. "No dead man has a say in that."

If only she had understood, if only Vix knew how little comfort her words carried but for the hint of a different path. "But they knew the guards were coming?" A hope Belladonna dared not hold flared in her chest. "Could one of them have told the guards?"

All of Vix's height showed as she stood from the bed. "Are you quite alright, love?"

In a way, Belladonna couldn't be quite sure she had meant to shake her head, her thoughts drunk on honey-toned words. "Someone talked to the guards; they knew too much. Could it have been..." her words faltered as Vix stepped close, but how tidy it would be, for the traitor to be dead, to be someone she never knew.

"No." A spark could turn to a wildfire, but how easily that hope had been killed with a single word, "Maybe after the first run, or the first few even. It's been years; even those idiots would know that any deal the guards offered obvious collaborators would be a lie at this point."

Some thought Belladonna had stored with a memory arose. "Not in person then, a note or a letter?"

"What would that get them? The runs would stop, but so would the gold," Vix said. So near to the question Belladonna had asked every moment since that night, what manner of reward could one of her inner circle seek in the betrayal? "Couldn't be anyway; the smarter half of that lot couldn't read."

"Suppose you can." Belladonna hadn't meant to say aloud, not a thought she would have had if not for the memory of a pre-dawn argument.

But something tinkled in Vix's driftwood-toned eye. "Well, only as well as the Mirri boys, but I wouldn't find that something to brag about." She chuckled — a joke Belladonna couldn't understand. "Why? Do you have someone else in mind?"

Belladonna stepped back, her staff nearly a crutch against the fog Vix cast over her mind. "There aren't many I'd like to believe would betray me."

"Not you," Vix said. "Anyone who knew so much would have known your name. But you haven't been arrested."

All at once the fog cleared. "I never said how much the guards knew."

Vix shrugged. "Enough to lay a trap on the right night in the right spot, but not so much to stop you before the run started," she said. "What about the safehouse keepers? They could tell the guards any story to explain their part in it. They'd have more to gain from selling us out too."

How Belladonna wanted to grab for the easy answer, cut away all the humans, and rebuild without them — it could have been so simple. But she shook her head and sent a long glance to the harbour tinted by orange silks. "None of them knew enough," she finally said.

"There was one, Nadia, was it? Your agent."

"Don't call her that," Belladonna spat. "We aren't spies."

Vix raised her hands, an effigy of surrender. "We aren't as far as you think, love. But she must have known enough if she was to get the runners together."

Belladonna so nearly forgot to stay silent, to not let slip the layers Nadia hadn't known, when so little could come of Vix knowing her suspicions. "I can't be sure."

A warm hand draped over Belladonna's shoulder, an intimate closeness from behind, but Vix gave no sign of noticing when Belladonna's breath caught. "Don't worry, love," Vix said. "We'll find them. And Xax can eat them with the rest."

Belladonna pulled away from the near embrace, if only for knowing how she would have stayed forever had she not. "I have to get back," she said as grace returned to carry her feet to the door.

"We're staying docked until after the festival; you know where to find me," Vix called to Belladonna's back.

She knew where, and yet somehow, in her heart, Belladonna hoped she wouldn't have to.

20
Belladonna
28th of Helenai, 447, Third Age

If it had been any other day, the gardens would surely have been empty during luncheon hours, but it would seem Southerners had not even the simple courtesy to keep the schedules of places they invaded. Still, had her mind not been miles away, Belladonna should have gotten past them. Her blood's grace should have carried her past Vix, as well, come to that. What her ancestors must have thought...

"Belladonna dear? Is that you?" the voice was of a stranger. Had Lyan'nyea taken a kinder god's hand, perhaps the face would have been as well. If only the woman, so near Belladonna's own age but who had seduced her father, could have vanished from the world as thoroughly as the previous day had banished her from Belladonna's mind. The truth could never be so kind. The damnable wench sat buried under furs that did nothing to hide the goosebumps as her bare arms reached for her teacup.

How Belladonna wished to ignore the greeting, to save her mind from the games behind it, how badly she wished to return to her allies, to choose possible enemies in place of certain ones. But as with all games, ignorance would only work when paired with avoidance, and, as with all games, the one she stumbled into had rules.

"Good day, Lady Gavrie." Belladonna's voice came out flat. Only a deaf man could miss its distaste.

A strange fool in a strange place Eugenia may have been, but so like every scheming Human of noble birth, she too knew the rules of the game she set. Not but a twitch of lips stood as a comment to the tone.

"I think we can dispense with all that," Eugina said. "We'll be family soon. Join me for tea?"

Belladonna knew the simple game of civility; she knew the script to follow, the prescribed words written by those clinging to advantage. She knew what was expected, but, on that day, not even the forces of The Seven Hundred could have made her call it a pleasure as she sat on the offered chair.

Such a put-upon shiver ran across Eugenia's body as she tugged at borrowed furs tangled over cream silks. "I must confess, I had thought your father exaggerated about the cold and how you live in such a drafty castle. I don't see how you can bear it."

"Evidently not."

"Well, not for much longer." Eugenia smiled. Her mouth was a thin, cruel thing. "We'll have it all redone after the wedding, panel the walls in proper marble, and we ought to have frescos like the Maker's Pass."

If nothing else could have revealed evidence of an interloper's false importance, she used the true name of the True Capitol while sitting across from one of King Elric's own blood.

"Will you be painting them?" Belladonna leaned back. The cold of iron kept at bay by cream toned summer wools. "Or did your father need to set your dowery so high?"

"And these roses! Of course, I'd heard the gardens were neglected under your grandfather, but I'd expected something of the legends to remain."

Belladonna couldn't be bothered to hide her scowl. "If we're disappointing, you might return south."

Eugenia's mask cracked with a frown, a disappointment so much more fit for a mother's face than a stranger's. "Now, dear, I'm sure that's not necessary. I'd like for us to be friends."

Every word came like a tongue to frozen steel as Belladonna forced polite words of someone else's mind from her throat. "If that's what you'd like, I'm sure it would be most convenient for both of us."

"Good." And with Eugenia's mask, the game shattered. "Have you told your father not to consummate our marriage?"

The shock came not from the interloper's words or their venom, although, perhaps, for a Human under twenty, the words should have been shocking. No, it was the story behind them – that the words of Belladonna's father had been earnest after she'd scorned them as a lie.

"I understand the city has a brothel," Belladonna said, a moment too late to hide her shock as anything else, "if that is so important to you."

"Filthy mongrel!" Porcelain cups shattered against the path as Eugenia came to her feet. "You think this is a joke? This will be my child's right."

"You're so free with that word, Gavrie." Belladonna had been so afraid when her father made his promise, but that fear was drowned, twisted, under the decades-old insult until only the anger remained. "Because this is *my* right."

"Don't be a fool." That fine shield of pleasantness returned askew as Eugenia sat back. "I'll be married soon and pregnant months before you can claim to be Lady Raylor."

That complication, that timeline to what Edmund called safety, had her parents been of the same people, had they been married under those fickle Human gods, that countdown to her Calling wouldn't have mattered. But a bastard she was, not Belladonna Raylor, only of the House Raylor until that arbitrary age of twenty. She didn't care for the title, for the name kept just a step from her own. She'd sworn to her countless gods that she didn't care. The same gods gave no wisdom for the challenge set before her.

In the absence of wisdom, Belladonna chose the easier option. "How do you expect you should get pregnant without my father's involvement?"

"They say you don't play the game," Eugenia sneered.

Belladonna matched it in turn. "I don't."

"Well then, you've convinced my betrothed his duties are to you. But he will see reason once he's restored."

"If I have him so convinced as you say, he won't be. And he can't be restored to the succession after he gave it up."

"If you had a proper mother, you would already be Lady Raylor, and we would be trapped by his mistake," Eugenia said, "but I haven't come to argue. I have an offer for you. You don't wish to play the game, and you should be so much more comfortable if you didn't have to. I've spoken to my third brother, and he is willing to adopt you and your dear sister into his household. When you turn twenty this winter, we will arrange a perfectly comfortable marriage, perhaps in one of the colonies. You can start afresh, far from this place you hate."

Out of sight. Wasn't that always her destiny? No. "I must have misspoken; your language is so simplistic." Belladonna's back straightened as she leaned in. "Lyria is my right."

"You can't hope for a better offer."

"I was given one," Belladonna spat, "when I was five. Do you plan for my grandfather to meet She who Waits before winter?"

Perhaps it was the malice of a goddess she hadn't known that had shaken Eugenia, but the words that passed her lips came so quiet, they couldn't have been meant for any but her own mind. "Someone will."

A line too far.

"You may threaten me," Belladonna said as she stood. Perhaps it was her hand that shook, or perhaps the intent that burned through her staff took form without a target. "Offer me your deals. But if you intend to remove me, you will have to do the same to Alyria. If you make a move towards my sister, you won't need to worry about consummating a marriage."

"You dare, you little Breaker spawn." The words came so near to a growl as Eugenia, too, stood. "Your Daemon magic won't help you."

"You fear Daemons? My ancestors fought them. Go on then, invoke your gods, and I'll invoke mine." Her mana found a candle's flame; it could have been so easy...

"Lady Belladonna!" a new voice called.

Both ladies spun to the sight of Edmund as he sprinted across the grounds. His hair stood matted with sweat, and his red face paled as his eyes crossed Eugenia.

"Mister Cardwell, to what do we owe the pleasure?" Belladonna said. How she wished to snap at him, yet she couldn't scold him for his carelessness, not when her own had so nearly gotten out of hand.

Whatever shock overcame the tailor passed as he turned to Eugenia. "I must apologize, Lady Gavire. I must borrow Lady Belladonna."

The excuse was given not a moment before Belladonna pulled Edmund away, but she needn't have bothered avoiding a final word for all the silence that followed the pair through the gardens. A silence she dared not break as they passed great doors nor as they climbed the spiral stairs of a near-empty tower.

Belladonna scarcely dared breathe until that off-key latch chimed at her back. She could nary hold her eyes on her lover for how he paced her room. "What's happened?" she asked.

"I went to see Nadia like you asked," he said.

"And?"

Edmund's tracks stopped at once, and his eyes finally found Belladonna's own. "She wasn't there. None of them were. The house was boarded up and empty. It was like they had been gone for months."

21
Kitty
37th of Helenai, 447, Third Age

The heat abated that day, and while sweat-matted hair no longer burned Kitty's scalp, those same clouds that brought The Maker's Blessed shade carried portent of the coming storms. The warning was made double in the humidity that summoned frizz from ebony curls. That morning, just another spent absent of any landmarks but empty prairie to both horizons and not half a week from Gentea, could well have been an easy ride, a relief from the sun, if it not for the cold silence from Wyvern far ahead, urging her horse faster every time he slowed, and for the cramping reminders of how long ago those stolen fruits had been eaten.

Kitty didn't notice Robin driving Ria close until a handful of grass landed on her hair. Loose green flooded her vision. She startled back, thoughts lost in the shock; her ears turned to Robin's cackle as he spurred Ria ahead.

"Robin!" Kitty half laughed and gave chase.

The game was different in the open plains, no buildings to scale or fences to jump. A straight and simple race with no end until the instigator was caught, unfortunate then, just like Robin clambering up a smooth stone wall, Ria was faster.

Still, Kitty spurred Shale on until Wyvern's cloud of near-white hair grew close. "Catch him, Wyvern!"

Laughter erupted from Kitty's throat at the puzzled sound Wyvern made when Robin raced past. A confusion that seemed to clear between heartbeats. No mortal of any kind should have been able to jump as Wyvern did from that unnamed horse's back.

It was a tumbling, graceless thing as Wyvern collided with Robin and pulled him from Ria — a doubly graceless thing when they hit the ground and rolled together, a tangled heap of limbs and cloth.

Robin managed to loose himself first; his head scarf askew and feathers ruffled, but there was a remorseless gleam to his eyes, a mischievous set to them. Kitty nearly fell from Shale's back for how she choked on sound when Robin plucked a handful of grass and dropped it on Wyvern's head.

The foot chase that followed was so much shorter than any Kitty and Robin had enacted in ten years together. The quiet melancholy vanished from that empty stretch of road — banished, forgotten to the mind's many vaugeries by how Robin squawked when Wyvern hoisted him off his feet. Kitty's eyes caught how Wyvern's shoulders relaxed, how little it took her to hold all of Robin's weight off the ground until he twisted from her grip, and the chase resumed. A pattern of catch and escape in rounds beyond number.

Kitty plucked the grass from her hair and held it; she so nearly steered Shale towards the cacophony of squawks and laughter. Her on horseback and them on foot, what a good head start she could have had if only being caught wouldn't have burned like the Dark Mother's own grasp. She let those grass blades fall away. Two horses, missing riders, gathered to sniff at the dropped pieces. Kitty let her fingers brush the nameless one's side. If only.

Something froze the air in her lungs.

Lost was the uproarious joy of the game in her ears, replaced by something else as she turned them. There was some new chorus beneath the rhythm of wind and shifting grass over the hard-packed earth.

Lost was the quiet melancholy of the road, replaced by something else. There was some new chorus beneath the rhythm of hooves on the hard-packed earth.

Had the sun been in her eyes, as with the previous days, Kitty may well have missed the first flash.

None could have missed the second.

Had she not been a witch, the flame may have looked ordinary; had she been born a human, she wouldn't have heard that never-whistle of mana as the flame chased a donkey and rider up the road.

Kitty's words gave no commands as she spurred Shale ahead; she had no need to wonder if her intentions were understood for the need to reach the tiny donkey before the flames did.

Only as furious hooves brought her close did Kitty see the true meaning of the fight: The donkey's rider, small enough to be a child, with eyes of such a blue they tore Kitty's eyes from the flames for a bare moment, a pause, a heartbeat's wonder, to see the donkey with singed hair, but how lucky the girl had been, so unlike the tinderbox-dry grasses around her, to be yet untouched.

The three that chased the blue-eyed girl were no mere bandits turned to witchcraft; she needn't have taken another step to recognize those many pointed star amulets identical on each chest. Identical too to those she'd seen that first night on the road.

Kitty raised her wand in concert with the cultist. But her spell never had the chance to fly, never grew past the beginnings of a thought before it was ripped away as Shale froze in his tracks, and shuddered in an all too familiar way. Something near and far from healing. His muscles shook in a losing battle beneath flesh as blood was wrenched from the heart's control.

Body for body, blood for blood.

Old magic, deep magic, the Daemons' first art. Pa's magic, but Kitty's mind spurned that connection as she was thrown from Shale's back. In the moment between air and ground, she saw nothing but the cut through the Blood Mage's hand, the crimson line that dripped from his blade.

A wand's sparks pulled her eyes as the earth knocked the breath from her chest. Mana cooled to a blizzard's pitch, but no thought of ice or magic came as her lungs screamed.

No inferno came. The second spark was blocked by the great black legs of a nameless horse; grey clouds were blocked by one of white hair. A wall that did nothing to hide the flames forced to the sky or the black song of a great sword through flesh, moments before the once witch fell to Kitty's level, missing her head.

And yet the wall of Wyvern's back hid the true foe, and relief stole her chance for a warning before Wyvern too shuddered in that terrible way; her pale skin flushed fever red, and stepped from her horse.

Kitty had only time enough to throw herself aside before Wyvern's sword cut a rent through the earth. She had neither time nor wits to fumble her wand into any manner of spell before the steel edge again carved the Dark Mother's call.

The wicked arch never struck. An axe clattered off the great blade, and a push of mere inches plunged the blade again into empty ground.

The Maker's mercy in Robin, but he had dared too close.

Wyvern turned on Robin faster than he could urge Ria away. The blade rose, and the spell Kitty had so longed for moments before crackled through her beating heart, the wand suddenly so sure in her hand. Wyvern's sword struck only against the wall of ice that grew before it. A shower of snow in place of blood.

Those pink eyes once again turned to Kitty. But Kitty saw not the sword, absent of its flame. Kitty had eyes only for the black-feathered head that emerged over the ice, his eyes so unlike himself, that look she had never seen before.

Her legs moved before her mind could realize she had placed herself between the two. "No!" she yelled.

Her feet hadn't yet the thought to stop when a massive hand sent her back to the ground. By only the Mother's true grace did she keep hold of her wand as she tumbled through the yellowing grass.

That tall shadow blocked the brewing storms overhead, and Kitty dared not search her eyes, cowardice, a prayer that nothing remained behind them. And yet, a contradiction: "It's not your fault," she whispered, with vain hope her friend could still hear it.

Ringing hooves in the back of Kitty's mind became so very real as a donkey with burned hair ran past her, and its blue-eyed rider leapt onto Wyvern's back. Such a tiny thing, surely a Dwarf but for pointed ears, shorter than the sword Wyvern so easily hefted, so little weight as to mean nothing. And yet, the great Fensmirri dropped to a knee as the strange girl scrambled down her back. When Wyvern's face rose, Kitty saw the life she had thought lost to her forever.

So slow, so slight Kitty may have missed it. She saw that cursed Blood Mage move, a shift for his knife. They had been lucky, just as Kitty knew nearly nothing of the black flames Wyvern called that first night, the blood mage had remained ignorant of their existence. Not even blood could touch that which its master didn't know to reach for. The Maker, even in Helenai, wouldn't, grant Kitty infinite luck, the blood mage knew his control of Wyvern was lost. And he knew Kitty to be a witch.

The ice had come so easily. All the mana left in its wake boiled within her veins; he wouldn't have it. Long worn cracks glowed violet as she raised her wand again. Like an omen of the storm to come, a bolt from the ground, there was no chance for the man to retaliate with his last breath – no blood remained in that wicked man as Kitty's lightning reached the sky.

That heat so different from a flame's warped the ice, just as it had once before, just as her mother's last defence had dripped down into such red ground.

"Kitty!" Only by Robin's call did Kitty keep her senses. Only by the sight of him did she find her feet and run. Had she not stopped just short, they might have embraced.

Only by the sound of a stranger's sword dropping did Kitty remember that third cultist; there was nothing left of the man when she turned, only the dust kicked by his horse and the growing stain across that tiny girl's tunic.

Kitty thought nothing as she stopped the girl's fall; her mind had no place for Hanson as the Dwarf girl's blood stained her hands. She had eyes for nothing but those blue ones in the growing dark.

22

Belladonna

29th of Helenai, 447, Third Age

The annual heat wave pushed east from the sea. Dark mahogany in furniture and panelling drew it in, radiating as if tiny fires. Even those obscured windows at the top of that lonely tower were thrown open for the hope of a breeze, but, as still, as the air always was ten days before summer's end, they only invited in more of that sun and heat.

It drove Belladonna to naught but floating layers of under things that left her corset and wrapped amber skirt fully unhidden. That same heat matted sweat through her hair and left a mess of strands stuck to her neck; the first of a list of problems she could scarcely count. A list furthered as Edmund brought Vix to Belladonna's chambers alone. Elysa's hand twitched to her hip when he did.

"Where's Xax?" Belladonna asked – words to fill the space a fight wanted to take.

The sound Vix made was one that couldn't have easily been separated between a sigh and a laugh. "You really don't want to know, love. If there are any dragons on this continent that didn't—" Vix's voice cut out as her eyes landed on Elysa. "Suppose I'll tell you later. Who is this?"

"An ally," Elysa said. The long sleeves of a modest servant were lost to the heat and, with them, any obfuscation of the long-ago charred flesh across her chest and arm. "One of Av'vella's, that is."

Vix's hand landed on the scimitar, so usual, so trusted on her hip. "Are you going to pull that knife, love?"

The memory twice forgotten, a sliver glint beneath those skirts.

"Enough!" Belladonna snapped, her effort to prevent the fight wasted and more given to stop its escalation. "Today of all days, pretend to get along."

"Of course, love." Even on that day, Vix wore every layer and yet seemed not a bit cowed by the weather as she wrapped an arm around Belladonna's waist. "I never did say how good it is to see you, Edmund."

"You–"

But Edmund's protest was cut short as a raven flew through the open window and, between beats of its wings, shifted, until only Xaxirion's golden eyes stood constant. "Seralie can't think herself so special now," he laughed, and draped himself over the cold stone hearth. "Four dragon riders left in her charge, and she's lost one."

"Mixed company, Xax," Vix said.

Her grandmother's gossip rang in Belladona's ears. Would the Seers claim she was giving up when she didn't push for Xaxirion to continue? That she didn't make him relive the hurt between himself and the Silver Dragon?

Golden eyes narrowed on Elysa, and, again, he laughed as his fingers gripped an arrow-head hung from his neck, so like himself and Belladonna's staff, a relic of ages past. "Now, what are you supposed to be?"

How it must have felt to be a Seer, to see all things in duplicate. A hint to that feeling as the same words were said. And how her little group's lack of the concept reminded Belladonna of how easily she had once trusted.

There were scars on Belladonna's hands, jagged from tiles shattered beneath a dropped bucket. An accident she had never once needed to worry after for the certainty her people would hide it. How much easier an enemy without had been, how she longed for a rallying point half as strong. For the unity, all Elves knew—a strange shattered mirror against allies who barely knew a shared cause.

An unknown enemy couldn't be held in common, and no trust came simply to a room that hid a traitor within its walls.

No false comfort could come in that sitting room, so crowded, made doubly so by the company and heat.

"Never mind that," Belladonna said to the growing racket of argument. But only as the silence grew in its wake, did she come to know that she hadn't the words to say. She hadn't lies to hide her suspicions. Or the strength to fight the silence.

It wasn't her voice that broke it. "She must have run off after she talked," Edmund said.

"You think Nadia was the traitor?" Belladonna asked.

"If not her, then who?" Vix asked. "Who else knew enough?"

Green eyes caught on Vixensha's storm of colour as Belladonna pulled away. A repeat of the question she had failed to find a lie for. In response to that honeyed voice, for but a moment, doubt flowed. Just a moment before the weight of her own knowledge stoppered it. For perhaps different words Vix carried had held more truth than Belladonna had known, for she had never trusted Human connections with the route beyond its first point. Never had she been such a fool to put true trust in a paid contact; no, she had only been a fool enough to trust those she called friends.

"We need to find her, traitor or not," Belladonna said. "If she's talked, she still hasn't told the guards who we are. She could still ruin us."

"It's my fault," Edmund said. "I shouldn't have complained so much about bringing her the money. If I'd been quicker—"

"No," Belladonna said, "it's not your fault."

A hand, rough yet slight, found its way to Belladonna's shoulder, a kind warmth in spite of the heat, such shuddering beats it sent through her heart. Those that stopped with her breath as Belladonna once more realized she hadn't heard Elysa move.

"It's not yours either," Elysa whispered just too close. "None of this is your fault."

"And what about you?" Edmund stormed forward to snatch away the warmth of Elysa's hand. "Showing up right after is a bit convenient, isn't it?"

"Convenient for whom? I'd love nothing more than to be free of this place."

Edmund scoffed. "That's what you say. But you admit you're from the Northeast."

"Oi now, most people are, especially humans. It's not such a good reason on its own," Elysa said. "I believe we're still under orders, pretending to like each other, was it?"

Edmund grabbed Elysa's wrist as its touch once more sent shivers through Belladonna's arm. "I won't lie to her to pretend I trust you."

Elysa wrenched her wrist from Edmund's grasp. "And yet you'd trust a Changeling?"

Xaxirion tipped his head, but his eyes remained fixed far away. "I'm not a Changeling."

Elysa's eyes narrowed. "Then what you are is worse."

Xaxirion didn't so much as move his eye to the servant girl. "Not many would know what that is."

"One knows their enemy." A Human wouldn't have heard that subtle way Elysa's accent slipped.

While Xaxirion still moved not an inch, Vix rose to that challenge, her advance only halted by her brother's hand on her arm. "And dragons are your enemy then?" she snarled.

Elysa stepped back from the half-dragon, just a step before an overstuffed chair stopped her retreat, but a liar's mask fell over her face as she shrugged. "Suppose not, no more than any other *beast*."

"Enough!" So many times, Belladonna had needed to wrench control from her allies that morning. "Have all of my allies been replaced with Fin'neshi-held children?"

Xax's gaze returned from that far-off place to pin Belladonna. "Every one of us is older than you, Bellavella."

"And you might, for once in your life, act like it, Xaxirion." Belladonna's temper flared under the humour in ancient eyes. "Or should I need to do Ellivar's work to find a decent ally?"

Words she hadn't meant to say, perhaps, and yet in no way an accident. That odd chorus of feigned apologies gave little comfort.

"We need to find Nadia," Belladonna repeated as she turned away. No words rose as she dug through the mess of her desk. Two lists of names, written only hours ago and yet driven by paranoia to be hidden beneath years of scraps – Anika's gifted drawings, illegible notes from those first months Belladonna thought the love of two families was an option, sketched maps of those corridors between walls long since committed to memory. Hoarded things were remembered and forgotten in the instant her prize was found. She gave both into the hands of her lover. "You and Xaxirion talk to these safehouses. Wherever Nadia is, we need to stop the ring until we find her."

Words gave truth and meaning to that step she hadn't wanted to take; she knew she had been so lucky her people hadn't come to harm for her delaying that step so long. None more could walk the hidden paths, could dare a chance of freedom, could risk more eyes while the means to destroy all they built still walked.

But still, she forced her eyes dry. "Come on, Vix," she started as she reached for the brown dress cast over a chair.

"I thought you might wear the grey one," Edmund said.

"Not today, love." Still, Belladonna's hand paused. "It's too much."

"You might, at least, change your underskirt then," Elysa said. "Amber with brown won't do until fall." there was a moment before Belladonna understood Elysa's words where she tensed – prepared herself for another round as unwilling mediator; she didn't quite know what her new role was to be when she grasped the side they landed on.

In understanding's absence, Belladonna shook her head. "It doesn't matter."

"But it does." Elysa held a hand to silence Edmund, a shaky alliance if there ever was one. "If you followed just some rules, held yourself as if you care about them even you might be treated as a lady, not a burden."

"It's a bit late to salvage my reputation," Belladonna said. "Leave it," she snapped as Edmund made to carry off the brown dress.

"So contrary," Elysa said somewhere behind her. "You mock the nobility as fools but put so much stake in their memories." The weight of the grey dress settled on Belladonna's shoulders; those fine embodied sleeves Edmund spent so many days crouched over caught the light as they slid over her hands. "Before they see your face, or even your ears, these people see your clothes. They see the colours you choose, the cuts you favour. They *are* fools. They only want to copy power, follow the leader as they might. But you won't let them."

Maybe it was because the words were obvious, things Edmund had said before but made so irritatingly simplified, that Belladonna didn't quite notice how Elysa's voice changed when she said them. "I don't stop them from doing anything."

"You should be leading them," Edmund said as he came to fasten her buttons, polished glass, cut to glimmer like the jewels Edmund had wanted to use but glass all the same. "We all hate this style we've been stuck in, but you won't let me make anything else."

Who was 'we' she wondered, the tailors most likely, all sick to death of keeping corsets spotlessly clean for display. It couldn't be the ladies; what great changes could they make anyhow with the decreed limit of three dresses a year?

"You can go on and keep blaming my grandfather's budget for that." Belladonna pulled away from her two allies' fussing. "But I've told you I don't care, make whatever you want."

"I want it to be what you want!"

Somewhere in the back of her mind, Belladonna formed a response destined never to come the words; what could she say about the futility of his passion without shattering his heart?

A hand tugged at her hemline. "This is fine work," Elysa said to the silence as her fingers ran across Edmund's embroidery.

"Out with it then," Edmund spat. "What do you want?"

The smile that crossed Elysa's face broke any sense she might have taken true offence. "Oh Edmund, I'm shocked, bringing Northeastern values all the way here, and here I was—" She broke off whatever little game she was playing and hummed as her fingers came to a point where the embroidery strayed from the pattern for just a couple of stitches. "Is this a fortune stitch?"

"A what?" Belladonna snatched her sight away to peer at that point she had never looked closely enough to notice before; it looked like a mistake, some error in the stitching.

"Nothing." Edmund made to grab for the skirt, but Belladonna batted away his hands, her eyes still fixed on those few stray stitches. "Just a good luck charm."

Elysa scoffed, "Not just."

"Leave it," Edmund said. "I know you'd tie your sleeves back if you had any, but—"

"And you'd never need to, but you'd have leggings under your skirts, no doubt," Elysa interrupted.

Belladonna didn't know what any of that meant.

"I know what it means," Vix said, not with the teasing tone she took with Edmund nor the honey wine flirtations Belladonna was often gifted. She offered her left arm, the crest of house Mirri inked to her wrist. It was hard to see at first with how warped and stretched the tattoo was but there they were, a few specks of ink that deviated from the pattern. "It's a sacrifice; the artist gives up some of their own luck and reputation so their love can get it back double."

"What now?" Edmund snapped to Vix, "I'm sure you have something to say about it."

"No." She shook her head, "You can have this; I'll never say a word against this."

"I can," Elysa said, still crouched by Belladonna's feet. "You haven't pushed it far enough. A fortune stitch is six out of line. You've done five."

"No, I—" Edmund grasped the hem. "Well, she hardly needs more wealth."

"Oh, is that the one you skipp – Oi!" Elysa's words cut off as Belladonna's foot caught her in the side.

"Enough of that," Belladonna snapped. She didn't care, didn't care if it was meant to be ten stitches out of line. She just wanted to keep looking at them.

"Well, fine then, Lady Master," Elysa spat as she came to her feet; the feeling of those amber eyes came to a fever pitch as they locked on Belladonna's. "If that what you think of speaking, I'll keep my mouth shut."

Elysa didn't leave space for a response as she left the room.

Doubt, what a rare thing, especially in her own chamber, especially towards herself. Lady master, that's what she had been called.

"Don't think about it," Edmund said. "She deserved every bit of that. Having a hard life doesn't mean she gets to make everyone else miserable." He paused. "I'll finish the stitch tonight."

"Right." Belladonna shook her head. "Right, Vix, we'll check the safe houses."

Another business she so wished could have been avoided.

23

Belladonna

29th of Helenai, 447, Third Age

There was no glamour in that cave, cold and dark on the cliffside. A safe house wasn't to be a beautiful place, a mere pause before freedom, pure function, but that hole in the rock, that crevice against the sea, could boast little of that either. It could have once, before the ring had grown to its Human members, but such a long time ago. So alone it stood, a place to be forgotten but for those siblings who called it home when they were still three together. So many years away from being a home, yet its walls still bore the scars, forever marked by the scratchings of a poet's soul.

"We can use this." Golden-eyed Nit glowed as a tiny sun in the twilight-dim cave. "So we can do big runs, and no one gets left behind."

"I said you could help her," Xaxirion growled from the darkness beyond the fickle sunlight in the entry. "I never said you could bring her here."

Winter wools, once red but ruined by frost and mud from that first climb to the cave, clung to Belladonna's legs, in their wake a chill not nearly from the cold. But a dragon's strike never came as Nit, a child younger and taller than Belladonna in the 442nd year, yet made to seem so tiny against her brother, stood as a shield between, a ward against winter, warm as the sun and twice as bright.

"I didn't need your permission," Nit said. "I'm your Favoured, and Vix calls me sister. I'm not your rider."

"Nit." The voice from darkness could have been said to soften if not for how it broke. "I never—"

"And you're helping too," Nit said.

"I'm not—"

"Well." A new voice joined the chorus as Vix stepped from the darkness at her brother's side. All cold and purple hues, the moon to her sister's sun. "We might."

"Why Vix?" Xaxirion asked as he, too, came to that meagre light. "Yesterday, you agreed with me."

"Maybe I didn't get a good enough look at her yesterday."

Belladonna couldn't help her scoff, disgust and protest driven by burgeoning affection for another.

"You can't join her insane mission because you think she's pretty."

"Why not?" Vix asked. "Is it that far off the reason you refuse to help her?"

The air thickened, knives of midwinter cold, transformed into those hot irons of tension before a fight. Not a word was spoken, but still Nit laughed.

"I'll take you home now," she whispered, warmer than the sun above, "he knows we've won."

Five years after the first time, spray from the Shivering Sea nipped the backs of the two women who lowered themselves down that cliff face. Just up the hill, the air was still as anything, but mere steps from the sea, hot air buffeted the cliff. Their arrival at last heralded by twin echoes as wooden heels scattered eternal puddles. Belladonna lingered even as Vix strode through the half-dark, even as her treacherous heart bade her come close.

"We didn't need to check here." Impatience flared in Belladonna's chest. The first stop was a wasted effort. "We haven't used it since I brought Nadia in."

But Vix gave no credit to Belladonna's words as she peeled off the damp coat; all and no circumstance followed the jewel-tone bundle as it crumpled to the ground.

"I didn't see it when we talked yesterday." Vix's hand traced absently over her sister's memorial. "When you talked about a traitor, I didn't think you meant it to be me."

Belladonna faltered, but what could any say against the truth? "I don't—"

The chime of metal as bracelets were dropped onto the coat. "You're a shit liar, Vella."

"Worse these days, it seems." Belladonna stepped past the threshold; only the heat of mana kept her from shivering. "At least to you."

"Oh, you can fool your nobles plenty. But that's just because they don't think you're clever enough to do so. I thought you were at least smarter than this."

Grey wool took stains by the very air of that place, perhaps it tarnished the power in Vix's voice just the same, for the first time in so long, Belladonna's mind stayed clear. "Is it so foolish to suspect?"

Vix scoffed. "I've been by your side in this since before you were properly bedding Edmund. So why?"

But here was a lie. There had been those long years spent apart, those cold days after Nit had died. Perhaps it was the lie that stole Belladonna's control, that drove her knuckles white around her staff.

"Because it had to be one of you!" Even her yell came as a trifle as the sea raged beyond. "And you've always wanted more from me."

"So, I'd tear it all down? Because you won't be with me? I hope I'm not that petty."

"You were supposed to meet me that night."

A Human wouldn't have heard the whisper. "I told you what I was doing!"

"You did," Belladonna said. "You *told* me."

"And you don't believe me." Perhaps only in Belladonna's mind, the sea stopped its howling as Vix's hand landed on her sword, an infinite moment before it, too, clattered on the pile. Before Vix finally turned. "I sent you my brother."

Belladonna shook her head to new doubts. "There isn't a trap Xax couldn't spring."

"Is that it then? My plan? You get arrested, and I rescue you. You would be so grateful you'd fall into my arms?"

"I never said that."

"No, but you thought it. I don't know if it would be a terrible plan, but *I* didn't think of it."

Perhaps Belladonna had. Or perhaps she had hoped it, for the crime to be of jealousy, of hate by another word. Perhaps too, she would have believed those words from any other voice; perhaps part of her heart still believed them from Vix's – from a person who never knew to stop talking, the only one who would argue against her own case for the sake of it.

"I don't know," Belladonna said. "I don't know why any of you would betray us."

Those crashing waves were all that echoed for a long while. Belladonna hadn't quite realized her legs had given out until Vix crouched at her side.

"If it was me," Vix said with that honeyed voice returned to its power, "I'd give up your name before I set a trap."

"What?"

Vix's hand settled on Belladonna's knee. "I could give proof too, but once I turned your grandfather towards this, I wouldn't have to. If it was me."

Comfort both came and fled from those words, and, for but a moment, Belladonna let herself get caught in those mismatched eyes. "This leaves me with nothing."

"Not being wrong is a great deal more than nothing. Or at least it isn't less," Vix said, "We can still find Nadia. If it was her, we can take care of it."

"She has to know something."

Vix nodded and held out a hand. "Right then, if you're not gonna kill me, let's get out of this place."

"You thought I was going to kill you?" Belladonna took the offered hand. Her fickle heart clung to that warmth even after they parted.

"I've never known you to hesitate, and if it would bring you peace, my life is yours to take, it always has been. Why else would I come here?" Vix asked as she pulled her possessions from the ground. "Elven bones, love; you couldn't scale this cliff with a body; Xax should be allowed to bury one of us."

It struck as if a Daemon, how sure Vix had been of the outcome, the certainty she had read from Belladonna's mere suspicions. How ready she had been. But then she had been ready, ready to join her sister, perhaps for those so easily forgotten years she had been missing from the ring Vix had been prepared for the end.

"You were wrong, you know," Vix said.

"About what?"

"Yesterday, you said support can't be unconditional. Mine is." Vix stepped into the entry's meagre light; a golden aura danced, resplendent, as if the light were her very own, where the sun hit her skin. "When it comes to you."

Belladonna stayed back. "You left."

"It wasn't you I had to leave." Vix turned her back. "Your grandmother knew my sister was going to die that day. She had to have. She could have said anything and the path would have changed. We know she's broken the rules before, but after everything Nit did for–" Vix's voice caught, a broken half thing not quite decided between a sob and laugh. Belladonna couldn't see what played over her face. "I couldn't look at your people without knowing that."

Belladonna took a single step closer, too far to touch, but only just. "And now?"

Vix looked over her shoulder. "When was I ever here for them?"

There was a power in those eyes, always the same one, and paired with honey wine words, stronger than winter drink, it went straight to Belladonna's head. So easily her own eyes drifted, drank in every inch of inked skin, followed the curves of flowers and dragons, a slow circuit until her gaze returned to those mismatched eyes.

She stumbled – caught herself against her staff – before stepping to Vix's side. "Vix, I-" No rejection ever came soft enough when one didn't want to give it, nor strong enough when they swore for their own mind that they did.

"What did I tell you, love? Unconditional."

Perhaps it was that last repeated word that broke the spell, that brought the world back into sharp focus. Unconditional, for her but not her cause. So why had Xax stayed when his loss was the same and he cared for neither?

But such thoughts fled as Belladonna glanced beyond the cave. So far below, she first thought it Fin'neshi's tricks, but no, no trick, and no lie either, the shadow of a man, so far away, and yet with such a certain profile she had seen but once before. Or perhaps a mistake, a simple one for how her heart still raced, but for the instinct that gave her pause, the same feeling that told her the names of guards with their faces hidden, and one that had her hesitate as Vix offered a hand up that short climb. "Go ahead," Belladonna said. "Elysa and Edmund can check the rest."

"Is something the matter?" Vix asked.

"No, only I can't be sure."

The sea spray felt so much colder as she left Vix's side, or perhaps it was only the descent to the sea, a heartbreak of every parting, and an Arh'hen blessed relief from the heat.

Belladonna knew she must have been a fool. Her mind's nagging, only newly familiar, chased her down the long hike to the shore, as fine embroidery turned dull and the waves soaked her hem. But her eyes had not lied; that man named Aroch stood unmoved, his face to the raging sea.

Belladonna didn't speak, not until she was too close to run; so far from the city, such a lonely cove, not a thing in sight to cause a mage any pause. "They call you Aroch?"

Pebbles flew under the man's feet as he spun. "I—it's you. That is—" The man so nearly fell to the sea as he stumbled a bow. "They don't. Not me. My Lady...only my father is Lord Aroch. I'm just...they call me Hector. It wouldn't have been right, keeping you from your family, that is, I said so to your friend. And we've never had no... that is never had any problems with your people."

"What?" Belladonna asked into the barrage of words and wind.

"Plenty of half-elves in the caravans. Lovely people, lovely singers, couldn't say a word against 'em. Them!" The sea gave such a spray to cover both of them as a look of dawning crossed his face. "My lady, you shouldn't be out here alone."

The ancient wood carvings left their memory as Belladonna's hand tightened. There was a moment of discord as rebellious claims of his lack of authority agreed with reality. "Nor should you."

"No, I shouldn't, we shouldn't. I needn't say I saw you, that is"—his fine shoes made such music as they shuffled over loose stones—"if you don't tell your friend I spoke to you."

"You mean Elysa?"

Could his eyes have gotten wider, they surely would have as he shuffled further back. "Just don't tell her we spoke. I have nothing to do with the claim," he yelled over the wind. "Just- just don't tell her."

Even if Belladonna had thought to ask what he meant, she would have lost the chance as Hector disappeared down the beach like so much rushing water.

24

Lane

Cycle 4722 || 40th of Helenai, 447, Third Age

P ain.
It came in waves, and yet all at once. A grey sea, lifeless as the ones no Lyrian map would show. Had she fallen to its depths? Was that why she couldn't breathe? No, lungs boiled with that first gasp; too hot. So why, then, couldn't she open her eyes? Or perhaps they already were. Were those her hands covered in blood? What a funny thing, she couldn't feel them. An island again, the waves crashed over her, so dark beneath the surface.

So hot.

Had the suns passed? Meet, pass, cross again, and a rhyme, where was the rhyme? Cross again, rise again, tet laviate? No, a different story. Phantom pages caught flesh ablaze. Eyes that wouldn't open.

Movement.

Hoof steps, the sea that pulled her under with every jolt. An escape? No, not Fen's gait. An escape. Flying free. The only reality in black earth as breath was stolen again.

Matching in hue, a clash of something older, eyes opened to the sky, Galet and Nesh'ran nowhere in those depths. Too old, and yet soon younger for renewal. Too soon, not time yet, push it back, fix the errors her life wrought. Leave this place, speak Her daughter's name, set it back. Can't wait. So hot.

When had the sky gone dark?

Voices. Strangers whispered words any could learn. She heard none of them for that rage of flame. Were her eyes open? Had she fallen there too, those places inked dark, lost to that all-black fire.

Had her braid come undone? Darkness, slim fingers that brushed it, no, she always put it back. Too loose, it touched her face; Hallei, she knew to put it right, she knew. More fell from its binding, flames wary of those spots strands tickled, taunting, teasing, tear it away, tet laviate.

No.

Sour herb's song, all she could see was that blue sky. Only one match for blue eyes.

Warnings.

"Quiet! They'll find you."

No, another story.

Helena watched through the clouds. They watched each other. How long until they should meet? Not long now. Should being would, could be late, could be early, too soon, too much left. Let go, fix the damage, leave this place, speak Her daughter's name.

Thei'nas annan mott'tir se't re'nnan.

Wait.

Change, seasons change, rise again those doomed to die, repeat the doom as echoes do. A bad year, a hard year. Choose a kinder hand. No, a season's change, sing to Bann'ni pray the season to spring. Moons crossed for autumn. Take a new hand before the time. It came too soon.

Wait.

And fire fled.

Lane's eyes opened again only so very long after the flames had gone. No grass touched her back; no wind cut to her bone. No sound at all broke the stillness of such heavy blankets and a wood-panelled roof. Her eyes found movement, such slight shifting, not but breathing, a black feathered Nestia sat vigil on the bed's end.

She knew him. He'd been on the road. All at once, the pain came again. She hadn't been careful. All the pain through her middle, the penance for it.

She prayed to Lilliana, her own in the storm of divine, let her see the sky. She would take the pain forever if she could only see Helena, if she could know she wasn't already too late.

25

Kitty

40th of Helenai, 447, Third Age

No tables matched in that Gentea Tavern, but neither did the floorboards nor the drapes pulled tight over windows that did little but turn the downpour to fine mist. That smell of salt, of fat and stewed meats in a patchwork place, so like those daylight refuges back in the Northeast Capitol. And so fortunate she was that even so far from the King's road, so far north of the civilised, the crossing town, that bastion on the northernmost crossing, wore both poverty and wealth in the same fashion as every other.

How fortunate she was that Wyvern was a citizen, that the coming festival scared travellers from the road, that the blue-eyed stranger had carried coin. Fortune, luck, poor things to be beholden to, even in Helenai. Especially at that luckiest month's end, any blessings granted by the fourth month would surely vanish in the fifth.

The soldier's map, carried so diligently from the journey's beginning, lay before her, near ruined parchment pressed flat by the damp against the table's chipped face. Kitty had thought herself careful with Sir Emmit's gift, with a possession she could never afford to replace, but still, blood she couldn't name spread from the Fens to the True Capitol, those notes that may have once given it a sentimentalist's value drowned within those dark eddies.

Had it not been for her battle with the Dark Mother over that tiny woman, perhaps Kitty might have thought to celebrate the arrival of their first destination, but then perhaps any such thing would have only delayed the position she found herself in. A goal achieved, true, but the next still as stubborn in its hiding. So little in their corner of the map, had that most recent fight been in any other direction, she would have been certain they travelled too far north.

She hadn't a plan but to reach the town. She thought the origin point might hold some clue, some way forward. But Lord Greyson, who commissioned the contract, was gone, travelled to the True Capital months in advance of a lady's Calling, and every door was bolted tight against Lord Mirri's abominations.

A battle for the words to say, and yet in spite of it all, peace in Wyvern's pale hands that, adorned by a ring of pewter and a ring of nine ruby stones, reached through the window.

"They have to be north." Kitty's dark hand brushed the stained parchment.

"In the Wild Lands?" Wyvern asked.

Red leaves and matching sap candies danced through her mind, that regular first autumn stop, cresting north before south for the winter, and those lords that played the hosts. What had they thought when the caravans never returned?

Her mind snapped back to its place, "If there's anywhere to hide, it's those trees; they must have gotten Routes from someone."

Wyvern's mouth opened and closed without a word, but still, Kitty knew the question she didn't ask, the absence of their own Routes. Hope that the Wild's tricks had kept the adversary to the edge could carry very little. Perhaps she was stalling, a hope that that stranger she'd held together for three days' ride could know better, could say they wouldn't have to face a place none could tame.

But Wyvern said nothing of the woods. Shadows shifted as she leaned through the open window, as the summer storms sent rivers down her matted hair, as Kitty wished she would come inside. When her words came, they came as that hidden thing Kitty hadn't dared call forth. "You might do better without me."

Wyvern couldn't have known how her words burned; the honest denial that roared in Kitty's chest, those words she never got to speak as taloned footsteps rang down that old staircase as Robin scrambled to her side. His breath came in gaps of haste. "She's awake."

The attic, that room to let, gave no impression of a temporary place, beneath years of soot clung to the roof, and humidity that stood ebony hair tall, was a simple place. Not but a bed packed with blankets worthy of a northern winter, and a candle's flames against rain-misted darkness, they called the place home far clearer than they had any right to in a place to be passed through.

The woman had seemed so small, bleeding on the road, a breath from the Dark Mother's grasp, so nearly mistaken for a child alone. But there, beneath blankets more in number than quality, something stood behind her smallness, an aspect of iron, some familiar nameless thing. Had Kitty not known herself truly blind to such things, she might have called it an aura.

"You saved me?" The girl, no, Robin had called her Lane, her voice so nearly startled Kitty. Those first proper words, un-slurred, un-muddied by delirium, a question only by its tone and an accent Kitty had never, even long ago in a previous life of travel, met before.

"I did – we did." Kitty nodded as she sat on the age-worn blankets. "I was wondering, did you know the people chasing you?"

Lane shook her head. "I would'ne 'ave. Was following the girl." Sounds missing, and words clipped, but no accident, a precision to the modification, the signature of a mother tongue.

"The girl?" Kitty asked under rolling thunder.

"They took 'er; I should'ne 'ave rushed."

Kitty's tail tapped the raindrops' tempo to the bedside. "You were searching for the children too?" Her haste nearly tore through abused parchment as she lay the map at Lane's side. "Do you know where they're hidden?"

Lane's eyes widened but a touch. "You chase them? Why?"

Kitty's hand found the contract on her waist, but some thief's instinct bayed her to leave it, to keep her cards hidden. "Don't you have a bounty to hunt them?" Yet she knew the answer, for how could she have one? She had been alone.

Lane shook her head; her hand shuffled together. "I was'ne 'ired."

The beat of Kitty's tail slowed, no longer a rabbit's heartbeat. It took hints in the lull of tides; perhaps it too, could have been mistaken for calm. "How did you know then, about Gentea's missing children?"

"Not Gentea, Northguard, taken east through The Pass."

"Why brave the Wildlands then? Why not take The Pass?"

A question easier for the mind than the conclusion of those words, an enemy that could venture so far east and west wouldn't meet her foolish hope, wouldn't have kept their hideout to the Wild's southern border. But why, then, should they take from Gentea and Northguard both? Towns of different provinces, a crossroads and a border, a trade town and an outpost. She had thought Gentea the target for its stature below the Spy Lord Tenor's notice, but what wisdom had they to risk the ire of two lords?

Those blue eyes settled on drips coming from that patchwork ceiling, ignorant and unbothered by those thoughts in Kitty's mind. "Pass was closed, Dragon sighting; I'll catch them through the other side."

Still, the acolyte's heart pressed for the question's other half. "But the Wildlands? You haven't got Routes, have you?"

"You fear the Never Song?" Those eyes cut through Kitty, pinned her as if a butterfly's wing "I 'aven'ne lost anyone; I shouldn'ne 'ear any voices I'd follow."

Carts came to a stop beneath bone-white trees; the evening count came one short. Elves held each other close in their mourning song; not one could follow.

"Why are you following them?" Kitty faltered, she'd assumed them traffickers, monsters of the living trade, but they'd had a witch, a blood mage too. "The... whatever they are."

For but a moment, those blue eyes met Kitty's, an ocean she could have so easily gotten lost in, but no, ocean was the wrong word entirely for such a shade. She had the word, the only word for such a colour, but beyond her reach, forgotten in a decades-old dream. Ice on a pond, the contact broke as those blue eyes blinked. "A cult of the Nine. I know what they wish."

"You know?" The parchment tore as Kitty jumped from the bed. "Why did they take the children?"

"You know a Reckoning?"

What excitement carried her to her feet died as Kitty shook her head. "Is it—" A glance to those pointed ears, "elven?"

"Not elven. They would bring the Old Gods, those to destroy us," Lane tipped her head, those eyes as if they bore molten into Kitty's chain. "Your Breaker."

Years of lessons, mere stories to scare obedience from the less devout. Those words, the only constant between Pa and every Speaker. Helena's bloody war against her sister's machinations. The annual fight, just days away, to keep back his champion. "Can they? Is that what the children are for?"

Blood beads pooled on Lane's hand, and those blue eyes looked far away. "They believe."
"What does that mean?"
"They believe."
Perhaps Lane may have said more, perhaps not, but Kitty heard no more from the Dwarf girl, her ears turned back at a wet crash, some commotion from outside, and a voice she wished had long since taken his rest.

26

Belladonna

30th of Helenai, 447, Third Age

Regular as those wretched temple bells, the heat broke for the wind, those gales that would carry in the week of storms, that final warning herald to the calm of the Dark Sky. Hooded cloaks and cream summer wools did little but catch in the wind, and chestnut curls flew wild like the prairie grasses to the east. That ancient staff was reduced to a walking stick against the worst gusts as Belladonna crossed empty gardens in step with Elysa. They had not spoken of the previous day – likely they never would.

"It won't work," Belladonna called over the wind as they came to those great gates.

Elysa's laugh caught on the wind, a simple note carried far away, the world's own song to Bann'ni.

"It will," she said and strode to the guard braced against the wall. He had lines to say, a script to read from, but he hadn't the chance to use it for Elysa spoke first. "As I said might happen, my lady's shawl blew over the wall. We're going to fetch it."

Belladonna expected a rebuttal, perhaps questions, or an offer to find the imagined garment himself. Had she Ellivar's own sight, she couldn't have predicted the guard would step aside without a word.

There was one proper road from the high cliffs to the city. It had once been a cobbled thing, but little remained of those patterns, once so carefully placed, for the missing stones and the grass and dirt that overtook the edges.

"He'll know we've been gone too long," Belladonna said to the wind as her feet caught loose stones.

"Of course," Elysa said. "The excuse is for if anyone sees us return."

"You think he'll lie for us?"

"I think he doesn't want anyone to know he's pursuing the captain's daughter."

Some scandal then, some Human drama she had little need for, an excuse perhaps that she hadn't thought to know if the captain had any family. "How do you know that?"

"Because a delivery boy broke a vase and was more than willing to tell me about his boss skimming off his orders, who in turn told me about a certain guard's meetings in his storehouse."

"Is this what you spend time on instead of helping?" Belladonna asked. If, in that tone, the humour could have been untangled from irritation, not even Belladonna herself could have done so.

"It got us out, darling." Elysa's hand snapped to the handkerchief still tied over her ears as it fluttered on the gale. "This is helping."

"I could have snuck out; you've seen me do it."

"Why waste magic?" Elysa asked. "You might need it today."

"This isn't going to be a fight," Belladonna warned, half a hope behind her tone. "I only need to *talk* to Xax."

"With his sister and without your tailor?"

In those first days, Belladonna hadn't noticed how her new ally did that, how she demeaned by denying names. It set Belladonna's teeth on edge, and how she longed to call it a Human trait, if only it weren't so familiar, if only she suspected the title wouldn't be accurate.

"If Edmund's there, you and Vix would be too focused on taunting him. I didn't ask Xax to bring Vix." Belladonna paused but a moment as the path levelled, her staff once more hidden beneath the cloak. "I didn't ask you to come either."

"You don't suspect her anymore?" Elysa asked.

An argument she had thought she'd evaded when Elysa hadn't questioned her story the night before, how she'd expected, with Fin'neshi's own confidence, the topic wouldn't return. "She knew I did, and she had no reason to do it."

"I've found paranoia to be a sign of a guilty conscience."

Belladonna's feet froze before that first house. "She was ready to die, Elysa. She knew she was innocent and still wouldn't fight me."

"I'm sure it was a very good performance," Elysa called back. Hurried steps to catch her ally before the market's crowds. "You want it to be her."

"I want it to be *somebody*." That mask of pleasantness slipped over Elysa's face, seamless and yet so wrong against her words. "You'd rather it be nobody so you can go back to how things were."

So wrong how her tone implied anything wrong in that wish, as if the way things had been hadn't been the only great right in Belladonna's world. But the accusation couldn't quite sting for its only half-truth. Hers was not a wish for no traitor, perchance in part a desire for it to be a stranger beyond her circle, but in truth, Belladonna's was a simple wish for it to be over; she took some comfort for, in that, she and Elysa wished the same thing. "I want a bit more than nothing to believe before I kill one of my friends."

There was a long silence as they made their way through the grey market, through crowds that spared not a glance to the pair until they reached the tavern. Its once-green roof was stained a different grey from its neighbours; its glass windows not yet replaced after the hailstorm weeks earlier. Had Belladonna believed the first persona, she might have thought Elysa's smile pleasant as her newest ally held the door.

"Whichever's done this isn't your friend," Elysa said. "Do try to remember that."

What anonymity the streets and crowds had granted was stripped away as Belladonna stepped into that place, there came a moment's worry as each eye turned on her, but worry faded away as the moment passed and none lingered.

"Vella!" Vix's summer wine voice called a moment before her arms encircled Belladonna's waist. "Another visit so soon? Your gods must be smiling on me."

"They wouldn't be." Belladonna made a careful dance to pull only half away from the intoxicating touch. "I only need your brother."

Vix faked a pout as she pulled Belladonna from the door. The place smelled of fish and forgotten ale, but no more eyes turned as they came to the table Xaxirion waited at.

"I couldn't possibly leave my brother alone with you and your"—Vix's eyes hardened as they met Elysa's—"servant."

"Suppose I thought the same of you," Elysa said as she pulled Vix's hand from Belladonna's. "But I'm sure *you* find this a respectable place, so perhaps I won't repeat such thoughts out loud."

Pressure built behind Belladonna's eyes, not a word to her tasks and already a distraction, another thing to mediate, another thing in the way.

But it wasn't her own voice that called the argument's end. "I think," Xaxiron said as he stood, "that the two of you might need a moment. Come, Bellavella, let's give them some space."

So lost in the dread of another distraction, Belladonna hadn't quite noticed her feet moving until Xax led her to the port. To a rocky shore beneath the docks, so covered from the wind, only waves broke the silence.

"I think they might be a bit busy until we get back," he said.

Belladonna couldn't help but laugh as realisation came with relief. "I think they might both be dead by then."

"Don't look so down about it," Xax said, "it would be two fewer problems."

A moment of relief was crushed by the bitter weight that followed. "But not the important one."

The humour in Xaxirion's eyes died with those words; his fingers ran through black curls that caught none of the damp. "You think this is taking too long—finding the traitor."

Belladonna let her cloak drop as sea spray soaked it, a small relief against growing irritation. "And I'm sure you don't think it's any time at all."

"It isn't"—Xax paused for a moment he wouldn't have any need to note—"but your lifespan won't be either."

"I'm sure that's not callous," Belladonna cut in.

Xaxirion sighed as his feet sent pebbles to the sea. "You've asked me to act my age; what do you think that means? When I'm older than your people?"

"And that's not patronizing," Belladonna spat. "Are we all just specks to you then?"

At once, Xaxirion became very still. "No." He shook his head. "No, but you are moments."

Belladonna scoffed. "And I'm sure you think that's any better."

"It's the greatest thing in the world," Xax said. "You have stories from the Fae; do you have any idea what immortality is?"

"Yes, Xax, I know that you'll outlive me, and none of this will matter."

"It's nothing, Vella." His tone came so different from the irreverent man she knew as he gripped tight that arrowhead strung around his neck. "It's lifetimes of nothing. It's waiting for a second of purpose that might never come again. I can't act my age; I don't know the number. I've been alive since before your people, but I've lived fewer years than you. I'm sorry that you're a moment; I'm sorry you think it's nothing; I wish I could be as lucky."

Heavy breaths clashed with the tide in the silence that followed, so close to that which came after a battle. And in the absence of wisdom, Belladonna chose the easier path. "This is a lecture, then?"

Xax shook his head, and the severity drained from his eyes. "No, I'm sorry. I was trying to say that you think this is taking too long, so I want to help you."

Belladonna kicked at the soaked cloak. What a bother how impulse had ruined it. "I don't think that's a good idea."

"Because you still suspect me?" Xaxirion asked. "Tell me, Bellavella, what could you do if it were me? You're a mage, you can counter my greatest power, and I couldn't ever speak Fae, so I've no chance to do the same, but I still have my claws. And I know you don't want to kill me."

"You never wanted to be part of this," Belladonna said, "and you don't love my people."

What a strange phrase, how her own words sought to reduce the venom she knew his heart held. Would she put it in those same words for herself? Would justice be served to say she didn't love humans?

"True on both counts," he said. "I won't deny that I once thought this endeavour was a waste. And we both know I can't forget what your ancestors did. But Nit wanted this. She believed in you before I believed in her, and I can't take back those wasted years where we were at odds. But this was her cause, too."

The sun was gone. Nit was gone. Felled by fear. The world darkened for her loss, a bright spot of hope gone forever. The news reached High Crest just days before the remaining siblings did. There was anger between the pair. Belladonna could feel it under the cold when she saw them part ways.

And so one remained, the dissenter in darkness but transformed in a world made to know not but those same qualities. Those golden eyes sang of stars. No substitute for sun, not by half, but light all that same.

"We'll need a new ship," was all Xaxirion said on that day. All he would say on the matter of either sister until Vix returned near three years later, just three months, just four runs before that cursed night.

"I don't want it to be you." It was all Belladonna could think to say.

"I don't think you want it to be any of us. I think you'd rather there be some enemy you never knew the name of."

She could have rebutted him, some fool's errand to keep her heart hidden, but for all Fin'neshi's hold, she'd been told what a terrible liar she was. "I'd understand why a stranger hated me."

Xaxirion's hand found her shoulder, but no warmth came from the touch, none of the conflict of any other's. "You might need to look beyond hate for your reason."

Belladonna almost laughed as she turned to those golden eyes. "Why do I feel like I'm being taught?"

"Because you've always resisted lessons you disagree with."

"What do I take from this?" Belladonna asked. "What if it is you?"

He shrugged. "Call it gloating. If you learn the lesson, a few lives lost won't matter."

Mockery, or so she hoped, but a close enough thing for that day. "Then I do need your help," she said. "I need Nadia found."

"Are you quite sure that's a good idea?" Elysa's voice was joined by the never-far-watched feeling as she strode through the hidden cove.

Xax raised an eyebrow. "Did you two make nice already?"

"Oh, don't worry, darling, enough common enemies for a battlefield alliance or an inch of common ground," Elysa said, "but I don't think dear Vella's thought this through."

Belladonna's initial irritation fell away for another kind under the scrutiny. "I have. He can search in and out of the castle."

"Haven't I shown you today how easily I can slip in and out?"

"Can we—" Belladonna started.

"Besides all that," Elysa cut in, "how would he know where to find a hiding human? Smart traitors don't stick around. Even the Lady Hunter might have survived if she hadn't."

"I'm not here to debate this," Belladonna spat. Something in that story she'd heard only part of almost gave her pause, but how foolish would she look to ask after it when she claimed no interest?

"No need," Xaxirion said. "If she thinks she can find Nadia, then let her. I won't die of old age in the meantime."

How she wanted to defend her first choice, to hold that point of control, but how easily she had been offered peace. Her eyes met those endless amber depths. What, after all, could be so lost in ten days? "I'll give you one week."

27

Belladonna

36th of Helenai, 447, Third Age

A break in the wind had sent the castle, familiar and strange to the gardens, a warble in that pattern which should have never changed. None on that day knew to see it as anything beyond a final respite before the storms.

Stockinged feet made nary a sound as Belladonna crept through those empty halls, alone at last. But the silence wasn't total, not the absolute emptiness a wandering mind craved. Hushed voices drifted like the old songs, and their music drew Belladonna ever closer, her feet behaving like dancers compelled by a rhythm until the familiar tones made themselves clear. Until she found them, her sister and the false maid huddled together.

"Elysa?" Belladonna called.

The scarred girl turned amber eyes from her machinations, and that watched feeling came like an iron wall.

"Yes, My lady?" Had Belladonna not known her so well, she might well have thought the courtesy in earnest.

"I'll walk the gardens. Fetch my shawl?"

There came no sound as Elysa left, no footsteps from two Belladonna knew born to grace, nor from one she only suspected. Only as that watched feeling faded did Belladonna trust they were alone.

"Why did you do that?" Alyria asked. "You hate walking the gardens."

There were questions Belladonna didn't ask for the trouble of answers, for the consequences of knowing a suspicions true. In that same vein there were answers she couldn't possibly give her little sister; if only to preserve the comfort of the ordinary, where Alyria's greatest worries were those rebellions she knew of.

Instead, her eyes drew to those glittering pins that held up Alyria's hair. Even with all Alyria was and did, it had been so long since Belladonna'd been reminded her sister wasn't an elf. "You should wear your hair down," she said.

Alyria crossed her arms; the corners of her mouth dragged downwards. "It's too hot."

"We aren't at war," Belladonna said. "It's disrespectful."

"All the ladies wear their hair up. Don't change the subject."

Belladonna shook her head and pulled Alyria further down the forgotten hall, always how a sister could see. "You should stay away from her; it's not safe."

Alyria pulled her arm away and stood firm in her tracks. "She's your maid."

"It's complicated, Lyri." It was a second desperate attempt to end the question.

"You think everything's complicated, and it never is."

"I don't—" Denials died in her throat as the sunset's glow washed over her sister, but, no, not in the eastern wings, not so early in the afternoon. "You've been practising?"

Tears sprung from those grey eyes. "Is there anything about me that isn't wrong? I didn't do anything."

Her sister's tears gave Belladonna a moment's pause before fear won. "Don't lie to me, Alyria. I can see your aura."

Tears dried in favour of a pout. "It was only on mice," Alyria said. "Nobody saw."

"You know that's not the only problem. What if the Blood Bound see your aura?"

"They can't talk, and grandfather can't make them."

Belladonna's knuckles turned white around her staff. How many times had they repeated the same argument? "Nobody else believes that."

"You hate the Speakers. Why do you believe them over me?"

"I don't need to like them. I want you safe." A breath to ground her spinning mind, to escape the circular argument. "Grandmother can help you hide it; she's already taught our cousins."

Alyria scoffed as she strode down the hall. "Jacob doesn't have an aura to hide."

Only a mite taller, but with all her height in her legs, it was nothing for Belladonna to keep pace. If only a calm response could have been so simple. "Don't be a child, Alyria—our real cousins."

"Our *real* family hates me," Alyria said.

Conversations and vicious words from not so far back fled Belladonna's memories. "They don't. They don't know you," Belladonna said with a gentle squeeze of her sister's hand.

Alyria snatched her hand back. "We've hardly seen you for weeks; you can't tell me I don't try."

"I have more important work," Belladonna snapped. "I can't spend all day coddling nobles."

"You're the heir! It's what you're meant to do." Footsteps echoed after Alyria's yell. "I've arranged a luncheon tomorrow, just for family and Lady Anika," she whispered. "I asked your maid to serve so you'd have more friends."

"Alyria, I appreciate that I do, but—"

"You have to come," Alyria interrupted, "I told Grandfather that you agreed. He was getting worried. I didn't want him to send guards to follow you."

All those times, she had thought she needed to protect her sister. It was a strange thought to think the younger had taken the same burden in return.

"Fine, I'll go," Belladonna said. It would mean a few hours wasted, but still, it was worth the smile across Alyria's face. "I'll go if you agree to see Grandmother."

28

Robin

40th of Helenai, 447, Third Age

The storm gave no signs of mercy as Robin crouched, his arm pressed to Wyvern's, beneath the slight shelter of a garden tree. What little sanctuary it gave from the downpour, it provided none from the cold that lanced through missing fingers. Pa hadn't properly taught him the name of the horrid god responsible for such things or even fully decided to blame the same each year. Under that tree, as soaked clothes dripped rivers into the soil, laying blame mattered so very little.

"We could find some better shelter," Robin suggested.

Wyvern only shook her head, her eyes never straying from that patchwork tavern. Robin followed her gaze, though he knew, as she must have, how little those windows with drapes nailed in place would reveal. Kitty would know what to do with the girl; she'd find a way to help her, but it was neither Kitty nor Lane his mind worried for that day.

"She'll be alright," he said after a long moment.

For a long time, the pattering rain was the only companion to Wyvern's silence. "I should go," she said, "before she comes back."

Robin's feathers ruffled against the water. "Don't." Lightning arched as Wyvern's eyes left the tavern. "You can't leave without telling her why."

"She doesn't want me here."

Mud gave no resistance, no hold, as Robin's talons grasped for grounding. "You know that's not true." He held that guileless gaze, easier to read than if, in the lifetime before Kitty, he'd been a Genteel instead of a Shadow. "You just want it to be."

"I can't stay. She...I...it wouldn't be right."

"I don't care!" Perhaps he, too, was shocked at his tone. "She'll blame herself. Is putting that on her right?"

A slurry of rain and leaves fell as Wyvern shook her head. "She couldn't. I'm to blame."

"Then tell her why. If you told her why you want to leave, you won't have to," Robin said. It was a pointless plea. What a thing it would have been to see both of them overcome their natures.

Leaves shifted as the young tree took Wyvern's weight. "I can't be what she deserves. I can't lie to her. Staying would... I'd be false."

The temptation returned, strong as the storm, to share what he knew of the feelings Wyvern was blind to. But her words showed another truth; she didn't wish for the comfort of reciprocation. She didn't dread Kitty's scorn. She longed for it. A tangle of a different sort and how the nature he so long ago overcame wished to pull at it.

So, Robin said nothing of that truth but, in its stead, gave another.

"I don't know your code. I don't know if this is your tenets or something else. But she's all I have, and I'll be dead before I let you break her over it." Whatever look crossed Wyvern's face disappeared in the lighting's flash. "You don't need to stay forever, but you will wait until she comes back."

An inclined head and a cascade of waterlogged hair over scale-dotted shoulders were the only responses Robin received as thunder rolled through the town.

The storm raged on, thunder distant as those far off and long ago battles of the Eighth and no less noble than the King's brother who had been tricked into leading them.

There was a comfortable quiet beneath, an almost rightness only shaken by the chill, but that pattern was all too soon broken, not by smooth-rolling thunder, but by hooves and wagon wheels over cobblestones. Black eyes opened once more as the source drew close.

Four identical horses, the lot of them white, pure as the rain was cold, free of marks from a traveller's life, drew forth a carriage of all colours. Naught but the driver were visible, but such a strange thing for nobility to travel north, to ride a carriage painted in a manner so reminiscent of a caravan wagon. A curiosity. The mystery was put to rest the very moment the occupants emerged into the storm.

Through a flash of light, their sigil came to sight, that mockery of the nine bleeding branches.

And under the thunder, a composition so like and unlike his own friends. Some would call all of lord Mirri's creations "kin," but Robin felt no kinship to that so recently famous group. Those who brought down the yellow dragon over the True Capital.

From behind an unfamiliar snake-aspected Salliten, all grey scaled and tattooed, came those he recognized. A Castilla, pale as Kitty, was dark; a Fensmirri, typical as Wyvern, was unique; and, too quickly, the leader of Mirri's Bastards, a Nestia with all the bearings of a blue jay.

Robin hadn't the time to duck away before the lightning's flash had his eyes meet those they matched.

Only by Wyvern's movement to his side did Robin realize he had stepped away from the tree. For a long moment, the storm was gone; for such fleeting ones, he was eight years old again. Over the roll of thunder, he didn't hear his father's words.

29

BELLADONNA

37TH OF HELENAI, 447, THIRD AGE

Should the castle have been abandoned, those gardens would still have known life. Perhaps then, there could have been no truer testament to Alyria's abilities than the horde's absence in the rose garden pavilion. Expected winds had yet to return, yet those storm clouds on every horizon carried the same promise. A ring no different, no darker from the path Elysa and Edmund tracked around that table, the looks they passed so much more real than distant lightning.

So, Belladonna watched the clouds and those birds that fled inland. If not for Alyria's hand on her own, her mind might have taken flight by their side.

"I must thank you for your help, Lady Anika," Lord Raylor said.

Belladonna turned her gaze back to her family's lunch, absent her father. "What's this about?" she asked.

Anika flushed red where scars allowed. "Oh, nothing."

"I would hardly claim that," Lord Raylor corrected. "She's been of great assistance with Jacob's homecoming. He's been in a dark mood of late; perhaps you could look in on him."

Belladonna shook her head. "Alyria would be better suited."

Alyria's eyes widened as she turned to their grandfather. "Might I?"

Lord Raylor gave a politician's nod, even as his eyes narrowed. "Of course, my dear, it can only help." His gaze fixed again on Anika. "Should I have another bachelor's room prepared for the ball?"

Whatever colour remained drained from Anika's face as her eyes dropped. "No, my lord, it won't be necessary."

Had Belladonna half the powers paranoia ascribed, her glare would have turned the Fin'neshi-touched man to ash, but as he nodded, it rang true; she hadn't even the power to make him notice.

"Of course," he said, "we expect quite a few guests from the southwest, some from the Makers Pass as well. I doubt you would have seen them in Ember Cove."

Belladonna so nearly could have smiled as her friend's eyes lifted if not for how her attention was captured by movement on the pavilion's edge. She turned in her chair to watch her father's approach, that wretched southerner by his side.

"Thei'nas re'thei kse ehia'a laietel ehia?" The elven words spilled forth, a message to her sister alone. A question, no, an accusation. How could she welcome that woman?

Grey eyes flashed, "Ehia'a'ne." A denial in turn.

The reply Belladonna yearned for never came to words as Eugenia clapped. "Oh, that must be Elvish, such a quaint little language."

Never had Belladonna wished for a blood mage's power, but how she wished to make that woman bite off her tongue. "It's not quaint."

Eugenia's smile was all teeth. "Well, I've certainly never met anyone who could make out a single word."

"I'm sure," Belladonna carried on in spite of Alyria's nudges beneath the table, "it's quite a bit more difficult than yours. I wouldn't expect humans to have the fortitude to learn."

She might have clawed back those words, regretted them for the look in Anika's eyes, if only Eugenia had remained silent.

"It must be hard to try to make sense of something so uncivilized," Eugenia said, "but it does sound pretty. My elves are always so sweet with their happy little working songs."

"They're not—" Belladonna was cut off by the hand on her shoulder, a presence she hadn't heard coming.

"Do you want to be right?" Elysa whispered. "Or do you want your songs allowed?"

Somewhere in her mind, Belladonna noticed how her sister flinched at the sudden arrival, but so much of it was taken by the war in Elysa's words.

"That is, they're Onari songs. They sang while working too." The lie tasted like poison, a mockery to the gods, worship and wayfinding reduced to a curiosity used to justify cruelty. The words burned, but Eugenia's look of triumph tasted far worse.

Under that long silence lay fantasies of candle flame leaping to life, of flame consuming the woman who should have been Belladonna's only concern. How she wished a fool noble could have been her greatest threat.

Wishes were interrupted when her father cleared his throat. "I apologize for our late arrival, Alyria. I hope we haven't spoiled anything."

But they had, as certain as two moons crossed the skies they had, yet the sweet daughter, the perfect daughter, Alyria, shook her head. "We were discussing Jacob's homecoming."

"Oh yes," Eugenia said. "Should I expect any familiar faces?"

Lord Raylor nodded. "I'm sure you'll recognize Houses Endair and Olliariah."

"Are there many great houses in the Southeast?" Alyria asked. The innocence of her eyes was so wrong, paired with her words. But how those eyes could distract.

"Not unless you like Dwarves," Belladonna cut in before the Southerner could say a word. For what a shame that bait would have been to ignore, and when her sister had set it so beautifully.

Eugenia's eyebrows pinched. "We are still recovering from the Eighth. That is, we shouldn't speak of such things." Her eyes snapped to Belladonna. "You must have known many a rebel."

Belladonna couldn't help the smirk nor the words that left her mouth. For it seemed such a pity for humans to forget the leader so many of her people blamed for failure. "Of course, my grandfather would have met his brother." Four glares had no power to sour the taste of Eugenia's scowl.

"And, of course," Elysa's voice rang through the silence as she tipped a bronze pitcher over Anika's goblet. "You will recognize Lord Tenor."

For a moment, Belladonna searched for Edmund. For what propose had she invited him, but to ensure the other's behaviour? However, proper as he had been, efficient and unseen, Belladonna hadn't noticed his departure.

"He'll be here?" Anika's fork clattered to the stone.

Lord Raylor tipped his head just slightly. "He will be. Invitations were extended to all of the provincial lords," he said as his eyes narrowed. "Where did you hear this?"

"Just a rumour," Elysa said as she picked up the discarded fork. "He was at your Calling, wasn't he?"

Anika's eyes went wide as they flitted around the table. "It was just because I was Called in the Northeast Capitol. He checks in on all the merchant lords."

"I'm sure," Elysa said, once more at Belladonna's shoulder. She thought, for but a moment, the closeness was another mockery, a joke she hadn't agreed to, but then her eyes caught the reflection in that rounded pitcher, impossible to find from any other angle. Edmund's disappearance answered at once as his reflection entered the maze, and almost as if watching her own reflection, Belladonna saw Erh'henni follow.

"That'll be all, Elysa." Concern hid beneath the guise of annoyance. "You can go."

Belladonna could no longer feel those eyes as Elysa disappeared into the gardens.

"But we've only just arrived." Eugenia pouted.

"You were late," Belladonna said as she pushed herself up with her staff. "Now, you'll excuse me. I have a fitting." Somehow, that lie came as easy as breathing

A sea of green, with each day of summer, the maze had grown wilder. Scarcely more than a ten-day week since she had spirited Anika into those depths, but those paths she had taken before were once more blocked by crawling vines. So late in the season, they must have seemed kin to the Wildlands. Fortunate then that Belladonna knew every route. Still, Belladonna thought her mind had played a trick until she found the pair deep in the maze.

"Av'vella," Erh'henni snapped, "I didn't know you were too important for us."

"What's happened?" Belladonna asked against the sting of her friend's words.

"I can handle this," Edmund said, "just go back; this shouldn't interrupt."

"No, Human, this should interrupt whatever nonsense she was doing," Erh'henni said. "I have three people hidden in the orchard and nowhere to bring them."

The world lost focus. "People are still coming?" Belladonna's words came breathless. "From where?"

"They sound southern," Edmund said, his hand becoming a grounding weight on Belladonna's shoulder. "Xaxirion was supposed to tell the out-of-province connections to stop sending people."

Erh'henni scoffed, her beauty twisted by that scowl. "She didn't ask you. And I don't care which of your Fin'neshi-touched friends is at fault. They came here for your help. So, help them."

All at once, the world stopped spinning. "Of course, I'm going to help them," Belladonna snapped.

"Donna, we don't have a plan," Edmund said, "and nobody sails this close to the Dark Sky."

Belladonna shook free of his hand, his words nothing against the plots forming in her own mind. "Get a message to Xax. Tell him to meet us at the first hideout tonight."

"You still think that's good enough?" Erh'henni asked. "You'll rescue three? Then you'll stop this ring? Are they to be the last three?"

"What do you want from me, Erh'henni?" Belladonna asked.

"We have people waiting for a sign. Have your dragon strike the first blow, and we'll follow."

Edmund turned on Belladonna's first friend. "Absolutely not."

"Do you think you have a say, Human?"

It was so tempting, Vix's standing offer, to run off with her only allies to ever get along. A thought she crushed. For the love of Edmund, she cast it aside. And for every way Erh'henni was right, she cast aside the wrong.

"I'm not debating this now," she said. "Keep them hidden until nightfall."

Mana ran hot as she left that place to the midday sun. By nightfall, she'd be home again at last.

30

Belladonna

37th of Helenai, 447, Third Age

As night fell, that column of empty sky closed for a cage of cloud, a cover in kind, and so came the storm. No Maker, but a marker, Bann'ni's hand, returned to a cracked pattern, the same storm as every year, and as it had every year, it wasted no time in a slow start.

Overgrown branches gave little cover as Belladonna scoured the orchard – a familiar place made strange by the blinding rain. As chestnut curls pulled taut, she heard it, her sign, a baby's whine captured by the howling symphony. It drew her, a winding trail through brambles to the wall. There she found them, three of them, two with matching auras of a mage's green; a jumping fish burned to her cheek, a crowned raven to his. And the third, so readily missed in the rain and rags, a newborn in the man's arms. She would be his daughter, but even just a glance told that she wasn't a mage and didn't yet have a name. Running gave so little room for ceremonies, and the gods hated to bend their rules.

"Ai'ihen and Lir'riyn?" Belladonna asked.

They started at her voice, but, as the woman turned, her eyes held naught but sorrow. "Ayir'riyn now."

The change of names, the work of the goddess Mai'iahai. Ayir'riyn had been the name of the eldest, and it became the name of the eldest remaining. Ayir'riyn, who had once had another name, would have felt the change, felt it in her blood, her bones, felt her womb quicken as her body took the position of eldest. She would have known the moment her elder sister died.

Belladonna's words rang in time with the man, Ai'ihen's, "Thei'nas annan mott'tir se't re'nnan." A poor night for fresh grief. So, she held out a hand. "It's time."

Those steep slopes, untouched by the single path, turned to rapids under the storm, each step a measure, a risk to be carried away by the current. They made slow progress, a meandering path through the waterfall by only the light of the city far below. A dark night, but not yet the Dark Sky, those lights unsnuffed by rain, defiant to the last allowed moment.

A mistake. A careless step directed by a wandering mind. Belladonna didn't have time to scream as the current caught her feet.

There was no sky, no ground, as water filled her mouth, as her chest screamed. As her staff was ripped away, and summer rain turned to a blizzard.

Darkness.

Then a gasp, clear air, hard-packed earth shifted and formed a wall at her back. As her feet found ground and her breath returned, the spire of earth wore again to mud. Her eyes found Ai'ihen's his precious bundle clutched in only one hand as the other held tight to a raven sigil amulet.

It hadn't struck her before; she had seen his cheek, seen both of their cheeks, their first-generation dim auras. It should have, but it hadn't; he was the first mage guard she'd seen to escape. So much sense came to Erh'henni's haste, two more mages to be gone from Lyria, to be beyond the next rebellion. How many could truly remain?

Belladonna had hoped, any more a fool wish would have been a song, but how she had hoped to reclaim her staff at the end of the slope. How cold the night grew as the ancient thing showed no trace. Every moment without it felt as if a slight against the goddess Maj'jri herself. How she wished to search, to scour the hillside for it. But the clang of metal boots on cobblestone told her how little time they had.

They crept through that grey market, deadened by night, pitch darkness in place of drowned torchlight. Thunder and rain gave cover to their footsteps. On that night, belladonna called them allies for how little cover they gave to the racket of armour. Under cover of a fishmonger's stall, they waited for the sound to pass.

It was a familiar dance under the storm's music, its steps in sprints, in dashes between stalls, in pauses when the metal steps came. No matter in counting steps for a pattern Belladonna knew so well. A butcher's stall from satins, a wine seller's from smells, and the dance began again until that grey place lay behind them, until all that stood before the docks and that cliffside cave was that white temple. Great braziers burned oil fires, that flickering light scattered over every drop of rain. An effigy of reverie. And a courtyard without cover.

But she knew the pattern so well. The dance well-practiced. So, she led her people in a final sprint, a final risk before they could slip beneath the docks, beneath the notice of those who never looked down.

Then came the metal steps. No, the timing was wrong; the pattern shattered, and guards stepped from the shelter of their holy place. They should have had more time.

Nails dug crescents into Belladonna's palms as mana pushed from within with no escape. Useless without that artifact left behind. Still, she stepped before the runaways as guards surrounded them.

She knew the captain for how he charged alone, his scowl, the sound of his steps, the weight of his arms as pommel met her ribs. That first hit sent Belladonna's knees to the cobblestone, her chest screamed for stolen air.

More metal steps rang as the captain raised his sword. Instincts warred as the arc began; before it stuck her shoulder, the older won. Pain erupted beside blood as her wrist stopped that blade. Not with power to sever bone, in no imagination a killing blow. Cruelty. How fortunate she was. The new enemy's evil was just the same as the old.

How stupid they were to let mages seize the initiative.

Beneath blinding pain, Belladonna heard the quiet, the storm's absence. With wheezing breaths, her eyes opened; that downpour sat paused and a dome of rain gathered over the square as Ai'ihen clutched his amulet. Those guards that followed their captain shook as they backed away from the monster they had created.

Raindrops that hovered turned as one to ice; the dome, in kind, became a wall cut by the temple. Screams echoed as ice flew. Belladonna hugged the ground as the indiscriminate storm raged. Chiming, louder than the temple's own bell, filled the air as the guards followed.

Then all at once, it ended, ice fell, rain followed, and, as Belladonna came to her feet, so did that cruel captain. His armour dented but, unlike his fellows, he had been spared from it crushing his chest.

The baby's wail had Belladonna's eyes stray from her enemy, and so came the answer to the spell's end. A first-generation mage, and his aura on that night had grown so faint, a flickering desperate thing, a deadly grip on that drop of mana no mage dared spend.

An old instinct had Belladonna duck just a moment before the wicked blade arced over her head, but again the flood stole her footing, and bruised ribs screamed as they hit the stone.

When sense returned, she saw only her adversary's back and heard only the baby's cries as his sword raised over the runaways. So often, her feet wandered; if asked, she couldn't have said if her mind had acted when her foot slammed into the captain's knee.

The enraged scream for but a moment, drowned out both baby and storm, Belladonna didn't see the man as he spun; her eyes fixed on her fellow's as he snapped the chain of his amulet and sent it across the square to her hands. In her hands it was sacrilege, wrongness, a cold beyond the absence of her own conduit, a coldness beyond betrayal. Her moment's pause broke as the armoured boot connected with her face.

Hot blood poured from her nose, and her vision blurred. For long moments, she couldn't remember how she came to be on the ground. Memory came blinding behind the pain. So much light, so wrong against the storm.

Wrongness, a wrong thing in her hand, wrong light in every raindrop. Oil fire, a witch's doom.

Sense returned. Those braziers called with the might of Seven Hundred, and the good soldier, Belladonna's mana yanked.

Flash fire, her perfect spell for guards' torches. She knew of instant devastation; she knew of limbs twisted on heat-sundered bone. She knew her enemies dead before their lungs burst and blood boiled.

Under the pouring rain, that cruel man didn't die quickly. His flesh and hair fashioned fuel for a blaze that made steam of the rain that sought to save him. The storm was no longer any ally of Belladonna's and yet no friend to a suffering man either. In Belladonna's ears, even the rain sat silent as fat boiled and the enemy fell still at last.

Then came a ringing that screamed for her ears alone until she led her allies into the cliffside cave filled with Nit's old etchings. Only once the runaways had settled did Belladonna let the frost-cold amulet fall from her hand. Maj'jri would surely understand. Surely, she wouldn't wish her own chosen, her own mages die or worse for a rule. The feeling of frostbite that persisted even without any mark where her hand had touched Ai'ihen's amulet didn't sing the song of a merciful goddess.

In the absence of the chase, of the battle, came the waiting, the dwelling on the broken pattern, but what thoughts she might have found never came as Ayir'riyn moved to her side.

"He's good with her," the runaway said with a nod to her Ai'ihen and the newborn across the cave. "My sister, would have liked that." She wouldn't use her sister's name, not anymore. Names were for the living, and if there was a living sibling to take it, it no longer belonged to the dead.

"Will you take her on?" Belladonna asked. That old question, the Fae had known its answer, the tradition they had passed on with an answer her people had rejected.

"I don't know," Ayir'riyn said. "I don't much like children; the name is wasted on me."

Belladonna remembered her grandmother's lessons, the eldest's blessing and responsibility, the assurance that she would never forget how her own mother had been one short. The lies her sister told to hide a barren womb. The sacrifices Alyria made to guarantee Belladonna didn't repeat their father's mistakes. "Will he be a good father?" A foolish thing to say.

"He didn't have a choice," Ayir'riyn spat. "You can't know what it's like being bound. I heard my family telling my sister that I was gone, that I was an empty shell. But I was there; I watched myself do their bidding, and I couldn't say anything. We stopped playing along when they brought the men for repairs. So they brought the Mage Guard to make more of us. The men couldn't scream — that was the only difference."

Ayir'riyn's breath was the only sound against the pressing din, and Belladonna had no words to break it for things none ever spoke of.

Only the throbbing pain of her ribs kept Belladonna company until her companion spoke again. "We knew him before the boys were separated. They brought the hogs when we were ten. They made a mistake bringing him two years in a row. My sister loved her daughter."

"How did you get free?"

"It was a small city; they only had one dark Speaker. The binding broke when she killed him." Ayir'riyn looked to the entrance. "And we left her."

"This is what she wanted."

Ayir'riyn turned back; tears ran tracks down her cheeks. "You don't know that."

"I do," Belladonna said, "I'd face the Seven Hundred for Liv'vella." Not only them, she'd gladly stand against the countless thousand elven gods, the humans' and dwarves' too, if only they weren't imaginary.

"She didn't want her baby to grow up as I did. She didn't want her to be a soldier either. Will you tell Erh'henni that? She didn't understand when I said it."

"She wanted you to fight?"

"I don't blame her; she isn't a mage. But I've been bound for two rebellions, and I heard everything the humans said. There are one thousand men in the mage guard; we had no more than three hundred in the Eighth; two hundred and eleven were killed and their conduits destroyed. We're dying, and magic will die if we stay here. I've not had control over myself since I was ten. Now I do, and my sister is dead for it. I'm not wasting it on another losing battle."

Only the familiar figure at the entrance saved Belladonna from reconciling those numbers. All came to their feet as the transformed dragon stepped, entirely dry, from the storm.

"Right," Xaxirion said, "we have to hurry. Dawn's coming, and I want to reach Narreth before nightfall."

Another crack in the pattern. "What about the Obsidian Isles?" Belladonna asked.

"I didn't expect a run until after the dark sky; my territory's a bit close to the Breaker's Reef for this time of year."

A superstition, a sailor's tale — as folly as finding luck in fourth days and the mid-summer month. Belladonna had thought him a pirate in name only.

"So, I'll take them to Thymiran's Forsaken Lands," Xaxirion continued, "and they'll work for her until I can get them home in the fall."

"What?" Ayir'riyn demanded.

"It's the best compromise I could get from her, but the Gold Dragon is reasonable. She won't put you in any danger."

"Xax," Belladonna said, "you know what they're coming from."

Xaxirion ran a hand through his hair, those golden eyes showing all of their age. "I do. And I'm sorry. If it was any other time, or if you'd given me more to make a better deal, I would have, but what Ellivar asked would have taken you from here, and I can't bring them home until Kendinus ends."

"Our ancestors killed dragons before," Ai'ihen said. "She will have my services for these twenty-three days and not a moment longer."

Belladonna so wished to protest, but Ayir'riyn, too, nodded.

"But before we leave," Ai'ihen said, "we ought to have an elder for the naming. But Mai'iahai has already been with us tonight."

As his words carried, Ayir'riyn began the song, the call for Mai'iahai, Giver of Names, and so joined Belladonna. Their part was a quiet thing, near a joyous thing, a chorus for a thousand voices carried by two, but their words weren't those meant to be heard.

"She will share her prefix with our saviour," Ai'ihen said as the ballad turned to a chant. "And for her suffix, I invoke Ryv'vyhan of the Seven Hundred. Let her sing as he does for a war's end. Let Mai'iahai know the name Av'vyhan!"

And the chant carried it, "Av'vyhan! Av'vyhan! Av'vyhan!"

The chant carried through Belladonna's mind as she returned to the castle, a line to hold as the last vestiges of battle fled, as the pain from wrist and ribs grew to a fever pitch. A substitute for comfort until she reached her chambers, and, leaning for support on her door, that watched feeling scattered all else.

"You ought to take better care of your things," Elysa called as she held Belladonna's staff.

"Don't touch that!" Belladonna hissed. Only her ribs held her back from snatching it.

Elysa smiled as she lay it on the sofa, over the grey gown Belladonna had ruined in that cave weeks ago; all became tangled as the staff caught on an embroidery hoop fixed to one of those patches too far gone for cleaning alone. "Would you have preferred I left it in the rain? Where the guards could have found it tomorrow?"

"You followed me." Belladonna winced as she lowered herself to a chair.

"Not quite far enough, it would seem. You left in such a hurry."

So many games, all the things always behind Elysa's words, and Belladonna hadn't even the energy to resent them. "I was working."

"Do you always lead?" There was an edge to Elysa's voice, the edge of a blade allowed to flash for just a moment. "Is it always you who brings them to the end?"

Belladonna closed her eyes against the embers in her ribs. "Is that so wrong?" she hissed.

"Not wrong, no." Elysa's voice came from behind. "Just stupid, is all. Be safer to have your pirates gather the runaways from the safehouses."

Belladonna shook her head. "No—" She winced, the fire's heat, no longer a comfort from the rain, sent its heat to that growing inferno in her chest. "They wouldn't know which ones are used. It would waste too much time."

"Your missing human, Nadia, would know. Could she not pass a note at the docks? Or one of those brothels your half-dragon likes so much?"

"It's too much risk."

"Oh?" Elysa asked as she came into view once more. "Is it so much more of a risk than exposing yourself? Or is it that you couldn't play the hero anymore?"

Instincts screamed for her to stand, but seven hundred voices couldn't move her back from that soft velvet. "Why would you say that?" The protest came as another instinct. "It worked tonight."

"Yes, I saw you got people out." Elysa crouched at Belladonna's knees. "When you told me it was impossible."

"Elysa, I—I didn't think—"

"I'm running out of time; if you can't help me, send me to someone who will, someone who can fight."

Laughing was a mistake as fire lanced through her chest. "You want to join the rebellion?"

"No," Elysa said, "I don't think your people would have me. But there must be others; don't you know anyone who isn't all the way elven?"

"I'll get you out. Just trust me." She didn't have a name for it, neither memory nor instinct, a pressure no more than a spark, a reminder of something unseen, but Belladonna knew in that moment she had missed something in Elysa's words. And in her own, passed a point of no return.

Elysa's voice came as a whispered artifice. "It isn't in my nature."

Truth in the lie.

Rain against the glass stood a blessed bastion against true silence. "Have you found any trace of Nadia?" Belladonna asked.

Elysa only shook her head.

Belladonna couldn't help the cry as she stood once more. With stumbling steps, she reached the wall, a crutch to guide her to bed. "Then wait for Xaxirion to return. I'll have him fly you to Narreth."

Under the waves of pain that followed her to the floor, Belladonna hadn't the mind to wonder anymore after her newest ally.

31
Robin
40th of Helenai, 447, Third Age

*L*anterns cast their tiny globes against the dark by the time Robin's work finished. If he looked ever so carefully, he could almost see the stars past the city light. Little memories of gods that lived in Lyria long before humans. He sang the names Pa taught him on his little journey from the forge to that house Ma's family built. That tree Ma planted when she could still see the sky towered over roofs, a beacon just the same as the old songs.

He could hear the crying from that little house, even under the never-quiet of the port, even under the scratched steps of his own running. She couldn't have gotten worse so soon; she had been fine. Pa would be a House Guard soon, and she would be fine. She only needed to hold on.

Had Pa been the sky, Ma would have been the clouds, but they were both wrong as Robin ran through the door. Her milky eyes reddened, perfect white feathers stained with tears.

No tears stained black feathers; if any fled his eyes, the mercy of a storm stole them away. That same rain ran in streams down mirrored armour and blue feathers as his father stepped into the storm. "Vaan'ni, how you've grown."

"Don't," Robin said as his talons curled into the earth. "I've never been that to you; I was her Little Night, not yours." If the hateful gods could have kept his voice even, they stayed their hands.

"Now, is that any way to greet your father?"

"You're not—" Robin cut himself off. Fury gave no peace; none of the Seven Hundred could. The past and its team masters of regret, its great lords of things to never be changed, no closure could be found in those halls. Robin's eyes met Cypress's. "I have nothing left to say to you."

Escape, that gambit of thieves, of spies, missing fingers burned with old habits, how readily he made for the tavern, for the curtain of strangers' scrutiny. How quickly it could have ended had his path not been blocked by that grey-scaled Salliten. Inked patterns announced the Poison Field as her first home, that amber glow from within promised a witch's gifts. A Castilla archer and a Fensmirri, to replace the last, who had replaced the first, came to his back. A team of four, a team to only be four. Four of five creations, or maybe they'd kill another dragon. How much fame would his father need to wrest a fox-eared Alta from Mirri's clutches?

He hadn't the chance to step around the stranger before his ears caught that familiar sound of a scabbard hitting the ground. Talons slid across cobblestones as he spun to Wyvern.

"Wyvern, don't," he begged. "They aren't worth it."

Cypress trilled laughter. "And you have a Talish." That name, the Fensmirri's first name, as if he still had the right to it. "Her breeding could be better. Don't you worry, son; my first was nothing special either."

As if he didn't mock the one who taught him the name.

Robin turned on his father. "Reed didn't deserve that."

"You have no idea what she deserved."

Robin's beak clicked without his say-so. "I know what you told her to do; it wasn't an accident you never found us again."

"You'd believe a traitor over your own blood." Cypress feathers flared against the storm's weight. "That's Opal's weakness."

"Don't say her name," Robin whispered. "Not when you killed her."

Cypress scoffed. "She was sick."

"She needed you! And you left!"

All night he'd left Ma alone. He'd promised to be home soon; shame burned as the first light hit Robin's feathers. He'd promised, but spies lied. They played their games; only the stolen scrolls in his arms tempered that shame. He had lied to Ma, but so too had he played for her.

They would have a healer. She only needed to hold on.

"Hello, Night," came that voice of shadows. "Did you find them?"

Cypress's beak opened, but what poison he deigned to say was drowned under a new voice. "Robin!" The song of Kitty's call rang across the street as she ran.
"You," Cypress hissed.
Kitty's back straightened as she reached Robin's side. "What do you want?" The quiver in her voice could have been from cold if not for her eyes. Robin cursed himself; beyond all else, she would still fight his battles first.
"To think I was almost proud of you, but you're still a follower. I thought you'd grown since Nico."
"That's nothing like this," Kitty spat, with her eyes narrowed.
"Can't he speak without his master's say so?" Cypress asked.
"Suppose I was right to come after you."
"What?" Robin's words caught in his throat.
Blue feathers preened against the rain. "I heard a rumour that a certain raven aspect Nestia had taken a contract. You didn't truly think I could let you kill yourself for something so simple, did you? But no need to worry about it anymore; it's in better hands now."
"You can't," Wyvern shouted over a thunderclap.
All at once, Robin saw how close both groups had gotten. Lighting flashed as witches reached for wands, as hands found hilts. Only a moment before too late, Robin caught Kitty's eye with a tiny shake of the head.
A pressure lifted as Kitty dropped her hand. "We should go; it's pouring," she said.
Robin never considered hesitating as Kitty walked back to the tavern, taloned feet stepping through ripples left by calloused ones.
"Robin!" Cypress yelled to his back, "We aren't finished!"
Somehow, in spite of it all, Robin believed his father's words, but still, they waged war with what he knew; Cypress hadn't held such a title for a long time.
He only looked back as he passed the threshold, past Wyvern's vigil at the door. He caught eyes that matched his own one last time before the wind slammed the door shut.

32

Belladonna

4th of Kendinus, 447, Third Age

Only oblivion behind closed eyes gave respite to the days passed in bed; the waking world held no escape from the flame that lanced through her ribs. When next Belladonna remembered to open her eyes, stars danced beyond her window, remnants of the storms scattered to the wind. The final month of summer had arrived.

There was a knock at her door, or rather another knock, an encore to that which woke her. And such a fool, Belladonna tried to stand. Her knees hit the ground before her feet felt the cold. Winer-heavy night things draped past her fingers as she gasped on the frozen floor.

Slowly, as ravens to a roost, her breath returned, and the flames retreated. Another knock. How many had she missed from the ground? As with breath, footing came slow, the wall her crutch until her feet found the path to her door.

The golden eyes on the other side allowed her to see the truth beyond the shaven face and guard's armour. She could have expected her ally's return; she couldn't, however, have thought to anticipate Alyria by his side.

"Xa—" her voice caught, broken from disuse. "What's happened?"

Dark curls slid, constrained by the false helmet; Xaxirion tipped his head towards Alyria. "I found her in the city; I'm sure you know where her room is."

"I do, thank you," Belladonna said and pulled her sister past the threshold.

Silence hung between the sisters until the door swung shut. "Who was that?" Alyria asked.

Belladonna couldn't help but sink to her chair as the right lie eluded her. "He's probably a guard."

"But I know the guards," Alyria said as she pushed aside the staff still lying across the sofa. "And he looked different when he found me."

"He's a friend, Lyri; he only wants to help." She tried to stand, to reach for her sister, but the only control she had in that fall was to bite back the scream as her bloodied wrist caught the table.

"Donna!" Alyria's voice came from Belladonna's side. "What happened to you?"

Sweat beaded as Belladonna forced herself upright. "I'm fine."

"I told Grandfather you'd been sick. I thought you were hiding from father." Alyria's warmth guided Belladonna back to the chair she hadn't managed a single step from. "I could have helped you."

"No," Belladonna whispered, "it isn't worth the risk."

"You take risks with your runaways, and we're supposed to report Changelings."

Green eyes met grey. "He helped you."

Alyria's eyes broke away with a glance to the door. "Your maid says we can't trust them."

"Did she?"

"Because they come from dragons," Alyria said. "She knew a lot about that."

"What else did she say?" Belladonna winced as she straightened.

For a long while, a shrug was the only answer between the sisters. "Why do you have her if you don't like her? She's nice."

Denial caught in Belladonna's throat, too complex to call truth or lie. "Why wouldn't I like her?"

"You hate humans." Alyria finally turned from the door. "And you got mad when all she did was talk to me!"

"It isn't her place."

"You don't believe in that kind of thing," Alyria scoffed. "She won't anymore. She just ignores me. It's not fair. I haven't done anything wrong, and they still hate me."

No flame in her chest could stop Belladonna from grasping her sister's hand, but how it tried. "No one could hate you, Lyri!"

"Grandmother does," Alyria cried as she tore away. "I saw her like you wanted."

A slow ascent, her good arm still clutched to the chair. "What happened?"

Alyria only shook her head. "She can't help me; she wouldn't anyway. She hates that I'm not what she wanted; they all do."

"They don't—" Belladonna started.

"They do!" Alyria cried. "They call me a traitor, and they won't use the right name. They wish I'd died with Mother!"

There was a knife in those words, and so readily, the pain of her body ceased to matter for its edge. "You can't think they want that." Belladonna scrambled to her sister's side.

Alyria scoffed. "Erh'henni said it."

"You can't think she meant it."

"But she did!" Alyria collapsed against Belladonna's chest. "They always do."

Belladonna gasped against the pressure, perhaps it could have been an excuse for her words had she not believed them. "They're family."

Relief from the weight off Belladonna's chest was shattered under Alyria's tears. "Half of this castle is family," she said. "Why do the terrible things only matter when they're said to you?"

"That's not—" Belladonna faltered. What wasn't it? "You have power over them, not just magic. It scares them."

"They're mad they can't threaten me with it anymore." Alyria shook her head. "They know Grandfather will believe me over them. They think yours is the only way to read auras."

"Alyria," Belladonna warned.

A warning that fell to nothing. "Erh'henni would be nicer if she knew I could see them too."

"Don't talk like that." Belladonna caught her sister's eyes once more. "You should be on the same side."

"But I can't be!" Alyria pulled from Belladonna's arms. "I can't be like you! Grandmother will never love me. If the humans hate me too, I'll have nothing."

"You'll never have nothing. I won't let that happen." Belladonna's legs gave out as Alyria returned her embrace. What a sight they must have been there, together on the ground.

Long after tears had stained Belladonna's night dress did Alyria speak again. "She's right, isn't she? Erh'henni? It's my fault Mother died."

No, never that, never her sister's fault; curses had rules and lords as well. Never her sister's fault that neither allowed her mother to escape them forever. Never her sister's fault that Mirri-crested letters would forever be cast to flame.

"No, Lyri," Belladonna said, "it wasn't your fault."

"But it was somebody's," Alyria said. Not a hint of a question.

"But not yours." Belladonna pulled away just enough to catch her sister's eyes. "They're far from here."

Alyria sniffed. "But you won't say who?"

Never.

"You won't ever meet them; they're nobody," Belladonna said.

"You're lying."

Belladonna shifted again away from her sister to link their hands once more. "It's better you don't know," Belladonna said, "I don't want you to be angry like me."

"What if I marry them?" Alyria asked. "You'd stop it?"

"That won't happen. You'll marry Jacob." Those words, how they gave light to Alyria's eyes, how angry it made Belladonna to know the ease an idiot prince would have in shattering it.

"Do you think so?"

"I know Grandfather wants it." Truth to overcome the lie of Jacob's intentions. "And our great uncle will love you the moment he meets you."

No more tears fell as Alyria once more pressed her head to Belladonna's shoulder. A moment to stitch to eternity, a moment to be brought low by a morning bird's call.

"You need to get back." Belladonna winced as she pulled her sister up. "Before someone notices."

Alyria nodded. "Will you take me through the passages?"

"I–" Belladonna faltered.

"I know you know them. I've seen you disappear." In Belladonna's silence, Alyria continued, "I wanted to try them tonight, but–"

"You wound up outside the walls?" Belladonna asked. Memories, how had her early days of exploring gone so differently? Her grandmother's guidance.

"I found the dungeons first." Alyria shook her head. "They don't make any sense."

"They were built for wartime; I don't know that they're meant to." A funny thing, passages built perfectly for wartime in a castle that hardly saw battle. Confusing twists under the facade built for vanity. But Belladonna had been directed by her grandmother's perfect knowledge, and deep in her desk, she had maps; seven entrances to the dungeons, all unseen. Which had her sister found, she wondered? "You mustn't tell anyone."

Alyria leaned close, a glint of mischief in her eyes. "I don't want to get *Edmund* in trouble for what you two do."

A trade, a hardly fair trade, security from her father's mistakes, an ancient spell from a different kind of war turned to the surety that Belladonna wouldn't face the natural consequences of a lover. That surety and freedom all for the cost of her sister's mockery, but on that night, it rang hollow. "This isn't a joke."

"I know, I promise," Alyria said. "Please take me. And let me help you when we get there."

That was it then, the true intention of the request, but Belladonna saw her sister's eyes, the summer storms captured in miniature. The war had been lost.

"Alright, then," Belladonna acquiesced and pulled her staff from its place. Completeness, after days apart, an ancient thing turned to a walking stick; she would be glad of the freedom.

33
BELLADONNA
5TH OF KENDINUS, 447, THIRD AGE

Evening sun marked the close of another fruitless day. Belladonna thought freedom from pain might mark a new start. Still, the day after was such a mirror to those before, as if she hadn't missed those last days of the mid-summer month, she might well have forgotten how near the Dark Sky and all its Human frivolity loomed.

As on all other days, those little sounds that drifted from her chamber gave Belladonna just a moment's pause before their pattern became a familiar one.

Her shoulders dropped as she pushed through the door, as she saw Edmund. "Have the others arrived?" she asked.

Edmund spun on his heel. "Donna! No, yet." He lifted a folded parchment. "I was just going to leave this for you, but you're here now." In moments, the parchment was reduced to ribbons.

Alone at last, a moment for just the two of them; how she wished to fall into his arms, to reenact that last night before he left for Jacob's Seeking. But there were words, words not her own that, in a moment of peace, she couldn't discard.

"Have you ever heard of the Hunter family?" she asked.

Edmund's eyes narrowed as he cast his shredded letter to the fire. "Where's this coming from?"

"Elysa mentioned them a few times; she seems to think everyone from the Northeast would have heard the story," she continued in spite of Edmund's scoff. "So, have you then?"

"A bit," he said, "my pa told me the Lady Hunter had been Lady Tenor's, that is, Lord Tenor's daughter's, spy before she eloped with Lady Tenor's betrothed. It's the same as every story about going against the Tenors."

A broken engagement, that great taboo of nobility. Only just greater than pursuing a girl before her Calling and only just lesser than such a girl falling pregnant. A human girl that was.

"Is that all?" Belladonna asked. It couldn't have been. A scandal for that Lord Tenor, true, far beyond reason enough to be stripped of their lands, but there was something else in the later story. "Elysa seems to think they were killed for it."

Once more, Edmund scoffed. "I don't know why you listen to her at all." He paused. "I think they were found to be witches after the Eighth."

Burned.

It echoed in her mind. A mage might be bound, but the Speakers' pyre was the only fate a witch could hope for. A mage's friend turned a witch's enemy, so natural in that order, bastardized by those who knew nothing of the oldest enemy.

"Is something wrong?" Edmund took her hand. "You've never cared about nobility before."

Belladonna shook her head. "Never mind that," she said. "Have you found the safehouse Xax missed?"

"No." Edmund shook his head. "But there were so many. It might be impossible to check all of them."

A moment, a hint of white on her knuckles. "Were?"

Belladonna let her head rest on her lover's shoulder as he pulled her close. "I was thinking," he said, "it might be better this way. We both knew it couldn't last forever."

"What's this now?" Xaxirion's voice echoed from the bed chamber, "Giving up so soon?"

Belladonna straightened, tears unshed burned hot, but it was her lover who spoke first. "It's been half a season."

Ebony horns caught the light as Xaxirion tipped his head. "Do you think that's supposed to be a long time?

Under the docks, wonderous incredible specks, how different it sounded, argued on her own side.

"Never mind that." Belladonna pushed between her allies. "Edmund, would you bring Vix up?"

"Oh, I wouldn't worry about that," Xax said in the moments before the door swung open.

"This is the most trouble I've ever gone to to get in a bedroom," Vix laughed as she slumped against a chair and kicked to the ground the gown Edmund still laboured to repair. .

"What are you doing!" Edmund hissed as he rushed to the door. "You could have been seen!"

"Relax; I didn't come in the door, and besides, no one saw."

"Vix," Belladonna warned.

"It wasn't hard, Vella. There are windows in your tower still missing glass from weeks ago."

Replacing window glass: it could have been called an elven job if one wanted an excuse to summon males from the work camps. Lord Raylor hadn't. A Human from the city had been called instead, one more face haunting the castle floor by floor those past weeks.

Belladonna tipped her head. "None on the ground floor."

Vix shrugged. "People can climb, and Lady Anika wasn't in her room."

All those weeks, and all through the summer storms, Anika hadn't said a word. A note to remember, a weapon to call against her grandfather's claims of hospitality. Only tempered by accusations against her own. She hadn't been told, but when had she given Anika the chance to tell? How many times could she truly claim she'd spoken with her friend since her return?

Belladonna shook her head. "Why?"

"Got tired of waiting for someone to bring me." Vix tapped her head. "I told Xax I was coming up."

Something nagged in her mind. "Edmund, you told Elysa to bring Vix?"

Edmund shook his head. "I couldn't find her."

Her eyes caught Xax's. "Have you seen her?"

"Why would *I* have?"

Belladonna shook her head once more. "She was supposed to find you when you returned."

Vix and Xax laughed in concert. "Donna?" Xax said, "I'm sure if your gods themselves told her to seek me out, she wouldn't be swayed."

"I thought she might compromise, given she stands to gain the most from this."

"So she says," Edmund cut in.

"Never mind that," Belladonna said as she moved to her desk. "I needed her here; I had her search the dungeons ages ago–"

"You think she did a lousy job?" Vix cut in.

Belladonna glared at her allies a moment before she resumed her search. "I forgot that I walk this castle differently from most. Nobody could search that place and avoid the guards without this," she said as her hand found its treasure, those old maps drawn in a child's hand.

"That's a neat thing," Xax hummed. "But if the task was impossible, why did she say it was done?"

Why indeed? But then, why had Xaxirion and Edmund claimed their own complete as well? How she had wished to speak with the false maid before she undermined work done, if only she had heard an explanation, no, if only she had been allowed to keep her passages a secret.

"And you've been keeping it from us," Vix whined as she draped herself over Belladonna's shoulder.

Belladonna savoured the contact for just a golden moment before she shrugged off the pirate's weight. "You didn't seem to have any trouble breaking in without it."

A honeyed laugh warmed her ear. "Impressed?"

The building retort was cut short by a sharp knock. "Lady Belladonna?" a guard's voice rang out.

Belladonna cursed and stuffed the map into Xax's hands. "There are seven passages in the dungeons; if Nadia's not there, she ran."

"I don't know what she looks like," Xax said.

"It's summer; anyone not at the work camps could be helpful."

For thieves, cheats, and elves born men, the Northwest didn't waste. Traitors and murderers may have burned away their little value already, but Naida was no killer, and the Dark Speakers didn't take humans who broke only mortal laws. She wouldn't be dead, not by a Speaker's sword.

"Lady Belladonna?" the voice came again.

"Just a moment," Belladonna called, and she ushered her allies into her bed chamber. "Go tomorrow, during the ball."

A nod was the only response as she slammed the curtains closed.

Retrieving her staff was the only natural movement as she opened the door. "What?" she demanded.

No words were exchanged as she followed them through her home's winding corridors. No instruction was needed as they held a door to the Great Hall.

Absent was that overwhelming press of bodies from the engagement announcement, not a raging sea at all, no strangers, only the familiar crowded into that space, enough space for air to carry the din of all crowds. But they stood unjostled, unmoving, and past that wall of finery, Alyira stood, a clear crimson rose at its head.

"What is this, Lyri?" Belladonna asked as she took her place.

"Donna! Where have you been?" Alyria hissed, though her face stayed cleverly neutral. "We've been greeting guests all day. Grandfather was furious when you didn't come this morning."

"I'm sure he was as furious at my absence as the guests were relieved not to see me," Belladonna said. "Didn't Anika cover for me?"

Alyria nodded as the storm of her aura settled. "She said you were still feeling unwell."

"Did Grandfather believe her?"

Alyria shrugged. "I said it was true."

Such a testimonial, and still she knew herself damned.

Some silent signal passed across the room. The ubiquitous chatter all but ceased as the great cranks groaned their warning. So abused they had been that day, no dust fell when those massive doors opened. Only a herald's running footsteps echoed under their protest.

"Presenting the high and honourable Lord Tenor and his ward, the Lady Hunter."

Unbidden whispers echoed the silent hall as that sharp-faced man, all grey-black hair and garnet silk, strode down that path, his sash adorned with that unblinking eye all traitors knew to fear.

Tagging in his wake with grey-sea silks in the style Anika wore, with fluttering silk sleeves that hung well past her waist, and carrying with her that feeling Belladonna had become so used to, strode a girl with a flame-scarred face and such amber eyes.

34
Kitty
1st of Kendinus, 447, Third Age

Rain washed, unyielding, over that tiny city as the lucky month ended. Every few moments, a cacophony of thunder, matched only by screaming wind, tore through the rattling boards and a flood to drive the likes of even Wyvern to the doorstep. A mirror in miniature to the pouring rain, Kitty's hair dripped its own river across rough tavern stairs.

Eyes followed her to that room, rented still by the gold taken from Lane's pockets while she lay in the Dark Mother's clutches. Guilt for such a theft should have kept Kitty from that place, but the eyes on her back, those whispers calling her Breaker Spawn, only spurred her faster to that room other travellers coveted.

Kitty's entry to that attic room received no notice from its occupant. The humidity had only increased in the face of the ongoing storm, as had the soot stuck to the ceiling. The candles burned low, though they had been replaced thrice already, or so the proprietor had complained. Much as it had become since she'd awoken, Lane's eyes strayed not once from the great book on her lap as Kitty wrung her hair into a half-filled bucket.

"It is much better today?" Kitty asked.

Lane winced as she sat straighter. "You 'av'ne left?"

Kitty shook her head. "Not until the storm passes."

Lane's book tipped down as the girl glanced to the window, the words on its page of the common tongue.

One for your fortune.

One for your health.

One that you'll always be kept in wealth.
One for your future.
One for your quest.
One for the little things and all the rest.

Kitty hadn't the time to decipher the odd rhyme before Lane pulled the book back. "It will end before the Dark Sky?"

Kitty nodded. "Of course." It would be clear for the festival, always clear as the moons crossed. Temple lessons echoed, for neither cloud nor flying bird might dare interfere with the sisters' battle. But lessons learned long ago halted for an instinct much older that ran down her tail. "Is there a timeline?"

"Eighth day."

Helena's Triumph, the eighth of the festival, the first of festivity, and by any measure the thirteenth of Kendiuns, but a day with only one name, and Lane hadn't used it. Walls of sandstone and unblinking eyes did war with the acolyte who longed to ask.

A war with no victor, for Lane's words came first. "You know your Daemon's name?"

"I'm sorry?"

"You're a witch. The one who gave you magic. You know his name?"

Stinging pins, lighting as if the storm broke through, ran down her spine as hairs stood. "I didn't say it was a man."

Those blue eyes turned from her book for but a breath as if Kitty, too, were a page to be inspected. "You're Castilla," she said. "It's all the same, your maker."

"Don't!" Kitty snapped. No, that wasn't right, it wasn't mockery; Lane knew not what she said. "He's not the Maker."

"But 'e's yours, and Sillas Mirri too," Lane said.

A vicious, poisonous rumour, Silas Mirri had wed and bed a Daemon to create his malformed creatures. But that wasn't a rumour of any evidence; a Daemon lived in those words because one lived in all tales. The harvest failed because of Daemons; the spring came late because of Daemon agents. The scapegoat for the witches they created and the mages they didn't. A blanket of blame to comfort each other with, a common enemy surpassed only by Elves for its effectiveness.

Still, the tale of Lord Mirri's hidden partner needed no evidence to be true and how worse the purges could have been if any proved its truth. If any could prove Lord Mirri's denial lies. If they only knew the name every Castilla and kin had etched into their very beings.

The acolyte won her war. "How can you know that?"

Tiny hands at once left the book and, in long silence, danced together, a practiced thing, a ritual, so nearly Wyvern's signs if not for how they scratched each other. "I do'ne know the name; I never 'eard it. You remember it?"

Kitty sat on the bed as she nodded. Perhaps a lie. The name she spoke all those years ago, could she claim to know a thing when she knew none of its sounds? "I won't say it."

"Aye, you would'ne know 'ow to send 'im back," Lane said.

That thing she could never correct in temple lessons, that risk her teachers could claim of all witches; Pa had never been so foolish. "We never called him here; it was in a dream."

Tiny hands grew still. "Never let them in your mind."

Possession, another rumour of all work, a misunderstood thing told in equal truth and lies. But Lane's words stumbled on the pure truth, the vulnerability in dreams the tricks of spirits and minds when granted an invitation. That knowledge she could perhaps excuse; no matter how Human the art had become, the first witches who fought the first mages had been of the Dwarves. She might have let it be had that piece come alone.

Kitty shook her head as thunder rolled. "My pa had a way; he could send him back if he tried to take us."

"No," Lane shook her head.

"No?"

"Only two ways to force 'im back," Lane said. "You did'ne 'ave them."

Thunder rolled over the city, and the flickering light wavered as the flame danced, threatening to leap from its wick and tear off its own shelter. As if flame, witch's friend and doom, knew itself without a side and readily bowed to The Breaker's.

"Most people fear Witches?" Kitty posed the question as Lane had.

"They fear magic."

"But you don't?" Kitty prodded.

Blue eyes shone in lightning's flash. "Not yours."

Scattered ashes tumbled from the candles. What hubris not to fear, but she'd spoken without bravado, without boasting, a tone calling itself proof where words gave none. Perhaps she knew, as

Kitty did, that every scattered ash on the wind held only a mirror to her future.

"What are you reading?" Kitty forced her ears up.

Lane proffered the book on her lap. "Stories I found."

Another glance to that book gave truth to the words, layers of twine and ribbon stitched through the spine, its pages uniform in packets but with not a prayer of uniformity. As Kitty leaned to the page, she was met with only characters she could make no meaning of. "What's this written in?"

"Lochni," Lane said as she pulled the book back.

"I've not heard of that."

Lane nodded. "It means spoken; you would call it Dwarvish."

"Is it—" Kitty leaned back from the reclaimed book. "Is it good?"

"It's Kiah Valire."

Kitty shook her head. "I don't know that..."

"Death mourned. You 'av'ne 'eard it?"

Kitty expected no explanation as she shook her head once more, but Lane turned the page back.

"When the first child of Calar 'ad no gifts to show, she despaired, and when Corin's rage fell upon Lomin, Valire stole 'er bother away. A new world beyond their father, without mother, beyond time. A realm their own, only 'er right as eldest. But first to come from life must be death, and no goddess of death could make life 'er own. The empty bodies, two gods made, sat 'ollow in a world no time could sway until a father's wrath followed sibling gods through veil and sea. There is evenness, a god's soul, sundered in even measures, woven to 'ollow forms, magic made flesh spun life even in those 'ands of death. Valire would not see 'er world torn by 'er father's 'ands; she sealed the world another place locked somewhere else."

A striking feeling to so casually be given something sacred. A trick that slipped it past an acolyte's learned defence, and it must have been one, if only for how familiar the tale carved through Kitty's heart, for how unworthy she knew herself to be. "These are Dwarven gods?" Kitty whispered.

Lane closed the book. "Valire is My Dark Mother."

But in that comparison, awe faded. Tales of life from Death, blasphemy even if by a different name. "You think she created the Other Place, The Fae and Daemons?"

"We believe."

"It's a good story." Kitty stood from the bed. "I should check on Robin."

"But you don't believe? You follow your Maker, so nothing else could be true."

Kitty paused at the door for just a moment. It wasn't kind. Silence had been easy in the face of Wyvern's mistaken beliefs. So much easier to know nothing and say likewise than ignore learned rebuttals. "Only the Maker creates; the others can only use."

Perhaps she could fake the confidence any of Lane's words held, perhaps Kitty could hold fast to Pa's version of "The Divine Truth". For what could Kitty be if, in this, she too was wrong?

35

Kitty

5th of Kendinus, 447, Third Age

Near four days passed before the storm did. Overnight, those black clouds fled, and in the pale light of morning, not but a wisp remembered them. Earth never forgot so easily, even tops of cobble unseen for the mud that buried them, mud that bore calloused footprints as Kitty led both her fellows from that inn.

A thief knew herself watched, through shuttered windows, in empty streets; she needed none of her home's eye-crested banners to know the weight. "Do you feel that?" she asked.

By Robin's nod, she knew it to be no imagined ghost.

"What?" Wyvern asked.

Kitty shook her head. "Something's wrong." She whispered as that urge to run grew heavy upon her legs.

Not a soul crossed them on the journey to the stables, but hidden away, whispers drew her ears with each step. Feet quickened over the slick ground, and still, those whispers followed as a wave. Until, from ahead, there was one voice she recognized. Kitty threw her arms out to halt her companions at that final corner.

Breaths came too fast, questions from her allies went unanswered – unheard over her own heartbeat. All went silent as Hanson's voice called out, "I know you're there."

"I know you're there," the man in black called as tiny feet carried the child through that maze.

Soot streams ran in rain that came too late. Black rivers scattered in a perfect hunter's trail; they would find her. No sense in the city; she couldn't see the sky. Too close. All too close.

"Come out, little monster," that voice laughed.

The little girl cried as the streets opened to a beacon of white marble. Nowhere to hide, no way back to the maze. She pressed against the ivory pillars. Those steps rang as Breaker's bells.

Her ears flicked all around as those steps faded.

"Found you." The man pulled her from the false refuge. Soot left a black stain over the white steps the girl slid across. "Give the Breaker my regards," he said with sword hefted high.

"Stop!" another cried as all the girl's world filled with white and gold.

"Are you going to make me come find you?" Memories snapped away with the voice.

Kitty's legs shook as she pressed against the wooden wall. She squeezed her eyes shut as she had so many times, but no nightmares ended with them open. Her breaths came sharp as she stepped from that wall into the mud-slick street.

There were three men of temple uniform – black of robe and black of beaded chain, midnight sky tangled in stars of witch's ash. Once and no longer healers, the Mother's Speakers turned to a darker call. Gloveless hands of the acolytes, the two, without binding scars to hide, held fast to the reins of two horses gifted names, of one that went without.

And at their head, marred beneath covers as his fellows were not, that man, that creature Kitty saw in each touch, all the same as her nightmares foretold. No bidding of hers could bring forth calm nor tear away the single thought that formed completely. There was a reason Speakers of The Dark Mother knew which scars spawned from blood magic.

Only shadows across mud told Kitty her companions had come to her sides.

"How?" The word came as a breath.

"Rumour had it some witch was stupid enough to kill a hog, but I thought even you were smarter than that, Kitten." Lighting scars stretched as Hanson showed his teeth. "Then I heard your rat broke a quarantine line. I knew I'd find you here."

Kitty shook her head, eyes squeezed closed. "No," she whispered.

"You couldn't expect to get away with it. You called me on plenty of runners."

Her eyes locked to the ground as her shoulders curled in. "We didn't touch anyone; we can't spread it."

"Did your heretic father teach you that? I thought I burned his stink away," Hanson said, "but I see you've gotten another rat; no matter, two heads are just as good as one."

Green eyes snapped to the object of their fear. "Two?"

"Oh, Kitten, I've no need for your head."

"But we—"

"Uh uh, don't interrupt, Kitten. I have no need for any heads. I could trust the word of a Mother's Acolyte, if she was to return to where she belongs."

Black feathers filled Kitty's view. "She won't," Robin snapped.

Hanson's voice lost its laughter. "Don't speak for your betters, Rat," he hissed. "Come now, Kitten, I won't wait forever."

Locked away, her eyes mere tower windows, how she begged for words, but none came past breaths of no air, no rescue in her old refuge as her window's edges turned dark.

For all the sound of her heart, it stopped as a crossbow's bolt tore through an acolyte's neck.

All in one moment, the world stopped, and an unscarred hand dropped Ria's reins as the body attached fell to the earth. Kitty saw not when Wyvern drew her sword, not until a second executioner lay in pieces.

She didn't remember running until she passed the dwarven girl who loosed that first shot. She didn't see as Robin lifted that girl to share his horse.

Her fingers brushed Shale's fine mane just as she was yanked back. Gloved hands dug bruises into her arm. "Don't think you can run again, Kitten."

Blood on her face, blood on ivory floors. False sanctuary, in those eyes, hunger beyond the years.

Kitty felt nothing of the skin that tore from her arm as she was yanked. She felt nothing at all, nothing but the familiar weight as she found her wand.

It had been such a very long time since she had felt her blood pull wrong under her skin. Something visceral, something old, unbreakable once bound, blameless, but for the shame. Still, all the gamblers on the Ember Docks knew more than to bet against a pickpocket's draw.

She saw not the lightning that threw Hanson a second time. Hardly felt the mana she spent. Neither did she see him stand, Maker's Guidance or Breaker's urging; it mattered not, she knew the monster lived by the rolling dread as she urged Shale to run faster.

She saw nothing of the city nor, not the crossing, nor the companions that followed, as memories overtook her.

36

Belladonna

5th of Kendinus, 447, Third Age

The Lady Hunter was waiting when Belladonna retired to her chambers. Under that flickering torchlight, green eyes met amber as the door latched shut. "What are you doing here?" Belladonna asked.

"Oh?" Elysa hummed from her perch; fine fingers brushed over parchment strewn about. Those long floating over-sleeves had been tied, looped around themselves so the knotted ends hung just past her elbows. Glimpses of white and red leaves glittered with woven gold thread, hints of a forest made unknowable by the knots. "I've always been welcome here?"

"I'm not playing anymore," Belladonna snarled. Her mana lanced out, always so easy in the cold night air to find her aptitude, her true ally. In a dance of colours, a storm of a new type, torch fires left their sconces and closed on the spy. "Why should I let you tell your master anything else?"

"Wait!" Elysa gasped as she scrambled off the desk. "Just think about it a moment."

Balls of flame hung suspended; the guards hadn't yet come, and no heavy boots invaded the tower. "You haven't told him?"

"See?" Elysa said through heavy breaths. "You can be clever."

Those little fires disappeared as Belladonna called her mana to heel. "Why?"

How quickly the false ally regained composure and what ease in restoring a shattered mask. "That would be telling. We all have our games."

Belladonna scoffed. "I'm not playing any games."

"Of course you are!" Elysa snapped, "Every day, you play at being a rebel. I can see your staff and your lover. Anyone at all can see how high above us you think you are for disdaining our games."

"I won't play along with people who think me and mine are property."

"And I see that too." Elysa smiled in that way of hunters before a kill. "How much you love to pretend the fix to your people's plight is beyond your reach; how you so dearly ignore the power your name could grant you, what the eye of the prince could grant anyone. But you'd rather fight the world and help your people a dozen at a time."

There was no reply Belladonna had for that. For a novel argument against those that followed her all her life. "Then why?"

Elysa tipped her head. "You think I'm to blame for your troubles. I'm not. I didn't know a whisper of your scheme before I found this." She held a parchment between two fingers. "Your traitor is lucky I caught this before it reached my dear guardian. They wouldn't have liked the result."

Belladonna's eyes locked on the letter as Elysa dropped it into the fire. "You knew who it was this whole time?" How those flames begged to strike as their kin.

"No, not when we first met. Your traitor was smart enough to leave it unsigned. I'd heard about that incident at the docks; I'm sure you remember, I was on my way when the letter crossed my path after. I thought they might go together."

The trap that ran so near to ruin and how that failure's spectre had hunted her since. She'd known, at least some part of her had known, that another attempt would surely follow. So why did she wish to claim the letter as a lie? Because it could have been simple? Because it had been destroyed? No, it was because she so wanted to reject that Elysa knew the traitor's name and that nothing Belladonna could do would pull that from her.

"How you must love your own voice," Belladonna spat.

Elysa laughed and tucked a stray hair behind her handkerchief. "I'm sure you would, too, if you had anything worth saying."

"Why did you care about that night?"

A smile grew across the spy's face. "There's the right question. I've been looking for someone; it's why I'm here. You know her: short girl, blue eyes."

Memories of that night played through her head — a girl of elven blood and no elven name, a runner with no intention to run, a new subject for questions Belladonna could boast no answers for. "I don't know her."

"And I'm sure you think that was convincing; you saw her at least. I know she was here. I've been tracking her since she nearly got the prince killed. I think you can help me find her."

"What happened to Jacob? What did she do?"

"I don't know." Elysa's hands raised in surrender at Belladonna's glare. "I don't know what she does. But there have been..." Elysa's voice trailed off. "Suppose we can call them events — several over the past five years. Some call it blood magic or a dragon rider bent on revenge; some call it The Breaker's hand pulling your old enemies into our world. But we know differently, don't we?"

"You think this Dwarf girl is to blame?" Belladonna asked in place of the agreement her once ally tried to force.

"I know she is, and so do you. I know you remember that night."

Again, Belladonna refused to give that woman the satisfaction. "Why are you telling me this?"

"Because I've lost her trail, and it's time for me to leave." Elysa's smile faded. "And I'm sure your grandmother will know where she is."

Belladonna pushed past her once ally to her bed chamber. "A Seer won't tell you anything."

"I think you'll manage to be convincing." Elysa's call caused Belladonna to pause. "What was it you said? I haven't told Lord Tenor anything. Yet."

It was odd – walking together again.

For the silence of the halls, High Crest Castle could have been abandoned. Still, under the sleeping castle that never-quiet drifted from the kitchens. That ever-familiar ritual of decent was tarnished by the presence of one Belladonna had once trusted too quickly. No children's chatter floated through the doorway, but under the eternal bustle came the soft tune of Bann'ni's song.

An'neira waited at the bottom of the stairs. "You want my help," she said in place of any greeting.

Elysa tipped her head. "Now, isn't that the point of you- Do you consider yourself elven or dragon kin? I'd hate to be inaccurate?"

Belladonna stepped between them. "Grandmother—" she started.

An'neira held a hand up. "I know," she said and turned to her room. "Wait for us, dear; I'll speak with Mirri's child alone."

Alone at the door, so many faces were unfamiliar and how their eyes lingered on Belladonna, an intruder in her own home. Belladonna knew not how long she had stood before she wandered from her vigil at the door. She found herself next to a woman she didn't recognize. "Is Erh'henni awake?" she asked.

The Elf shook her head. "I've not seen her. Not since Liv'vella's visit," she said. "Did you need something?"

That couldn't be.

Belladonna shook her head; a quiet dread she dared not name dug claws in her gut. Alyria hadn't said a word, but why would she? All named enemies in their own terms; none mourned them. "No, I was only—" What way to tell a stranger how wrong she had been? How she'd so scolded herself for mourning a loss before its time.

Thei'nas annan mott'tir se't re'nnan.

Mourning Belladonna hadn't the time to ponder as Elysa strode from An'neira's room and slowed not a step on the way out. Belladonna pursued without a moment's goodbye to the stranger.

"Did she tell you what you wanted to know?" Belladonna asked as the two strode through empty corridors.

"Rather hoped she wouldn't be so eager to," Elysa said as corridors turned to gardens. Silence stretched until they reached the wall.

"What now?" Belladonna asked.

"Now," Elysa said as she pulled a knife from beneath the gown. Belladonna hadn't a moment to see a threat before Elysa turned it on her own skirts; fine silks fell away in sheets until not a scrap reached bellow Elysa's knee, and the soft hide legging beneath hid no longer. "Now, I go east by the Northguard Pass."

"Wait," Belladonna said. "How do I know you won't sell me out?"

Amber eyes caught distant light as Elysa turned from the wall. "Because now you know I'm going east by the Northguard Pass. And you might guess that I shouldn't like to be followed by any interested parties."

"Did you do something to Lord Tenor? Or is it only that you aren't human?"

Those eyes turned on her one last time as Elysa pulled free her handkerchief, and a fox's ears twitched under the moonlight. "So bloody clever."

All at once, that feeling left, and Belladonna was alone in the gardens under a pale moon, its edge caressed by but a fragment of black.

37

Wyvern

5th of Kendinus, 447, Third Age

The sky grew dark long before they slowed. Wyvern might only have guessed how far they would have fled into darkness if not for how her horse faltered, for how Robin's struggled under a second weight. She knew not why the dwarven girl with far too blue eyes had come, another to that list of things she didn't know about her companions.

In that wild blackness, Wyvern knew not the road, nor when they strayed from it, not but the free night on all sides, and still she knew Kitty to be right when she refused a fire. What a beacon it would be in those flatlands north of the crossing, how it would draw those that hunted.

Those that would hunt Kitty and more that followed Robin. It wasn't anger in her heart, only sorrow for those secrets they clung to, and shame for she had thought them good, beyond the common lies of that strange place. In the ink-toned night, no leading light, no path away, and still, how silly of her, how she clung to that little she could see. How she drew to the silver moon that danced in Kitty's eyes.

"Who were they?" Wyvern asked the night, but neither Kitty nor darkness deigned answer. "You lied."

"No, Wyvern." Even as Robin spoke, Wyvern couldn't make his form from the dark. "She didn't."

"You did too," she cried to formless space.

"We didn't lie to you," his voice came again, placeless.

"You kept secrets." However could grass feel so much the same as a ruined marble floor? "You didn't tell the truth."

"It's not the same."

"It is!"

"No." Kitty's voice floated, a battle-chipped ring, a winter's grave, wrong choked thing in that dark. "It's not."

Wyvern knew her Tenets, branded as they were across her mind, written in blood between her fingers. She knew Kitty's words to be wrong by how near identical they were to her own long ago. Admonishments died in her throat. Tenet breakers, wrongness, the absence of good: a single sign, no difference given to things always true together. Only they couldn't be; what a lie it would be to deny goodness in Kitty, no greater a lie to deny all the world. And still, in darkness, only the lies shone under that moon. "Why was it a secret?"

"I hoped I wouldn't meet my father again," Robin said. "You didn't need to know about someone you would never see."

"But I did meet him."

A quiet click sounded. "I didn't know that would happen."

"You never know when you keep secrets." Impossible to know, she had never thought – No, she should have.

"Would it have changed anything?" Robin asked. "Your knowing? If I told you of him two weeks before you met him, would it have made a difference?"

"I could have warned you when I saw the carriage."

"What would that have helped?" Robin asked. "It wouldn't have changed him, wouldn't have changed the things he said."

"I could have taken them by surprise." True words, but not those Wyvern reached for; she could have helped, and he could have let her help.

"You couldn't have fought them." Tiny sounds of grass pulled from its roots drifted through the night in his hesitation. "Cypress, he... he has a power you wouldn't understand."

Wyvern bristled. "You're keeping that a secret now?"

"You're not owed my pain! Even if I told you what he is, you wouldn't believe me."

Fingernails drove their marks into Wyvern's hands; how she wished to see her companions, to see Robin's eyes as he told more lies. "Why not?"

"Because you're not an Elf!" the snap of Robin's voice startled Wyvern to stand. "And you don't believe in their gods."

Her gaze turned again to the silver light in Kitty's eyes. "But what about—"

"Leave her alone," Robin said. "You know mine. Isn't that enough?"

Half a truth, a distraction, no, never enough. "I need to know why they're hunting us."

"It's not your right to know."

Kitty's voice, that musical thing, cracked and raw, cut off Wyvern's retort. "Are you leaving?" The question gave Wyvern pause. "I know you want to, but you're too polite to say the words. He doesn't care about you; you'll be safer if you leave me."

Would it be a lie for Wyvern to claim surprise when her voice broke? "I don't want to."

Light danced a flash as Kitty met her eyes. "Then it is your right," Kitty said. "His name is Hanson; he was made to be my guardian when I was an acolyte." Tiny jingles echoed across the night.

A secret answered by revealing she'd had another. "Why is he hunting you?"

"I didn't know he would." Kitty's voice caught. "I—he—when I... I'm sorry, I can't."

"You said," Wyvern started.

Reflected light vanished. "I know. I know you can't forgive me, but I just can't talk about it."

"It wasn't your fault," Robin said.

If Fensmirri had the vision of their aspect, or if she'd only had that of her peers, mayhap Wyvern wouldn't have missed the way Kitty shook her head or the tears that fell to damp earth. Perhaps then she wouldn't have spoken again. "Telling is important."

Even wind fell prey to the silence between them; creatures of the night dared not call until Kitty spoke, her voice edged as her aspect's claws. "Then why haven't you told us why you left the Fens?"

38

Wyvern

Spring, 437, Third Age

However the lies that came later clouded her memories; there were truths in those early days, truths incorruptible, beacons through the haze. Her homeland was a scar she had been made to fill, Parsifal's truth. She was safe only as their warriors earned her safety, Steward's truth. And she knew herself a woman years before her declaration festival, a truth for the future, for on that night, though she knew it true, she was but a girl.

Fourteen years, near grown, she should have known better; she should have trusted the tenets she knew so well.

None but warriors might leave the Fens; nevertheless, Wyvern crept through that abandoned town named for storms, unclaimed by vocation, destined for the priesthood by her black flames.

Not ever again to be imprisoned, not ever again to step within walls, but, still, she crossed that once temple's threshold and sat on the nest of furs laid over cracked marble floors.

No secrets, no lies; even so, under morning's cold light, she would sign not a word.

Nothing above the collective. Why, then, was she so ready to break four tenets – to also send the fifth crashing by her lies? Worries to plague her journey, but how they vanished when Parsifal came to her side.

So long after they had nothing left to teach, they sat together in that place her people never wanted but for its emptiness; that place the humans fled. Talish and Human together, impossibility proved by Tempest's own state. Peace in being together, in the words they no longer had need to learn, but one Wyvern would break that night, that beautiful night, that night to be made to last, for she knew how it would be the last.

How she later wished it had been.

"Par," she whispered as her head left his shoulder. "We can't meet anymore."

Ice blue eyes grew stricken. "What? Why?" Parsifal asked.

"Tomorrow is my fifteenth festival. I can't sneak away from the priestesses as I do from my Steward."

"But you said you'll be grown after you're chosen." Parsifal shook his head. "Grown means you can do what you want."

Wyvern couldn't help her scowl; it should have meant that. Humans could do as they wished, as could her brethren-creations. How unfair that her elders demanded her wishes be theirs, to claim it as the cost of being highest. "We have rules."

"So do we. I can't do anything until my Seeking—" His voice faltered. "What if we didn't have to leave each other?"

So many things to leave: her pack sister River, her pack brother Aspen, to be claimed by warriors and hunters, to all separate, to forget fifteen years of nesting together, to be as nothing, separate as birth broods. Nothing above the collective. No sign for River's beauty, no sign for how she loved them both, no sign for love. But she had the words. She had Parsifal's beautiful words. And come the morning, she'd have none, none but the collective and a priestess's pewter ring. A mean thing, a cruel thing to hold hope, but still, so young, so foolish, Wyvern reached for it. "What are you thinking?"

"I have a plan, but it can't happen until autumn."

Autumn, a long summer away, but what a beautiful beacon, and such a better thing to wait than to never see him again. A precious thing she could hold for a little longer. It could stay a secret for just a little longer.

39

Belladonna

Dark Sky Festival: First Day

Beyond high castle walls, no light dared shine, save for those auroras that danced over the sea. Even Helena's eternal light stood dampened, silver covered by that first sliver of black, a pebble to coming tides, a delicacy consumed by the great beast of Helena's Dark Sister. None would dare defy the dark until that night of total eclipse, that night of triumph. Soon, not even the castle lights would glow. But as it always was on that first night, even as peasants hid in darkened homes, High Crest Castle stood as a beacon.

Cloth-covered lanterns and powders sprinkled upon torches sent shimmering sparks in hues of neither nature nor magic across the halls. Not an old tradition, not one of their own, an eastern thing, an interloper's design, what other than invasion to turn a court of earth tones to such a rich palette? Invasion, indeed, but familiar in its undertones, beneath sweet Carsi Bells and great brass horns hummed the din of all crowds. Belladonna listened not to the southerners as they mourned the structured gowns of the true capital, nor those strangers she cared not to meet who drifted about her and Anika.

Thread ravens hunted their kin along jewel green velvet sleeves, ridiculous things to tangle her staff and to kiss the ground with Belladonna's every move. Somehow, she couldn't bring herself to hate the annoyance, for down on the skirt just above the floor, one of those ebony ravens had just six stitches out of line. Her eyes danced across the doors in turn. With every shift in light, she searched for her allies, every disappointment a ringing warning of his lateness, but even still, as moons climbed, Belladonna saw no sign.

Only Anika's sudden laughter startled Belladonna from her search. Between the blinks of returning, she saw her friend twirl before the two young men who hovered, further invasion without invitation, arrived without Belladonna's notice, thieves past a sleeping guard.

Tiny ships of red sails made their merry voyage across sea blue skirts; a sea turned choppy as Akina stopped. Her over-sleeves, tiny things that made it not a quarter way to her elbows but bright red and stitched gold with every symbol of ship and sea, fluttered with her every breath. "Oh, Donna," Anika said through giggles, "Isn't Lord Kanis so charming?"

Just barely past a boy and already the lord of his house? An orphan then, or perhaps left with his mother alone, and even perhaps of interest to any others in that hall. "Quite." Belladonna gave not but a nod. "If you would excuse me."

That tide of bodies parted, if by reputation or staff alone she knew not, for on that night as all nights, it mattered not.

"Was Ash'heiren great?" The words more than that voice gave Belladonna a turn as Lord Tenor's sharp face emerged from the crowd. His black velvet sash of office with its shocking green eyes hung like a wound against a coat of darkest crimson. Those eyes burned as if real, as if daring any to try escaping their gaze, as if the lord who wore them stood before her not as the lord of the Northeast but still as the King's Spymaster.

'What did you say?" she asked as those few who remained close scattered.

The danger behind a pleasant tone, the one her traitor wanted for a trap. "I want to know if your mother was great."

"Why would you care?" Hostility, disinterest, wards for a different arena, how bare she felt.

He chucked softly as his thin lips curled. "Because I want to know you. My mother always told me greatness skips a generation. She always had so many ways to say I was disappointing. I imagine she was great – the Elf who survived reading Mirri's scrolls."

Belladonna's fist tightened unbidden around her staff, another useless ward. "How do you know that?"

"With great difficulty, my dear. The same way I learned her name. But I must say when I spoke with your father, he gave me a different one. He could have been lying, but I don't think so. I'm sure you'd know why he and the Mirri boy had different names."

There was something about the question, perhaps simply the curve of his mouth, perhaps how the eye of his crest bore through her; Belladonna wondered then if any answer she could give would be one he hadn't heard before. "An Elf wouldn't tell you."

He nodded, just slightly. "No, I don't imagine they would. I've never met a people more loyal than yours. I'm envious, really, loyalty without expectation; it's a fine thing."

A trap in those words, only in how they were wrong, but an Elf wouldn't speak of those things either. "I think my sister needs me," Belladonna said as she started to turn.

Only the laughter in Lord Tenor's voice made her pause. "You truly don't play," he said. "I was certain Lady Hunter had lied about that."

With a breath, Belladonna turned back to the sharp-faced lord. "I might say she played enough for both of us."

"I'm sure. Were you close?"

"I don't think we were," Belladonna said.

"She seemed rather quite interested in you," he said. "Did she tell you she was leaving?"

Games in every word, and how simply she could have refused his game, told him where her once ally had run to, but Lady Hunter knew too many truths, and it would be far too simple for her to know who gave her up. A raging storm against every instinct, every comfortable learned thing, Belladonna tipped her head as she knew Alyria would. "Didn't she tell you?"

Lord Tenor's lip quirked up. "I'm not so close with the Lady, but I should like to know where she is."

"If we weren't close, she and I, I'm sure she wouldn't have told me, and if we were, I'm sure I wouldn't tell you."

Eyes of thread gleamed in tandem with the lord's own. "You have potential. You could be so great in Maker's Pass."

Belladonna shook her head. "I'm sure your ward told you why I don't play."

"She told me that you think you can avoid the game by not playing."

"I have no interest in games."

"I can see that. You strike me as someone things happen to." He nodded to where Eugenia had gathered a crowd of her own. "Do you think she'll be your only competition?"

"I don't think she's much of a threat." Belladonna forced her hand to relax, never let him hear the truth behind those words.

The lord shook his head. "You're a worse liar than you think, my dear, but she won't be the only one. People talk. I've heard them whispering about the half-elven heir."

"I've been the heir for nearly fifteen years. Why should anyone start to care now?"

"You know why. An elven heir is a novelty until she comes of age. Especially when she has the eye of the prince."

"I have no interest in Jacob."

Brown eyes flicked to the crowd for but a moment. "Because you're loyal to your sister. I understand that."

Fool. She'd thought herself clever, but how readily she'd been taken. "I have no interest in playing your game either."

"It isn't mine, and you are a part of it," Lord Tenor said. "Should you wish it, if only for your sister's benefit, I could teach you to play it properly."

"Why would you do that?"

"Is it so hard to believe I'd want an ally in you? Should you play well, the queen's sister would be a fine ally to have."

Before the thought could become words, Belladonna saw her grandfather's eyes catch her own. "I'm needed."

"Of course," Lord Tenor said. "Do think about my offer."

She thought to turn back as she left, a last glimpse, a final chance to catch what lay behind those of the man who lay claim to all eyes, but, as the crowd shifted around her, the Spy Lord had vanished.

Her grandfather's eyes didn't again meet hers until Belladonna came to his side. "You should be more careful," he said. His own wine-toned sash didn't shine against a charcoal coat, a play at how natural the garment looked on his person, such the inverse to the Spy Lord.

"Should I?" A blanket in winter. She couldn't help the smile that formed as she slipped back to her own ways. "In what sense?"

"You can't trust him."

"If even your lot know *that*," Belladonna said. "I'm sure I might have figured it out."

The lord shook his head. "Don't get too friendly."

"I'm not a complete fool. I didn't invite him."

"What did he want from you?" Lord Raylor turned back to the dancing masses.

"For me to be different from what I am," she said. "It was a better offer than you've ever given."

Lord Raylor scoffed, "You can't be considering it."

"I might; if I think it'll scare your lot." Her eyes cast over the hall and caught, for just a moment, on where Anika stood alone before she found Alyria's ruby gown with its ebony ravens nested on silken branches; a crimson glow under coloured lights.

"You might have stayed with your friend; she had such hopes for the Kanis boys."

Belladonna searched the floor for the two that had hovered around her and Anika so closely, but for all her searching, she couldn't remember their faces. "I didn't make them leave."

"You could have made them stay. Should you have had an interest in the older, the younger surely would have been compelled to entertain Lady Anika."

Belladonna turned to her grandfather. "Is that all you think she deserves? The younger brother of a fortune hunter?"

"She hasn't much to offer a suitor."

"She's better than the lot of us," Belladonna snapped.

"The Kanis boy may have realized that if you had kept them around," he said, "as Jacob may see Alyria."

Belladonna sighed. "Are you sure you don't trust Lord Tenor? You want all the same things."

Lord Raylor gave no reaction. "I don't imagine it will be much trouble finding your cousin."

Belladonna glazed over the crowd for but a moment before she caught Jacob's eyes watching her. "No, I don't imagine it will be."

Belladonna's eyes held Jacob's even as she left her grandfather's side and once more waded into the parting sea. A crown of gold sat on the prince's brow; perhaps one day he would learn to wear it, but on that night, his first ball as a man, it shifted under his every move. Belladonna watched as he twitched for it with every step.

She thought perhaps she might scare off the gnats, a plan she needn't have made for how he ran from them at her approach. His spun gold ravens danced across their night blue field, a graceless thing under the crown's weight. "Belladonna!" he panted.

"Jacob." She nodded.

The boy's hand fidgeted with glimmering sleeves. "I-I think you're supposed to curtsy to me."

How she wished to simply send him away, some useless errand to have him gone. "I'm not going to curtsy to you, Jacob."

He nodded with a hummingbird's beat. "We're family, so of course, you don't have to."

A sigh went unbreathed as Belladonna turned. "Walk with me," she said.

Belladonna didn't wait for her cousin before she strode towards a glimpse of crimson. Just the tiny clinks of a crown that didn't quite fit spoke to his presence at her elbow.

"I was looking for you," he said. "I wanted to ask you to dance, but then you can't dance, and I didn't want to embarrass you."

Belladonna's face grew hot with Jacob's every word. "Alyria dances," she said.

"But I couldn't dance with her."

In an instant, Belladonna had stopped, and Jacob continued for another moment before he turned around. "You've danced with Alyria all your life," she said.

"That was before. And she's just a kid. I need to dance with women now."

"You're not a man, Jacob," Belladonna said as she strode past him. "You're sixteen years old."

Should Jacob have made a response, Belladonna didn't hear it, for as the crowd parted at her arrival, she saw him, without his horns and dressed as a guard, golden eyes met her own.

"I'm needed," she said without looking at her cousin.

"I could—" Jacob started.

"No," Belladonna snapped. "I'll find you. Don't follow me." If he listened, she would not learn for many nights, but that mattered not as Belladonna lowered her staff and pushed a more subtle path to her ally.

40

Belladonna

Dark Sky Festival: First Day

The dark stone, immune from even summer's warmth, should have been empty, but for the guards set to patrol abandoned halls, still far too early for work camps to be closed for winter. Even still, Belladonna could have been a stranger and known that the woman in those bedrock-carved tunnels was no guard. Not by her horns alone, but just as well by the buttons left open on the red velvet dress uniform, and the sleeves pushed up to show the fine tattooed skin beneath.

Vella," Vix sang before she turned on her brother. "See, it didn't take you long to find her."

Xaxirion shook his head as his own horns reemerged. "She doesn't blend in as well as you."

"Don't be jealous; I'm something of a master." Vix laughed as she wrapped an arm around Belladonna. Even as the air showed their breath, Vix's skin felt as if warmed by the sun. "Remind me, Vella; we were to get you if we found *anyone* down here, right?"

Belladonna nodded. "That's right."

Vix smirked and held a hand to her brother. Belladonna couldn't help her head from tipping as Xax dropped a jingling pouch into it.

"What's all this?" she asked.

While Vix only chuckled in response, Xax spared her a glance before he stared down the tunnel. "He doesn't look like a Nadia."

Words rang true as Belladonna led her allies from a door made to look as if stone; the prisoner huddled in that frozen cell looked nothing like Nadia, but neither, unknown to her allies, was he a stranger. His eyes harkened to memories years old, from those early days before her ring was any more than her and Nit's shared dream. "John?" Belladonna whispered as she abandoned Vix's warmth.

Nadia's husband flinched at the voice, but his shoulders dropped as he turned to the party. "My lady, what are you doing here?"

"Your family went missing," Belladonna said as she crouched and lay her staff across the rough stone. As she peered into the cell, his isolation bore ill portent. Those Humans who feared their made-up gods never spurned their Mother's Blessings, never dared separate those they joined under her. "What happened, John?"

Belladonna fought every part of her heart that cried for escape as John grabbed her through the bars. "The guards came for us. They knew who we were, what we did," he gasped. "Beth and Isobel — they ran. You have to find them, my lady."

Belladonna's first thought, a selfish notion the girls may have seen something, was pushed away only by the worry that Edmund hadn't found them. For all their father's hope, a black dread that they too had been caught settled as a stone deep in her stomach.

Dread replaced anew by the voices that drifted down the tunnel. She gripped John's hand tight for but a moment. "I'll find your daughters; I promise you," she said. "Listen, John, we don't have much time. Do you know where they took Nadia?"

She wasn't dead. She couldn't be. Speakers wouldn't raise swords to their own when it had only been a king's law broken.

The clever and cruel made other arrangements.

The dread failed to lift as John met Belladonna's eyes. "They mock me with it, the Grey Fall."

That cursed ship, the nightmare to make the workcamps seem a mercy. That place traitors and heretics waited in turn for She Who Waits Behind All Doors. Who could have given such evidence for such a sentence without the provincial court learning of it? She knew, those same three she had always known, to think until that very moment she had a single spark of hope to blame Lady Hunter still. "We have to go," Belladonna whispered as she tried to pull away, but John held fast.

"You can't leave me here, my lady."

"They'll know we were here," Belladonna said.

"Please, my lady, don't leave me."

Here was another proof positive of Erh'henni's cruel words, another death to the naive hope she'd once held, that her troubles would end with her traitor, that she could one day return to the home she'd built. She glanced again to the corridor from whence came the voices her companions would soon hear. "The door, Xax," she said as she finally pried her hands away from John.

"Are you sure?" Xaxiron asked.

Belladonna gave but a nod and had time only to retrieve her staff before the scream of tearing metal filled that narrow space.

Distant yells filled that place as Belladonna led allies deeper, through corridors that surely would have filled with dust if ever touched by life, to that lowest of passageways. Its entry was not stuck by age, as it should have been, but was blessedly made simple by the misadventures of one who knew not the ways of the passages.

Deep below creation, they fled until carved stone gave way to earthen corridors filled with those ancient songs. Sister moons had long since vanished for cold dawn before Belladonna led her allies out of those tunnels no Human remembered.

She emerged with three, but only alone, with those thread ravens trampled and frayed, did she return to a ballroom of dwindling celebration. She needed time and only prayed, a song in her mind, that her gods would grant her enough for a plan.

41

Kitty

Dark Sky Festival: First Day

There was a spot on the horizon.

"They'll drag you down with claws and teeth! Beware, beware the reef." Lane's discordant rendition of the familiar traveller's song skipped in and out of time with both Robin's clapped rhythm and the horse's steps. It might have been an inappropriate thing to sing of the Breaker's Reef during the days of Dark Sky. Still, unharmonious and heretical as it was, Kitty blessed the break in silence.

The acolyte still longed to scold Lane, not for the song, but for that insistence through action that she come along in spite of her wound. Some other part of her born of the Northeast knew they needed every hand to find the Cult Lane claimed as the monsters behind the missing children. And another part still wondered what help any of them would be in the Wildlands without Routes.

Kitty'd taken the rear position that day, an ill place for an ill leader, last to glory, first to die in ambush, vanguard against pursuers, eyes to watch ahead, ears turned to watch behind. In self-imposed exile, she had but a moment's warning as Wyvern's horse faltered, nearly fell. Once more, its flagging steps carried the pair to Kitty's side. "Sorry," Wyvern said as she tried to spur her horse forward amidst its protests.

"Wyvern, wait," Kitty said. "I'm sorry, I shouldn't have asked about Parsifal." What could be more sensitive than one's first love?

Wyvern shook her head. "I couldn't even tell you everything. I shouldn't have said those things to you."

"I deserved it. But you see now how hard it can be?"

Some days ago Kitty would have hoped the way Wyvern shifted was only for the odd angle riding set her tail at. There was no more cover for such pretences after that last night. She had thought herself almost used to the awareness in silence. She'd thought Wyvern's coldness to her a matter of anger. Anger was simple; anger was injustice or hate. A wrong word said could bring anger. Kitty could accept anger, for to do otherwise would be to call herself above fault.

Wyvern's anger wasn't lacking, Kitty found, in the past night's darkness, but it wasn't pointed to herself, nor even to Robin, perhaps not outward at all. It didn't make the silence easier. Perhaps when she thought it was only anger behind Wyvern's eyes, she could accept it better than whatever lay at the heart of another emotion. Whatever it was that her heart could sense but her mind still rejected.

The silence was filled with only Lane's song. "Beware, beware the Breaker's beast. Beware, beware, its eyes that see. They'll drag you down with claws and teeth! Beware, beware, the beast!"

"I don't understand her song," Wyvern said. "Is it elven?"

Kitty couldn't help the laugh that rang across the plains. "It's a sailor's song." Kitty turned to the lead horse before Lane could begin that cursed final verse. "Lane, do you know any elven songs?"

Lane gave no reply but to begin a song that Kitty could understand no more than she could recognize. Its melody, slower than the last, a near mournful drone. Foreign words cut and clipped, a single voice unskilled to replace a chorus, loneliness, nothing so great a sorrow.

Longing for lost days, if she closed her eyes, she could near imagine the wind just the same, a different melody carried by a hundred voices, the smell of healing herbs. She hadn't realized her smile until Wyvern's voice pulled her back.

"Did you know many elves—" Wyvern cut herself off. "Sorry."

That sunlight joy Kitty had only just felt crumbled with Wyvern's frown, marble features pulled by sorrow, a penance to know it was her own doing. "No, it's my fault; we should talk."

The quiet was broken only by strange music for a long while before the idea came to Kitty. "Robin," she called as she spurred

Shale closer. "Do you remember that question game you made up?"

Lane's singing ceased as Robin answered, "Are we going to play?" When Kitty gave but a shrug, he turned to Wyvern. "It's simple: we go in a circle, anyone can ask a question on their turn, but it has to be one they can answer about themselves, and they must answer it if their question is answered."

Kitty nodded. "Wyvern? Do you want to go first?"

It was a long moment before Wyvern spoke, "When did you become a priest?"

Kitty opened her mouth, but no words came; she could pass, but on the first question, a poor leader indeed to consider stepping aside from her own idea. "I was nine. It was in the spring of 430, after..." Her voice faded.

For a long moment, she wondered if her companions knew – if any but Robin understood. A canny glance from blue eyes, one of them did.

The silence was broken by Wyvern. "I was fifteen. We're always fifteen when we choose. I thought I might be a Steward, but the Black Flames came when I was eleven."

An acolyte's curiosity, longing to know more, to know of the black flames Wyvern called to her sword, to know if her companions felt her choice had been stolen, to know *her*, was thrown aside by the rules of the game, barred by the very same questions she couldn't speak of for herself. "Right," she said. "Lane can go next."

Blue eyes turned on Robin. "You were a thief before?"

Robin nodded, but Kitty had to speak. "He was punished for both of us because I got away."

Robin shook his head; even from behind, Kitty knew his face. All that could have turned between then was cut by Lane's answer, "I was a Courtesan."

Robin straightened, if Nestias could blush surely his face would have been red. "I'm sorry."

"Why?" Lane asked, for once, a question phrased as one. "I asked and answered. Is it your turn?"

"Is it?" Robin asked. "I guess I'll ask you, who's the most powerful person you've known?"

Lane's braid swayed as her head tipped. "I don'ne know I can say."

"Oh, that's my turn then," Robin said. "That leaves you, Kitty."

She knew it would be a question for Wyvern, it had been only moments since she learned Wyvern called herself a priest. A priest of what? What gods did the Fensmirri follow? The city's rules didn't apply in this game of Robin's, she could ask. What to give in return? A true Speaker would never let the lay know that the divine truth was a debate, so which version to tell? Was The Maker the sole Creator, or had The Breaker created evil?

Was Helena The Maker's bride or The Mother's last true child? Had she been born with her healing gifts and unbreakable shield, or had they been given to her? Was Kitty to present the truth of the Speakers or that of Pa.

Kitty began a question, but her eyes were, in an instant, drawn from her party. The shape, once just a spot, had grown. "Robin, do you see that?"

All at once, the aura of play dropped. "It looks like a caravan," he said, "but I think all humans."

The glimmer of homesickness at the word caravan died as it was born. "Keep an eye," she said, "we'll just have to pass them."

As the sun reached its peak, the dark shape began to take form. As it began to descend, Kitty could see the humans that swarmed around something at their core. "Robin, can you see what they're carrying?"

Kitty saw nothing of Robin's expression from the front of the party, but his voice told every tale. "It's a cage; I can see a man in it. Kitty..."

The summer air all at once felt cold. "It could be anything; we don't know that he's a witch." She almost wished any of her companions would protest.

It was only as the sun kissed the horizon and a partly blackened moon started its climb that Kitty's party came upon where the caravan had made camp.

"Halt!" called a man styled as a knight. "Who would pass The Maker's justice?"

"We're—" Kitty's voice broke as she pulled Shale to a stop. "We're only passing through."

"What business do you have—" the knight started but was cut off by another.

"Kellor! What are you on about?" A young man adorned in pale leather that matched his hair emerged from the camp. His tirade cut off with a breath as his eyes landed on Kitty. "You're a Castilla!"

Kitty had no time to answer before the young man strode to her horse. "Lord Ason!" the guard hissed.

But the lord paid his guard no mind as he held a hand to Kitty. "Lord Ason Aroch, at your service," he said.

Kitty ever so slowly placed her hand in his; their skin touched for perhaps an instant before she pulled it back. "They call me Kitty," she said, the tremble so faint she could so near deny it.

"Kitty," Ason said. "It's as lovely as you. You must tell me, Kitty, do you know of the Mari Group."

The blond boys ducked between carts, all at once, one with the caravan children. The little girl watched them as she packed sweet-smelling herbs for their father. She wondered if she should have the chance to play before the caravan moved on. Doubt by the changing leaves, but no matter. There would always be more summers.

Heavy shifting of Wyvern's horse anchored Kitty's mind against that breeze of all summers. She nodded. "I was born in the Mari Group."

Lord Ason must have seen something hidden in her eyes as his face fell. "They're gone then?" he whispered. "I prayed the Purges wouldn't find you."

Kitty fought the thief's instinct as the knight approached. "My lord," he said.

Lord Ason looked from his guard back to Kitty. "Share our camp tonight," he said.

Kitty looked between her companions as her tailed drummed against her leg. "We couldn't... impose?"

"Nonsense, I must insist," the lord said with a hand that ceased his guard's protests. "The last of Mari Group will always have a place at my table."

Kitty gave but a shrug to her companions as she dismounted, and the young lord pushed her reins into his guard's hand. "Will you walk with me, Kitty? Kellor will see to it that your companions are taken care of."

"Alright," Kitty said without breath to refuse and a final glance to Robin.

Ason spoke in a constant stream as he led Kitty through that camp. "Father marked autumn's start by your visit. It was the tradition." Blasphemous words, a marker beyond the Dark Sky.

Kitty nodded along with his deluge of words until they passed the caged man. "Who is he?" Kitty's words slipped from her mouth.

Ason turned from his meandering. "Oh, him," he spat, "a dragon rider. He attacked our party in the Wilds. Father insisted we take it to the Northeast Capitol. I don't see why. We could have dealt with it ourselves."

"I thought they were all killed."

The lordling glared at the cage. "Not all of them. Do you want to get closer? You can take a swipe at him for Prince Michael."

"Maker keep us." Kitty shook her head. "I've never seen one before."

"A dragon rider?"

"A dragon."

Ason turned away from the caged man. "They're getting bold; every season, we see them in the Wildlands, and one of those that attacked the capital is still out there."

"Did you kill it? The dragon?" Kitty couldn't help how her eyes traced the sky.

The lord scowled. "Damn beast flew off."

Kitty shuddered as Ason resumed his endless flow of words she needn't add to.

"Are you going to the Wildlands?" the young lord asked.

Kitty took more moments than she should have to recognize the question. "We are," she said.

"Isn't it a bit late in the season?" he asked with a glance to where Helena was part blocked by her sister.

Kitty couldn't help the shiver that wracked her body. If only they were in a city, they could have hidden from that dark gaze. Regret for their Gentea departure held but a moment before Lane's blasphemous portents tore it by the roots.

"We have a job to do," she said as her eyes caught identical shivers across Ason's arms. "It's far north through the Wildlands."

"We must all do our duty to the Maker, especially these nights."

Kitty couldn't help but nod at his words when he looked towards her companions; all mismatched in the sea of green and gold. "I'll have my men prepare another horse for your party."

Kitty shook her head. "We couldn't—" she cut herself off at his raised hand.

"I insist, for my sake, so my father won't accuse me of being a poor host. And you'll have my routes as well. They aren't old, but they reach the mountains. They should get you close."

Kitty gave only a nod before the lord wandered off and she found her own way back to her companions.

The caged dragon rider wandered from her mind until morning dew clung to the saddles of three familiar horses and one new. The camp was changed by the dawn light; early risers shuffled about in hooded cloaks, guards on final watch slumped over where they succumbed to sleep's call. She received sidelong glares as she was handed a gilded list of instructions for a Route marked by carved stars. Whispered sneers, and the word "beast" followed them from that camp, so bold they became while their lord slept.

It was Robin's gaze locked on the cage that brought the man back to mind. Kitty only shook her head. "There's nothing we can do; it's not our place," she whispered.

She only wished he would give words to those protests he left silent.

42

Wyvern

Dark Sky Festival: Second Day

To what end would a horse need a name? Personhood bestowed to something unneeding, a beast to be ridden, and no separate thing from a hunted beast when its use ended. Wyvern had thought it strange, a quirk of that strange place they lived when Robin and Kitty gave names to them, but again, when Lane had been gifted one, she too had named it. Laviate – a word Wyvern knew not the meaning or even the language of – a name for a beast. She had once thought herself wise of outsiders' ways, that Parsifal's stories had given her that much, but on the road, she knew only that she had been mistaken.

As it had been the previous day, only by Kitty's prompting did Wyvern's eyes search the forward horizon. They caught on those banners of green and gold, a beacon under the setting sun, an effigy of those great old trees that grew near. Not so uniform as those about the caged dragon rider; those golden eyes and arrows mingled with other hues, other sigils, all so unfamiliar.

All but one.

Wyvern couldn't hear the calls of her companions as she urged her horse onwards. She truly noticed very little until her feet touched the ground beneath an ebony banner branded by a tree of nine bleeding branches.

If not for plate mail steps, Wyvern may have lost herself to the memories. She turned only fast enough to watch as knights marched a ring around her.

She saw again her companions just as they were halted by that circle. Wyvern couldn't act but to watch as Kitty leapt and ebony curls deeper than that banner's fathoms, wove between armoured men.

"Are you alright?" Kitty asked as she stood between Wyvern and the Knights.

"I—" Wyvern started.

Those words meant for Kitty were never spoken.

"Wyvern?" Knights parted at the voice. There he was, cleaner than he had ever been in her memories. All dressed in red. Parsifal Mirri.

"Do you like it?" he asked as the ring of nine ruby stones slid against that one of pewter she'd worn all that lonely summer. "I had it made to look just like my grandmother's."

His plan after all those months apart, his plan to never part again. "My broods will be Fensmirri." Only Fensmirri, had he been Salliten as Wyvern's brood father half of the brood could have been like him. But Parcifal was human, there would be no halves as the elves had, not for her kindred, Parcifal's humanity lost. The price of being highest.

"I know," he said, "my grandfather knows. I think he likes it that your people will share our title properly."

Two rings turned to ice. *"You told him."*

"Of course. I needed his blessing." Blue eyes, so perfect, what a clever plan it had been; he'd been set free of the secret, and soon, too, so would s he.

If only they had kept it just a little longer.

The warm touch of Par's hands fled as Kitty stepped from behind Wyvern. "Lord Parsifal," she said with half of a nod, an unfamiliar kind of curtness.

"I am," he said, "and you are?"

Kitty's eyes met only Wyvern's. "I'll give you some time. But," Kitty shook her head. "I'll give you time."

That silence in Kitty's wake held none of those comforts it did on that cracked marble floor. Even that scrutiny of knights, that buffer of an audience, disappeared as Parsifal led her to a tent.

His side beckoned, to be with him again, to be as her oaths demanded, but that place he led, those walls of canvas, the heat of sun and candles alike, how impassible that open doorway became.

Those pale blue eyes caught her lingering. "Second Tenet." He nodded as he sat just within those canvas bounds. "I'm sorry, I forgot."

For all her desire, Wyvern couldn't break the silence before Par. "It's been a long time," he said finally.

"Ten years this fall."

"It's almost time then for them to be reborn."

"They should be before winter."

"I don't suppose my word could mean much to your assessors on their behalf."

"Don't talk about them," Wyvern snapped. "We should be at war."

Blood of the unborn, blood between nine ruby stones.
Don't go.

The fifth tenet broken, shattered and ignored. Oathbreaker her, oathbreakers her elders all.

"I'm sorry."

Wyvern shook her head. "Why are you here?"

"I was at a Lady's Calling. I'm meeting Micha in the Central for another." Those canny eyes — how easily they must have caught the way Wyvern tensed at his brother's name. "I'm sorry. I shouldn't have—"

"I'm fine." The lie tasted of tar as it dripped off her tongue.

"I did look for you. I had Lord Tenor look for you." That name again, that name that made Kitty flinch. How wrong she had been to think she knew any outsiders' ways. "I didn't know you left the Southwest."

"I come north in spring; the Warriors find me if I stay still."

He hummed as he came to his feet, a rhythm as they began a trek back and forth across the tent. "You're different. I guess we both are a bit."

Wyvern found herself picking at scales that had regrown so many times already. "I'm not a liar anymore. I don't— I try not to keep secrets."

Parsifal ceased his pacing. It took just a moment to recognize his face, the one from their first encounter. Eyes for a stranger. "Everyone has secrets; it didn't make us liars."

Wyvern forced her eyes to the ground. "My elders would have stopped us if I told them."

"They would have killed you."

"Not if I told them right away, after the first time."

Trampled grass flew as Parsifal sat once more. "Then they would have killed me the second."

"Yes."

And others would yet live, two to be reborn before winter. To many unborn who couldn't be. Couldn't ever be again.

"Do you really regret all of it? Don't we have any happy memories?" he asked. "It wasn't your fault; I should have kept it a secret."

"Secrets only hurt. There's a woman; I love her. But I can't be honest with her."

"No one could blame you for not speaking of that day."

Wyvern shook her head. "She doesn't care about that. I can't tell her that I love her. It wouldn't be right."

Parsifal placed a hand on her arm. "How could it not be right?"

"It would be dishonourable."

"To whom?"

Wyvern couldn't help but feel the weight of her rings, "To her." Of the oath she had sworn already broken. "To you."

The gentle weight of his hand lifted from her arm. "I won't regret loving you. I can't stop loving you. I wanted to believe there was a reason you still wear that ring," he said as their eyes met. "But if it's only for honour, I wish you would leave it behind."

"I could love you again."

Parsifal shook his head. "I would wait forever for that day. But I won't be the thing that keeps you unhappy."

"She wouldn't feel the same."

"At least you'd know you could find someone else to love."

Wyvern kicked at the cloth-covered ground. "It was easier when it was us."

"We aren't kids anymore," Parsifal said as he walked to the door. "You should go; She – that is, your friends – will be waiting."

With a ripple of fabric, Wyvern was left alone. Two rings slipped off her hand; only a pewter band found its way back on.

On the ground, perhaps as it should have been long ago, a gold ring with nine tiny stones was left alone. Its metal cooled for the first time in a long time as four riders vanished to the north.

43

Elysa

Dark Sky Festival: Third Day

    A funny thing, names; the bear never needed one to catch a fish – who never needed one to swim, and still their hunter clung to hers. Hunter, Poacher, Runaway, Spy; titles, names, one and the same, powerful only by the power believed behind them. Impermanence, given by a king, taken by a mere lord, their only natural power a chance to take more.

    Home again at last in the ghost-white Wilds.

    Her target was, as the Seer promised, on that intersection of routes. That path of the interlopers, carved stars guiding north that bled sap down pristine white, such an amateur attempt against her own, so old the trees, carved with marking eyes, no longer resisted their place as waypoints. But both Routes, so like all the other carefully carved paths of safety from the Never Song's call, were impossible to know without a guide or jealously guarded instructions. For Elysa, on that night, it had to be the former, always those summer seasons of childhood spent memorizing those corridors her ancestors had marked, learning the borders her father dared not stray past, poaching off her own birthright.

    But a homecoming no more surprising than the truth in a Dragon Kin's words, the blue-eyed Dwarf Kin sat with three whom Elysa, perhaps, could have thought kin if hers hadn't been so easily forgotten. The gathered four were nothing of a matched set and she hadn't a name for any.

Her target's mystery should have been great enough by her dwarven blood. A people so seldom seen few on the surface thought to question why. The elves' fate after they lost The Landing War was so cruel, so front of mind, it cast a long shadow over the dwarves' lesser punishment. Exile to their ancestral home underground must have seemed a fair price to see their older enemy crushed into unending torment.

It wasn't the girl's blood that gave the greatest mystery. Until she had left the Northwest, Elysa thought the greatest of the dwarven girl's strangeness would lie in whatever power trailed death in her wake. How absurd that the answer to her quest was no longer her greatest question. That honour lay in the Seer's odd half-cooperation. Why did the White Dragon want this girl dead?

The greatest mystery that her goal might align with that beast's.

A pair of contradictions – the dragon and the other – bore through her mind those three days' hard ride on three different horses: the Seer's need for the quest's success against her desire to watch Elysa fail, how similar the elves and humans were.

The murmurs of no real chatter failed to reach even her own fox's ears over Lady's soft breathing, over all the other sounds of night they captured, freed from their disguise after so long.

The Castilla's ears turned on Elysa as Lady's hoof came down on a twig. "Is someone there?" the dark-skinned woman called.

A good time? An opportune moment? Perhaps not, but the time presented nonetheless. Slowly, possibly with more trepidation than the illusion needed, Elysa led her horse into the clearing. "You shouldn't call out to the sounds in these woods," she said.

The Castilla's ears flattened, but what words she might have said were silenced as Blue Eyes turned on Elysa. "You're an Alta?" the target asked.

Elysa let a smile dance across her face as she cast her eyes over the group. Missing fingers on the Nestia that faded into the night with shifting light. Perhaps, then, not followers of law. "Of course not," Elysa said. "Who would ever admit to that?"

"A Half-Elf then?" All eyes turned to the Castilla when she spoke.

"Have you known many?" What lay beyond those green eyes? Not scorn. Perhaps sadness, or longing, a Caravaner then? Perhaps not, for her city accent, but who else to know, without judgement, the lies of that better other? "Half-Elves, that is?"

"Every Elf I've met." Cat eyes twinkled in the firelight. "Share our fire?"

She allowed a smile, a nod, simply another traveller, glad to be welcomed. Certainly, none could blame a stranger a second glance, a closer glimpse of that party. Armed but without armour, the picture of mercenaries, novices, amateurs, all the more to have strayed so far from the cities. No, another glance, their leader hadn't fit, a diplomat, perhaps, a face without the need for base weapons, a vain hope. Tattered clothes held by unmatched threads banished such foolish notions. Not nearly the same, but how Elysa's scars burned with that warning of a witch.

All eyes traced the leader through that long silence, a pause longer than politely plausible, a prison before she and that silence broke as one. "What brings you this far north?"

Those other words, Elysa could see in her eyes the true meaning behind the ones spoken; who was she to stray from shelter, to dare fire on those dark nights? If only she'd had the thought to reclaim that servant's dress before her flight. Pity, it could have been such a better mask, that rough-cut gown turned tunic would play its part. Her precious over-sleeves lay folded in the pack she'd taken along with her current horse in Northguard. A good thing she had put them away, beloved as they were over her arms, that leader with the not quite pure northeastern accent would recognize that one symbol that no change in fashion could shake. As for the rest, she might have prayed that night's dark as much as her opponent's penniless upbringing would obfuscate its fine make had such things had any utility. But useless trifles hadn't a place in her mind as she shifted and twin daggers, fangs in half black moonlight peeked from her hem. "I suppose it must be the same as you."

"The kids?" the target blurted.

Elysa kept at bay the grin that threatened to show itself. "What else could bring me this far north?"

"You can't have a contract," the Fensmirri said. "They don't give this one to single people."

"Suppose the village I got it from wasn't too choosy."

"What village?"

"Latia," her home village slipped out unbidden. Idiot. "Just south and east of here. I don't think they have many mercenaries north of the crossing."

"Let me see it," the Fensmirri said, "you should have a contract."

Her eyes slipped from the albino back to their correct place on the leader. A moment later, and perhaps she wouldn't have seen how the Castilla's eyes flicked to the sky, the way her hand ghosted over something beneath her dress. "Do you fear Helena's sister?" Elysa asked.

The leader's eyes turned to her again, "You aren't a believer?" It almost raised concern, how willing the leader was to turn the conversation, though the Fensmirri's eyes only hardened, her demand evidently not forgotten.

"Oh, I don't doubt she lived once. But I don't fear the dead, or the moon." Only the slight warbling laugh drew Elysa's eyes to that patch of shadow her gaze kept slipping past. "I suppose you don't either, then."

Eyes Elysa couldn't quite remember if she knew emerged from the shadows. "Wrong gods," he spat.

His anger, the way his eyes flicked off hers before it settled across his face. Perhaps he knew the game, a check before showing, or perhaps nothing at all, a stranger's wariness. Very well then, a check of her own, just a momentary distraction, drowning in those black eyes. "The singing pricks can rot just the same."

Shock matched only by her own rippled across the circle; she might admit those words came too truthful, more by half than she had meant, but only a second thought behind watching the Nestia, those eyes, the only without shock, without admonishment, a halfway kindred spirit.

No.

Elysa shook herself and leaned back as heat washed over her scars; whatever the Nestia's spell, she knew better. "You'll have to excuse me; I don't get much conversation on the roads."

"Why not?" the Fensmirri asked. "We've met dozens of people. Why won't you show us your contract?"

Elysa almost began the show of searching her clothing for a scroll that didn't exist.

"Enough, Wyvern," the leader said. The hand, which once only brushed, gripped tight to the chain hidden away. Another piece to tuck away for the time. "You weren't half this hard on Lane."

"I can appreciate wariness." A war to keep back her smile at the Fensmirri's glare. "Though I might think meeting dozens of people would inure one to the practice."

"It's hardly been dozens," the leader said. "Just two groups, really. Didn't you see them at all?"

"I didn't take the main road. But tell me, who's travelling south? Old Aroch isn't one to hide from winter now?"

Idiot, another slip; how the Northwest had made her sloppy, and not so lucky to go unnoticed again. The leader's head tipped just so slightly at the name, but her tail drummed a far clearer pattern. "A Calling. They said they were going to the Central for a Calling."

Elysa couldn't stop the scowl quite fast enough. "The future Lady Raylor – they'll want to mark their place before their sons have the misfortune of meeting her."

It was only the target, the one called Lane, that turned for the spat words. "She is'ne bad."

Elysa shook her head. "Maybe not then. But you said two groups."

"They were dragging a man to be killed," the Nestia said.

"I see. A whole group for that?"

The leader's tail stilled. "He was a dragon rider."

"Good." The word slipped before Elysa could think. She could have been blind to the Nestia's face and would still have known it was the wrong one.

"You can't mean that," he demanded.

Couldn't she? Presumptuous lowborn.

But another thought, and what a phrase to remind her, how she wished to laugh, what would that once false ally have given for that morsel she'd learned by accident? The temptation to use it, to give the Black Dragon, means to further war against the Silver. Blue eyes in the dark pulled her from that happy fantasy. Her own quest returned; foolish words would drive her from that party's hearts, but still, on that night, she had to win but one.

"I won't wish for anyone to be burned alive." Elysa pushed back that sleeve she hadn't the heart to cut, had her face not been enough, perhaps the carnage wreaked across her arm would be. "It's a terrible fate. But I can't be sorry there are fewer dragons."

"They didn't kill it." The leader's words near stopped her heart.

"What?" Elysa hadn't realized how stiff she had become until a feathered arm brushed against hers.

"If you don't like dragons," Wyvern cut across whatever words the Nestia could have offered, "you should just turn back; I've heard they come from up north."

Elysa pulled herself away from the offer of comfort. "Trying to scare me off? I suppose you don't want to split the bounty. Here I thought you wanted to join our efforts."

"We don't need you."

"Don't need to split the money another way?"

"Enough," the leader snapped, "Wyvern doesn't speak for us."

Wyvern had the look of protest, but not another word passed her lips.

The leader once more met Elysa's eyes. "Lane is still hurt; the three of us can't fight an entire cult, not if we don't have to do it alone." She continued, "The money isn't as important as saving the children."

"Of course," Elysa said, "I feel the same way."

The leader finally smiled, but the victory, even the chance to learn Lane's secret, perhaps it was the White Dragon's influence that made it hollow.

"I guess introductions are in order then," the leader said. "You've met Wyvern and Lane. They call me Kitty. That just leaves Robin."

Elysa let herself smile once again for Kitty, but her eyes settled only on Robin. "My name is Elysa."

Robin's face shifted, only for a moment. Subtle, specific, games upon games. So, she did recognize him.

44

Belladonna

Dark Sky Festival: Third Day

Sleep was snatched from Belladonna's grasp only a bare moment before the knife would have plunged through her side. Just one instant long enough to roll clear of the cutting edge.

"Edmund!" Belladonna cried as she pulled him to the floor out of the reach of the second assassin.

She had only the time to see his eyes snap open before she was yanked from his arms.

Familiar chambers spun around Belladonna. The flight ceased prematurely as wood panels cracked under the collision. She took a shuddering breath before her mind remembered the pain. All the world spun around her, no assassins in sight until the blade slashed her chest.

A hand wound through Belladonna's hair, an unrelenting tear until she stood upright. Faces that could have fit in any crowd stared back at her. "Bit unprofessional," one said, "but we were told to make you suffer. You understand."

Belladonna yanked against the grip, graceless, a feral thing of screams and tears, a dance of desperation, fruitless until her teeth met flesh. Blood filled her mouth as her hair was released.

"Bloody bitch bit me," a voice yelled.

But Belladonna paid no mind. She hadn't hit the ground before her feet were moving. Frigid night air cut through her slip as she ran to her sitting room.

The staff waited, a prize amongst discarded clothes.

Mana flowed as her hands closed around it. A grasp for fire was aborted for another. Air turned solid just as a blade should have plunged into her back.

So cold. No flame. Her entire knowledge of air shown in a shield.

Maj'jri would understand, or so Belladonna hoped, as she slammed the ancient staff over the assailant's head. The shock returned through her arms, but the man stumbled for but a moment.

A moment not wasted, for Belladonna's flight carried her to the flint stone on her mantel. She snatched the treasure an instant before she was once more thrown against the wall.

A crack once more echoed from the wood as all breath was knocked from her chest. Belladonna bent double as she sank to the floor, both fists tight around their prizes.

"Get the staff away from her."

"I'm not getting close to that thing."

"Just kill her."

Belladonna let the precious staff rest on the ground for just a moment as she took a stone in each hand. "Come on, come on." Her voice came rapidly as they struck with no effect.

Had the assassins acted on the dropped staff, or had they understood her purpose? Belladonna would never know as, from the stones, burst a shower of sparks.

Precious light fell, born with only the right to die in an instant, until a mage's fingers touched her staff.

Flash fire.

Flesh charred off the once-assassins as flame, born of a single spark, exploded, born with such vigour to light the room with the audacity of suns, to make ash of curtains and books caught in its wake.

That quiet that could only live in spaces after combat settled over the tower. Belladonna spared a thought for whether Anika heard the commotion. Surely not—the stone walls were built for winter, no sound should have travelled beyond their watch. What a winter cold it was. For, even as she watched the rugs that still smouldered, her mind lingered on a truth that she had come to once before so recently, how close she'd strayed, again, to Vix'xhella's waiting grasp for lack of flame.

New sounds came from the quiet, but of them all, Belladonna heard only her lover's footsteps.

"Donna?" he asked. "Did they hurt you?"

Belladonna shook her head even as blood trickled down her chest, the pale chemise a battlefield of soot and crimson. "They didn't hit you?" Her legs screamed as she pulled herself up; a weapon of ancient design submitted to its place as a crutch.

Edmund's eyes widened. "They weren't after me! This is why we need to be more careful."

Belladonna shook her head as her lover disappeared into the bed chamber. "It wasn't about that."

"How do you know?" Edmund reemerged and threaded a robe of deepest charcoal over Belladonna's bruised arms.

How foolish. So quickly after she'd said them, her words, her defence to Lord Tenor's warning, had proved false. Not such a threat, indeed. "My grandfather isn't one to send assassins for a job he has guards for," she said. "I can guess who sent them."

The thought came as she kicked a smoking foot out of the remnants of a boot. Her lover wasn't given notice save for a curse only elves could understand before Belladonna bolted from the room. If her lover had tried to follow, all he could have hoped to have seen was a stone wall settling back into place at the tower's base.

Alyria's rooms lay across the castle from her own. It was nestled in the tower of women just opposite the great hall, from that which housed their father and grandfather. Corridors had been abandoned for the lateness of the hour, torches cold for the festival.

In that pitch dark, Belladonna had no need to knock at the door that lay ajar.

She found her sister curled behind an overstuffed chair. Bloodied hands shook even as they gripped fistfuls of nightgown.

"Lyri?" Belladonna whispered no louder than the gentle click of the closed door.

Alyria's head shot up at once. The blood of her palms smeared against the blood of a split lip. "Donna?" Alyria's voice broke as tears welled in those storm-grey eyes.

Belladonna let her staff clatter to the ground as she rushed to hug her little sister. "She still waits." The elven blessing, bastardized, flowed under Alyria's sobs.

Alyria only burrowed deeper into Belladonna's arms. "I thought we were safe here."

Belladonna pulled away just enough to lift her sister's face. "We will be. Did they get you anywhere else?"

So close her word came to admonishment, dark sky moons carved through those perfect hands by their own nails, but not that night, not when she cared only for how long her little sister should wear gloves, not when she begged for a song to forbid scars.

Alyria wiped a scabbed hand over the split lip but only renewed the bleeding. "They didn't." She pressed a hand to Belladonna's ruined night dress. "You're bleeding."

"It's not bad," Belladonna said, even against the warmth of Alyria's fingers. "Where are they, Lyri?"

Alyria nodded to the bedchamber; her hands tightened for just a moment before Belladonna pulled away.

Had Belladonna not seen all the ways a flame could rend and warp, had her grandmother kept secret those ways of war, the abattoir of that room could have sent her to the grips of She Who Waits.

There were no clean cuts; the two who knew not what they faced any more than those first humans on Lyria were shredded. Bones were broken such that burst-through skin rendered even the faces something beyond recognition. The fists used for such deeds, as well, made to splinters. Humanity's cruelty leashed to tear each other apart.

"What are we going to do?" Alyria asked, her head again tucked between her knees.

The orchard was silent that night; even bugs dared not chirp as a pair of sisters dragged things that were once Human to the edge of a pit touched by no spade.

Had guards not feared the wasp's nests in the very stone of that section, they may have heard the night sound return when the sisters left. They may have noticed how they ceased as one when the sky lighted, as the elder sister returned with another, as they dragged two more unfortunates to a pit that magic filled before the sun could chase off that half-black moon.

A mage and a tailor didn't speak until they had once more hidden away in that newly scarred place, and even then, only with words to lie about the vanished cut that had once marred Belladonna's chest.

45

Kitty

Dark Sky Festival: Third Day

Those hours of last watch, when moons fled behind the trees, when there were still hours before reprise of sunrise, were the loneliest times, made double by the road or lack thereof, the absence of port din. Kitty sighed as she leaned over the dying embers; even such an excuse for a leader couldn't pass off her turn for the loathed position.

Anyone could have seen it, a fox's ear twitch in the grey-toned night. City instincts to leave it be reared for but a moment before obligations of her unwanted position won out. "You're awake?" Kitty asked.

Elysa pulled herself from a nest of blankets. "My ears gave me away then? Damn things."

Kitty rolled onto her heels. "Didn't you ever learn to still them?" Kitty knew her father had mastered the skill even as it evaded her own grasp.

"I usually keep them covered." Elysa held a hand over them. "I can pass."

"I knew a few half-elves to try that," Kitty said, "It didn't end well."

"No, I imagine they didn't."

Silence stretched for a long moment against darkness. Kitty could feel the newcomer's eyes even as she turned her own away. Primal darkness, the nearest she could hope for privacy, for the questions she imagined no peace from. However much she wished to let things lie, she was the leader, her people came first. If there was a threat, she needed to know.

"Who are you?" Kitty asked.

"I told you."

"No." Kitty let her eyes lock with amber ones. "Who are you really?"

"I'm not sure—"

"I'm not a spy," Kitty cut in as her ears pressed flat. "I don't play court games. But I've lived in the Northeast long enough to tell when someone lies to my face."

"If you knew, then why—" Fox's ears twitched. "No, I see, you're desperate, is that it? Why would you take a job you don't think you can do?"

Those words she had shared as the storms still raged, those words she swore were not but Lane's stories. Devout, Kitty claimed to be, how weak to so easily fall to doubt. "I've learned things about this job."

"Yet you still – oh," Elysa said, "you can't give up, can you? You can't bear to let them down. So that's it then, you want bodies between your people and some new evil you've discovered?"

For the first time in so very long, Kitty meant to draw her wand; fox eyes turned round as Kitty let her conduit rest on her knee. "I didn't ask about me."

"Hunter," Elysa said, "the name I gave you is mine, but Hunter is the one that matters."

Kitty's mind drew up dusty lectures in the temple, histories and sigils she had long past forgotten. "I know that name."

"Wondered if you might. We're camping in my birthright."

Had that been so? Kitty only knew the Speakers spoke little, if at all, of those before Aroch, for how little it mattered on that night. Still, she wondered if that truth might still be sanctuary for lies she didn't see.

"You aren't really here for the contract, then?" Kitty asked.

Elysa shook her head. "No."

"How did you find us then? It can't have been an accident."

"I was playing a game with the Northwest's miserable heir," Elysa said. "Her Seer told me to find you."

"Why would a Seer send you here?"

Canny eyes narrowed on her, the cadence of words chosen carefully. "Do you know the power behind Seers?"

"What power?"

"Then I don't think you'd—" Her voice faltered, and two sets of ears turned as one. "Do you hear that?"

That rustle from the forest all around wasn't careless, no broken twigs, no knocking into trees. Instead, there was a pattern — damp leaves squishing into the undergrowth, and under that, tiny metal clinks.

Her hand, for a bare moment, snapped to Robin, but she drew back before it ever touched. Wake her people, the first thought, then doubt, what if she'd heard wrong, heard only what an untrusted stranger wanted her to hear. What trust could they have for someone so gullible? But what more trust could she boast if she ignored the warning for fear of ridicule?

"Stay here," Kitty said. "I'll see what it is."

"That's stupid," Elysa said.

Kitty sat and blinked a moment, an odd thing, an insult and proof positive for her first thought at once. She felt a warmth beyond her body as she shook Robin's bedroll. "Wake the others," she said to him. "I hear something."

She might have explained that pattern to sleep-addled companions; they might have trusted her word without. She never had to find out. All around them, the forest erupted.

Kitty spun to four that lunged at her. An arc of lighting left their lead a smoking husk.

Three once-attackers turned before their feet reached what remained of their leader. Instinct against rationality, Kitty found herself rushing into those trees after them.

Ebony curls snagged low branches that ripped their marks into bare arms. Grace made for the chase covered steps that stumbled when she fumbled to catch the golden ring that unclasped and tore from her hair. A curtain of curls hid the attackers for mere blinks as the trees ended, but where she chased three, the clearing had but two.

Her wand was raised when the twig snapped behind her. The man who leapt for her back had no time to scream as Kitty pushed far too much mana through the flame. So, like that very first night on the road, Kitty only stared as the charred flesh crumbled to ash.

She froze as calloused hands threw her across the clearing, but the only memories were of soot and mud as she tumbled across fallen leaves.

Kitty called for another flame, another inferno, but her mana couldn't offer more than glimmering sparks.

Kitty sunk deeper into the mud as her attackers laughed. The drawn knives reflected no stars in dulled and cracked blades.

As they approached, Kitty knew herself watched.

The figure dropped from above, her legs wrapped around the attacker's shoulders. Fluid, a move no separate from the fall, Elysa plunged her knife through his chest.

The only man remaining turned on the newcomer; his knife surely would have found Elysa's throat, but Kitty found her feet. She slammed into him just a moment late for the blade to miss entirely; a crimson stream flowed out a shallow cut through Elysa's arm.

Kitty had little time to worry about her new companion and less to debate whether she should. Her legs tangled with the attacker's as she rammed him, a poor man's gamble to send them both tumbling to the ground.

Kitty froze as his hand stole her air. The pain hardly registered as her head was slammed hard into the soft earth.

All the world turned black at the edges as Kitty fought for air.

The man's hands went lax.

Air returned to Kitty in choking breaths. Braced for another attack, she saw the knife in the dead man's back as he tipped to the side.

Elysa gave a smile so much more suited for ballrooms than battlefields as she retrieved her blade and held out a hand.

Kitty almost shook her head as she stared at the old burns all around the proffered hand. Her chest screamed as she pushed herself up.

Something gave in the silence, or, perhaps, she only just noticed it, the absence of true quiet, a hum that wasn't music, not quite, a song sung by one raised without, the opposite of a song and yet its notes drifted in her pa's voice.

There was a drifting pull; her feet so often moved before her mind. How had he hidden so long? Why had he left her alone? Of course, he had escaped — what blood mage could be killed? And what right had she to question his choice to hide? She had returned to him, all would be right, all would be good.

A line snapped as Kitty hit the ground. Once more, she felt more than she saw those amber eyes. "This is getting to be a pattern," Elysa said as she once more offered a hand. "Your first time hearing the Never Song, innit?"

Kitty's chest tightened. "The route — the others—"

"We haven't stepped off the route, not yet. You and I have a lot of advantages over humans, but not here."

"You hear it too?" Of course, she could, and, of course, she hadn't been fooled.

"I don't recognize the voices," Elysa said, "and neither do you."

"What? No, I—"

"You don't." Something in Elysa's voice slipped, overcome by an edge of formality. "You don't recognize them, you don't know them. You've never heard that voice in your life, wouldn't you agree?"

As if it was a borrowed and gifted coat, that certainty enveloped Kitty. Those beckoning tones lost her father's voice, and, of course, they had to; he was gone, and she didn't know them.

"Your game failed," Kitty said as she pushed herself once more to her feet. "You could have left."

"I think you and I both know that *you* don't know what my game is, and only I can say if it's worked." Elysa's hand dropped back. "And you could kill me now if you wanted, and only you can speak for that."

"Then *tell me* what your game is." Kitty's words were strained by her fight to put her hair back into the golden ring. "Seers don't give anything away."

"I'm looking for something, information, that is. It's important to me. I'll never find it alone. You are the only people that can help me with this," Elysa said, "but you could be rid of me. You and I know it might keep your people safer, and you could have done so an hour ago. So, what say you?"

Bone white trees rattled with that unsong of a family long lost. She didn't recognize the voices.

"What is it?" Kitty asked. "Where does the song come from?"

"If we could answer that, we'd both be dead. No one comes back from stepping off the Routes. Why?"

"They came from here, and they ran this way," Kitty said. "What were they running to?"

A horrid notion, a worse plan, Pa's lessons of that place, Elysa's same warning. She could keep them on the Route, keep her people safe, but what next when they reached the Pass? What, then, if she found nothing? What then, a traitorous, heretical piece of her mind asked, if Lane's words held truth and she had but five short days to find her quest's end?

Those amber eyes, filled with impatience, gave something of a fire poker's prod. "Would you think me an idiot if I followed their path beyond the route?"

"Oh yes." Those eyes flicked to the path trampled by Kitty's earlier pursuit. "But I dare say you wouldn't be going alone."

Kitty stepped from that clearing. Her steps echoed so much more in the quiet after combat. "You were right," she said. "I do need help; I don't know if we can defeat this cult, every time we fight them, it's worse."

Elysa appeared at her elbow. "I'm sure we can't."

"But you're here anyway, and you've all but told me you're still hiding something."

"It's not much hiding if you know what I'm doing."

"Can I trust you?" Kitty asked.

"Of course not," Elysa said, "you know I'm a liar, but you've been around us all your life. If I could fool you, I would have, so you keep your eyes on me, and while you do that I'll watch your back."

A promise so like her home city, so foolish she believed it, and more by half in how she still wanted the words. "Can I trust your word in that?"

"Everyone falls in behind you. It has to be your decision."

Kitty smiled. One day, perhaps she'd ask again. One day, she'd hear the words she wanted. "I'll take that for a yes then. I want to trust you."

46

Kitty

Dark Sky Festival: Fourth Day

The little girl cried when she killed the cat. A price to be paid. That dark place, the circle of blood stained by three generations. Call the name, and he will come. In life or dream he will come to us. A name of no mortal sound.

Grey skin and so many ocean-deep eyes, a spider in all but face. A Daemon's words, so like his name, no sound to make sense of. The monster of ancient times returned from whence he came by Maker's might when the little girl took the wand and the magic a cat's life had bought.

Water pooled then rushed around the girl's feet; the cave melted as wax to that blue sky.

Smoke.

And so began the screams.

Smoke lingered as Kitty scrambled from her bedroll; tears burned surely as smoke. Red leaves tumbled as to flame.

"That's common."

Kitty spun at the voice. The scream halted in her throat, but she couldn't stop the ice as it flew from her wand. Ice drew a glittering carpet until it stopped all at once when it hit Lane's knees.

Kitty gaped at the almost carnage. "How did you?"

Lane tapped a foot on the frost melting before her. "The Za– The Daemon's magic can'ne pass me."

"Is that a Dwarven skill?" But what other could it be? For all the proclaimed half-elves shared of their ancient enemy, what Fae could have passed such a skill? A strange thing, though, in all the hateful tales of the past, they painted Daemons and dwarves with the same vitriol. Whatever had transpired to bring Lane into the world?

"No," Lane said, her eyes cast to the sky. "You know her story?"

Kitty's eyes latched to the moons. "Helena's?"

"I've seen the plays. They teach it different in the temple?"

Kitty's hand found her chain, but the words were older, teased out by wagon tracks and dying fires.

"They say she was made by the Mother's own hands, a gift to her husband, his voice and sword in our world. They say even war couldn't tame her beauty, that no sword could touch her, a shield against wickedness, and where the shield did falter, faithful were healed by her song."

That was an addendum, unique to the Lyrian sect. Those texts before, Elves put no mention of song, but Pa had, and the Speakers of her childhood said the same. Moments of synchronicity to be blessed, at least she knew the matching parts were pure truth.

She paused at that part where lessons of two lives again diverged, where she chose the older.

"When her sister, untouched by his grace, saw how Helena was beloved, her heart grew hard. She called down the Breaker and set upon the faithful. For years she did lay siege, warriors of light turned to stone in her wake, until Helena, too, took the field, and in battle, banished her dark sister to the sky. A final sacrifice, Helena followed her sister to the heavens that she might never escape and that we never again live without the Maker's light."

Night's quiet life was cut by the scratch of Lane's quill across the parchment. A glance gave Kitty only those same Dwarven characters that had long confounded her.

"Is that how your plays tell it?" Kitty asked.

It wouldn't have been, not when the Speakers attributed the sister's fall to The Breaker's careful corruption instead of her own mortal folly. It was just a single-line difference, but it changed the meaning: The Speakers' warring against turning from The Maker became Pa's against reaching for what she could not have.

"I 'av'ne 'eard it from a Speaker before."

Kitty shook her head. "I wasn't a Speaker." An apprentice, an acolyte, never a full Speaker, never a hope to earn that title. "I couldn't have been."

"You still follow their gods?"

Their gods, someone else's, a fact without malice, a burn just the same and twice as bright. A throb in her chest, not for her own, but for the faith of Mari Group, sat by His side. "They're *my* gods. My Pa taught me Helena's story; he made sure none of us forgot her name."

Lane's eyes flicked to Kitty's face for but a moment. "It's my name."

"What?" Kitty straightened from reminiscing.

Lane's voice came bitter and cold. "'Elena. Pa could'ne say it neither; 'e thought it was a joke. Only 'Allei calls me that."

"Kitty isn't my name," Kitty offered. "It's not what my pa called me."

Lane's book closed heavy on melted frost. "You changed it after the purges?"

"The Speakers called me Kitty. It's my fault; I didn't want to tell them." Kitty's tail drummed out a heartbeat. "My pa called me Jacqueline."

"He taught you of your Maker?"

The chain of beads rang its chimes to the night as Kitty shifted. "He was a leader; they all made sure we followed the path."

"Not the Elves."

Kitty tipped her head. Lane's words were so sure of something she'd never seen. "No, they did too."

"Were'ne Elves."

"They claimed to be half-elves, but—" Kitty tried.

"No such thing," Lane said. "Elves or outsiders, blood's not enough. You were witches?"

"Most of us." Kitty's wand rolled between her fingers. "Pa was a witch first."

"Chose blood magic?" Lane's voice held none of the scorn Kitty knew it deserved.

Her fist curled tight. "He was our healer; he didn't have a choice."

The cheater's art, magic without mana, blood sacrifice for blood control. Cheat once and lose true magic. She remembered all the mage's nicknames and barbs and how easily their scorn was hidden away when they needed Da's gift. They learned; Da said they would learn, even as no mage child was ever sent to apprentice.

"Not Elves," Lane said again. "Would'ne live with the enemy's magic nor their deep art."

"And you?" Fingers turned bloodless for their tension around her wand, always the same thoughts for Daemon's magic; how foolish to think someone knew both truth and compassion.

"Not an Elf," Lane said in spite of her pointed ears, her hands lifted from parchment to scratch each other. "I do'ne follow their gods, and My sister 'ad the deep art,"

"Had?"

"Not 'er calling, did'ne choose it forever."

A lie, by only its contradiction of truth, of Pa's warring and the elves' barbs both, draw from blood once and burn her mana forever, no escape from the oldest art. And still, how could Lane's eyes hold nothing of obfuscation? "How did she go back?"

"Forward, not back," she said, "did'ne bleed all her potential."

"That's impossible."

Those blue eyes blinked. "I've only read the rules; my sister knows them. Mine were given more mana than yours."

"Where is she now?" Kitty bit her tongue at the implication.

The stone settled ever further as Lane reached for a blue feather, her eye's same hue, hung from her neck. "Somewhere else." Euphemism, careful words, how similar they rang to those of plague towns. "Can'ne leave 'er 'ome."

A rock that hadn't quite settled lifted. "She's alive then?"

Copper scent filled the air as beads of crimson bubbled from Lane's hand. "Why would'ne she be?"

Kitty forced her tail to still. "A lot of people react badly to learning about a blood mage."

"They fear magic," Lane said. "They can'ne fight a god's gift."

Kitty tried to keep her face even, her ears still, but how her hackles raised, so much an accusation to trained ears, how she heard Breaker behind words that danced around gods Lane meant. "You said your god of magic is gone."

"Dead," Lane said.

An acolyte's instinct to refute. "If it's a god's gift, as you say, how can you have magic with no god to grant it?" she asked.

"You can'ne; she was born when magic returned to this place of mortals." Unmatched pages turned together, a fine addition to night's symphony. "We do'ne know 'er name; we see only 'er champion in Seralie."

"Why doesn't she have a name?" Kitty shook her head. "Your goddess, that is."

Lane looked up from her book. "The elves call her Maj'jri for their mages."

"But that's an elven goddess; why don't the Dwarves have a name."

Lane tipped her head. "She is'ne an old god."

Again, her mind found itself in that rainy inn. "Old god? Wasn't that what you said the cult follows?"

Something compelled her to pull out the amulet she had taken that first night on the road. Before, she'd only glanced long enough to see many points on the star; on that night, she counted nine.

"Vallire, Coar, Calla, Miche, Nari, Raille, Doran, Nori, Colhen, Lomin," Lane read from her book. Somehow, it felt important that she hadn't said them from memory, or that she claimed nine gods and said ten names. "Our nine names are the Onari's, their aspects the oldest gods."

Kitty's brow furrowed. "The Onari weren't the first to make up gods."

"All before were lost in the Last Reckoning. All we 'ave now will be lost to the next. The first survivors name the next."

Doubt over doubt, faithful, acolyte, shoved aside but a moment, a leader's responsibility. "This Reckoning, you've said that before. That's what you think the cult wants? That's why they've taken the children."

"The Old Gods break through Vallire's veil to destroy their mortal creations. This is a Reckoning. The children can'ne 'elp them."

"Why take them then?" Kitty's voice raised before she caught it. "Why lay traps for people that try to stop them?"

"I do'ne know. There are keys in mortals. The three great powers." She turned her book to the very first page. "By old gods, by new, and by dragons. These are Ellivar's keys to end the next."

A name Kitty knew nothing of, but she heard the sentiment, the warning in those words. "But keys can open as well?"

"Easier to find keys to open, but they can'ne 'ave the new gods' champions." Those last words were so much like a prayer. "Too soon to choose their singers."

Hair stood on Kitty's neck; that question she hadn't yet the courage to ask burned as she gave it voice. "Why? Why would any gods want to destroy their creations?" The acolyte over the leader, her role to defend her Maker from those wicked that would defile his name. Why? The question why echoed, not the acolyte, the little girl who saw the purges enacted under House Mirri banners.

Those eyes gave not an inch of retreat nor an ounce of sympathy. "We believe they do," Lane said. "We saw the last those thousands of years ago. We rose from the ash first. Mine knew only our own gods to give blame when it ended, and so it became."

Kitty so readily would claim that nagging fear left with those words, faithful incredulity should have so easily given peace. "Your proof can't be the story of something I don't believe happened."

A weight came over that blue-eyed gaze, a pinning thing before they flicked to the dark moon high above. "But you do believe. You told me *your* story of it."

47

Elysa

Dark Sky Festival: Fifth Day

For another day, The Never Song grew louder as they cut through untouched wild. The bone-white trees shivered as that circle of riders passed; early red leaves dropped in their wake, scarlet beads, a bleeding wound responding to the intrusion.

The others of lesser hearing still heard not the call of loved ones lost. Elysa didn't recognise the voices. As if clockwork, by the hour Kitty's head shook, nearly an impressive thing, she only had to be told once the rules of that place to keep them, to ward against the call in quiet moments.

How Elysa loathed quiet, its maw as open as western fields, those places where words held no power. How fortunate Elysa was then, that those companions she found warded against it all the same.

"Robin"—Lane winced as the horse, far beyond her measure, stumbled on undergrowth—"both your parents were Nestias?"

Elysa might have called it a guess if not for the pattern in Lane's questions, she never phrased them as such but for a rising tone. It might have been a guess in any case, for it would have been impossible to tell. If only their beast blood could have been diluted as elven blood. Within two generations any hint of Elf could be gone, But Mirri's lot would always be abominations, the price they paid for whatever Daemon's deal their creator made. She'd have made any deal for her father's ears in place of her mother's.

Robin, for his part nodded to the question. "That's right?" His voice trailed off, those black eyes fixing somewhere far away as his horse turned to the deeper woods.

Elysa didn't think about why her heart seized. "Kitty!" she called.

Robin's leader needed no more prompt to spin her own horse and seize Robin's reins. Whispered words floated between them. "Opal," was the only one Elysa's ears could make sense of. The Nestia shook when Kitty resumed her place, but no longer did he make for the sound.

"I should have told you before," Kitty said. "I hoped we wouldn't come so close, but Lane, Wyvern, you'll probably hear it too."

Kitty's eyes met Elysa's. Perhaps the leader hoped she would speak, would give her family's long passed-down warning of the woods. But given nothing, Kitty continued.

"There's something hiding in the woods; you wouldn't have heard of it if you've never travelled here before. House Aroch calls it the Never Song."

The house of interlopers, that house of thieves and frauds, as if they named the danger, as if they braved its call before the routes were cut. "All you need to understand," Elysa snapped, "is that you don't recognize the voices."

"That is true." Kitty nodded, her eyes more relieved than angered at the interruption. "You might think you do, but you don't."

"We've left the Route?" Lane asked in her way as the group resumed their journey.

"Yes." Kitty nodded. "You don't seem to hear it yet."

"Ah, nay. I won'ne," Lane said.

A curiosity, any more curious to be a complication, so keen she was to reach for that to understand her target, another mystery or a mere quirk of the land's oldest blood in her veins. So cautious she was to leave to words as they were, to reach for others in the growing unquiet.

"We're still playing, correct?" Elysa asked, "I believe Robin has to return the question?"

"That's right." Robin turned back to Lane. "One of them being a Nestia would have been enough for me to be one. But both were. What were yours?"

Such an odd thing, her mother's first game turned to such an innocent lens. Elysa gave Lane's response no mind; for all her mystery, her parentage was of little consequence. A Dwarf's stature with an Elf's ears. But in those eyes, an outlier from both.

Around in circles, the questions went. One, for its like in return, innocently stalled at that first step. Only by Wyvern's call did Elysa return her attention. "Elysa! How did you travel the woods without us?"

Elysa sent another smirk to Kitty. The leader's face was tight against laughter and scorn in equal measure. "Pass," she sang.

Wyvern growled. "You can't pass on every question."

"Can I not?" she asked. "It seems I have so far."

"You only get to ask back if you answer."

With a nudge, Lady sped in time with Wyvern's horse. "I suppose," Elysa said, "your answers are worth less than mine."

"You're just hiding things on purpose."

Elysa pulled Lady back into position. "I don't know why you're so upset; you're winning."

Wyvern turned in her saddle. "Robin made the game. There isn't any winning."

"Really?" Elysa shot a glance to Robin; so many ways to play that kind of game, but with only a slight shake of the Nestia's head, she relented. "I supposed you would know it best, this game Robin invented. What was the question?"

Wyvern gave a huff as she turned back. "How did you travel the woods without us?"

"I see," Elysa said, and how worth the pause to see Kitty's ears tick. "Pass."

What fun to see those pink eyes alight with true rage, and what a perfect time since Wyvern wanted the game so desperately. "Do you want a real answer from me?" Elysa asked.

"Honesty is the heart of this party," Wyvern snapped.

"Then this is the deal I'll give you; you can ask me any question that you haven't asked me before. I'm sure you can be honest about that." Elysa let her eyes settle on Robin. His widened eyes gave only a tinge of hesitation; he had, after all, brought it to that, brought a spy's game to the lay. "And in exchange, I can ask you any question at all."

Forward movement in the game, a test of unknown potential value, a trap, but one Wyvern so easily snatched. "Fine," she spat. "Why are you here?"

Rules, Mother's drilling of that game's only true rule, but no rules said truth came with explanations. "A Seer sent me."

The Fensmirri scoffed. "You're lying."

"No, Wyvern," Kitty called, "she isn't."

"Why would a Seer send *you*?" Wyvern asked.

Elysa leaned against Lady's neck, red hair against black, an effigy to ember, so like the fury she stoked. "Oi now, Wyvern, I only promised you one answer. Don't go back on our arrangement now."

"Fine!" White skin flushed. "Ask your question. *I'm* not hiding anything."

"I'm afraid you're mistaken. I never promised I'd ask it today, I trust you'll remember that you owe me one."

Wyvern's snarl was interrupted by the leader. "Let's maybe play a different game," Kitty said.

"I know another game," Elysa said. Recollections of Lord Tenor's early training carried the old riddle forth. "Have you ever heard of a desert problem?"

"Let's hear it then." Kitty's hesitation was palpable in that late summer air. "How does it work?"

Elysa nodded. "You're wandering the Sandy Wastes, and you come across a person dying of thirst. You only have enough water for one person; what do you do?"

Silence stretched for but a moment before Lane spoke. "Who is the person?"

"It doesn't matter."

"Do I know them?" Lane asked again.

Elysa shook her head, and she'd thought the half-Dwarf half-bright. "Let's say it's a stranger."

Kitty's voice came almost in a whisper. "Giving my water to them would be the right thing to do."

"Is it?" Elysa asked.

Kitty's ears flattened. "It's right to be selfless."

Against all bidding, Elysa's ears twitched. "To the point of self-sacrifice?"

"I think so." Kitty nodded, her face set. "I'd give them my water."

How odd, a will turned to iron under that same prompt that had so many turn tail. Perhaps Lord Tenor had yet more ways he hadn't shared.

"Where is the Waste's edge?" Lane called.

"That doesn't matter," Elysa said.

That rope of a braid danced as Lane shook her head. "Do I know where the Waste's edge is?"

"You know it's too far to go without water."

"Desert's cool at night," Lane pressed. "Can I travel then?"

Wyvern's voice rang before Elysa could add another correction. "How heavy is the person? Could I split the water and carry them?"

"You can't win," Elysa snapped. "There are only two options."

"Could I be a witch?" Robin asked.

Elysa could have snapped at him until dark eyes, creased at their edges, met hers. A game in an entirely foreign meaning. "It won't help you," she spat. "The Stranger's a Speaker now."

Bird song forged to a laugh rang over Lane's protests; silver met by returned songs of true birds. But of course, his was the answer she didn't need. That one she wanted never came.

The beastly screech beyond volume rent peace from the sky. Trees snapped to splinters, shattered, so simply beneath the serpentine body; a never known peace was swallowed as the dragon leapt forth.

Dull yellow scales wrapped all around as the great beast tore through the Wilds. A maw of fangs split open in a scream of the storm's own kind, the right in reverse, thunder mere moments before lighting leapt from its throat.

Horses scattered.

She could have, should have, held fast, but those eyes found hers. *No pain like dragon flame, no whip nor corruption dared claim sway under inferno's name. Frozen, ice to stone and return to dust. No escape on legs that wouldn't run. Only those eyes. Those eyes that saw her, those she saw before nothing at all.*

Elysa was yanked back as her feet found earth. That titan's maw lifted again, thunder's cry before the onslaught. A blur of black and green pushed her to the forest floor.

A bird shouldn't have been able to scream as Robin did when that lighting lanced, an arc's edge glance, across his back.

The beast's head swung around as a blast of flame slammed into its wing.

Robin fell, a broken puppet, when those jagged ribbons vanished.

Elysa scrambled past the whimpering broken body before her; a hand twitched for a blade, fruitless, a mere dagger against that wall of armour. A monster. No blade came as her slim form slipped beneath a downed tree.

Fox's ears twitched to Wyvern's familiar yell; the Fensmirri served only to turn the beast from its search for the witch. The tail swung around to meet her. A splintered tree fell under the force of a white scaled back.

A cry from the trail, a pitiful thing, prey; Robin should have stayed down; another blast of lightning struck out for him as he came to his knees. But that golden arc never struck; a wall of ice turned it away as Kitty ran in front of her friend.

All for naught, the wall shattered under assault from a taloned hand.

"Idiot," Elysa whispered, though to whom, she couldn't say, as her knife soared for the dragon's eyes.

A shallow cut just two days old, a stiffness in pain's place, a muscle moved just wrong, a dagger that missed its mark. Still, the beast turned; flying wood ripped its vengeance through Elysa's flesh as she rolled from that blast.

A first trial in creation, failure, deprived of the cat's grace, a leap for the path failed to find footing, not a dash to unbroken trees, made to be a stumbling thing to the open.

So open, so seen. Empathy for those under her own. Those eyes.

Decade-old burns roared as they once had.

Thunder's cry as the maw opened.

The dragon shrieked as arrows pierced its eyes. Five newcomers moved as one, all uniformed in images of bleeding branches, a blue Nestia at their head; the leader, with two swordsmen at his back, charged the reeling beast. In one movement, as to a dance, three swords cleft the dragon's neck.

Arrows harried the beast as it fell. The last cry of a monster rang as the first sword came alive with light, a song beyond words, a sword beyond measure, as blue feathers flew and it cleft off its bleeding head.

The five newcomers were strangers to Elysa, yet still she knew them; for who in Lyria didn't know the group that slayed the yellow dragon over the True Capitol just three years back.

The leader of Mirri's Bastards spat as his group gathered at his back. "You're out of your depth, Robin. Go home."

Presumptuous lowborn.

Elysa found herself at Kitty's side; all five of the mismatched party stood together, a shattered mirror to those that would claim their maker's name. Disharmony forgotten for but a moment against the challenge of those who turned from them.

Elysa dared not waver until the other group disappeared down the trail. Only as their backs were hidden by red leaves did the memory of flame take her.

48
Elysa
Dark Sky Festival: Fifth Day

Dragons didn't rot. Flakes of ash fell over the party as to early snow when they made camp under the dead beast's shadow. Even as golden embers grew across the beast, the true sight was Kitty. Gone was the skittish woman she'd known those few days, replaced with focus, pure and unadulterated, as those delicate hands tended to Wyvern and Lane.

The Dwarf girl's absence in that fight was clear after the beast's wrath ended but readily excused by an old injury, an unfamiliar horse, the panic of a moment. Excuses Elysa knew she had not the right to call judgment on. Had she not also frozen, chosen to hide away? No, her true irritation was only that her curiosity had been unsated; the girl had run, her mystery remained unknown.

And the deaths in her wake just the same.

"She could help you too," Robin said as he appeared from the shadows, a bundle in his hands, "if you ask."

"I'm given to understand she would insist on helping. I'm fine," Elysa said, even as the blood down her back named her a liar.

"You don't look it."

Elysa shifted away as Robin sat by her side. "Aren't you meant to be resting?"

Talons dug into the earth. "I feel alright now."

"So, we're both liars then?"

Elysa dragged her fingers through rough-cut hair; perhaps if she waited long enough, he would broach the subject both of them knew lurked in every silence.

The ideal of a Genteel, never a Shadow, hardly an infiltrator, never the patience, such poor traits for an ambush predator. Elysa turned her eyes to the ash that gathered on Robin's scarf. "I know you," she said.

"If I admit it"—his talons curled tighter—"will you let me help you?"

Buttons of the once gown came undone as Elysa turned from Robin. "Would denying do any good at this point?"

Gentle fingers peeled the garment away but paused at the corset beneath, a new thing, free of those slashes and scars of the old, that which kept debris from emulating a rival's blade between her ribs. She had almost half an intention to thank Lord Tenor for the wonderful gift. Thoughts of that man were driven off by soft hands. "May I?" Robin asked.

The name 'lowborn' drifted past her mind with no venom, for which of her kind would dare? Almost a true smile crossed her face, almost. Elysa sighed. "My corsets have stopped knives; I doubt sticks got past it. But, by all means, do what you must."

"I didn't recognize you at first; it's been a long time," Robin said as he started at the laces.

"I don't think I could forget someone I caught breaking into my room."

Robin made an odd chirp. "I'm sorry about that."

"Don't be," Elysa said. "If, for nothing else, I was the one to lay eyes on Nico's weapon."

"I thought you would come after me."

"I thought I might, but Nico lost you. It caused quite some talk—his weapon vanishing."

Deft hands paused. "My mum died," Robin said. "Just after that. I was only playing for her."

"I'm sorry for your loss." The platitude felt empty as Robin continued his work.

"And I suppose you've just met my father." A hardness so rare in that voice.

"The Bastard?"

Robin's laugh rang like silver chimes. "I can't fault the name he chose."

Not a dozen words between them that day. How a father could turn down feathers to iron. How disappointing. She'd once thought the dragon killers to be allies even from afar — saviours of The Maker's Pass. The gleam so tarnished by his failure as a parent.

"I've never seen someone kill a dragon without magic."

Robin's beak clicked. "He didn't, not really."

Elysa turned her ears, a command, for once, obeyed. "What aren't you saying?"

"What did you call them? The singing pricks?" he asked. "Do you know the name Ryv'vyhan? Does the word 'champion' mean anything to you?"

Not nothing, something of an old memory, made by the Mother's own hands, a gift to her husband, his voice and sword in the world, dusty lessons. And with those temple lectures, doubt that the dragon killer would heal allies with a song.

Elysa shook her head. "Very little, I'm afraid, but I might understand. Would it mean he's made a right ass of himself?" That she pulled from her own eyes rather than any speaker's tale.

"You could say." Robins's laugh filled the mournful, near-moonless night.

Those bells of camaraderie froze as Robin pulled the corset free. Elysa knew a mere slip couldn't hide the scars. She could count them, the lash lines, some white, almost innocent, next to those burned shut, to those others hardened turned black from old corruption. Half a season alongside the Black Dragon and she'd never envied him so, but what she wouldn't give to wipe those marks away, to be pretty as her mother had been, not twisted by fire and lash.

"What?" Robin's question tumbled like so much ash.

"And now you've met my father." That need to hide, to pull back her clothes, burned deep. "I wasn't born Tenor's ward."

Nine years and only two with her father alone, only her own fault it hadn't been fewer, only her own fault it had been so few. How humans feared witches, how after Mother, a mere child's word had been proof enough of her father's imagined guilt.

A damp rag wiped over the cuts. "Did you get away from him, Lord Tenor, that is?"

Elysa's ears flattened. "Not quite; I don't think I can ever leave the game, not as you did," she said, "but unless I misjudged someone, he doesn't know where I am. Suppose I might be dead by now if he did."

Fox's ears turned toward laughter from across the camp. "I won't repeat anything you've told me," Robin said.

Elysa nodded. "Likewise," she said, "I suppose Wyvern doesn't know you were a spy."

Rough bandages turned such a contrast from Robin's hands. "She means well."

"She's self-righteous and entitled," Elysa said.

"It's the only way she knows to be good."

Elysa scoffed. "Real good doesn't exist, not in this world."

Robin crawled to sit by Elysa's side. "We can only do our best."

The corset was ruined, and in the light of the fire, it seemed nearly torn in two. What a wonderful gift it had been, she tried not to mourn the days she'd have to spend without it.

"This job, do you really think we can do it? We'll be against your father." Elysa pulled her overdress back on, heavy silk still marred by the blood that would never come free rubbed against the old scars through her slip; graciously, its uncut sleeve still hid her ruined arm.

"Why do you care?" Robin's head tipped. "It's not why you're here."

"No." She let that truth fly, perhaps a shield for her lack of honesty in explanation, "Perhaps I didn't want to die in the meantime."

Eyes too canny narrowed at the proffered reason. "If that's what you say," he said, "do you think it will take until our contracts end?"

Elysa scoffed. "I could be done tonight."

"But you won't be?"

She forced her eyes still, not a glance to the target. "I haven't quite decided I want to do it yet, not until I know why a Seer cares so much. But you didn't answer my question."

Black eyes flicked to his leader. "Kitty thinks we can," Robin said, his voice carrying more certainty than their leader's could have dreamt of those few days. "I trust her. So can you."

49

Belladonna

Dark Sky Festival: Sixth Day

Auroras danced beyond counting in the primal dark. Belladonna cast her eyes to them – remnants of the Fae's entry, so said Ryt'tyiv's song. Perhaps they would grant her strength. But wandering in a dark street gave her no victory, so, as to a mouse, Belladonna ducked into the safe house.

A waste of a night perhaps; her people had checked them all weeks before, but something in finding Elysa's so-called search of the dungeons to be a lie cast doubt beyond reason to all others in kind. And there were reasons beyond her own; she had made John a promise.

The cellar smelled of damp and stale air. Grain baskets lay empty, awaiting the new harvest soon to come. But famine-ridden baskets were not all that held no treasure; in such a small place, the children couldn't have hidden for more than moments.

Tiny jingling bells danced through silence; such tiny music should have been silent to any others on any other street. But their song of arrival filled her ears as Belladonna turned to the cellar door.

"I can't ever sneak up on you," Vix hummed as she held out a hand.

"You hang bells from your horns." Belladonna's breath left for but a moment as she let herself be lifted from the cellar. "Where's your brother?"

"Why?" Vix grinned as Belladonna started towards the next safe house. "Would you rather meet with him?"

Belladonna shook her head. "I asked him to help Edmund sort through the records. We still need to find the Grey Fall."

"Didn't your tailor find anything?"

Belladonna's eyes hardened on her colourful ally. "No," she said, "so where is Xax?"

Vix's fingers drummed on her sword's hilt. "Seralie's missing dragon died yesterday; he went to see who did it."

Sweet Nit's laugh danced across her memory as Belladonna put a hand on Vix's clenched fist. "Was it the same people?"

Blue feathers on parade, those that gave themselves Belladonna's first title. "He'll find out if they are." Two moons reflected in a single eye, a fading thing as tears blinked away.

"This is the last of them," Belladonna said as she stopped before a long-since-loved stable. Pilled rags and broken furniture spoke to its many lives before and since its induction into smuggling.

"You work fast," Vix purred.

"Lot of good it's done so far." Belladonna pulled her hand away from Vix's as she strode inside.

The stable had been lived in, but an observation worth little at all, for a place like that always had been. There was dread with that knowledge. What little could she find if thieves and urchins had returned? A worry confirmed by those clothes hung from the rafters and rags piled into rough beds all around. But empty of life, no, beyond that emptiness, a sound, a shifting of straw.

"We always find the nicest places," Vix mused.

Belladonna held a halting hand. "I hear something."

The shifting grew only louder as Belladonna ventured deeper past mould-stained walls. Then she caught it; those grey-blue eyes that watched her back from behind piled crates. "Isobel?" Belladonna whispered. "Is Beth with you?"

One pair of eyes became two of a matched set as the girls crept from their hiding place. "M'lady?" Isobel, the taller, the older made to lead, asked. "We thought you were caught."

"We were going to rescue you," came Beth's hoarse voice.

Belladonna knelt before the shivering girls, and Vix's coat draped over them. "You were?"

The girls nodded as one. "We didn't know where to go."

"You've been here all this time?" Belladonna asked. "Someone should have come looking."

Isobel's head shook. "No, we didn't see anyone."

"Vella." Vix nudged her arm, "Sun rises soon."

"Right," Belladonna said as she stood. "We're going to take you to your father."

A safe house on the path, a familiar route, but to walk with children not yet raised to pass unseen, a task reprieved only by that total darkness. A strange route to walk with people not her own, so much like an intrusion. One worth every close call as filthy children bounded up a pirate's gangplank to a ship freshly painted black with new, nearly golden sails. Whatever new name Vix gave the ship after the last run, Belladonna couldn't make out in the darkness.

"How long can we hide them here?" Belladonna asked the night.

"Until we find their mother." Vix leaned against Belladonna's arm.

"We *have* to until then." Belladonna pushed against Vix just slightly. "How long before your ship is suspicious in port."

Vix gave Belladonna an odd look. "We have until the festival ends at least; nobody's leaving port."

Only then did she see how many ships sat lightless aligned to the port beneath the cliffs that grew to both sides of the city, and further still, dark ships sat anchored in the shallows. "What happened to them?"

"You spend too much time in those walls, Vella," Vix said, "they're not going to risk the dark sky storms."

Belladonna pulled away from her ally. "There's never been a storm during the festival."

"Not over land. All the sea is Breaker's Reef these nights."

Superstition, that drunken sailors chorus. Belladonna couldn't help but shake her head. "Don't tell me you believe all that."

"Do you think Xax leaves his territory for the Dark Sky because he likes being so close to Seralie?" "Ask him what happened to the last Black Dragon."

Belladonna shook her head, fingers that had turned white around her staff relaxed. "But all ships stay near the shore. Why didn't you tell me this?"

"Why would it matter?"

"We've been searching for the Grey Fall for days." Belladonna couldn't control what slipped through in her voice. "Why would you keep that?"

Keep hidden that puzzle piece she needed. All those days searching for a ship's route.

"What should that matter? I thought you send prisoners to work camps," Vix snapped.

"Not for this!," Belladonna snapped back, "You're Lyrian; you should know that!"

"I left!" A plea of ignorance. "You might have seen the regard I give your laws."

"It's fine." Belladonna couldn't believe her own words even half as much as she wished to believe Vix's. "It is a ship."

"Then it will be near to the shore until the eclipse ends."

Belladonna nodded. "Good. Can you get Xaxirion back here for tomorrow night?"

Vix's arm brushed again against Belladonna's own. "I can. You have a plan, then?"

"Most of one." Belladonna allowed herself to feel Vixensha's warmth for just a moment. "I should have the rest tomorrow."

And all too soon, that day would come as moons began their descent; too soon, she too would no longer have ignorance to claim.

50

Elysa

Dark Sky Festival: Sixth Day

There was an air to that party, a way to the routines she found herself grafted to. They spoke not of the fight ahead; riding days were filled with games of that innocent definition, guessing games and finding games. There was nary a mention of the reward they sought, nor debate for how a prize for three would be split for five. Confounding mercenaries. And how easily they all fell behind their leader, such confidence in a woman who held none of her own.

Such simple small wonder, she drifted listless on that rhythm, shifted away from those raging flames they built. Only in greater mystery did she seek their company; only by that strangest was she joined in night's cold by that presence unseeable but for the flame's distant glow.

"Your accent is different," Robin said as he sat.

Amber eyes pulled from those flames, too close, still too close. "Is it now?"

"I keep thinking how you couldn't have been young enough to lose it," he said, "but you don't sound the same."

"Is there a question you want to ask?"

"Will you want one back?"

She let half a smile grow. Clever Shadow. "Tell me this then, if we'd never met before, would you believe I'm high born."

"No." A pause. "And I wouldn't think you're from the city either."

"The accent Mother taught me has its uses." She let the old cadence fall into place. "Oh, *my* lord, I *am* so pleased to make your acquaintance." With a laugh, the mask returned, "But there are so many low-borns in the country; lot harder to pick from a crowd."

Hard to pick from a crowd? What a joke. Perhaps from behind, perhaps if her face hadn't been ruined. Only Robin hadn't cared for the joke, or perhaps he hadn't heard it as one; he only nodded. "What about me then? Or the rest of us?"

"You?" Elysa asked. "You're from the city, or at least arrived young, never worked a ship."

"Really?"

"You don't drop g's." She waved off the question. "A lot of manners for a thief. I'd think tradesman before I thought spy. But then you were a shadow; both could be true."

"My parents could have been merchants," Robin said.

"They could have been, but they weren't."

"But you wouldn't know that." Robin's beak clicked. "If you were only judging my accent."

Wisps of hair brushed her shoulders as she shrugged. "Wouldn't know you're a thief either, come to that. I'd hardly be playing to win if I ignored what I know."

"The others, then." Robin shifted closer. "You wouldn't know them."

Amber eyes turned to those three around the fire. "I hear Southeast from Lane." Perhaps it was a risk, to speak first of the only she had truly listened for that first night. "But that's not most of it. I've not met any dwarves before, might be that which makes her butcher Common."

"Don't be nasty."

An error to let the hunter's feelings for her target slip. "Wyvern didn't teach herself," Elysa continued. "Not her voice but the words she uses. Do you think her teacher was highborn?"

A lie in that question, things she wouldn't have heard if not for the rumours.

"Lord Parsifal?" Robin asked.

Her gaze snapped back to Robin. Had he, too, heard? How very far had those stories spread? "It's true then?"

Those black eyes blinked at the question he evidently hadn't understood. "We saw him on the road, is all."

All? No, something else in that tone, so near a warning, static before a storm.

"Shame then," Elysa said, a turn from the danger, a broken dam's diversion, the trick of pretending to have left without noticing. What lay beyond the warning saved away. "I hadn't thought it the older."

"Who?" Dark eyes softened.

"A certain member of house Mirri has been courting the future Lady Raylor." Her ears flicked, a smile for the memory of that game. "Though all but his first letter have been hidden from her."

"You hid them?" Robin asked.

"Not me." Flame-hued hair wrapped around a finger. "It would take more than my ability to make her seem appealing. So, ravens arrive, and ravens are returned, and the lady knows nothing."

"It doesn't seem very fair." Robin shifted again closer. "Planning someone's life without them."

The sentiment of those free from legacy, an envied sentiment, those words so much easier to hear from one with that freedom.

"She chooses not to play; she thinks she's above it all," Elysa spat, with the ease of that defence from Robin, such a contrast to one with no right to it. "She could have used her advantages, but she doesn't. She could turn her mongrel blood into an army, but she won't. So, all she'll ever be is a pawn, and she won't even notice."

"Or they'll kill her." Frank words, but that voice of mourning. Sympathy for such a stranger?

"They'll try," Elysa admitted. For what point was there in denying that girl's abilities? "I wouldn't give many assassins too much chance against a mage."

"Is she really a mage? I'd heard that but..."

"Oh, she is," Elysa said. "Never lets anyone forget it either; carries a staff like it's the Second Age."

There was a long quiet, only distant popping sparks and chatter she turned her ears from interrupted that chaos of the Wilds. "Hai-Sheira could kill a mage," Robin said at last.

Those dragonkin of far Narreth, scaled and tattooed, that card she'd known Tenor to play but once. That move to win a silent war, those nights she couldn't forget. "They could." Breaths came shallow at the memory. "But a title chaser couldn't afford them."

A rebuttal of little comfort, how fickle, such fear they might tread the same land.

"What about Kitty then?" A turn, a shock to draw her mind back.

"What about her?" Elysa hummed.

"Her accent?" Robin asked. "You never talked about it."

"Oh." Elysa shook her head. "Quite a bit like yours, something older there, something she tried to lose. Was she a caravanner?"

Robins's words came staccato, stumbling things. "I ah, I wouldn't ask."

"Oh?" Elysa pushed into the little space between them.

"Her past is..." Robin shifted back as his voice faltered. "She's fragile."

Fox's ears pressed flat. "Low opinion you have of your leader," Elysa spat.

"No!" Talons dug into the earth. "I'd follow her anywhere."

"But she's too weak to talk to; you must hate her for dragging you out here. We're all going to die, and it will be her fault."

He'd claimed once in the day's games he'd never kill. How his eyes refuted that claim. "I don't think that!"

Still, habits, she couldn't help but prod. "Don't you?"

"No! Nobody could think that about her."

The reason for the issue that contradiction in confidence, a chance for a piece of progress.

Elysa let her eyes drift to their leader. "She does; she thinks you lot do too."

"She can't," he whispered. "We're her friends."

"You won't talk to her!" Elysa snapped. "Wyvern is too damn smitten to see anything past the version of Kitty she's created, and Lane has said six words that have made any bloody sense since I got here. What is she supposed to think?"

"I talk to her every day." He, too, must have known it was a weak rebuttal.

"Not when she needs it; I've seen you. I see how you go quiet whenever she needs to make a choice. You never disagree."

Undergrowth tore beneath those talons. "I follow her; I trust her. And she doubts herself. I know if I criticized her..."

"So you let her assume the worst? Make every decision her responsibility alone?" A fruitless battle to keep her voice calm, such a strange thing, for what reason should she care so to lose composure for those near strangers?

Perhaps Robin, too, saw that struggle, those questions in her eyes. "You don't know us," he said, "you wouldn't understand."

No, she certainly didn't. She couldn't make sense of a great deal of that party, but in some things, she was certain. "Kitty?" she called across the clearing. "Might I speak with you?"

Soft hands grasped her arm. "What are you doing?" Robin hissed, but Elysa only shook him away.

"Is something wrong?" Kitty asked as she crouched by their sides.

"Robin, here, was telling me of how you got this contract," Elysa said. "Seem rash, dragging him and Wyvern out here."

"It was Wyvern's contract." Those first words stumbled forth. "She couldn't do it alone."

"Still, just three people?" Elysa asked, a mock kind of sincerity only allowed in that literal truth. "And are any of you truly trained? Seems irresponsible."

There it came, that piece she'd been looking for, something iron behind those green eyes. "Somebody had to do something. We were the only ones who made it far enough to try."

"Suppose. But why you?"

A step too far, attack too swift, that iron threatened to crumble. "I—" Kitty's voice broke over non-words.

A step back then, a retreat, an invitation to reinforce. "Suppose they do say a witch is worth ten men; suppose that gives us fourteen, then... Well, twelve, if you include Wyvern."

"She's a good fighter," Kitty snapped, a rare bite in those words.

Defence of her people, no, not simple defence, not wounded pride for an attack on them, honest care, an unusual mercenary indeed.

"Suppose we'll see then."

"You will." Kitty stood from the pair. "We're leaving at dawn; be ready."

Elysa didn't quite let the smile show until the pair were again left to their own. But Robin claimed the first word. "What was that about?" he demanded.

"I noticed it during Hail's Rite. And it reminded me, once Tenor asked me why a warrior could fight off a thousand opponents but fall to the Crest just the same as anyone else. He meant it to mean infiltration, to tear my enemies apart from the inside."

"So, you'd tear her apart from the outside?"

"She can't fight her own mind. Nobody can." That dying fire, still too close. "If she doubts herself, she's wrong, even if she made the right choice. If I doubt her, she can defend herself."

Dark eyes cast to the ground, roots beneath his feet dreaded to ruin. "What if coming here wasn't the right choice?"

"It would hardly help us to worry about that now, would it? You said you'll follow her anywhere. At least now she won't falter." Elysa sighed. She could nearly convince herself that was the entire reason. "I've seen her when she forgets to doubt herself. She could be that person every day; that's who you follow, isn't it?"

Something revealed in those words, some few words too many. Robin's eyes lifted. In the dark of night, how their canny danced in dying embers. "You want to know her."

She scoffed. "I think I've proved I do."

"No." Robin shook his head. "You want to know what we see. You want to know why we follow her."

Her ears flattened, how she wished to tie them back. "It's no mystery why Wyvern follows her," she hissed.

That silver bell laugh echoed through the night. "You truly don't know how to talk to people, do you?"

"I was just talking to her," Elysa spat. "And, besides, I could find any lord and know him in ways his own mother doesn't."

"But Kitty isn't a lord; she's just a person," Robin said, "and she's too canny for games."

"Everyone thinks they're too canny; that's why it works."

"But it hasn't worked. Not on her."

Elysa came to her feet. "I don't know why I tried to help you; you hate that I'm right."

Feathers didn't so much as ruffle. "I can admit that you were right. But so am I."

Those ghost-white trees welcomed her as she stormed from that place; her knuckles turned to match those trees at whispered assurances she would soon return, how she hated for Robin to be right on that account as well.

51

Wyvern

Dark Sky Festival: Sixth Day

Sweet-smelling grasses had drawn her from that warm place about the fire, a smell so like that pouch Kitty had emptied those days past. A gift. An apology for hiding the truth for so long. Parsifal's words still flooded her mind; every memory of touch yet screamed dishonour. No, lies of her own mind, her dear Parsifal, an outsider, never again to be what they were, but never a liar, not to her ears. Find another love. His bidding. So pale hands clung tight to those leaves and grasses, an apology for hiding the truth so long. A mind made to hide no longer.

A quest so ready in her mind as she passed those trees of her same colour, a stumble in that quest when that newcomer, that interloper brushed past her to the clearing. Wyvern's feet stalled as Elysa reclaimed a spot at Robin's side. That little patch the pair had claimed far from the fire. Far from the group. No whispers passed as Wyvern diverted from her mission, silence at last as her feet carried her to their side.

"Why don't you two come closer?" she asked, the next question too clear in tone to be left unspoken. "What were you whispering about?"

Venom in those amber eyes, a poison to kill a Salliten. "Mind yours, Oathbreaker."

Herbs fell from Wyvern's hands, how her heart begged retreat, for her return to Kitty's side, but how her legs froze.

"Elysa, don't," Robin warned.

"She likes the truth, doesn't she?"

Wyvern's tongue came unstuck, only too late she realized the warning for her as well. "You don't know what you're talking about."

"Don't I?" Elysa stood from the ground, such a tiny stature against Wyvern's own. "You owe me an answer. Tell me. Do you care at all that you've ruined Parcifal's life?"

"What are you talking about?" Wyvern hissed.

"Do you even care?" Elysa asked, "What a broken engagement means for nobility?"

Something there she should have heard, some knowledge the newcomer shouldn't have had. But hidden from her ears by the other, Robin would have told the newcomer of her lost love, or perhaps Kitty. They thought her a friend; they should have thought it nothing to hide.

Her eyes flicked to Robin but found nothing in those depths. "I know I've dishonoured him." A glance back down to Elysa. "But he's free now. We can both find love."

"Ha! Did he tell you that?" Elysa laughed. "You've ruined him, and yourself if anyone should care."

"Stop!" Leaves crumpled as Robin, too, stood. "You're being awful."

Wyvern shook her head, the tangle of white strands and braids matted deeper with each move. "He'll find someone better; he's high born."

For a moment, Wyvern thought Elysa's nod a concession. "That he is. Not many higher born than the Mirris. But I can't say that helped Lord Tenor's daughter much after her betrothed ran off for another."

In her heart, Wyvern begged for denial as her eyes settled on Robin. His word she knew true; with his word, Elysa's could be just more lies.

Those black eyes bore through Elysa, the click of his beak an echo under that near black moon. "It's true she never married, but—" The words came as a scramble up wasteland dunes. "But it's not a rule; there were other rumours about her; she doesn't matter here."

False assurances fell on deaf ears. "But... he said—" She couldn't breathe.

"Her fate was the best of the three." Elysa's words came a mocking song.

Cold air hit Wyvern's lungs. "Three?"

"Did you think the woman Lord Hunter ran off with was unscathed?" Elysa sat back. "No, she died first. Burned as a witch."

She couldn't help how her eyes found Kitty. How they locked on those green eyes. A cat's eyes. Reflecting starlight in the dark. So perfect. She hadn't the mind to see them turn to worry. Nor ears to hear Robin's admonitions. Those sweet herbs forgotten in the dirt as her legs carried her back past the trees.

Somewhere in that primal darkness, those wild vines tangled her legs, a pain she couldn't feel past her heart as her back slammed to the earth. Those two moons passed the red-leaved treetops. Light being eaten away by darkness. A shiver for that wickedness she could see in them. A new kind of hunger from the dark. A kind of fear she'd never known all those eclipses, all those non-festivals in the Fens, all those years hiding in the fringes. Perhaps she'd never known to look up.

Blood, blood on her hands, blood beneath two rings. Her fault, her fault. Run, run, run from it all.

"Don't run away, Wyvern, come to me. I never left." River's voice, her Brood sister's voice, on the wind, Aspen's as well. Impossible, but yet.

No.

Another voice in her memory alone, Kitty's words always right, always true. She didn't recognize the voices on the wind. They were gone, gone near ten years, soon to be reborn. Dew soaked her back as the wicked chorus became strange, unfamiliar, a predator stripped of its disguise.

Taloned feet through the undergrowth stirred Wyvern to sit up from the soft earth. "Don't listen to her," Robin said as he crouched by Wyvern's side. "She was being cruel."

She couldn't meet those black eyes. "Was she lying?"

"She only said it to hurt you."

"Was she lying?" Wyvern snapped.

The silence grew a long time before Robin shook his head. "No."

That barbarism her people had escaped, her own magic protected, safe as Kitty never could be. A pyre in her mind. "They burned her, the other woman?"

"It was after the Eighth," Robin said. "It had been years since they eloped."

Those words carried none of the comforts Robin must have hoped for. Only a single thought in her mind. "She would never be safe."

"Kitty?" Robin asked.

But Wyvern had no response. No gift of apology to give for keeping that secret.

"I wouldn't happen here," Robin said. "Elysa said it like that so you would think it, but it isn't true. I only had to see Parcifal once to know he isn't cruel like Lady Tenor. Or Lady Hunter, come to that."

"He'll hate me for it."

A shuffle of torn leaves as Robin shifted closer. "You aren't nobility; you didn't know." The feathers of his arm brushed the scales of hers. "He knew what a broken engagement meant, but he didn't tell you. He wouldn't have wanted it to change your mind."

"I can't—" Words Wyvern had no end to caught in her throat as Kitty stepped through the trees.

"Are you alright?" Those words and eyes for Wyvern alone.

Only Wyvern had no words to return.

"We were just hunting." A lie, how smooth, how easily it fell from Robin's mouth. "We'll be right back."

Ebony curls danced as Kitty tipped her head. A standoff in silence for but a moment before she turned back to the camp.

"How do you do that?" Wyvern asked long after they were once more alone. "How can you lie to her?"

"It's not a lie if she knows," he said. "She doesn't believe we're hunting."

Her hands curled into the dirt. There was nothing to hold, nothing solid to keep her in place. "Why say it?"

"It means I can't tell her." His body turned. A trap, nowhere to look but his eyes. "Because I can't tell her you love her. It's not my secret."

Wyvern shifted away, and that trap released without a hint of a fight. "You told Elysa. She knew to say those things."

Robin shook his head. "I told her nothing. I didn't have to. Anyone could see the two of you."

Night air stilled. "Two?"

"I can't say it," Robin said as he came to his feet. "As I said, it's not my secret."

How hot the air grew as Robin left that place, or perhaps it was simply the blood that rushed to Wyvern's cheeks. It was kind, what he tried to do. Even such little hope. The mind she had made up such a short time ago shattered, but that such little hope, a ladder from the pit. For that night, it could be enough. When their job finished, when the interloper had moved on, then she could see more than a pyre in Kitty's smile. Then she could tell her.

52

Kitty

Dark Sky Festival: Sixth Day

Their end grew near. That not music of Never Song deafening in her ears. Those trails they trod split in dawn's early light, turned away from the routes she was gifted. The feel of that new trail, younger and older than those Aroch traced. An abandoned hall with footprints in the dust.

She led no games as the sun passed its peak, nor did her group break that quiet; perhaps they, too, felt the end's portent. But a settled kind of quiet, something shifted after the row she knew inevitable. A tension line snapped, but a war turned cold. The peace between rebellions, how easily a single word could end it too.

And those scraps of words she couldn't help but hear, those meanings that needed no context. Had Robin known she would overhear when he gave voice to Wyvern's mind? Or had he hoped she would? A spy's instinct for lines, a thief's for crossing them.

A line of thought cut. The air smelled of blood and the forest was silent.

At her hand, horses slowed in a mismatched jolt before the trees ended. "Robin." Kitty nodded to the tree line.

Without a word, Robin slid from Ria's back, talons designed for another wood made not a sound as he crept ahead.

At his wave, Kitty dismounted and edged to her friend's side. A caution proved unnecessary; all who had once stood at the tunnel's mouth lay dead, rotting in the evening sun.

"Oh, dear." Elysa's voice came from Kitty's back. "Seems the Bastards got here first."

Crunching leaves portended Wyvern's arrival. "It's a cave." Her voice came breathless.

"Onari tunnel," Lane corrected.

A correction that finally turned Kitty's eyes from the dead. "How do you know?"

With neither warning nor apparent caution, the blue-eyed girl strode past the dead and lay a hand on the stone entry. "It's carved."

That tiny hand traced a curve, a perfect smoothness – anathema to the natural, untouched by centuries. But that ancient stonework, a worry far greater than the name. The stories that remained of that underground kingdom, of twisting traps and spirals to oblivion. A place for its makers alone, so fierce a challenge those descendants could boast but a corner. A descendant to stand at that darkness's edge and know its name.

"I–I don't..." Wyvern stumbled over her words.

All manner of stories forgotten, for Kitty needed none to remember her companion who leaned through windows, who stood in the rain.

Wyvern's head shook as she stepped backwards. "I can't?"

"Wyvern, I—" No, intention irrelevant; Kitty knew then those words Wyvern dared not give voice, those words that made hers unfair. "We need you," Kitty said.

If Wyvern's face could lose colour. "I'm sorry, I can't."

"If she won't," Elysa said, "neither will I."

Kitty's ears flattened. "I'm not sure you're helping."

"I'm not dying for a coward."

Wyvern rounded on Elysa. "You could never understand."

Kitty placed herself between the two. "Enough, Elysa, watch the cave."

Perhaps a surprise, the word her mind grasped for at that moment, after a fight never came as her words were followed. A reeling moment, a missed step as she was left with Wyvern.

"You have to come," Kitty said.

Wyvern crossed her arms while her eyes still tracked Elysa's path. "I can't go in there."

A mind's fire lanced up Kitty's arm as she placed a hand on Wyvern. "Look at me," Kitty said. "You chose this job, and now you have to follow through."

"Other people are already here."

"Do you trust them?" Kitty turned from her company as her feet carried her to the cave. A bite she had thought dead forever entered her voice, for but a moment, she needed no assurance for her choice. "I can't make you come along, but if you don't, then you'd better be gone when I get back."

Kitty never saw the signs Wyvern made as they gathered at the entry, but she could feel the press of all her companions as she pulled forth her wand and stepped into blackness.

53

Belladonna

Dark Sky Festival: Seventh Day

When Helena rose that night, only a sliver of light would remain, and as she reached her peak, even that would be inevitably consumed by her sister's darkness. Only when she set the same as every day, when the sun returned and proved that light hadn't been lost forever, would the celebrations begin. She'd have her answers long before that first light of dawn.

It wouldn't be long; the sun hung low, and the last golden rays trickled through ocean-facing windows. It had been a day of rest, readying her mana for what was to come. By tradition, it should have appeared the same for all, rest and settling early on that night of the darkest sky, but even as dusk fell, nobles scurried about. Layabouts given purpose by a wedding that should have been Belladonna's challenge for the season, a challenge pushed to the wayside, superseded by circumstances, and ignored by will.

So different from the days and weeks proceeding, Eugenia was impossible to ignore when aimless wandering brought Belladonna into her path. Like a summer storm tearing through the halls, her face just as fierce. Jewel-toned ladies flitted around her debris to the cyclone that parted crowds.

Belladonna nearly stopped as she came upon them; darkness hadn't yet fallen; surely she had time enough to pull victory from that never-finished argument. All the better that the sycophants could witness. She readied herself for it and smiled, an ingenuine thing, when she caught her opponent's eyes.

A plan halted as elven ears caught a sound, a single choked sob for whence the women had come. That pattern of the summer reared its head, and Belladonna once more ousted Eugenia from her priorities. With hitched gasps, the ladies parted as Belladonna pushed through their party. She knew the cries of that voice.

She'd known them for years.

Ankia sat huddled on the ground, her back to the stone and knees to her chest, ocean blue skirts rumpled where flame-scarred hands pulled them over her eyes. A wig of auburn hair lay by her feet. She made no sound after the first, scarcely moved but for how her shoulders shook.

"Ani?" Belladonna approached slowly.

Anika startled and dropped her skirts in favour of clutching her scalp. Her hands only lowered slightly when her eyes caught Belladonna. Fresh tears fell. "I wish the Dark Mother had taken me." Fingernails dug into scarred flesh. "Watching the sky would be better than this!"

Belladonna didn't feel the cold when she dropped her staff, nor the stone when she fell to her knees, not until she grasped her friend's hands — until Anika's warmth filled that void. "What did that woman say to you?"

"It doesn't matter." Anika shook her head. "she's right. There was no point in Calling me; no one would want me."

"That's not true."

"Isn't it? I couldn't beg my way into a dance. Even you've gone off me." Anika pulled her hands away. "I can't blame you; you aren't a lonely little kid anymore. You've outgrown me, and you've more important things than sitting with me."

"That's not-" Not true? Not in any way she should have known about. Not unless she, just like Edmund, had been counting down the days until winter. An opposite thought for the same date. Belladonna sat at her friend's side and leaned close until their arms touched. "It's been a bad summer."

Anika wiped tears on silk sleeves. "She told me to stay away from the wedding tomorrow. She said I'd be a distraction at the temple."

"You don't have to listen." Belladonna pulled the wig from the ground; tangled and kicked through dust, her fingers worked through the disarrayed strands.

"She doesn't want me there," Anika said, "I don't want to be anywhere I'm not wanted."

"I won't be there either then," Belladonna handed her friend the tidied wig. "Let her explain that to my father."

The shadow of a smile crossed Anika's face as she put it back in place. "were you ever going to be? I thought they were going to have to dress up the elf who looks like you again. Like the painting."

Erh'henni in a temple; it almost made her laugh until she remembered. They couldn't, not anymore. Anymore? She had said again.

"What painting?"

"From when Alyria stopped aging. They couldn't find you. I told them you were sick, and they had her pose instead." Anika stood; a last fading ray of sun caught her skirt and danced, like auroras over the open sea, before vanishing to that growing dark. Those first stars caught in the tears her eyes hadn't yet shed – constellations that grew together and threatened to spill forth. Who could ever see the scars when she could capture all the sky in those eyes? "I'm going to bed."

Belladonna pushed herself upright; her staff still abandoned on the ground. "I'd like to spend more time with you again," Belladonna said, "after the wedding." After her season's problem was resolved.

Anika smiled, a true, genuine thing even against the something else that lingered in her eyes. "Try not to stay out too late. It's still bad luck until tomorrow."

There was no reason to refute that superstition. The sun was gone; it was time.

54

Wyvern

Dark Sky Festival: Seventh Day

Those weeks on the road to Gentea, those camps in darkness under the bright moon, there was a rightness there, a justice to that dark. No right could live that cave's black. A pressing thing; Wyvern couldn't breathe for the closing walls. Closer, every shift they got closer. No air. So hot. How could it get so hot in that place the sun had forgotten? A breath-like drowning. Had water risen so fast? Too close. Water raised to her back; no, only sweat dripped from her hair. Walls pressed closer, and air vanished. It smelled like blood.

Oozed through her fingers, crimson under rings. So much, too much, the Fens stained red. River, don't go.

A feathered wall hit her chest. Robin. Why had he stopped?

Light, a pinprick far ahead, walls retreated their attack, an instant thing as if they'd never pressed so close. A beacon against the dark that still shrouded all. Only the absence of Robin's touch had Wyvern walk again.

The light, salvation from the dark, such relief to have her forget the danger of that place. Her eyes danced up high cavern walls; pillars like great oaks stood proud. Those walls – smooth as poured steel; the ceiling vanished from the darkness above. An impossible place. Such was its splendour she near forgot to look down, nearly missed the carnage of bodies. Rag-dressed humans lay dead around the bodies of a grey Salliten and one of her own kind matched in bleeding branch armour.

She thought the wreckage all rags, mere bodies, dead in another's wake until Kitty stepped into the light, and cultists stood from where they lay next to their dead compatriots.

A trap.

Wyvern struck before the walls remembered to close; she pushed past Kitty and Robin. She called back to the place of power, from whence their creator pulled the magic to make her people, to that thing that had stolen all choice of vocation – that marked her with pewter. To black flames, from across realms, they wreathed her sword.

The nearest was cleft at their waist before they could think to hurt Kitty.

They came as a wave; gouts of flame decimated their numbers, and yet still they came for her. Her sword swung with no doubt, each strike with the power of the Fensmirri behind it. No grace, no swordsman's dance. Strength alone was her guide. Strongest, highest, each swing a testament to the Elders' truth.

And still, they came.

She could never be an archer, not when a few dozen steps could rend all shape from her foes, nor could she trust herself to pull a wall of black flame with any aim. But with a sword, she had assurances: she would never hit a friend by mistake; she would always be close enough to see her enemy's face.

Faces full of rage in one moment slackened to nothing beneath blade and flame.

The man came with a swiftness opposite strength. He ducked beneath the hefted blade, twin daggers so like teeth as they ripped across scaled arms.

Too close, she tried to raise her blade to him, to kick him back, but with every failed strike, another cut claimed its tithe.

The menace mistimed; last she saw his blade moving, not a second to heft her sword, she let it clatter to the stone as she drove a fist through the cultist's nose.

She didn't see the witch until his wand was raised. She braced; a finality she knew in Kitty, she wouldn't make it to ten years; who would speak for them? Who might be close enough? A gout of flame born in an instant died the next as a tiny hand yanked the witch's wrist.

An odd moment of incomprehension, as the witch's eyes turned to Lane, hung from his arm. A moment cut as Elysa sprung from shadows to plunge a knife through his neck. The question on his lips drowned in blood.

Elysa's raised brow turned to a smirk as Wyvern caught her eye. A stance of combat turned to a bow.

Wyvern gave no response to the irritant as her sword came down across the final foe.

All that remained was that same quiet she knew well — that presence in the un-quiet of a stone hall dripping with viscera.

"Mirri's Bastards didn't clear the room?" Wyvern asked.

"They did." Lane pulled herself from the dead witch. Her hand pressed hard to the old wound. "More came."

Wyvern's eyes fell on that matched armour. "They left them here?"

Robin shook his head. "They would have."

Kitty's delicate steps made their own echoes. "I see four tunnels. Lane, do you know where the children might be?"

When Lane's only answer was a shrug, Robin's voice rang out. "Don't you see the glow from that one?"

For all she tried, Wyvern could see nothing but black from where he pointed.

"I don't see anything," Kitty said.

"Colour? asked Lane over Kitty's denial.

Wyvern knew not the meaning of the look the two shared before Robin spoke. "Grey, maybe, I can't describe it."

Lane nodded. "That way."

Only her heart's pull to Kitty had Wyvern follow. Still, it froze over cold as she did. It shouldn't have mattered. She had already stepped past the threshold, already broken the tenet for the first time in ten years, but every step down below creation burned her mind. In a battle of attrition, her heart gave more – as they all drove deeper, back to the darkness.

55

Kitty

Dark Sky Festival: Seventh Day

Flames. All at once, they sprung from that primal dark. And with them, torch-bearing cultists raced forward.

She called for flames her own, for lightning, for ice. That last drop of mana warded against her grasping, too jealousy-guarded, so far beyond her reach.

A body slammed against her as each spell failed. Chaos and trampling feet, distant echoes, her head meeting the ground.

A foot slammed into her wrist. It was nothing, a memory of less, except for the cold shock as her wand slipped from her grasp.

Had she screamed as that piece was lost? Was it her own voice that cried in the sound of no language?

Metal against stone, a sword fell. The clatter of hatches to the ground. Feathers splayed where Robin fell.

Kitty's only thought, in blurred sights and dull sound, was of a desperate flight to reach him.

Not again.

That regret as a boot met her head.

As blackness took hold once more, she noticed it. Lucidity in delirium. Three bodies on the ground. Three weapons dropped. Two were missing from their number.

56

Elysa

Dark Sky Festival: Seventh Day

Three ahead and one behind, in blackness, footsteps made their own pattering chorus. Elysa needn't see. A failed first draft, perhaps; how her kind failed against Castillas in grace and sight, but how their ears matched. That five-part symphony tapping, tapping, echoing off walls. A map of where they'd been.

Her ears turned when those steps behind grew faint. Scarred fingers pressed to the wall, the map of sounds ignored as Elysa backed away from her companions, each step up the slope measured until her fingers found the tunnel Lane disappeared down.

The darkness in that tunnel wasn't total. Veins of glowing blue cut, like roots, through stone, blue opal they called it, all the same as those from old Narreth, but for in that total darkness, that black beyond the darkest sky, those blue veins gave their glow, sent a frozen cast to that tunnel.

Elysa slowed when she spied the dwarven girl. Lane's hand traced the pulsing veins of her eye's same hue; the other clutched to that feather amulet. Her mouth moved, but with no curse or incantation, no tongue of Onari decent. What echoed down the tunnel was the sound of no language, cracking ice, a snake's hiss, rain over tile rooves.

Knives came to Elysa's hands as she stepped from the shadow. "Oi! What are you doing?"

Lane flinched, a jolt to send her stumbling against the wall, to tear that blue feather from her neck. "You found 'ere?"

"Followed you." Elysa closed the space between them; the grin she fought to keep at bay burned as Lane's eyes widened. "What are you?"

"Your meaning?"

"Elody's point, Nox, most recently High Crest..." Elysa let the list flow. "You are well-travelled, but it seems death follows you. How do you do it?"

That was the crux of it, the reason she found herself complicit in a dragon's schemes. How could a girl of no apparent magic cause such swaths of death?

Lane's back pressed to that glowing wall. "You're 'ere to kill me?"

Elysa stepped back from the girl. "Ellivar certainly thinks I will," she said.

That recognition she'd hoped for danced across Lane's eyes, but that startled fear fell away with it. "A Seer sent you." Lane nodded.

She knew? Or at least she had known of the White dragon's intentions; perhaps then, she knew also the reasons the Seer refused to disclose.

"But I haven't decided yet, so I want to know—"

"You can'ne kill me today," Lane interrupted. Her emphasis all wrong for a plea, not the tone to beg. A thing familiar to another life – letters of regrets, notes asking to reschedule: delays instead of cancellations.

Those words, so near her expectations, but for that disparate element, a stair she'd forgotten to count. Elysa let an eyebrow raise. "Can't I?"

"Not in Ellivar's name." Lane shook her head. "Not strong enough, not close enough. She does'ne understand. You don't know Her daughter's name." Those blue eyes met Elysa's, a pinning gaze, a matching hue to the glow clashing all the same. But what caught most was one word: how Lane's accent had changed for the word 'her' as if it wasn't to be trampled by her natural speech, as if it was foreign, as if it was a name. "We can'ne let them win. The Reckoning's already too early."

She let her blades lower just a hair. "You will have to explain that one," Elysa said.

Lane's shoulders dropped. Had there been any more light, perhaps she would have pulled out that book. "They would bring the old gods to this world." She shook her head. "Should'ne be possible, should'ne be champions names for twenty years."

Old gods. Near a foreign term, near blessed ignorance of such affairs, she'd heard that term before. Not so long ago. Some vestigial name for one who mages claimed dead and replaced. She shook her head against the useless tale. "You'd have me believe this? That I should believe that some imaginary gods are coming to destroy us?"

Those blue eyes turned on Elysa, so much deeper, cannier than all those nights around the fire. "You do," she said, "you can'ne 'ate what does'ne exist."

No defence to those words. No retort nor rebuttal. She stood, a butterfly pinned to the wall, indignant display, every marking to be shown. No wisdom against those cuts. And in the absence of wisdom, of defence, Elysa chose that other option.

Knuckles turned white as she once more raised her daggers. "And the death that follows you, is this some cult's fault too? Or maybe it's some Old Gods' then?"

What tightness had left Lane's shoulders returned in force as the girl scratched at her hand. "Uh, nay," she said as scabs reopened. Drops made black by the glow trailed down to that feather.

"Then explain that." Elysa's voice was harder than she had, perhaps, intended.

"I can'ne."

Elysa advanced on Lane once more. "I try to keep my goals from aligning with dragons. If she didn't want you dead, you already would be." Elysa said, "I don't know what your trick is. But I'd put my life on it that, from here, I can move faster."

Copper scent filled that tunnel. "I have a s—"

Her voice was cut by the ring of clashing steel. Elysa's body turned faster than her ears, impatient to a fault, but she never rushed, never left a game unfinished. Still, her legs carried her back, back to where companions travelled through the darkness.

57

BELLADONNA

Dark Sky Festival: Helena's Triumph

Past every claim, every lie of Belladonna's life, were two truths: Alyria kept her in Lyria, and Anika kept her sane. In that world of nobles, rebellions and rings, a great many things could boast little sanity; in dragon riding, there was none.

To her eyes and her mind, there was no understanding of the true size of an elder dragon. Even as Belladonna clung to Vix's waist against screaming winds; she couldn't look over his wing's expanse without her eyes burning, a pressure in her head beyond wind's bite. Under that barest ring of silver moonlight, black scales could be seen only when wings rose to block auroras and stars above.

And by those deafening winds did Belladonna understand, at last, why Draconic was a language between minds. If she had called out to her friends, they could never have hoped to hear before her words were lost to the wind.

Long grey sleeves flapped in that created wind. The repaired stitching caught the last slivers of Helena's light just the same they had before the damage had been done; perhaps new stitches had no need for the memories of the old; somewhere on her skirt, five of those stitches were out of line.

Perhaps her plan had been half mad from the start, she couldn't have dreamed of finding a ship in the great wide ocean. But a ship that clung to the shore? She hadn't thought it a mad plan until Xaxirion took to the sky when the city and all the ships around it faded away and the wind became her only companion.

Time became as unreal as it had been in her ancestor's homeland. She had guessed north for their direction; had she been wrong, there wouldn't be another soul to see until they hit Northguard.

So far from flame, so much in air's domain, its essence whispered to her in words without words. If she gave up every piece of her natural aptitude, she could fly herself.

Temptations were cut short by Vix's hand on her thigh. There was a ship on the horizon.

That ship, lumber made damnation, a lonely thing hours or minutes north from the city ports, grew from a speck on the horizon. The smell of rot, of those waiting hands, found her past the rushing air. As they closed on the wretched thing, its mast showed their patches and tears, its wood grey with spotted mould. She Who Waited there surely did not wait long.

Perhaps her first thought had been wrong. Perhaps there was sanity in the dragon riders before the prince; perhaps the dragon she rode was insane. Darkness hid how high he had flown until Xaxirion circled the ship and dove. Belladonna's heart pushed through her throat as, in a single motion, Xaxirion slowed his descent and transformed into the shape of a mortal.

Belladonna found nothing but a graceless roll as her hip slammed against the rotten deck.

"For an Elf," Xax said as his eyes turned to the western horizon, to roiling blackness that blocked dancing light, "I'd expect more grace. You have ten minutes."

Belladonna shouldn't have expected their entrance to grant any more than a moment of confusion, a moment wasted grasping for a retort, as horns sounded into blackness and the deck filled with swarming guards.

No light but that little of the sky touched the ship, not flame nor hope of spark. Bizarre superstitions, a parody of irony that, on that night, it had protected those guards. Wrongfooted, dizzy from travel, Belladonna stumbled against that first hurdle.

Before her on deck, Vix and Xax held attention with fists, claws, and a sword passed in a crimson relay.

Another stumble as she reached for hold with any spell she knew, a shock not in finding nothing. A sensation so familiar to sneaking under the walls, so wrong for a ship, an array on each corner. Barrels of earth.

A shock with a meaning. A meaning come to the light as earth raised around Belladonna at a command not her own. It was only as dirt formed to stone did she see the Bound Mage with his raven-branded cheek and raven-crested amulet.

That first volley of stones bounced against walls of air. The second broke through. Bruises raised as stones struck her arms, and tore through wool sleeves. Cries from the deck, stranger's cries, a spell never taught to discriminate.

Belladonna wouldn't be caught again, but there was nothing her will could bend, nothing she could make alone. "Xax!" she cried as a third volley rose.

He hadn't needed further instruction to understand. Tiny against his form moments before, a dragon of red scales rose from the deck. None were so unlucky to touch that breath that raked down the ship's centre. But Belladonna hadn't needed a stranger's lack of luck.

The warmth of home gathered as she pulled those flames, a dancer's ribbon to her staff, a wave like the tides she sent at the bound mage. That wave was blocked by a wall of earth. She never made a second wave; salvation in flames was ripped from her grasp and ordered to die.

Belladonna's cry of outrage cut as that stone wall rushed forth and stole the air from her lungs as it sent her flying over the ship's edge.

Frigid cold and darkness beyond the night. Wools, soaked through, dragged her from that precious surface. It sang a song she knew not. Beyond a washing bucket, beyond a hill's flash flood. A vastness beyond the mind. A stranger.

She knew her friend in flame, curled in a pile for hearth's warmth, blazes set to aid a lie; she knew fire's curls, its contours. Her first friend.

How strange to die by its opposite, a mage drowned. Stubbornness, to keep loyalty as the Fae would, as the first would.

Something moved in that far-off dark, a glitter of bronze, a lure of treasure, a sparkle of sunlight. Until those eyes opened, that colour of sickness for a name Xaxirion refused to speak. Beware, beware the Breaker's beast.

Between beast and bargain, Belladonna chose the latter. She reached for that frigid stranger all around, a handshake for a friend. The Shivering Sea reached back. The pull of the moon, the pull of the tide, breaths her chest burned for. Riptide's hidden blade, a flow frozen against hot blood. A wildfire tamed, those hottest flames cooled. How her heart broke as those furthest, most favourite, doors sealed forever.

Her staff swung through resistant sea, and unending black lifted as Belladonna was carried forth, risen in a column of the sea. A torrent crashed around her as her feet landed once more on that deck.

Her adversary had turned his back, a hand stretched to harry a dragon with his own flame. A mistake. He never saw that ice Belladonna pulled from her clothes – not until the spear pierced the bound boy's chest.

A peace in silence that couldn't last a moment. The scream of a lungless thing came from the sea as many dozen clawed hands grasped and crawled up those rotting ship walls.

Only as she readied her staff did Belladonna quite realize she hadn't mana to spend lest she lose it all. Her heart stopped for a moment of panic before her arm was grabbed. Not a clawed hand, rather warmer, rather more familiar. "I can give you four minutes," Vix yelled as she shoved Belladonna to the door. "Find your person!"

Her nature reached to argue, but as that storm grew close, she ducked below deck.

Had Belladonna thought the smell above deck was overpowering, she learned that day she had never known the meaning of the word. There was order to that place, even rows of cells evenly spaced; only the yelling of prisoners defied that order.

Nadia's once black hair lay streaked with new white as it covered her face. At the sound of footsteps, the woman pushed to the back of her cell. "What do you want?" her fists raised.

That sight – her ally cowering away – the coming storm, the creatures beyond their essence vanished from Belladonna's mind. She stepped close to that cell. "We intended to rescue you."

Nadia's eyes, so drained of colour, found new light as she ran to Belladonna. Her hands grasped damp wool through the bars. "Merciful Mother," she sobbed. "Beth and Isobel, they ran."

"We found them," Belladonna said as she lowered herself and the shaking Nadia to the ground, moulded planks left their patches on her ruined skirt. "They're with John."

Sobs grew ever louder. "I thought you'd abandoned us."

Belladonna pulled Nadia from her chest to catch her eyes. "Why?"

"Your man – he said not to bring any others after the last group. He said you wanted to stop."

It wasn't possible, and yet... "When did you last see him?"

Nadia shook her head. "He wanted to know where we'd be during the run; I told him we'd be at home like always."

Why?

A question she hadn't even the time to voice as Xaxirion burst down those stairs. In a breath, he tore that cell door from its hinges. "We have to go." Xax grabbed Belladonna and Nadia both. "He's here."

Over the screaming of her mind, she could hardly feel Nadia's arms around her waist. She didn't dare look when that great shape moved beneath the water, and a ship of twice-dammed souls vanished into the blackness where no one at all waited.

58

Elysa

Dark Sky Festival: Helena's Triumph

Mother had spoken, so many times before she was taken, of that bond between witch and wand, of her conduit, more precious than a limb, more painful to lose. In the light of dying torches discarded in that chamber, Elysa rolled Kitty's familiar wand between her fingers.

No bodies, only blood told of where they fell, defeated, not dead; those scant crimson stains were too small to proclaim that just yet. Amongst those torches left lit on the ground lay her allies' weapons, a sword and hatchets, the wand she held, discarded without a care.

"When does an ambush not end in death?" she mused.

"Capture." Lane crouched over the stains. "They were dragged from 'ere."

"And why does a cult take prisoners?"

The answer she already knew rang through Lane's voice. "Sacrifice."

Elysa tucked away the wand, a precious thing. "Suppose I believe that your cult can do what you say they can."

"They believe."

Her teeth clenched, all the wicked done for belief; what a sight for it to be right. "Suppose they can, then. Why do they need sacrifices?"

"Ellivar has a list to end the Reckoning," Lane said. The book made a dull thud as she pulled it out. "Of Old gods, of New, and of Dragons."

Prophecy, that trade of fools. Elysa herself, the greatest for having staked herself to one. It would seem in the pursuit of theirs the cult had bet on another type of fool falling for their trap. Innocents stolen away, what perfect bait for heroes.

"And I suppose the key that locks the door can open it as well?" It could have been such an easier thing to lean on the simple, to spit and call nonsense, but faith nurtured in animosity alone gave no room for the comfort of simplicity. "Out with it then. Does your little cult have these?"

"The New God's Champion who kills dragons." Lane nodded, then hesitated.

"You passed a dragon rider. What odds would you give the cult finding them too?" Elysa asked.

Lane gave no answer to that question and only flipped a page. "A witch should'ne be enough."

"You care so much that they truly believe, but you think they'll follow Ellivar's rules?" Elysa asked.

"Can'ne be broken." Lane shook her head in a flurry of flipped pages. "Nay, easier to open. If they 'ave the dragon rider, they do."

No good in gods; dragons just as well. Confounding things, all best left to those debates of fools. But what a witch couldn't fight could be solved with no knives. Elysa scoffed. "I suppose you want to go after them then."

"We can'ne let them succeed." Those blue eyes caught her own eyes in a way they never had before. "You 'ate the gods. 'elp me fight them."

And she'd thought none of them could play.

Elysa stood from her crouch; she let the chuckle echo barely more than a breath. "Go on then; you can see in the dark. Lead the way."

As torchlight lit their backs, Lane's voice came as a whisper. "You plan to kill me."

"Not at the moment."

"If we can'ne stop them, could you? In Her daughter's name? Could you mean it?"

Darkness overtook them before Elysa could find honest words. "I think you'd better hope your trick holds down here."

59

Belladonna

Dark Sky Festival: Helena's Triumph

Skies lightened over the lightless castle as Belladonna awoke to her grandmother's voice. Cold stone pressed to her back, gatekeeper to a stiffness she hadn't known for years. "Av'vella, you must wake."

The elder Elf stood over her in the passage; she hadn't made it back to her chamber; what a disappointment Belladonna knew herself to be – a mage too afraid to face the one who waited there. The blow doubled for that way her grandmother always knew the coward she would become.

That cold lingered through the numbness as her grandmother led her, hushed to silence through the tower. That little mana sleep had afforded rose as that familiar door opened. A coward's defence, for no traitor waited in her chambers, not that day, not when all would be preparing for the wedding. "You didn't warn me," Belladonna said as her soiled dress dropped.

An'neira pulled a gown of green brocade from its display. "No, I didn't."

Belladonna allowed the gown to be threaded over sea-stained underclothes. Perhaps another day, it would have felt a betrayal, such a fine thing, such a work she'd once called love, to be ruined after but one use. But the hand it came from – one betrayal couldn't match another. "You could have."

"No, dear." An'neira's fingers brushed through Belladonna's hair. "There was nothing you could do. A friend can be a fine thing, but you couldn't save her."

Belladonna's staff dropped as she spun. "Who?"

An'neira's eyes widened. "I see. I'm too early."

"Who couldn't I save?"

"I can tell you tomorrow, but, by then, you'll know," she said.

"If I tell you now—"

"Grandmother, if you don't tell me, I'll—" Belladonna faltered. A Seer wouldn't know a lie, but her grandmother would; what true leverage did she have? "If you don't tell me..."

An'neira nodded before she walked to the door. "We may speak after the wedding."

"Lord Tenor knows Mother had two names." A bone-deep exhaustion she'd thought impossible just months ago drove those words to honesty. "Tell me, or I'll tell him why."

For a long time, or perhaps only moments, there was silence between two frozen elves, a stalemate, a tide rising to a fight, a portent that felt like an end. A match of stares shattered by temple bells.

"Now I may tell you," An'neira said as she held open the door. "I am sorry about Anika."

Belladonna had neither time nor mind to retrieve her staff before her feet carried her down that spiral star case. A journey to her friend's chambers never finished for the voices that turned muscle to stone. "Common Ivir, or do you want Thymiran to know your doubts?"

"I thought she was supposed the be an Elf."

"Did you see anyone else in the tower last night? Don't cause trouble."

Her only strength to stop shaking enough to peek past that wall, hair and scales of matching blue, arms wrapped with tattoos, fire named itself no longer an ally for how her heart burned as two Hai'sheira stepped from Anika's door and vanished down the tower.

Belladonna's hand clutched for an absent staff as shaking fingers pushed open her friend's door. Sobs, so far from silent, escaped as she saw all that remained.

She could have been asleep, her eyes fixed closed. Perhaps Anika had never woken up. If Belladonna could pray for the past, she'd sing that she didn't. An illusion of sleep shattered by the stain of crimson that grew from her throat.

No dozen words. The gods themselves could have heard her scream.

Hairpins drew blood as Belladonna strode through the gardens, all celebration of her father's new marriage lost to the red of her sight. She saw them, all smiles, as they took their place at the head table; for all the guards they had, nobody stopped Belladonna as she approached.

Reverie of a wedding she should have dreaded more. Weeks she'd had warning, warning but no mind, she'd thought herself safe after that first failure; she thought she had longer. A fool.

"Donna," Alyria began to cheer as she came to her place.

But Belladonna hadn't that slightest intention of finding her own. Eugenia's dinner knife found its way to Belladonna's hand and slammed between the bride's fingers. "You wicked bitch!" Belladonna spat.

"Belladonna!" Her father cried as guards shuffled between the revelry.

"Anika was the best person in this damnable court! You couldn't give up after your first try?"

"I'm sure I don't—" Eugenia started. Her ivory gown rumpled from how she flinched. How brilliant it would look in red.

"That was you?" Alyria's voice came soft under the yelling, a hurt her sister should have heard.

"That's enough!" Lord Raylor stood, stern-faced, from his seat. "I'll hear no more of this. Belladonna, you're excused."

Those words she'd fought for every dinner, every ill-conceived luncheon, were hollow for unfinished intentions. She leaned further over Eugenia's quivering form. "Did you think I wouldn't know it was you? Little Elf too stupid to put it together?" she asked as her eyes held the Human's. "You *can't* hurt me. My grace reached only so far as you *failed* to hurt my sister."

Eugenia leapt from her seat. "She—" The coward fumbled her words. "She threatened me! Guards!"

Plate mail steps echoed through the garden, and all who might have blocked them, might have ever taken the right side, stepped aside. How Belladonna wished she could burn the lot of them.

As her heart yearned for that forgotten staff, a miracle of the old songs, carved Ashtana pressed to her hand.

"A Seer wishes you'd hold onto this," came Lord Tenor's whisper before he clapped. "I'm sure all that isn't necessary; the young lady's had a shock, is all."

"This is a family matter," Lord Raylor growled.

"I'm sure. And this is a day for celebration." Belladonna couldn't help but turn her eyes to the Spy Lord. "But a sweet girl has died today, and we must make allowances."

A murmur rippled through the crowd. It was news to them then. Of course, they hadn't noticed her absence. Hadn't paid attention to her. Had Belladonna done any better those past weeks?

Lord Raylor sat back in his seat. His face gave no reaction to Anika's death, but then he didn't care, did he? None of them did. Not one of the damnable crowd had the decency to show grief. "Lady Belladonna may apologize to her stepmother."

Belladonna scoffed as she turned. "I've been excused."

As her feet carried her from the party, as roses gave way to wild trees, Belladonna wished those footsteps behind her weren't so familiar.

60

Kitty

Dark Sky Festival: Helena's Triumph

Wakefulness came as lighting against a stone floor. Her eyes opened to Robin's as he crouched over her. She needn't ask the question; the bars behind his head and those other cages all around told her so much. And so much more she needn't eyes to see.

Her wand was gone.

The absence of a thing – it was a poor excuse for a leader who thought of that first. She felt such hot shame that her first thought hadn't been for her people, but still, she couldn't turn her mind from it. Its feel gone, not merely from her hand, not the biting itch of it stuffed away in a pack. Gone. Lost. Perhaps forever. Her mind was a shameful mess, but still, she knew her words couldn't be of mourning, not for lost power. "Are you two okay?" she asked instead.

"We're alright." Robin shifted against the confines, mere inches that gave Kitty view of Wyvern, her nose bloodied, trails of crimson running down those pale arms.

Her nightmare, her fault, her half-made scheme to prevent that fear brought it to light. She couldn't help the tears that burned hot as she came to her feet.

Her ears twitched as tiny sobs suffused the suffocating air – those children they'd sought to rescue. But under that sorrow, silence, other cages lay free of tears, far across the wide cavern, stripped of their armour, a group of five turned to three, led by a blue Nestia.

And closer, still all alone, a man Kitty had seen before in an entirely different cage. It must have been his dragon in the forest.

Five turned three, a mirrored circumstance. She searched the cages beyond once more, but those missing faces eluded her. "They're not here," she said.

"Who?" Wyvern pushed to her side.

"Lane and Elysa, they weren't at the ambush."

Wyvern spat, "Elysa probably ran off."

"Maybe," Kitty said, "but Lane wouldn't. She... She had ideas about this."

"They could have got lost," Robin offered, but Kitty hardly heard.

"I'm sorry," she whispered. "I'm sorry for dragging you two into this."

"It was my idea," Wyvern said.

But Kitty only shook her head. "I'm the leader; that means I'm supposed to keep you safe. It means it's my fault."

"You couldn't keep me from danger," Wyvern said, "I'd follow you anywhere. Kitty, I—"

Wyvern's words were silenced when the door screamed its open, and cultists wielding wicked knives stepped through. "Give us the witch."

Wyvern stood as a wall between Kitty and the enemy. "I'll die first."

"No." Kitty stepped around as knives were readied. Her failure, her responsibility, she wouldn't see that nightmare to its end. "You won't."

Rough hands pulled Kitty from her friends. Their eyes were all she saw as she was pushed to a platform of three pyres. Cypress was pulled to one, the dragon rider to the last. Fire, her immutable destiny. She was surprised only that the hand lighting it was a stranger's.

Pink eyes turned red with tears. And, as her hands were tied, those last words came. A response to those that had been interrupted. "I know," she said, "I love you too."

61

Belladonna

Dark Sky Festival: Helena's Triumph

That web of tangled trees had long started their turn, their march into autumn reds. Those trees knew nothing of mortal desires for time to cease, to hold. Bann'ni's hand was just the same as the years he didn't hold fate's. So little time since Belladonna thought she knew a man, how quickly summer had come to an end.

She couldn't look at the man who followed her deep into that once orchard. "That wasn't being careful," he scolded. "We agreed!"

Belladonna had no words for him even as he came to her side.

"You didn't come back last night, and then Alyria—-" His voice hitched. "I don't know what she did to that man. I thought you'd died when you didn't come back."

Belladonna's heartbeat tapped a rabbit's rhythm over the torrent of words. "Alyria came to you?"

"I rather think she wanted to come to you, but I wasn't going to send her off alone covered in blood. Why would you call so much attention to yourself?"

Finally, Belladonna forced herself to look at her once beloved. "Did you tell the guards about Nadia?"

To all the gods, she begged. To the Seven Hundred, she'd wage war against Lyan'nyea herself that he'd deny it. "I had to," he said. "I had to for you."

"Why?"

Edmunds's hand reached for her shoulder, an offer of ground against shivers that wracked her body, but Belladonna pushed him back as tears sprung free. "You were too reckless," he said, "you were going to be caught, and I thought that if Nadia was, you'd see how dangerous it was."

"You thought I would stop? Who do you think I am? That I would stop trying to save my people?"

"I thought I was your people!" Edmund placed both hands on Belladonna's arms; the man bent double as the staff caught his stomach.

Belladonna couldn't help her stumbling steps. "I thought so." Her retreat halted as wild trees clung to her hair. "I was wrong."

"You weren't!" Edmund cried through gasps. "Donna, I love you! I told the guards Nadia was the leader. As long as you stop, they'll never find out it was you."

"I haven't stopped! You sold her for nothing!"

"It was just one more time." Tidy hair fell in shambles. "I can convince them it was a coincidence."

"Did you think Lord Tenor would give up the hunt easily?" A cruel corner of her heart lifted as his face paled. "Lady Hunter showed me your letter. You couldn't do that if you love me."

"The guards weren't working fast enough; if they didn't act, you would keep going, and they'd figure it out. I thought his name would scare them into moving. Everything I did was because I love you."

Hot tears burned as they marked tracks down her face. "You're wrong; you can't love me; I don't know who you are."

Those tiny drops of mana the night had returned laced to the earth at her feet, a spell not unlike her favourite escape, one she'd seen so recently as its form warped and hardened. A blade made of stone. Belladonna heard not the pleas of a man she loved as she turned away, as the stone found a home in his chest.

An Elf said no prayers for the dead as a traitor joined assassins buried, forgotten, deep in those woods.

62

Elysa

Dark Sky Festival: Helena's Triumph

Every novice spy knew they ways of shadow, knew how to move unseen, unheard. She who hunted and ran from spies, doubly so. Those cultists hadn't a hint of her presence as they gathered about pyres, as they prepared to burn alive someone Elysa could admit respect for. They noticed not the shadows moving, with eyes cast down, before she leapt on a robed man's back, her blade an anchor in his chest.

Then they saw her.

A stunned pause. Then, like a mage's flame, every person in that room sprung to their feet and froze. Elysa rolled as her victim fell, both knives ready, but she had lost her advantage, her single trick; all eyes could see her.

Under still silence, that moment before minds moved, she could see her goal: pewter keys hung from the waist of a man in a porcelain mask.

Initiative won by the adversary, the cultists moved first, blades sparked against the stone Elysa had crouched on moments before. A defensive wall arrayed, her way to those keys blocked by a press of bodies.

Her feet moved with the grace of practiced crisis; an iron cage became a wall to spring from as she rolled between legs, her knives extracting ruby tithe from those she passed.

And the opening, a bolt struck before the cultists' second volley. Tiny victory in another moment of hesitation from robed men. Between breaths, Elysa's hand found the keys; in another, she tossed them to a cage of dragon killers. Beast Bloods stared as they landed in the hand of a grey Salliten. "Is this a Dark Sky Play?" Elysa spat as she ducked from another blade. "Pull your weight."

Chaos, the moment that first cage opened, a focused pursuit became a kicked anthill. That room a blur of crimson until Robin's shoulder bumped her own. "Get the kids out," she hollered over screams.

"What about you?" Robin called as Elysa dove back into the swarm.

As to a ballroom, Elysa danced between pressed bodies until she stepped above the ants to a stage of pyres. "Oi!" Elysa called as she tossed a knife to the grey Salliten, who tugged the ropes of his leader.

"Elysa?" Kitty's voice came hoarse as Elysa hacked at the binds.

"You dropped your wand," Elysa said, a strained mimicry of optimism while oil-slick ropes defied her blade, "thought I might bring it to you."

Just as ropes began to tumble away, a torch dropped on oil-soaked wood. Flames burst as if from a witch's wand. Elysa stumbled back, deaf to how Kitty screamed as a white blur tossed her aside.

A tumbling roll ripped away her blade, if not her footing. Elysa saw the masked man's knife only a moment too late, her arm stiff from injury raised just too slow to block it. The scabbed-over cut was struck through by a blade that scraped bone and continued on as Elysa stumbled.

An arc of her own crimson blood flowed as it found its mark. And rent a hole through her beating heart.

63

Robin

Dark Sky Festival: Helena's Triumph

Thief, spy, on that day, he'd become a shepherd, his back a shield against the chaos that might take those children. Focus at the forefront as he herded them from that room. He heard nothing over screams and clashing steel. Still, some tingling instinct had him turn.

He was too far when the flames caught. Wyvern was a pale blur to his eyes as she pulled ropes to shreds, as Kitty slumped against her chest.

He heard his own scream as Elysa fell upon the altar of stone; her eyes never closed. A scream of his own voice vanished through air that shifted all wrong.

That huddle of children fell as ragdolls to the corridor as Robin ran. Something shattered as those flames grew, a sourceless fog that hid shapes behind sight, beneath hearing, below touch and taste. They danced around those pyres atop that altar, eyes and hands beyond size.

The cultist's leader, the man in a mask of white, swung his blade as Robin ran for him.

A shallow cut couldn't slow Robin at that moment; his borrowed knife cut deep through the wicked man's wrist. Two blades clattered to the ground.

Under the mask was hair Robin's fingers found purchase in. The monster's mask cracked as his head slammed against the altar.

Again.

Again.

So easy, just like before, too easy.
Only a sharp breath from a dead woman ceased his assault as Elysa sat up.

64

Elysa

Dark Sky Festival: Helena's Triumph

Nothing, so much as anything, so much as everything. She hadn't survived. Waiting, always waiting. Not waiting anymore. A mouth to speak and hands to bargain.

Grey plains and a woman's voice gave way to that cave lined with cages; Elysa clutched her chest as a sundered heart knitted together. That thing with a woman's voice echoed across her memory.

But chaos gave no time to dwell, an excuse and cover, to convince a coward's heart it had always been whole. That third pyre, a man she didn't know, still burned, and, as his screams died, eyes in fog flickered and blinked, a thing brought to a tipping point without its needed weight. That fog faded. And in the moments before they, too, disappeared, those eyes turned to the dead.

And those dead, servants past their last, stood, with empty eyes and flesh glowing with black veins; they stepped, shambling towards screaming children to where Wyvern carried an unmoving Kitty.

"Go!" Elysa yelled as she leapt, unarmed, to the back of the once-man who rushed the pale Fensmirri.

Nails did little but turn the monster. Its steps a shambling circle, as its own nails tore at Elysa's legs. Monster, freak, liar, beast, what was she but another animal? Predator turned prey. Black blood that tasted so much more of ink than iron flowed past her lips as she sunk teeth into the creature's neck. For the second time, she rolled from that man's back as he fell.

Her bleeding arm scraped a cage as she regained footing. Her path out was clear, all of the creatures pushed for the centre. She shouldn't have rushed back to the side of people she didn't care for.

Her back pressed to Robin's as he pulled a creature off Lane. The three of them stood together as a ward against the wave, a crumbling wall with every attack.

Screams grew quiet as the children fled from that place. But that wave which crashed over the three who remained grew only stronger. A dull thud as a final blot flew into that ceaseless sea of shambling dead.

Lane.

Mission and mystery. A girl with a trick, a last resort, but a trick that couldn't abide witnesses.

Elysa found herself taking a handful of Robin's scarf as she shoved him to the passage. "Go!" she yelled to the weaponless man. "We're just behind you."

His protests echoed, half-formed, for but a moment before he disappeared into the darkness.

"You've got a trick," Elysa panted as her blade was wrenched from her grip. "Might see if it works here!"

Blue eyes met amber, the raging dead vanished from mind for but a moment, their wrath replaced as Lane spoke, and the air went still. A word of no language, of no spoken sound.

Nothing in the air shifted as the creature stepped through it. No, that wasn't quite right; the creature, almost a woman, tall and grey-skinned, with legs of a deer and Lane's same blue eyes, hadn't stepped through anything. She'd stepped forward, and if Elysa hadn't seen the space the creature stood empty a moment ago, her eyes could have sworn it had always been there.

Don't say his name, somehow, she knew then her mother's old warning against their creator had never been about Lord Mirri.

She'd made no witch's bargain, nor had she any tale to draw an ancient adversary, but Elysa knew then – more certain than she had ever known herself to be, with little need for superstitions, little need for anything, to know when she gazed upon a Daemon.

"Hello, Helena." That creature smiled.

Fox ears couldn't help but hear the screams as she ran from that place. A strength she couldn't name burned as she dragged Lane behind her. Echoing cries of things without voices, a haunting memory of grey plains chased her, a relentless pursuer. Even as she reached her own in dawn's first light.

65

Belladonna

Dark Sky Festival: Helena's Triumph

Night was split by commotion when Belladonna, at last, found the strength to stand from the ground to return to her home. Nobility ran about as jewelled ants, but still, they jumped from her path as she trod that familiar route. An empty tower gave no peace for the knock that came at her door.

Alyria wore only night clothes, heavy and long sleeve things for winter, her face lit by a single candle. "I—I... you have to come see."

Belladonna followed as a ghost while her sister ran through crowded halls. A path cleared for the two girls, who never slowed until they reached the men's tower. The home of their grandfather. But Alyria stopped only halfway up the tower, at the chambers of their father.

Even those door guards, sparkling and useless, stepped aside as Belladonna strode inside.

She knew the smell of blood.

Her father knelt against the bed with a bloody hand clutched in his own.

That bed showed no colour but red, and the carpet beneath, while slow to join, pushed to become the same way. Eugenia's eyes were fixed on the ceiling, a silent scream locked forever on her face. Her nightdress was torn from chest to waist, one of her hands still lodged inside the jagged hole that was once her chest.

Belladonna's father looked up when she approached. "You," he hissed, "you did this!"

Belladonna took a step back. "What?"

"Guards!" he cried, "arrest her!"

The Lord Raylor said nothing, only nodded to his son's command as guards, who had blocked the door, closed in on Belladonna.

That same reason she knew he hadn't sent the assassins when he had guards to get their hands dirty. Guards for his traps. And wasn't grief the cleanest excuse to be rid of a problem?

Only a glance at Alyria told her all she needed. Her sister hadn't set the trap but neither would she have stopped it had she known. None to take her side, none ever for her defence. Belladonna pressed her staff into her sister's hands as guards seized her arms. Screams, cries and jewelled nobles were all a blur as they dragged her from that room.

66

Elysa

Waiting. Grey lands of fog, that dammed voice, a hand extended. Take it.
Take it.

At once, they snapped away for those red leaves fluttering against ivory trees. The stream still ran past her feet; she stood unmoved from where she'd been when the cold hit, when that voice and memory came again.

Sombre voices filtered from their camp, a cave of no tunnels she always knew the way to. A place to which she never wanted to return.

A mournful place. Neither Wyvern nor Robin left Kitty's side. The burns down her legs would never heal; the smoke in her lungs should have long passed, and still she slept. So the pair who had joined her first sat a funeral vigil for one who hadn't yet died. Lane hadn't spoken a word since that cave; her quill, a constant scratching against parchment. Perhaps they were, all of them, the dead returned, aimless wanderers.

Elysa's arm burned as she peeled back rags. Robin swore Kitty could help it when she woke. When. Such hope, such faith. But what help could she take from a woman all but dead to the world still after days of camp and travel? Blood and foul biles oozed from the twice cut wound as Elysa scrubbed it with frigid water, a screaming burn deep within until she wrapped it once more, her once wish to have that arm left unmarred, a contrast to the other, ruined one.

She knew he was coming from the break in voices even before talons crushed leaves behind her. "How's Kitty?" Elysa turned to Robin.

His head shook. "She'll get better."

Elysa sat at his side, her feet still in the stream. "I hope you're right." Perhaps another could have prayed.

"We could have done better."

"We saved the children." Saved them only for Mirri's bastard to run off with them, to keep the glory they hadn't earned. That was twice then. "If we believe Lane, we kept a terrible thing at bay." Only a temporary respite, that voice from beyond echoed again through her mind without words.

"We didn't save everyone. I keep thinking of how we could have done better."

Could she say differently? Could she wish to save a dragon rider and mean it? Lane's question refracted with time. Her answer was no different.

There was no help in wishes nor regret. Elysa stood and offered her scarred hand. "Come now; it's just a new game. I think we've mourned long enough."

Robin took her hand. "So, what now?"

"Suppose we have to know what the game is."

"And then?"

Her smile was of years of practice. Her speech was of gentle lies so often only for her own ears – perhaps, just once, it could be true. "Then?" she said. "Then we can win."

Manufactured by Amazon.ca
Bolton, ON

44402740R00208